A True
and
Faithful
Brother

A FRANCES DOUGHTY MYSTERY

A TRUE
AND
FAITHFUL
BROTHER

LINDA STRATMANN

The
Mystery
Press

To
Mark and Katie

First published 2017

The Mystery Press, an imprint of The History Press
The Mill, Brimscombe Port
Stroud, Gloucestershire, GL5 2QG
www.thehistorypress.co.uk

© Linda Stratmann, 2017

The right of Linda Stratmann to be identified as the Author
of this work has been asserted in accordance with the
Copyright, Designs and Patents Act 1988.

British Library Cataloguing in Publication Data.
A catalogue record for this book is available from the British Library.

ISBN 978 0 7509 6994 9

Typesetting and origination by The History Press
Printed and bound by CPI Group (UK) Ltd

Layout of the Lodge room at the
Duke of Sussex Tavern

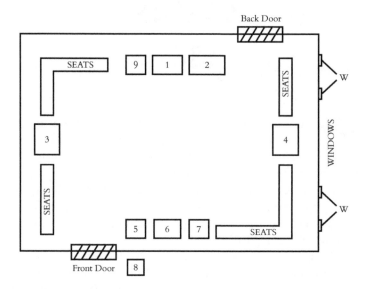

1 Worshipful Master
2 Immediate Past Master and Chaplain
3 Secretary and Treasurer
4 Junior Warden
5 Inner Guard
6 Senior Warden
7 Junior Deacon
8 Tyler
9 Senior Deacon

LONDON
1882

Frances Doughty unfastened the top three buttons of her gown, thankful for the sake of decency that no more was required. She was comforted by the fact that the man who stood beside her, calm and solemn in his dark attire, had performed his duty many times before, and would be both her guide and support. Facing her was a closed door. In a few moments it would open, and once she had passed into the next room there could be no turning back.

Although she had been prepared, it was nevertheless a shock when the hood of white fabric was placed over her head. The world vanished as if in a fog and suddenly she felt alone, helpless and vulnerable. Aware that she had begun to tremble, she tried to conceal her apprehension and breathe as evenly as she was able, hoping to face the mystery to come humbly and without fear. Moments later came the descent of the hempen rope around her neck, its weight resting on her shoulders and tightened by the loop of the noose. Her throat was dry, her palms moist, and she could feel the deep pulsing of her heart.

There was the sound of the door opening. It was time.

As she felt a steadying hand on her elbow, encouraging her to step forward, Frances could not help but cast her mind back over the remarkable train of events that had placed her in this very unusual situation.

CHAPTER ONE

In the autumn of 1881, a series of catastrophic incidents had culminated in the arrest of the notorious killer known as the Bayswater Face-slasher. Despite this welcome resolution to the appalling crimes that had struck terror all over West London, Frances Doughty, lady detective, felt that she had little with which to congratulate herself, and a great deal to regret. Certain deaths had struck close to her heart and although no one had suggested that she should be blamed for them, especially since she had never been hired to investigate the case, she could not contemplate those losses without a strong sense of failure. Surely, she reasoned with herself, again and again, there must have been a way in which she could have prevented the tragedies, if only she had been cleverer or braver or more determined. She had been left with the conclusion that taking up the profession of detective had been, as she was so often advised, a foolish thing to do.

As a result, Frances had resolved to give up all except non-criminal enquiries. This change in her career had been announced in the local press, and clients who came to consult her in the hope that she might make an exception for them were politely turned away. Straying pets and long-lost relatives were her domain now, as well as research in libraries and reading rooms, and the drawing up of family trees. She also continued to carry out the occasional secret mission for the government, which mainly involved the delivery of messages she was trusted not to open, or simply making careful observations of an individual.

The one enquiry on which she ought to have spent time, solving the mysteries in her own family, she had felt reluctant to pursue, as she believed that her personal history was part of the reason for her deficiencies. The more she had learned about her past, the more it became apparent that she was tainted by the inheritance of character flaws that she could only suppress but never fully escape.

Frances had been brought up under the stern unloving eye and firm hand of an aunt. Her father, William Doughty, who had maintained a chemist shop on Westbourne Grove, had regarded her as little more than an unpaid servant, and lavished all his paternal attention on her older brother, Frederick. William had rarely spoken of his wife, Rosetta, a subject he found too painful to explore, saying only that she had died when Frances was three. Only two years ago, however, Frances, then nineteen, had uncovered the shameful truth; her mother had not died but had deserted the family home, her husband and children in the company of a man.

In 1864 Rosetta Doughty and her paramour Vernon Salter had been living together in humble circumstances when Rosetta gave birth to twins, a girl who had died in infancy, and a boy, Cornelius, who still lived. It was not until after William Doughty's death that Frances had learned that it was suspected that she too was the child of her mother's lover. This had been distressing enough, yet Frances had retained the hope that somewhere Rosetta and Vernon were together and now that Rosetta was free, they would finally marry.

That hope had been extinguished by her recent discovery that in 1865 Vernon had deserted Rosetta to marry Alicia, the only daughter and heiress of wealthy philanthropist Lancelot Dobree.

And this was why, despite everything, Frances could not resist taking on one more case. She had just been informed that Lancelot Dobree had disappeared from within a locked and guarded room. Her client, Mr Algernon Fiske, knew nothing of her unhappy connection with the Dobree family, and Frances hoped he never would.

As Frances considered the peculiar problem that Mr Fiske had brought her, she was inevitably reminded that it was he who had first engaged her as a professional detective. He had been concerned about the unauthorised distribution of unconventional pamphlets at a school for girls, an apparently simple conundrum that the governors had felt required the feminine touch. Frances' enquiries had resulted in the exposure of scandals, destruction of reputations, solution of murders and her first meeting with the prime minister. It was the best possible proof that one could never know where an investigation might lead.

Mr Fiske, a mild-looking man of about fifty, was an enthusiast of English literature, who wrote a regular column for the *Bayswater Chronicle* under the pen name 'Aquila', in which he reviewed new publications. He was also a Founder and a Past Master of the Bayswater Literati Freemasons' Lodge. This organisation, a private club for gentlemen of culture who liked to meet and dine and enjoy good conversation, also provided generous financial support for local schools. He was, thought Frances as she faced him across the round table in the parlour where she interviewed her clients, a little more portly, a little greyer about the whiskers, and had less hair on his pate than at their first meeting. He certainly looked more worried. According to Mr Fiske, two nights ago Lancelot Dobree, a guest of Mr Brassington, the current Master of the Literati Lodge, had vanished from the Lodge room while a meeting was taking place, during a part of the ceremony in which the lights had been extinguished.

'People do not vanish into the air,' said Frances, soothingly. 'They do not leave locked rooms unless they have a key and unlock them.'

Fiske made a helpless gesture. 'I know, I know, but that is what happened! And he left without taking his coat or hat or regalia case and his overnight bag. In fact, he was wearing his regalia the last time we saw him; he would not willingly have stepped out of the building dressed like that. It is against all proper practice.'

'That is worrying, I agree.'

'Then you will look into it?' he begged. Frances had already told Mr Fiske that she had given up her detective work, but he looked pathetically hopeful that she would relent on his account.

'Very well, I will.'

Her new client breathed a great sigh of relief.

'But should he reappear, and I have every confidence that he will do so soon, you must let me know the very moment you learn of it.'

'Of course, of course!'

Frances opened her notebook and took up a freshly sharpened pencil. 'Before I begin, you must tell me in your own words exactly what transpired.'

Mr Fiske nodded and collected his thoughts. Frances poured a glass of water from the carafe on the table and he refreshed himself gratefully, then blotted his brow with a handkerchief. It was, thought Frances, anxiety rather than the fire that crackled cosily in the grate that had produced the excess of perspiration. 'The regular meetings of the Literati are held at the Duke of Sussex Tavern in Kensington. Dobree and his son-in-law Mr Salter are members of Mulberry Lodge, which meets at the same location. The night before last, Dobree attended our proceedings as a guest of the Master, Mr Brassington.'

'Was his son-in-law also present?' asked Frances, trying not to appear overly interested in the information.

'No, I understand he is away on business.'

'Please go on.'

'I arrived at the tavern a little after four o'clock, as did Mr Chappell our Director of Ceremonies, whose duty it is to make sure that the Lodge room is secure and in good order. I should explain that the room, which is on the first floor, has two doors on opposite sides. One leads to the rear of the premises and is always locked during our meetings. The other door is the one we use as an entrance and leads to the landing and main staircase. Chappell checked the room as soon as he arrived and he is quite certain that when he had done so, both doors were locked. Shortly afterwards the other brethren arrived including the Master, Mr Brassington, and his guest Mr Dobree.'

'Who has charge of the keys to the Lodge room?'

'When the Lodge room is not in use the keys are kept in the office which is on the ground floor. Mr Neilson, the landlord, checked immediately after the meeting and the key to the rear door was still there. That door remained locked throughout. Mr Chappell took charge of the key to the entrance door when he went up to prepare the room. He checked everything, then relocked the room and that door was not opened again until the meeting started.'

'So during the meeting the rear door was locked but the entrance door was not?'

'The entrance was bolted from within and guarded. Mr Manley is our Inner Guard and he sits by the door inside the Lodge room. Mr Neilson acts as Tyler.'

'Tyler?' queried Frances, making rapid notes.

'The officer stationed outside the Lodge room with a sword to prevent unwanted entry. Mr Neilson was on the landing beside the door throughout the meeting.'

Frances was always wary when weapons were mentioned. 'Is it a real sword? I hope he never has occasion to use it?'

'It is real, but not very sharp. For ceremonial purposes only. Neilson tells me that he also checked the room before the meeting; that would have been earlier in the day, before any of the brethren arrived, and it was quite secure. That afternoon there was our usual convivial conversation in the lounge bar, as the brethren gathered, and then at five o'clock we all went upstairs. There is a small anteroom next door to the Lodge room where we leave our coats and hats and put on our regalia, the larger Lodge room is where we hold our meetings. We always enter the Lodge room through the door on the front landing. Dobree was undoubtedly with us then. We all remember him being there. But there is one part of the ceremony where the lights are extinguished. We were in near darkness for about ten to twenty minutes. There is just one small candle by the Master. When the lamps were re-lit —' Fiske paused and shook his head, and there was a heavy sense of failure in his expression, 'I suppose no one expected a man to be missing, so we didn't look about for him. But as we were about to file out, Mr Brassington wished to make some remark to his guest, and realised that he was not there. He asked where Dobree was, and it was then that we realised that no one had seen him since the lights were dimmed.'

'Does the room have windows?'

'There is one exterior wall, but if a man did open a window and scramble through, I doubt that he could do so without making a considerable noise. And even if he could there is a sheer drop to the street.'

'And no secret exits? You mentioned that Mr Dobree's own Lodge also meets there so he would have been familiar with the room.'

'If there are any trapdoors or priest holes I certainly don't know of them, and neither does Mr Neilson.'

Frances reviewed her notes. 'So what it comes down to is that anyone leaving the room must have used one or other of the doors. Is there a possibility that Mr Dobree could have unbolted the main door and left without either Mr Neilson or Mr Manley noticing?'

'None at all, I would say. And after the meeting the door was still bolted from within. How could he leave and do that?'

'Did you check afterwards to see if the rear door was still locked?'

'We did, and it was.'

'Supposing Mr Dobree had obtained the key of the unguarded rear door, left under cover of darkness, and then relocked it. Where does it lead?'

'There is a staircase going down to the ground floor, where there is an outer rear exit of the building. That door is locked at all times apart from deliveries, and its key is only in the possession of Mr Neilson, so Dobree could not have gone out that way. One can, however, go from the foot of the stairs, past the door to the cellars and into the storeroom. There were men working there during our meeting and neither saw Dobree. To leave the building he would have had to go through the storeroom, and then through the public bar without being seen, and from there onto the street. In fact, he was not seen by anyone at all in the building after the lights went out.'

'So he entered a room in which one door was locked and the other was bolted and guarded by two men, and then he disappeared.'

'Exactly.'

'Without taking with him any possessions he might have been expected to take if he had left voluntarily.'

'Yes.'

'And wearing regalia, you say? What did that consist of? Is there a special robe?'

'No, he wore a plain suit as we all do, but over that was an apron, a short half apron the size of a stonemason's, and then there was a collar,' Fiske's hands moved from either side of his neck to come together in the midline of his chest to suggest a shape coming to a point. 'And pinned to his coat there were a number of breast jewels as we call them. They look much like medals.'

Frances wrote this down, then tapped her pencil thoughtfully on her notebook. 'During your earlier conversation with him, did you notice anything unusual in his manner? Did he seem well?'

Fiske paused to explore his memory. 'He seemed well enough, but there was something on his mind. He told us that he would not stop to dine with us as he had another engagement, but he did not say where or with whom. I had the feeling – now I think about it, yes, I had the definite feeling that it was not something he wished to discuss, other than giving it as the reason he could not stay.'

'He did not receive a note or a message?'

'Not that I saw.'

'What did you do when you found he was missing?'

'We naturally assumed he would return, as his property was still there, so we waited for him. After a while we became concerned and searched the convenience in case he had been taken ill. Then we searched the rest of the premises; the stores, the cellars, the upper floors, everywhere. And then – it must have been about half past six o'clock – a carriage arrived, one that Dobree had hired. We had to send it away.'

'You said that he left an overnight bag?'

'Yes, we examined it for clues but there was nothing unusual in it. A change of linen, toilet requirements, and so on. Nothing to suggest where he was going.'

'Did the driver of the carriage say where he was to take Mr Dobree?'

'No; I'm not sure he knew himself.'

'It was a hired carriage, you say. Does Mr Dobree not keep his own carriage?'

'He does, but this was not his.'

Frances thought that tracing a carriage driver for such a memorable fare would not be hard. 'So after the tavern closed, what did you do then?'

'I went to Dobree's house, taking his property there for safe-keeping. I told Neilson that if Dobree returned to the tavern he was to say what I had done.'

'And who did you speak to at the house?'

'Dobree's manservant, Jeffs. He said that his master had told him he would be away for a day, so he wasn't expected back that evening. Mrs Salter was out, she had taken the carriage, and Mr Salter had been away on business for several days.'

'Did the servant know where his master might be?'

'No, although there is a family owned cottage in the country; somewhere in Berkshire I believe. Dobree uses it in the summer when he wants a few days of peace and sunshine, and Mr and Mrs Salter like to take the children there in the school holidays. Salter sometimes uses it to stay overnight if he is late coming back from a business trip.'

'So he could be there – but without his coat or hat or bag, which is strange. Did the servant comment on the property Mr Dobree left behind?'

'If he had an opinion he didn't express it to me. He seemed to think that if his master was at the cottage then he had all he needed there.'

'What action did the manservant say he would take?'

'He said he would speak to Mrs Salter when she returned. But Dobree was only supposed to be absent one night. I called again today and learned that he was still not home, and no message has been received.'

'So we have a departure from what might be considered usual behaviour, and a disappearance that doesn't make sense. How old is Mr Dobree?'

'Above seventy, but very hale.'

Frances was reminded of the shocking decline of William Doughty, the man she still thought of as her father, after the brain fever brought on by her older brother's death. William had been just fifty. Had something similar happened to Dobree; had he lost his memory and wandered away?

'Has Mr Dobree been at all absent-minded of late?'

'No, he seemed as sharp as ever. You would have sworn looking at him and speaking to him that he was scarcely over fifty-five.'

'So, on the first evening when Mr Dobree was not expected back, his family was probably not too concerned, but by now they will have taken some action. If they have alerted the police, then contact will have been made with the station nearest to the cottage and a constable sent there to check. Have the police been to the tavern?'

'I went first thing this morning and they hadn't been there yet, neither has Neilson heard anything. Do you think you can find him?'

'I will start by instructing my agents to make searches, and also interview Mr Dobree's friends. Were all the members of the Literati Lodge there on the evening Mr Dobree disappeared?'

'Not all. I can provide you with a list of members and those who attended. There are always some absences due to indisposition or business duties.'

'Do you have a portrait of Mr Dobree?'

'I'm afraid I don't, but I am sure his family can provide one.' Mr Fiske looked acutely miserable. 'And all this had to happen just as I am relinquishing my role as Almoner and taking up the office of Lodge secretary, which I can assure you is no sinecure.'

Frances closed her notebook and put it into her reticule. 'Well, let us go to the tavern. There may be some clues there. I will need to look around and also speak to the landlord.' Despite her previous vows Frances realised that she was actually looking forward to starting a real investigation once more. While she did not wish any ill to Mr Dobree, she knew that if she arrived at the tavern to find that he had reappeared, she would, along with a natural relief, feel quite disappointed.

CHAPTER TWO

On the morning of Mr Fiske's visit, Frances' assistant, Sarah Smith, with whom she shared her apartments, was absent from home on a case of her own. Unlike Frances, Sarah had not withdrawn from detective work, and her specialities to which she brought all her considerable strength and persistence were domestic and family issues. The mere appearance of her burly form and an expression that meant she would stand for no nonsense were usually sufficient to resolve matters. Frances, unsure how Sarah would take the news that she was engaged on a new case which promised more excitement than the hunt for a lost kitten, wrote a note explaining the reason for her absence, left it on the table and departed with Mr Fiske.

Leaving the tree-lined peace of Westbourne Park Road, their cab plunged into the teeming thoroughfare of Westbourne Grove, where shopping was both a compulsion and an entertainment, a passion fuelled by Mr William Whiteley's growing retail empire. Escaping the great crush of traffic, they turned south along the sweeping curve of Pembridge Villas and its tall cream-coloured houses, elegant with pillars, porticoes and balconies, before heading in the direction of Notting Hill, where Bayswater shaded into Kensington.

Only a year before, London had been blanketed in snow for the greater part of January, bringing the business of the great metropolis almost to a halt. Travel, post and deliveries had been near impossible for weeks. Now, by contrast, the weather was unusually mild for the time of year, and predictions exchanged across the tea tables were that the capital was not to suffer another frozen winter. There were the occasional squally winds and showers, but once the early morning fogs had vanished, leaving only a ceiling of grey cloud, all was remarkably calm.

'This is so very kind of you,' said Mr Fiske. 'Really, I hardly knew where to turn. I may of course have panicked unnecessarily and then I will look foolish, but better safe than sorry, and you will of course be recompensed for your time.'

'I only hope he is found soon,' said Frances. She reflected on what she already knew about Lancelot Dobree, stemming from the enquiries she had made into her own family. A retired silk mercer and a man of considerable wealth, known chiefly for his devotion to charity, Lancelot Dobree enjoyed an unblemished reputation. She determined, however, not to reveal her possession of even that slight knowledge as she wanted to see what would be volunteered. 'We must not of course ignore the possibility that despite the thoroughness of the initial search of the tavern, Mr Dobree is still somewhere on the premises. Is he a large man?'

'No, not especially tall, and middling to portly in build.'

'If he became suddenly unwell he might have felt confused, and then he could have gone anywhere.'

Fiske nodded. 'We too wondered if he had been taken ill or suffered an accident, perhaps stumbled and fallen, but I spoke to Neilson this morning and I can assure you that he has made a most diligent search of the entire premises from top to bottom.'

'Very well. Let us assume therefore that Mr Dobree has left the premises. If he simply wandered away without knowing where he was going, then he should have been found by now. If he has been placed under medical care his family would have been notified. I assume he carried a card or pocketbook that would have identified him. If he left deliberately, however, he must have had a reason as yet unknown to us, and some means of leaving the Lodge room and the building without being noticed.' Frances wondered if Dobree had fallen victim to a robber, but that did not explain how and why he had left the tavern without his hat or coat on a cold day. She wondered about the prevalence of dangerous criminals lurking in the streets of Kensington, a subject with which she was unfamiliar. The other possibility was that he had been abducted, but why and how were also obscure. 'Tell me something about Mr Dobree's family,' she went on. 'I will almost certainly be obliged to speak to them.' Even as the words fell from her lips Frances felt a dreadful hollow open in the pit of her stomach. The last person she wished to interview was her natural father.

'He is a widower. His wife died many years ago and he never remarried. There is a daughter, Mrs Salter, and three grandchildren who are away at school. I don't know of any other family.'

'What business does his son-in-law pursue?'

'I believe it is something in the jewellery line. Dealing in silver-ware, trinkets and similar. He travels a great deal.'

'Does he have a business premises?'

'I don't know of one.'

'You mentioned that Mrs Salter used her father's carriage on the night he disappeared and was expected back at his house. Does she live there?'

'Yes, she and her husband occupy the whole of one floor of the house.'

Frances, who had searched the Bayswater directory during her earlier enquiries, now understood why the name of Vernon Salter had not appeared there, since it just listed the householders.

'Dobree is extremely fond of his daughter. He speaks of her with great affection. I have the impression that his would be quite a lonely life if she had a separate establishment. I have rarely met Mrs Salter myself, but she has her own circle of friends.' Fiske made an extended pause as if he was about to say more, but thought better of it. 'She and my wife were at school together,' he finished weakly.

Frances wondered what Mr Fiske was leaving unsaid.

The Duke of Sussex Tavern was a solidly built four-storey edi-fice, its exterior woodwork painted a dark glossy green. It sat proudly on a substantial corner site which marked the junction of Kensington High Street, a broad thoroughfare lined with com-mercial premises, and a narrower quieter road, Linfield Gardens, a terrace of tall residential properties. Mr Fiske, expecting Frances to enter the tavern as soon as she had stepped down from the cab, was deferentially ushering her towards the door, but she decided first to examine the building from the outside.

The main frontage, which faced onto the High Street was hung about with gas lanterns, and boasted a wide welcoming entrance and large windows with advertisements in gold lettering for premium ales, port, brandy and good dinners. Frances tried to imagine Lancelot Dobree emerging from the tavern onto the busy shopping promenade at a time between 5 and 6 p.m. He would have been hatless, still wearing his Masonic regalia and without even an overcoat. It seemed an unlikely thing to do. Although the sun would have set by then, the street would still have been well lit both by the lamps with which it was generously provided, and the illumination from shops, its pavement crowded with strolling pedestrians, the road a constant parade of cabs and carriages. Dobree was almost certain to have been noticed, but he would have been able to hail a passing cab without too much delay. The shop next door, which shared a party wall with the tavern, was a well-patronised confectioner, the window displays of fancy cakes and cascades of pretty biscuits surrounded by shelves piled with invitingly crusty loaves.

Around the corner, on the side of the tavern that faced Linfield Gardens, there were more windows and a smaller more discreet entrance with a sign that showed it led to the lounge bar. The exterior was hung with colourfully painted wooden menus, and high on the wall a carved stone plaque announced that the building had been erected in 1860. If Dobree had left by the lounge bar exit he was, thought Frances, far less likely to have been seen by passers-by, and could easily have entered a nearby house unnoticed. As she considered this possibility she saw a police constable descending the front steps of a house further down the street. He paused long enough to write in his notebook, then walked on to the house next door, climbed the front steps and rang the bell. Clearly Mr Dobree had not reappeared and the police were making enquiries, which, Frances observed thankfully, would save her a dull and arduous task. She walked a little way down Linfield Gardens and soon came to a narrow alley called Linfield Walk, which divided the rear of the tavern from the first house of the terrace.

Mr Fiske, who had been following Frances in her inspection, appeared by her side. 'The alley is only for deliveries,' he explained.

'I don't think it is ever used by customers.' He was about to turn back, assuming that Frances would do so too, but to his surprise she walked along the roughly cobbled way, and he hurried after her. 'Surely Dobree couldn't be here?'

'I rule out nothing.' Frances reached a door with a brass plate engraved 'Duke of Sussex Tavern. Deliveries only'. She tried the handle but, as Mr Fiske had previously advised her, it was locked. 'You said that the landlord, Mr Neilson, keeps the key. There is not another one?'

'I'm not sure. We can ask him.'

Further down, past the single small gas lamp that was the only lighting in the alley, was another door, its signage announcing that it was the rear exit of the confectioner's shop. Frances tried that door too, finding it also locked. There the alley ended with the back wall and small high windows of a warehouse. Anyone who entered from Linfield Gardens had no choice but to return the way they had come. Directly opposite the two doors was the perimeter wall of the end terrace property, about eight feet in height, and with a stout gate. Frances tried the gate but it too was secure.

To Mr Fiske's astonishment Frances next proceeded to open the covers of the ash bins that stood outside both the tavern and the confectioner's and peer inside. 'What are you looking for? Oh my word, you don't think —?'

Frances didn't yet know what she thought, and said nothing. She had sworn never again to undertake enquiries into a crime, but old habits meant that she had to consider all possibilities. To the relief of them both, there was nothing of any note in the bins. 'Very well,' she said at last. 'I would like to speak to Mr Neilson, and be shown around the property.'

Returning to Linfield Gardens, they entered the tavern by the side door. The lounge bar was warm and comfortably furnished, its interior promising good wholesome fare and a companionable atmosphere. Some respectable-looking gentlemen were seated in leather armchairs at oaken tables enjoying glasses of ale and light luncheons of meat pie and potatoes, the savoury aroma of the food lightly spiced with cigar smoke. Behind a faultlessly tidy bar a young man in a crisp white shirt, waistcoat and bow tie was polishing glassware with a linen cloth. It was all quite different from some of the less salubrious public houses of Bayswater to which Frances' enquiries had occasionally taken her. Her appearance seemed not to attract any special attention, from which she guessed that in the lounge bar at least, lady diners in the company of gentlemen were not a novelty.

'What can I get for you, Mr Fiske?' said the barman, trying to look cheery but unable to conceal his concern at the circumstances that had brought his customer there.

Fiske glanced at Frances questioningly, but she shook her head. 'Thank you,' said Fiske, 'we require nothing for the moment. Could you tell Mr Neilson that I am here and wish to speak to him?'

The barman nodded solemnly. 'Of course, Sir.' He bustled away and soon returned with the manager.

Mr Neilson was a smartly dressed man in his late forties, his pointed beard liberally speckled with grey. He clearly believed that the traditional dirty apron preferred by some publicans was not for him. Mr Fiske made the introductions. Neilson looked surprised but did not object to the arrival of a private investigator.

'Miss Doughty is one of the foremost detectives in London,' enthused Mr Fiske. 'Now that the famous Mr Pollaky has announced his retirement she must surely be the leading agent in the west of the city. You will recall how she recently effected the arrest of the notorious Bayswater Face-slasher.'

Frances would have preferred to forget about that dreadful business, but knew that this would never be allowed. She decided not to comment.

'She is also very discreet,' added Fiske.

'I am aware that your fraternity is open only to men, so I will only ask what questions are needed to resolve this mystery,' Frances reassured Mr Neilson. 'I remain hopeful, however, that Mr Dobree will be found very soon. I see that the police are making enquiries.'

'Yes,' said Neilson gloomily. 'They came here to question me not an hour ago. Let us talk privately – we can go into the office.'

He led them through a door that linked the lounge bar with the larger, busier public bar, where clusters of drinkers were perched on high stools, some deep in significant conversation, others contentedly alone with their pipes. The air was cloudy with blue smoke, its scent mingled with the tang of beer. The patrons, recognising Mr Neilson, nodded to him respectfully, and glanced at Frances in curiosity. In front of a roaring fire, and looking for all the world like a thick brown fur coat that had been carelessly thrown into a heap, snoozed the largest dog that Frances had ever seen.

'And this fine fellow is Wellington,' said Mr Fiske. 'If he could only speak, he would have some stories to tell.'

'He has the freedom of the premises at night, and I am happy to say that we have never suffered at the hands of burglars,' said Neilson. 'Some have tried, but he always gives the alarm.'

Wellington opened one eye. It was a large, deep, dark eye, and it spoke eloquently. 'I may appear to be asleep,' it said, 'but put your hand in the till and I will bite it off.'

They continued through the public bar, on the far side of which was the entrance to a corridor. 'This way,' said Neilson. He led them past a door marked 'W.C.' There was an exit at the far end, but before they reached this Neilson opened another door marked 'Office, Private', and they went in. Frances looked about her carefully, trying not to make her thoughts too obvious. She saw a desk, chairs, shelves of ledgers and directories, document cabinets, and a small safe. There was nowhere to hide a body.

Mr Neilson gestured Frances and Mr Fiske to sit. Outwardly he looked at his ease as he took the chair behind the desk, but his eyes betrayed his anxiety. 'What do you wish to know, Miss Doughty?'

Frances took her notebook and pencil from her reticule. 'I understand that a very thorough search of the premises has been conducted, and you are satisfied that Mr Dobree is not here?'

'Yes, Mr MacNulty, my bar manager, and I examined every room from attic to cellar, and the police have conducted another search. He cannot possibly still be here.'

'Did you learn anything from the police?'

'Yes, I mentioned to them that Dobree has a cottage in the country. I thought that perhaps he had gone there, but they told me that they knew all about it and had confirmed that he never went there that night or has been there since.'

'We must assume that he has left the building.' Frances assumed no such thing, but kept her darker suspicions to herself. 'How long have you known Mr Dobree?'

'Above twelve years. I can assure you that nothing like this has ever happened before.'

'The questions I want to try and answer today are how and why he left, and was it voluntary or forced. I notice that there is a confectioner's shop next door. Is there a door connecting your premises with theirs?'

'No. There are only three exits from the tavern, the main one from the public bar onto the High Street, one from the lounge bar into Linfield Gardens, and one for deliveries which opens onto Linfield Walk, an alley at the rear. On the night Dobree vanished the first two were of course open, but the rear door was locked. It is always locked except when deliveries are brought in, or we might attract pilferers to the storerooms.'

'How many keys are there to the rear exit?'

'Two. One is on a bunch I keep on my person.' Neilson patted a pocket. 'The other is kept in the safe, here.'

'Who has access to the safe?'

'Only myself and Mr MacNulty. I should mention that he has worked for me for the last fifteen years and has my absolute trust.'

'And at the time Mr Dobree vanished you were outside the Lodge room guarding the door with a sword?'

'I was.'

'Where is this sword normally kept?'

'In the anteroom upstairs; we have a trunk containing materials and books relating to Lodge business.'

'I saw an exit at the end of this corridor – where does that lead?'

'To the storerooms, kitchens, cellars, the rear exit into Linfield Walk; and there is a back staircase leading up to the first floor.'

'It would be helpful if you could conduct me over the premises, so I can understand how the rooms and floors are connected,' said Frances.

'That sounds very sensible,' agreed Fiske.

Neilson assented and before they left the office he removed a ledger from a shelf and opened it to reveal that it was not after all a ledger but a shallow box. A row of six hooks was fastened inside the box and a labelled key hung from each hook. 'These are the keys of the inner rooms of the premises,' he explained. He extracted two of the keys and slipped them into his pocket.

'Who knows where these keys are kept?' asked Frances.

'The senior staff, and certain members of the Lodges, that would be the Directors of Ceremonies whose duty it is to see that the room is in order. Mr Chappell of Literati and Mr Pollard of Mulberry.'

'Would Mr Dobree have known?'

'I don't think so,' frowned Neilson. 'He was Chaplain of Mulberry; he recited the prayers.'

'Has he never fulfilled the role of Director of Ceremonies?'

'Some years ago, yes, he did, but that was long before I lighted on this scheme to keep the keys secure. They used to just hang on a board inside the door, but after an attempted burglary a few months ago, which I am pleased to say Wellington thwarted, I wanted them out of sight. It's rather good isn't it? MacNulty had it made for me.'

They returned to the public bar at the rear of which was a winding staircase leading to the upper floors. It was well carpeted, and a man might easily walk up and down without his steps being heard, however, it was clear that anyone creeping down those stairs would also have been in full view of many of the customers. Frances was first shown the attic rooms, one of which stored tools, spare furniture, chinaware and cleaning materials, the other being where two of the male staff lodged. On the second floor were three rather superior sets of apartments, one of which was Mr MacNulty's residence, the other two being available for the accommodation of gentlemen of business visiting London.

There were three rooms on the first floor, the largest of which was an elegant dining room, with a menu board announcing that it was open in the evenings for dinner. There was, Frances noticed appreciatively, no stale hint of dinners past, but all was fresh and polished, with vases of hothouse flowers gracing pedestals about the perimeter, and tables ready laid with spotless silverware, glassware and napery. Mr Fiske intimated that this was where the Literati and Mulberry Lodges held their festive boards, meals enjoyed by the Lodge members after meetings. The next and far smaller room was provided with a row of hooks along one wall so that the brethren could leave their coats, hats and bags there and attire themselves in their regalia. Mr Neilson opened a large leather-bound trunk with a key he kept on his person, and revealed some items of paraphernalia, leather-bound books, and a handsome full-sized sword in a scabbard.

'This is the sword used to guard the Lodge,' he explained.

'Could you show me where you are when you do this? I know that you do not allow ladies into your ceremonies, but I assume there can be no harm in showing me what occurs outside the Lodge room.'

'None at all,' said Neilson. 'My duty is to be stationed outside the door during the ceremony, guarding the Lodge from malicious or simply curious persons.'

He was about to replace the sword in its trunk, but Frances said, 'Oh, and please do take that with you.'

Mr Neilson complied, and after relocking the trunk led them to the upper landing again. There was a third door next to that of the Lodge's anteroom, and here Neilson paused. 'When Lodge meetings are held there is a chair by the door for my use. I remain outside, with the sword, throughout.'

'I can see that it would be very hard for anyone to leave through that door without your knowing,' said Frances.

'It would, yes. Impossible, I would say.'

'Is the sword drawn?'

'Dear me, no, it is purely ceremonial. It rests by my side.'

'I would so like to see it drawn,' she asked, in a manner that disarmed all possibility of refusal.

He smiled and complied, but was careful to keep the blade out of dangerous proximity. 'It is not very sharp.'

Frances gazed at the sword in admiration, although her object was quite different. If it had been recently used there was no sign of it. 'Would you be able to show me the Lodge room? If I am to discover how Mr Dobree left it, I really must see inside.'

'By all means,' said Fiske. 'We do have lady visitors who ask to view it, not during a meeting of course.'

Mr Neilson permitted himself a slight smile, showing that he had anticipated Frances' request. 'I would be delighted for you to see it,' he said. He sheathed the sword and after replacing it in the anteroom, took one of the small keys from his pocket. He unlocked the Lodge room and they entered.

CHAPTER THREE

rances was not sure what to expect but saw something that reminded her of pictures she had seen in history books, impressions of how temples of classical antiquity might have looked. The room was oblong, its floor covered with a chequerboard of black and white tiles. On the wall opposite the entrance was another door. There was a single row of seating around the perimeter. To her left was a small desk with two chairs, but on the other three sides of the room she saw a kind of high wooden plinth, displaying a number of objects that she did not recognise but which she felt sure must have Masonic significance. Behind each plinth was a carved wooden armchair, one of which, the one facing the entrance door, was more ornate than the others, and on a low dais.

'That is the chair occupied by the Master of the Lodge,' explained Fiske. 'The others are for the Wardens, and the secretary and treasurer sit at the desk.'

'Do you recall where Mr Dobree was seated during the ceremony?'

'I am sorry, I don't remember. But he took no part in the ceremony, so he would have been either in his seat or standing in front of it throughout. A guest usually sits by the member who invited him, but since Mr Dobree was a guest of the Master that didn't apply in this case.'

The wall to Frances' right was the only exterior wall of the room, with four tall narrow windows hung with thick curtains. Frances approached to examine them, but the gap between the back of the row of seats and the wall was too small to accommodate her skirts. She thought it might have been possible for a slender gentleman to squeeze through the space to reach a window, and asked for one to be opened. Mr Neilson obliged. Drawing aside the curtain of the window nearest to the far wall, he turned a bolt, then, grasping two curved metal handles, and with some effort, slid the lower section of the window upwards. All these operations made an appreciable amount of noise, and Frances concluded that it would have been impossible for anyone to carry them out without attracting the notice of those seated in the chairs immediately in front of the windows. She peered out. The paving slabs of Linfield Gardens lay about fifteen feet below, with no means of climbing down or breaking a fall. The idea that a man of more than seventy could leave by that way even under cover of darkness, without alerting others in the room or suffering injury was one she dismissed at once.

'Is there no other possible exit from the room other than the doors and windows?'

'No, none,' said Neilson. 'I have worked here for more than twenty years – my father conducted the business before me – and I can assure you that all there is, you can see for yourself.'

The window was closed and fastened again, and Frances crossed to the rear exit door and confirmed that it was locked. 'Could you let me have the key, Mr Neilson?' He produced the second of the two small keys and handed it to Frances. She examined the label, a thin wooden rectangle carved with a number and letters, '1.L.B.' 'Floor one, Lodge, back?' she queried.

He smiled. 'That is correct.'

'Have they always been labelled in this manner?'

'No. I used to number them, but this seemed like a better idea.'

Frances inserted it in the lock. As the key turned it emitted a metallic creak. 'Does it always make that noise?'

'I suppose so. That door is rarely opened.'

'I have been told that Mr Dobree vanished from this room while the lights were out. If the key had made that noise during that period would you have heard it? Was there any other sound that might have occluded it? Speeches made? Hymns sung?'

'There was the address,' said Neilson. 'Mr Fiske spoke it, and rang a bell.'

'Was the bell rung continuously?'

'No, just every so often.'

'But Mr Dobree would have known when to expect it?'

'Not necessarily. The address is not spoken in all Lodges, in fact it is not done in Dobree's own Lodge, Mulberry, and when he was invited here he said how much he was looking forward to hearing it.'

'But he could have used it to cover the noise of his exit if he had had a key.'

'I suppose he might. But no key is missing.'

'Is the other key still in the safe?'

Neilson saw her meaning. 'I expect so. I had better go and bring it.' He hurried away.

Frances didn't seriously think that Lancelot Dobree had come to grief from the combined actions of his brethren, but the sword had started her thinking, and in Mr Neilson's absence she found herself taking a careful look at the Lodge room as the possible scene of a crime. Several objects had the potential to be used as weapons. There were gavels by the Master's and Wardens' chairs, which were probably too light to do a great deal of harm, but she also saw a substantial wooden maul, three large heavy wooden boards, and two rocks, one rough-hewn and one cut smooth, any of which would have been deadly in the wrong hands. All surfaces were carefully cleaned and dusted, and there was no sign of blood anywhere. Mr Fiske, mistaking her examination for curiosity, was kind enough to explain some of the significance of what she saw, and Frances obligingly made notes.

On passing through the back door Frances found herself on a small landing, from which a narrow staircase led down to the ground floor. The stairs, which were uncarpeted wood, were little worn, suggesting that they were not used often, but there was no noticeable dirt. Directly opposite the rear door to the Lodge room was a small window in the external wall. Frances peered out but saw only the alleyway, Linfield Walk, and the open yard space of the house opposite. Any light illuminating the upper landing at night could only have come from the small gas lamp further down the alley and must have struggled to pass through the thick glass of the windowpane. She thought it unlikely that opening the back door of the Lodge after sunset would have admitted much light.

Frances was hoping that when Mr Neilson returned he would reveal that the second key to the rear door of the Lodge room was missing from the safe, together with the second key to the tavern's exit into the alleyway. It was the simplest explanation. Dobree had somehow managed to purloin both keys, left the Lodge room under cover of darkness and the sound of the address and the bell, slipped down the back staircase and out into the secluded alley, locking both doors behind him. To Frances' disappointment, however, when Mr Neilson returned he brought with him the second key to the back door of the Lodge, which when it was tried in the lock was if anything creakier than the first.

'May I see the other rooms now?' They left the Lodge by the rear door, which Neilson locked behind them, an action that produced another squeak of protest, and descended the stairs. 'Were there any deliveries expected during the time the Lodge was meeting?' asked Frances. She reached the ground floor and saw on one side an internal door leading to the storerooms, and on the other the rear outer door, which was secured with a large bolt.

'No. There had been one shortly before, but all was locked up after that. Deliveries are always supervised, usually by me but sometimes by Mr MacNulty. On the night Mr Dobree disappeared I was checking on the Lodge room prior to the meeting, so MacNulty oversaw the delivery.'

'And provisions are brought from vehicles in the alleyway through the rear door and from there into the storeroom, kitchen and cellar? Not up the back stairs?'

'That is correct.'

'I don't suppose you noticed just now whether or not the second key to the external door was in the safe?'

'Yes, it was in the same box as the key to the back of the Lodge room. And I see what you are thinking. No, all the keys of the tavern are accounted for and in their proper places. I checked them myself soon after Dobree went missing. And the back door was bolted from within. Even if he had somehow been able to leave that way, he could not have re-bolted it.'

'Someone might have found it unbolted and bolted it,' Frances suggested, hopefully.

'I have asked all my employees. No one found the door unbolted or noticed anything out of the way.'

Frances looked over the storerooms, which were tidy enough, with small dusty high windows, obviously undisturbed, and far too small for a man to squeeze through. The shelves were fully stocked, and as far as she was able to see there was no space to hide a body. She even explored the cellar, but unless Lancelot Dobree's corpse was floating in a beer barrel, slowly pickling, something which would surely become noticeable before too long, he was not concealed there. Had this been an incident in a sensational novel, she thought, Mr Neilson would have dispatched Dobree with his sword, cut him up, and removed him from the premises piecemeal, the entire membership of the Lodge conspiring to conceal the crime. It seemed unlikely.

Neilson took them to the lounge bar again and supplied luncheon, gratis. Frances decided not to have the meat pie.

CHAPTER FOUR

'Have you come to any conclusion?' asked Mr Fiske eagerly as he made short work of a glass of ale.

Frances, as she sipped her mineral water, saw that he was hoping that her tour of the tavern had somehow resulted in her solving the mystery. She was obliged to confess that she had not. 'It is easy enough to see how Mr Dobree could not have left the building, but I cannot yet determine how he did, and knowing that could well tell us why. You told me before that you thought he had something on his mind. Were there family troubles that might have demanded his presence?'

'Not as far as I am aware,' said Mr Fiske. 'But he might well have kept personal matters to himself.'

'I know of nothing of that sort,' said Neilson.

'Was there any business reason that might have made him leave so suddenly?'

'He was a silk mercer, but long retired from trade,' said Mr Fiske. 'He is still a very busy man, although nowadays his interests mainly rest with charities. You must have seen him mentioned in the newspapers; making donations, and giving prizes at schools.'

'I have. Is there anything in that area that might have caused him concern?'

'I don't believe so,' said Neilson.

'He didn't reveal where he was due to go that night?'

'No, but he ordered a meat pie, a bottle of ale and some bread and cheese for the journey, so he wasn't expecting to dine anywhere.'

Mr Fiske looked pensive. 'He did mention quite recently that he wished to found a school in the name of his late wife. Her loss was a grief from which he never truly recovered.'

'Whereabouts is this school to be?'

'In Kensington, I believe, but it is all just a plan at present.'

'Do you know if he had bought a premises, or was hoping to buy one?'

'I'm afraid not. Of course his brethren in Mulberry Lodge might know.'

Frances hesitated before asking her next question, and the interlude that followed the arrival at the table of a basket of warm bread rolls, fresh butter and potted cheese allowed her to decide how best to word it. 'This is a difficult question, but it is one that I am sure the police will ask. Do either of you have any reason to suspect that Mr Dobree was involved in an activity which was against the law, or questionable in any way?'

Fiske and Neilson glanced at each other but it was not a guilty look. Neilson coughed discreetly. 'You should know, Miss Doughty, that if a brother Mason breaks the law, his brethren do not, as so many people believe, draw ranks and protect him from the consequences. On the contrary, we are duty bound by our obligation to report him to the authorities. Such a man would certainly be expelled from freemasonry. Speaking in my capacity as Tyler to both the Literati and Mulberry Lodges, I can advise you that we have never suspected Dobree of anything illegal or underhand. Neither have we ever had occasion to question his morals. As his friend, I can reiterate that statement.'

Frances took out her notebook. 'I accept your assurance. Mr Fiske, can you provide me with the names of all the members of the Literati Lodge, and let me know which of them were present on the night Mr Dobree disappeared?'

'Of course, once I have examined my records. Although not all those who attended that night were actually in the Lodge room when the lights were extinguished.'

'Oh? Why was that?'

'The ceremony which was being performed that evening, the one where there is a period of near darkness, was what we call a raising. I should explain. There are degrees in freemasonry – ranks, I suppose you might call them – and brethren only attend those portions of the ceremony appropriate to their degree. A man is first initiated, and that is the First Degree. When he is ready he is passed to the Second Degree. The next stage is raising to the Third Degree. A raising is only attended by the candidate and those who have already achieved that rank, so those of lesser standing would have been outside the room.'

'In that case,' said Frances, 'I will need to know exactly where every member who was in the building that night was situated during the ceremony.'

'The signature books are held in the trunk upstairs,' said Neilson. 'I will fetch them.'

As the manager departed, a thought occurred to Frances and she turned to Mr Fiske. 'I had assumed that the lights going out was a usual part of your ceremonies. What you have just told me suggests that it only takes place during some of them. Is that the case?'

'It only happens during a raising and not at any other time,' said Mr Fiske. 'Is that important?'

Frances had no idea if it was, but she made a note of it all the same.

Mr Neilson returned with the books, and as luncheon proceeded so the pages of Frances' notebook filled, and she was able to establish that twelve members of the Literati had been in the Lodge room at the time of Lancelot Dobree's disappearance, and six others in the lounge bar. There were in addition five members of the Lodge who had not been present at all.

She was just completing her notes when a new arrival joined them at their table. Frances was introduced to a Mr Herman, who she saw from her list was a member of the Literati who had not been present at the last Lodge meeting. A gentleman in his middle fifties, he was tall with a dignified bearing, wavy hair the colour of slate, well-trimmed whiskers, and anxious grey eyes. 'I have just returned to town to hear the news about Lancelot Dobree! Do say that all is now well!'

'I am afraid not,' said Fiske. 'Dobree is still missing, the police have been called, and we have engaged Miss Frances Doughty to look for him.'

Herman, looking upset, made a cursory nod to the barman, who obediently brought a glass of beer and a hot beef turnover to the table. 'I was due to have a meeting with him at my office this afternoon.'

'What was this concerning?' asked Frances, reopening her notebook.

'I am an architect by profession and we have been looking for a suitable property in the area for him to purchase and convert for use as a school. Some days ago Dobree said he thought he had found the right one and wanted me to come with him to look at it.'

'Do you know the address of this property?'

'I'm afraid not, but I had the impression that it was not far from here.'

'Is the property currently occupied? If so the police may already have visited it or will do so soon. They have been making enquiries at all the nearby houses.'

Herman swallowed a deep draught of ale and bit thoughtfully into the turnover. It looked appetising enough but he hardly seemed to taste it. 'I do recall him mentioning that it was empty. A former lodging house, I believe, in need of renovation, but he thought it most suitable both in size and location.'

'If it is locked up then the police may not have been able to gain access yet. Do you know who has the keys?'

'No, but there is a property agent only four doors away. Munro & Son.'

'Then I think we should ask them.' Frances gathered her papers and put them away. Mr Herman took the hint and quickly dispatched his informal luncheon, while Mr Neilson took the signature books back to the anteroom. They were ready to depart in minutes.

At the agent's office, Mr Herman, who was known to the proprietors, took the lead in the enquiries and spoke to Mr Munro, a trim and active individual with a head of short dark curls and a neat moustache, undoubtedly the 'Son' of the partnership as he was aged no more than thirty-five. In the rear of the office a rather more elderly gentleman, dressed in an old-fashioned but faultlessly turned out ensemble, was casting experienced eyes over some weighty ledgers with an air of quiet authority. Young Mr Munro readily confirmed that Lancelot Dobree had recently made enquiries regarding properties for sale that could be converted for use as a school, and had been intending to view a nearby premises, a former lodging house, much in need of refurbishment, which had lain empty for two months. Mr Dobree had not thus far made an appointment for the viewing and nothing had been heard from him for several days. Knowing that Mr Dobree was a busy man, the agent had not been especially worried. The house, as it turned out, was the end terrace property in the next street, number 2 Linfield Gardens, the very one overlooked by the Duke of Sussex Tavern. Munro, on being informed that Dobree was missing, was naturally anxious and seeing the implications, at once went to fetch the keys.

'Is that the only set of keys?' asked Frances.

'There are two, and both are still here,' said Munro.

'Could Mr Dobree have obtained another set?'

'Only if he knows the owner, and I am fairly sure he did not.'

'Do you think we should summon the police?' asked Mr Fiske, nervously.

'It would be for the best,' Frances advised him. 'I suggest that we notify a constable of what we have learned and bring him to the house. But I don't want to delay. Supposing Mr Dobree had somehow obtained the keys and decided to explore the property in advance of his meeting with Mr Herman. If he is in the house and has had a fall or been taken ill then he might still be alive and urgently in need of help. I am competent in rendering medical aid.' Frances hurried away, feeling sure that the worried gentlemen would follow her, as they did. On the way, Mr Fiske quickly hailed a messenger boy and dispatched him to bring a constable.

CHAPTER FIVE

Frances' immediate thought was that if Lancelot Dobree was still in the house then he would be easily located, either lying on the floor or crumpled at the bottom of a staircase. It was her intention to do no more than cover those possibilities, leaving any detailed searches to the police. The prospect that he would not be found alive was one that she felt sure was in all their minds, but no one was choosing to voice it.

'Two months empty?' Frances queried, looking up at the exterior of the building.

Number 2 Linfield Gardens was a four-storey terraced house, with some architectural pretensions in the shape of slim pillars on either side of a portico enclosing the front steps, but the exterior was coated in the accumulated exudations of sooty chimneys, paint that had once been white had peeled in large dun-coloured flakes from the low wall surrounding the area, and the hedge behind it had been cut back so savagely that it had given up the struggle and died.

'Oh yes,' said Munro, brightly. 'Just one owner in the last thirty years, an elderly lady now living out of London.'

Mr Herman grunted. 'Two months empty and thirty years neglected,' he muttered, and Frances did not disagree.

'I can see that it requires some attention,' said Frances, diplomatically.

Munro waved aside all objections. 'Oh a coat of paint and it will look as fresh as ever!' He indicated the houses further down the street that had been rather better cared for, apparently implying that it would be no effort at all to bring the dilapidated property up to the same standard.

Mr Herman did not look convinced. As they mounted the steps, which were clogged with dirt and appeared not to have been swept for some years, Frances noticed that there were three keys on the agent's bunch, one of which Munro used to open the front door, from which fragments of dark blue paint were hanging in clumps like the scales of an ancient lizard, leaving weathered wood exposed.

'What are those other keys for?' she asked.

'This one,' said Munro, showing her a small key, 'unlocks the rear door leading from the kitchen to the yard, and this,' he held up a much larger one, 'opens the yard gate which leads onto the alleyway at the back.'

The interior of the house had a sour, abandoned smell, with dust that pricked at the nostrils, but the hallway was high and wide. 'New wallpaper and some polish on the lamps and this would be most attractive!' declared Munro. 'As you see, the accommodation is substantial.' Frances fought the urge to sneeze and carefully sniffed the air. There was no stench of decomposition but since the weather was cold and the house unheated this was not surprising.

The visitors were shown two large front reception rooms, as well as a dining room and parlour, all bereft of furniture apart from some pieces of wood that were fit only for the fire. A few rolls of old carpeting were stacked against the walls, the edges frayed and shredded as if gnawed by small sharp teeth, and there was broken lamp glass and china under foot.

'It is a very handsome property with many possibilities,' said Munro, 'not only as a school, which was what Mr Dobree had in mind, but I can easily imagine it as a business premises with suites of offices, or divided into separate apartments, or indeed as a large family home.'

'I would like to see the upper floors,' said Frances, thinking that if Lancelot Dobree had suffered a fall then the staircase was the most likely culprit.

Munro led Frances and her three companions up the unwelcoming stairs, the loose cords of its threadbare carpet threatening to trip the unwary, its boards sagging like old sponges. Frances became suddenly aware that the gentlemen, apart from Mr Munro, were not as young as they once were, and was obliged to pause on the landings and wait for the older men to catch her up. Mr Neilson seemed agile enough, but Fiske was puffing with the effort, and Mr Herman grimaced and knuckled his hip. 'Old war wound,' he said, and Frances wondered how many men old enough to have fought in the Crimea described their sciatica in that way. There was a grimy bathroom with dented plumbing, and no one had bothered to remove the faded curtains, old bedsteads and cracked porcelain that were undoubtedly bound for the rubbish heap. The little party looked in every room and soon satisfied themselves that Dobree was not there.

Mr Herman wore a serious expression. He prodded some stained patches on the walls, sniffed at them with distaste, and explored some areas of floorboard with a cautious toe, then shook his head. 'I am afraid the internal appearance tells all the story of this property. The previous owner has sadly neglected not only the interior but the fabric of the building, too. If I had examined it with Dobree I would have strongly advised him against purchase.'

Mr Munro looked displeased but made no comment.

They returned downstairs. 'Is there a coal cellar?' asked Frances, thinking how easily a man might open a door and fall down unlit stairs.

'No, but there is a fuel store in the yard,' said Munro.

'I suppose we had better see the rest of the house.'

The kitchen, pantry and washroom were bleak and dirty, and scatterings of dark brown droppings, trail marks in the dust and greasy smears on the walls confirmed what Frances had already suspected – the property had been liberally infested with rats. Any food scraps were long gone, however, and she hoped that the vermin had moved on to find better pickings elsewhere.

The back door of the kitchen faced out into the yard, although the glass panels were coated with black dust and little could be seen through them. It was locked and a stout bolt was in place from the inside. Frances reasoned that had Dobree entered the house he would have let himself in by the front door, the lock then clicking into place behind him. Since the back door was bolted from the inside, he could not have left that way, but must have retraced his steps and returned through the front door to the street. This was assuming he was unaccompanied, but so far there was no evidence that he was not alone.

'Was this back door as you last left it?' she asked Munro.

'Yes,' he replied. 'I showed a potential purchaser the property about a month ago. He was unable to appreciate its many promising features, however, and did not return. Since then we have had a number of enquiries at the office, but no actual views had been arranged until Mr Dobree suggested he might be interested.'

'When you show someone the house, do you always enter by the front door?'

'Yes.'

'I assume it wouldn't be possible to get in from the rear without breaking windows or doors.'

'That is so, and as you see, the exterior is quite undamaged.' He waved a hand at the grime-coated windows with some pride that they were not actually broken.

'Nevertheless, may I see the yard?'

'Of course.' Munro slid the bolt of the back door and unlocked it. They entered the roughly paved yard, where there was an ash bin with an ill-fitting lid and two brick outhouses, the smaller of which Munro indicated delicately was 'the usual offices' from which Frances understood it was the servants' privy, the larger being the fuel store. The unevenly paved ground was littered with wood splinters, small coal and grit, while a heap of rotting planks lay piled against the far wall. The heavy outer gate was also secured from within by a large bolt.

Frances peered into the ash bin but it revealed nothing more than the usual debris cleared from cold stoves and fires, some broken furniture, and stained curtains. Neilson glanced into the privy and wrinkled his nose, while Fiske, with some effort because the catch was stiff, opened the door of the fuel store. At that moment there was a loud knocking at the front door. 'I'll go,' said Munro. 'It might be the police.' He hurried back into the house.

'And not before time,' said Fiske staggering back, a look of horror distorting his features. Frances hurried up but he turned to her gasping 'No! No!' and held up his hands to prevent her from seeing into the store. Despite this she caught a glimpse of the dark interior, a pile of wooden planks, and something writhing.

'Is it —?'

'I don't know,' he gulped, 'but I fear there may be a body in there.'

Neilson and Herman peered into the store, and both started back in alarm.

'It's moving!' cried out Neilson.

Fiske pressed a handkerchief to his lips. 'I think those are rats.'

CHAPTER SIX

There were questions to be asked, but Frances was firm with herself and decided to leave the official enquiries to the police. Munro led the constable into the yard, and after some explanations as to why they were there, and what they had discovered, Fiske indicated the open door of the fuel store. The constable was a stout fellow, old enough to have seen most things, but even he recoiled at what he saw. He closed the door of the fuel store very quickly. 'Nothing to be done for the minute,' he said. 'If you would all be so kind as to return indoors and wait to be questioned, the Inspector will be here shortly.'

Obediently the party trooped back into the kitchen, Mr Fiske looking very unwell. Frances felt sorry for him, especially as there was nothing in the house which could have provided a restorative, and suspected that an early return to the Duke of Sussex was in order. It took little time for Frances' natural curiosity to reassert itself. Extracting the least unpleasant cloth from an abandoned pile of rags, she coaxed a spurt of brown water from the tap and scoured one of the windows. 'I want to see what is happening,' she explained. There were only two chairs in the room, which Mr Neilson examined for cleanliness and robustness. The company decided to remain standing.

'Mr Fiske, do you feel able to tell me what you saw?' asked Frances.

That gentleman, who appeared to have recovered a little, heaved a deep sigh and nodded. 'There was a loose heap of firewood, but clearly it had been laid on top of something else. I saw —,' he gave a whimper and Frances wondered if she should guide him over to the sink, '— it looked like a hand, but the fingers were gnawed by vermin. There was blood … and finger bones. At first, because of the movement, I thought there might be someone alive, but then —,' he gulped. 'I saw the dark bodies and little eyes and I knew what it was.'

'I don't suppose you could see who the individual might be, or even if it was a man or woman?'

Fiske clasped his bunched handkerchief to his mouth and shook his head.

'It is probably a vagrant who crept in to keep warm,' offered Neilson. 'He might have scrambled over the wall. Rats can attack the living as well as the dead.'

'The door had a latch,' said Mr Herman. 'Could someone have gone in and then the latch fell back and accidentally locked him in?'

Fiske frowned. 'The latch was closed. I had to lift it to enter. But no,' he shook his head, 'it was quite stiff – I don't think it could have fallen back as you suggest.'

'Mr Munro, did you notice anything unusual when you last showed someone the premises?' asked Frances. 'Did you look in the fuel store? Could the latch have been left open and you closed it?'

Munro wore the unhappy look of a salesman who had just seen his property suddenly decline in value. 'I don't recall looking into the fuel store; I think I just pointed out that there was one. I don't believe the customer looked inside. But if a man was trapped in there, he would have been able to break out, even if it was locked.'

'Unless he was weakened by starvation or illness,' said Neilson. 'I am sure there will be an explanation.'

Frances peered out of the kitchen window, but the constable was simply guarding the fuel store and had not moved from his position. 'Anyone who entered the yard from the alleyway would have had to climb in. Do you think Mr Dobree was capable of scrambling over the outer wall?'

'I shouldn't like to attempt it,' said Fiske, 'and I am more than twenty years his junior. Also the mere idea of a man in his position climbing over a wall while wearing his regalia is quite ridiculous.'

Frances agreed. 'Mr Munro, could you tell me who else apart from Mr Dobree has shown an interest in the property since it was offered for sale?'

'The gentleman I conducted around a few weeks ago is a Mr Johnstone of Notting Hill. He owns a number of properties in London and rents them out as lodgings. I am sure the body can't be his as I saw him in the street only this morning. Then there was a young man who didn't give his name or the reason for his interest, he simply asked if the house was still for sale and promised to arrange a day to view it, but nothing came of that. I suppose someone active could have climbed the wall but it does seem very strange.' He sighed. 'I wish the Inspector would come.'

After what felt like a long wait, a police inspector arrived, introducing himself as Payne of the Kensington constabulary. A morose-looking individual with a surly manner, he was in his early thirties and might have been considered handsome if his features had not been marked by ill temper. 'I won't keep you long,' he said. 'If I can just have names and addresses for now and I'll question you later if need be.'

'Do we know whose body it is?' asked Fiske, tremulously. 'You know that Mr Lancelot Dobree, the well-known philanthropist, is missing and he was last seen in the Duke of Sussex Tavern across the way?'

'Also he had expressed an interest in purchasing this property,' added Herman. 'That is why we thought to look for him here.'

'But he didn't have the keys,' Munro quickly pointed out.

'When Dobree was last seen he was wearing his Masonic regalia,' said Fiske. 'He is over seventy years of age, and we are very worried about him.'

Payne nodded. 'Wait here and I'll have a look. I'll send the constable in to take your names.' He went out into the yard and, after a brief word with the constable, opened the door of the fuel store and peered inside. His expression did not change, and he went in.

The constable rejoined the visitors and started to record their names in his notebook. 'Do you think it is a body?' Fiske asked him anxiously. 'I am rather hoping I was mistaken after all, and it was just a dog or a cat. Then I would be very embarrassed of course, but it would be such a relief! Have you found Mr Dobree yet?'

The constable shook his head. 'No sign of him, I'm afraid.'

Inspector Payne, with more sangfroid than seemed healthy under the circumstances, emerged from the fuel store, closed the door and returned to the kitchen. 'Well, all I can tell you is that we have a body which, from its size and the remains of the clothing, is that of an adult male much disfigured by vermin. There is nothing obvious on the body to identify who he is. No apron or collar, I can tell you that much. Even rats won't eat metal fittings.'

Fiske heaved a sigh of relief. 'If the man is not wearing regalia then it cannot be Dobree. He must have been called away on some urgent matter.'

'What did I tell you?' said Neilson. 'It will be some vagrant who went there to keep warm. At the tavern we are occasionally obliged to turn out undesirable persons and those who cannot moderate their consumption of alcohol.'

Frances was curious to know the cause of death, but realised that it might not be apparent until the body had been examined, and Payne was unlikely to reveal his suspicions. He had already frowned heavily when he read the constable's list of names, and favoured her with a hard look. Before too long he would have confirmed that she was that nosy lady detective who so often troubled the police.

'You can all go about your business now,' said Payne brusquely. He took charge of the house keys and ushered them out, leaving the constable to guard the property.

Munro hurried away to give the unhappy tidings to his office, and the others, as Frances had anticipated, returned to the tavern where they sat around a table in the lounge bar. No one had any appetite but there was some thirst in evidence. Frances asked for a glass of water. She needed a clear head.

'What is your advice now Miss Doughty?' asked Fiske after a hearty restorative had been swallowed.

'At present we must still regard Mr Dobree as missing and possibly in danger. If you can let me have a full description of him and a portrait if possible, I will make some enquiries. There are agents I employ to carry out searches of this nature, and they are very efficient.'

Frances was referring to the team of messenger boys managed by a young relative of Sarah's and known throughout West London as 'Tom Smith's Men'. Tom was an enterprising youth whose hours were devoted to the art of making money. His best 'man' who was known only by the name of Ratty, aspired to be a detective and commanded his own little battalion of boys who assisted Frances in her enquiries. If there was a lost puppy anywhere in Bayswater they could find it, and they were certainly able to find a missing man if he was above ground. 'Of course, if the body we found today is that of Mr Dobree then my involvement in the matter is at an end.'

'It is?' said Fiske, surprised.

'Yes. You engaged me to find him, no more. If, as seems more likely, the body is not that of Mr Dobree, then the police will continue to look for him, as will I.'

With the assistance of Mr Fiske and Mr Neilson, Frances wrote down a description of Lancelot Dobree and what he had been wearing at the time of his disappearance, but apart from the regalia it seemed that there was not a great deal to distinguish him from many another man of his age and position in life. She wrote a note for Tom Smith, which she would deliver on her way home, asking him to instruct his agents to keep their eyes open for the missing philanthropist.

Frances had other concerns. She did not say it but she still had to be convinced that Lancelot Dobree was the paragon of all the virtues he was said by his brethren to be, a man with neither vices nor secrets. The possibility was in her mind that if the body found in the fuel store was not his then he might have been involved in the death of the unknown man, and that was the reason he was missing.

CHAPTER SEVEN

It was the middle of the afternoon by the time Frances returned to her apartments. Sarah had prepared a luncheon of meat broth with bread and cheese, and, in view of Frances' habit of forgetting to eat when preoccupied, took some convincing that her companion had already eaten and tried to tempt her with bottled gooseberries and custard. Sarah had had a busy morning dealing with a complaint made by a washerwoman against her neighbour who, she claimed, had been deliberately dirtying the linen she hung up to dry in order to steal her customers. The neighbour had arrived with her own loud complaints, and Sarah had been obliged to break up the resultant fistfight. Further enquiries revealed that the source of the dispute was less a matter of laundry than the wandering eye of her client's husband. Strong words were needed to restore calm, but there was little Sarah could do to resolve the situation, and the two women had stamped off separately with glaring expressions. At least now that the trouble had been aired Sarah would know where to look if one of the three participants was murdered.

Over a generous portion of bottled fruit, Frances described the visit of Mr Fiske and the events that had followed. To her relief, Sarah, the only person who knew the full extent of Frances' unhappy discoveries about her family, fully understood why she had been unable to resist following up the enquiry.

'Are you going to interview Mr Salter?'

Frances strove to deduce from Sarah's expression whether her assistant thought this was a good idea or not. Perhaps it was something of both. 'I suppose I am hoping it won't be necessary.' She had eaten only half the fruit and had no appetite for the rest. She pushed away her plate, and for once Sarah did not urge her to eat more.

Once the dishes were cleared Sarah went out. She was due to instruct her regular ladies' exercise class at the sporting academy run by expert pugilist Professor Pounder. The classes had become increasingly well-attended during the reign of the dreaded Face-slasher, and even though that criminal was no longer free to strike terror in the residents of Bayswater the demand had continued, since the academy on its ladies-only days was considered a respectable and healthful meeting place. Sarah had recently been obliged to engage another lady to take additional classes, a Miss Harrison, a diminutive yet deceptively powerful individual who taught club-swinging, her face set in a snarl of fierce determination. Frances, after some hesitation, had been persuaded to sample the art, and found it both stimulating to the bodily system and calming to the mind. She now had her own set of clubs kept propped against the wall just inside the parlour door where, said Sarah, they would be of use if required for the pacification of burglars.

Frances very much doubted that their home was a potential target for burglars, since Sarah and Professor Pounder had been walking out for some while, and the Professor had recently taken lodgings in the ground-floor apartment. Professor Pounder was a tall, muscular, handsome fellow, economical with words, and softly spoken when he uttered them. His devotion to and admiration of Sarah was obvious to the most casual observer, and the fact that he was one of the very few men who had ever earned Sarah's trust said all that Frances needed to know. Any suggestions of future marriage or even romance were, however, robustly denied by both Sarah and the Professor, although Frances had noticed that recently the denials had been firmer and more readily provided.

Frances studied the notes she had made of all she had learned that morning concerning the disappearance of Lancelot Dobree, but no new ideas suggested themselves. She was not expecting a visitor but when the doorbell rang she peered out of the window and with a sense of resignation saw Inspector Payne on the doorstep. He arrived with his unvarying serious expression, but there was a new keenness in his look which told Frances that he had been making further enquiries about her. He surveyed the little parlour with more than the usual polite interest and she saw his gaze rest on the purple sashes of the Bayswater Women's Suffrage Society which hung proudly from a wall bracket, the embroidered cushions depicting Britannia and Boadicea, and the exercise clubs propped by the door. The cushions, though he did not know it, were gifts from Miss Gilbert and Miss John, joint leaders of the Suffrage Society, and were far too ornamented for Frances' taste, but she kept them on display in case the ladies called without warning, as they were sometimes wont to do, since she did not wish to offend them.

'So,' he said, taking a seat and leafing through his notebook, 'Miss Frances Doughty, private detective. And you reside here with a lady companion, a Miss Smith, I am told.'

'That is correct.'

He glanced at the two sashes again and sniffed. 'You were recently present at the arrest of the Bayswater Face-slasher.'

'If you don't mind Inspector, I do not wish to discuss that,' said Frances.

His glance evinced a slight trace of what might in a good light have appeared to be sympathy, but it soon vanished. 'Also, as I understand, you were responsible for the arrest of the notorious criminal known as the Filleter.'

This was true, as Frances had at one time been convinced that the Filleter, a grubby and unpleasant individual who had once haunted Bayswater like an evil shade, had committed some of the crimes to which the Face-slasher had later confessed. 'I have already said that full credit for that arrest is due to Inspector Sharrock of Paddington Green.'

'Nevertheless those who witnessed it have another story to tell.'

Frances refused to be drawn. 'I still find it hard to believe that he was never charged with any crime.'

Fortunately, the most dangerous part of the Filleter's criminal career was over. Believed to be responsible for multiple assassinations with the thin sharp knife that was his signature, following his arrest last October he had been lodged in the cells of Paddington Green police station when he had been seriously injured in a roof fall during the devastating gales that had swept through West London. Cleared of suspicion of the Face-slasher murders, he had lain close to death in the workhouse infirmary for some weeks before being spirited away by some no doubt criminal confederates.

'Well he won't trouble us again. I've heard he's gone south of the river, working a team of boy pickpockets like a regular Fagin. Southwark police have got their eye on him, so they'll get him sooner or later.'

Frances made no comment, but she was relieved that this lurking threat was a thing of the past.

'So, perhaps you could tell me why earlier today you were at an empty property when the body of a man was discovered?'

'As I am sure you know Inspector, I no longer accept enquiries in criminal matters. However, Mr Fiske, who is a former client of mine, came to me very concerned at the disappearance of Mr Lancelot Dobree. At the time I felt sure that there had to be a simple explanation; he might have been called away suddenly on an emergency, or taken ill or suffered an accident.'

'Do you still believe that?'

'It still seems the most probable explanation. Has the body been identified? How long has the man been dead? Do you know how he died?'

Payne gave a twist of the mouth that might have been a smile. 'The inquest will open tomorrow morning at the Duke of Sussex Tavern so we may have some answers then.'

'I will be sure to attend. Are the police still searching for Mr Dobree?'

'We are. There is no further news and he is officially regarded as a missing person. There is especial concern in view of his age and constables have all been issued with a portrait and are making careful searches. Are you personally acquainted with Mr Dobree?'

'No, I have never met him. Do you have a copy of the portrait? I should like to see it.'

Payne hesitated.

'I have asked my agents to look for him. It would be a useful thing for them to have. Of course we will notify the police at once if we should discover anything.'

Payne pulled a bundle of papers from his pocket, printed engravings that looked to have been copied from a photograph. He handed one to Frances. A simple line drawing, it showed the head and shoulders of a man with receding hair and side whiskers, but no special features that would have marked him out in a crowd. 'If I might have another I will see that my agents have one and keep the other for myself.'

He grunted but complied. 'Well let us hope he is found safe and well very soon. There have been several informants at the station saying they saw an elderly man getting into a cab, and we're following those up. And then perhaps he can tell us how he managed to walk out of the tavern either through two locked exits, or by escaping through a properly guarded and tyled door.'

CHAPTER EIGHT

The inquest on the unknown man was convened in the first-floor dining room of the Duke of Sussex Tavern, an event which required that the tables should be moved aside, one remaining for the use of the West Middlesex coroner, Dr Diplock, while the chairs were arranged in rows for the jury and observers. Frances and Sarah both attended, and Sarah took the opportunity to familiarise herself with the layout of the premises before they took their seats.

Since the body had not yet been identified, Frances would have expected little more than the amount of interest usually generated by the finding of a corpse in an outhouse, such occurrences not being altogether unknown in the winter months, although she suspected that they were rarer in Kensington than other parts of London. To her surprise, however, the room filled rapidly, and many of the onlookers were members of the press, representatives of the Paddington and Kensington newspapers, some of whom Frances had encountered on other similar occasions. It was obvious that the rumour had quickly spread that the corpse might be that of the missing philanthropist, and even if it was not, a body half eaten by rats always sold newspapers.

Mr Fiske and Mr Neilson were there, and a number of other gentlemen whom Frances had not previously met, who she suspected must be members of either the Literati or Mulberry Lodges, or representatives of the Dobree family. She studied the faces of the gentlemen, wondering if one of them might be Vernon Salter, the man she believed to be her natural father. Would she recognise him, she wondered, or he her? Since Frances did not resemble William Doughty, she had until her recent discoveries assumed, in the absence of any portrait of Rosetta, that she looked like her mother. Frances was unusually tall, taller than either William or her older brother Frederick who had died in

1879. It had been her uncle, Cornelius Martin, Rosetta's brother, who had finally told Frances that she did not look like her mother, but that Rosetta had once been seen in conversation with a very tall man of distinctive appearance. Frances, with her angular jaw and sharp-featured face, knew what he must mean. She looked about her but saw no man present to whom she might bear even a passing resemblance. She was obliged to admit to herself that this was a relief. She knew she might have to face him, but felt far from ready for that encounter.

The jurymen filed in, fresh from viewing the body. Several looked pale and the features of one were unhealthily shiny, and a little green. If the exposed flesh of the corpse had been chewed by rats it could not have been a pleasant sight. They were accompanied into the room by a slight odour of brandy, which suggested that some medical restorative had been necessary. Even Dr Diplock, as he took his seat and placed a folder of papers on the table, was tucking a cigar case into his pocket.

Inspector Payne arrived, and after a quick look about the room to see who was present he slumped into a chair, studying the pages of his notebook. He did not give Frances a second glance. Sarah, who had not seen the policeman before, looked briefly at Frances. She said nothing, but her face revealed her thoughts. Sarah habitually warned Frances against closer acquaintance with any single man of even halfway reasonable appearance and vaguely marriageable age. It was her decided opinion that no man could ever be worthy of her companion, but in the unlikely event of Frances meeting someone she considered suitable, she was prepared to inform her of the fact. In the case of Payne, however, no warning was necessary. After the Bayswater Face-slasher case it had been clear to her that Frances was avoiding any but formal relations with men. The only exception to this rule was her dear friend and close neighbour, the flamboyant Cedric Garton, a gentleman of refinement with a taste for poetry and the fine arts, who was both intelligent and amusing company and a confirmed bachelor.

When Dr Diplock had reviewed his papers, he called the court to order and opened the proceedings by stating that the purpose of the hearing was firstly to establish the identity of the deceased and second to arrive at cause of death. If it was not possible to conclude business that day, and he believed that that might well be the case, then it would be necessary to adjourn to allow time for further enquiries.

The first witness called was Mr Fiske, who, struggling to control his nervousness, explained to the astonished onlookers the circumstances under which he had come to be at 2 Linfield Gardens where the body was found. His account naturally mentioned the inexplicable disappearance of Lancelot Dobree and his decision to call upon the services of a private detective. Several gentlemen turned and stared openly at Frances and Sarah, and the men of the press scribbled busily. Inspector Payne then told the court in strict official language how he had been called to the scene, and after establishing that there had been an unexplained death had proceeded to seal the property pending the arrival of Dr Northrop, the police surgeon.

Dr Northrop, the next to testify, had the air of a man who had seen worse corpses too many times to mention. He confirmed that the body was that of a well-nourished male who he estimated to be between sixty-five and seventy-five years of age, although the hands and face were considerably damaged by the action of rats. He believed that death had taken place between one and three days previously, but a factor that complicated his estimate was that he was far from sure that the man had died where the body was found. There was nothing on the body to identify it, and much of the clothing had been gnawed by vermin. The quality of the remaining linen and suiting suggested that they had been purchased by a man of some means, although it was impossible to say if the dead man was the original owner. His preliminary examination showed that the man had been in very good health for someone of advanced years. The only thing discovered so far that could account for death was an injury to the head, which might have been caused either by a fall or a blow. He would know more when he had had the chance to make a detailed post-mortem examination. There were no obvious identifying marks on the body, however he had noticed that the deceased had a slight club foot, a defect he must have carried with him since birth, and his shoes had been specially made to correct this.

Northrop returned to his seat and the coroner next questioned Mr Unwin, Lancelot Dobree's personal shoemaker. Unwin identified the shoes found on the body as those he had made for Dobree, and brought with him the last on which they had been formed. He had examined the feet of the corpse and had no doubt whatsoever that the body was that of his customer.

The next witness was a man of about forty-five with a manner of carefully studied calm, who gave his name as Thomas Jeffs and said that he had been manservant to Lancelot Dobree for eighteen years. Whatever his feelings about his master, either alive or dead, these were so carefully hidden as to be indiscernible. He had viewed the body found in the fuel store and had no doubt at all that it was that of his master. He confirmed that Dobree had a slight deformity of one foot, something few of his intimates would have known.

There were no more witnesses and Dr Diplock asked Dr Northrop how soon he might be able to complete his report. There was a clear implication in the coroner's tone that since the evidence was tending to suggest that the body was quite probably that of the noted philanthropist and not a homeless vagrant, it would be advisable to accelerate the proceedings. Dr Northrop quickly took the point and replied that in view of the importance of the case he would give the matter priority and felt sure that he would come to a firm conclusion in three days.

Dr Diplock addressed the jury. While it was not yet possible to arrive at a cause of death, would they be willing to deliver a verdict as to the identity of the body? Offered the option of retiring to consider their decision, the jurymen did not trouble themselves to do so. There was a brief whispered conversation and much nodding before the spokesman rose and announced that they were content to identify the deceased as Lancelot Dobree. Dr Diplock then adjourned the hearing for three days, adding that in view of the immense public interest the resumed inquest would inevitably attract, the next hearing would take place in Kensington Town Hall.

Several of the pressmen hurried away, burning with the news, but a number of the younger ones hovered hopefully around Frances. 'I have nothing to say,' she insisted and Sarah quickly interposed her bulk, folding her brawny arms and making it known by her expression that she would not tolerate any annoyance.

Payne rose smartly from his chair and approached the gathering. 'Now then, clear off quick or there'll be trouble!'

'We have to get the story, Inspector,' whined one of the youths.

'There's no story here – move on!'

They slunk away and Frances was intending to thank the Inspector but he had already turned and left.

Another gentleman was present. He had a quiet, businesslike manner, and carried a leather document case. He did not approach Frances, but looked at her with interest before he departed.

Mr Fiske and his brethren remained behind, consulting with each other, their faces heavy with grief. Frances went to sit with them. 'I am so sorry that you have had bad news.'

'I can hardly believe it,' said Fiske, dejectedly. 'I had hoped it was another man, of course. We all did.'

'Did you know about Mr Dobree's club foot?'

Fiske shook his head. 'There was no sign of it in his walk.'

'Well, let us hope that when the final report is available you will know more.'

'Will you be attending the resumed inquest?'

Frances had half expected this question. 'I was only engaged to find Mr Dobree. Since he has been found, there is no good reason for me to do so.'

'Could I ask you to attend on our behalf?' pleaded Fiske. 'You have more experience than we do of these unfortunate occasions, and we would like to have your observations.'

Frances hesitated. 'Very well. I will watch and let you know my thoughts, but you know my position. If the cause of Mr Dobree's death is an accident, then there is nothing for me to do. If there has been a crime committed, then there is nothing I should do.'

'I understand,' said Fiske. 'The past has taught you to be cautious, but all the same I would welcome your advice even if you cannot take matters further.'

'It looks a lot like murder,' said Sarah in the cab home.

'It does,' Frances agreed. 'Of course his death might have nothing to do with why he left the tavern. He could have gone out for a reason we have yet to discover and been attacked by robbers in the street. He might have been injured in a fall and then robbed by someone who chanced by. But now we know the body is his we have more mysteries. Dr Northrop believes that Dobree did not die where he was found. Even if we can find out how he left the tavern, how did he manage to get into the yard of the house? He appears to have had an extraordinary ability to move through locked doors. And while I can understand that robbers might have taken his jewellery, money and even the regalia, which I assume must have a value, they had also removed other non-valuable items which could have identified the body.'

'A robber would just have taken stuff and run off,' said Sarah. 'Why risk being caught by taking time to hide the body?'

'The only reason I can think of is to prevent or delay recognition. Which suggests that whoever hid the body knew who he was. Perhaps it wasn't a random attack after all; perhaps Mr Dobree was targeted for murder.'

CHAPTER NINE

S oon after they arrived home, Max Gillan, a senior reporter with the *Bayswater Chronicle*, arrived with a sparkle of antici-pation in his eyes. Frances and he had come to an agreement some while before that she would grant him exclusive interviews on the condition that he promised not to distort the truth, and he in return would supply her with any information he had gleaned about cases in which she was interested.

'Is it true what everyone is saying?' he asked eagerly. 'Are you taking up your detective work again?'

Frances spoke carefully. 'Not precisely. I have been undertaking searches for lost relatives and pets, and helping clients construct their family trees, but I am not engaging in criminal work. I was asked to look into the disappearance of Mr Dobree, which could have occurred for any wholly innocent reason, and until the next hearing we will not know the answer.'

'Would you be able to tell our readers your opinion on the matter?' he asked with what he must have hoped was a winning smile.

Frances would not be won over. 'I would never presume to anticipate the verdict of a coroner's jury, especially since there is more evidence to be presented.'

'But it is all over Bayswater that you were there when the body was discovered! Did you see it?'

'Thankfully no, since I was told that it had been much damaged by the action of rats.'

His pencil moved rapidly over the pages of his notebook, scat-tering the impenetrable lines, loops and dots of shorthand. 'Eaten? Oh, please say it was eaten.'

'I can't comment in any detail. The hands and face had been attacked, which made identifying the body difficult. If you want something new to print, then I can give you all the circumstances of the finding of the body.'

'I'll have to be content with that for now,' he conceded.

Frances supplied the story, hoping that an account of the unusual disappearance of Lancelot Dobree would stimulate the memory of any witnesses who had seen him on the fatal night.

'Will you be at the adjourned inquest?' Gillan asked.

'I will, but as an observer only.'

'So you do think Dobree was murdered?'

'I can't answer that question. But should the jury come to that conclusion it will mark the end of any interest I have in the case.'

Gillan smiled. 'I know you, Miss Doughty, and if it is a case of murder I think you won't be able to resist looking into it.'

Frances was spared making a reply by a loud knocking on the front door. She looked outside and saw a group of press-men gathered on the paved approach and steps. 'I have said all I am going to say to the press, and if you could do me a very great favour, Mr Gillan, on your way out could you tell the gentlemen to disperse before their presence constitutes a nuisance and I have to summon the police, or, worse still, Sarah.'

He grinned. 'Right you are!'

Frances had no more news of the Dobree case on the following day, and expected none, but it remained prominent in her thoughts. Mr Gillan had been right about one thing, the puzzle continued to intrigue her.

There were two clients to see in the morning. Frances interviewed a lady whose son had been truanting from school. The usual chastisements had failed to have any effect, and she wanted him followed to find out what so diverted his attention from his studies. It was a case made for Tom Smith and his 'men' and Frances prepared a note with the information they required.

A single young lady arrived with a letter she had discovered that had been placed on a path where she walked, and was clearly intended for her. The writer professed to be a young man of good character and paid her compliments in refined language to which no one could have objected. He wished to meet her with the object of making her better acquaintance, and suggested a time and place. The lady had very prudently declined to make the assignation, but appealed to Frances to discover the identity of the sender. Frances decided to turn that case over to Sarah. It was not certain whether the writer had any criminal intent, but it was as well to test him out.

Her afternoon was devoted to work on behalf of a Bayswater businessman, Mr Cork, who had asked her to draw up his family tree. Mr Cork, a manufacturer of cravats and cummerbunds, was in a state of permanent rivalry with his former partner, Mr Wren, whose business was of a similar kind, and the two alternated between being bitter enemies and close friends. Both were well known to Frances and it had once been necessary for Sarah to restore calm between them through the liberal application of alcoholic beverages. It had been Mr Cork's hope that she would discover that the family legend that he was descended from nobility would turn out to be true, in which case he would never permit Mr Wren to forget it, but Frances was going to have to disappoint him. Not only were his great-grandfathers all fishmongers, but it also transpired that he and Mr Wren were distant cousins. How that would affect their tempestuous relationship she could not guess.

Sarah was due to go out that evening in the company of Professor Pounder, and Frances had expected to spend some quiet time by the fireside with a little reading and cold pie and cheese. Having just enjoyed a pot of tea, she was choosing a book to read and trying to convince herself that a novel would be the best thing to calm her busy mind, when the volume that really appealed to her was the Bayswater Street Directory. Sarah was doing some mending but appeared to be unusually unsettled as if her fingers, usually so strong and nimble, had suddenly lost their ability to direct a needle.

'Is there something troubling you?' asked Frances.

'Well, it shouldn't,' said Sarah. 'I mean, it's just a fish supper.'

'That sounds very enjoyable.'

'It will be.' Sarah didn't look convinced. After more fidgeting with the sewing, she suddenly gave up and threw it down in her lap. 'You could come with if you like.'

Frances was surprised. 'Would that be acceptable to Professor Pounder?'

'I don't see why not.'

'But if it's just the two of you —'

'Well that's it, isn't it? It's not just the two of us, we're having supper with the family. So there.'

It took a moment or two for Frances to understand the import of this information. 'You mean that you are introducing Professor Pounder to your family?'

'In a manner of speaking. He hasn't met them before and they want to meet him.'

'Does this mean —'

'No,' Sarah cut her off. 'It doesn't mean anything.'

'But you are worried they might not like him, or he might not like them?'

'Anything's possible. I just don't want it to end in a fight.'

'Do you think it might?'

Sarah shrugged.

'But isn't one of your brothers Jeb Smith, the Wapping Walloper? So there is a mutual interest in the art of pugilism. That is a good start. Your parents will surely think well of the Professor and his successful business; and he has very good manners.'

'That's as maybe, but Ma is old fashioned and don't like Irish.'

'I didn't know he was Irish. But he is an excellent man and I know he will win her over.'

Sarah looked as though she was trying to convince herself. 'Would you come with? I know they'd like to meet you.'

Frances laid her book aside. 'And I would very much like to meet them.'

Sarah's relief was all too obvious. Soon afterwards, Professor Pounder, clutching a bunch of flowers and a box of sweetmeats, called to say their cab was ready. He said nothing when told that Frances would be accompanying them, but Frances thought that he too was relieved, though she could not imagine how she might be of any use if a fight broke out. Young Tom appeared, wearing his best suit of clothes, his face scrubbed to a shine, and they departed, Sarah carrying a parcel containing two plum cakes she had made earlier.

As they left the wooden paving of Bayswater, which reduced the sound of their carriage to a dull rumble like a looming thunderstorm, they passed through the teeming heart of London, where the clatter and crunch of wheels and hooves was almost enough to drown the cries of drivers trying to work through what looked like a dangerously random melee. Their journey took them through the heart of what Frances thought a mighty city should be, the shopping emporiums, the homes of the ancient guilds, the great banks, the offices of the press and palaces of law and government. Tom, the only person not regarding the visit with nervous apprehension, looked out of the window at the fine buildings as if counting up the money of those who worked there.

Heading past the street markets and the Tower into the commercial east end, they reached the part of London dominated by the docks, a reminder that London was and had been since ancient times, a seaport. Warehouses, factories and the homes of labouring families were clustered close together, dwarfed by a forest of cranes. Buildings wallowed like sinking ships in the stench of industry, which mingled the odours of smelting, metal casting and sugar refining with the dark smoke that boiled from blackened chimneys.

Sarah rarely talked about her family, and she had never revealed exactly how she and Tom were related, occasionally referring to him vaguely as a cousin, although Frances suspected that the connection was rather closer. Now, however, Sarah, perhaps trying to still her nervousness by talking, began to tell some of her history. Her father, she said, had worked in the London docks since he was twelve. Now aged sixty, his legs were weak and he was only able to do light labouring. Her mother had married at sixteen, and brought up a family of eight boys and two girls in a small apartment on the Ratcliffe Highway. It was a tribute to her hard work and devotion that she had only lost one child, a daughter who had died from scarlet fever. Sarah's eight brothers had initially been destined for dock work like their father, and four of them still toiled there, but family fortunes had taken a better turn when Jeb had discovered a more lucrative metier in the boxing ring, Henry and Sam had found employment at Charles Jamrach's Animal Emporium, which dealt in exotic birds, beasts and curiosities, and Jack became apprenticed to a tailor. Sarah's parents and the four sons who were still unmarried now occupied a three-room apartment above a draper's shop.

As they drove down the busy highway, Sarah, who liked a bloodcurdling tale as much as anybody, told the story of the horrible murders of 1811 and the time when Mr Jamrach had saved a young boy from the jaws of an escaped tiger. Far more fearsome in her estimation was the prospect of the promised gathering and as the cab drew up in front of the draper's, Professor Pounder squeezed her shoulder with a surprisingly gentle hand.

Mrs Smith, who came down the stairs to greet them, was a small wiry woman with grey hair and strong hands, knotted and darkened by hard work like the branches of an ancient tree. She led them up to the parlour and introduced her husband, a broad shouldered but mild-looking man, with a well-used pipe and a penny whistle sticking out of his waistcoat pocket. A large fire was blazing in the grate and the room burned hot and smoky. Salutations and gifts were exchanged and Mrs Smith, after a cautious look at Professor Pounder who towered over her, accepted the flowers and sweets and seemed much taken by them.

All of Sarah's brothers were there, with four wives, Jeb's intended and several children, although there was not room for everyone in the parlour, and the three younger brothers, two wives and all the children had had to crowd into an adjoining room, and be brought out in twos and threes at intervals to be introduced to the visitors.

The scrubbed table was hardly large enough to do more than lay out platters of food, and there were so many chairs in the room, many of which must have been borrowed from neighbours, that once seated it was almost impossible to move without disturbing several people. The food was plain, fried fish, boiled potatoes in butter, white sauce, and pickles, with foaming jugs of beer. The conversation tended to family matters, Jeb's recent success in the ring and forthcoming wedding, the wild animals that Henry and Sam had, at considerable risk both to themselves and the population at large, recently transported to a menagerie, and Jack's progress in the art of gentleman's suiting. The four dockworkers seemed not to resent their brothers' more elevated employments but looked on with cheerful pride. All were dressed as if for a Sunday and the young men, while respecting their father, deferred to their mother in everything. The meal was rounded off with cake, sweets and tea, and then someone sent out for more beer.

Frances was questioned about her work, since all were well aware of the dangers she had faced and the criminals she had brought to justice. She was regaled with stories of the old hanging dock where pirates had met their end, and asked for her opinion on whether John Williams, the man suspected of the notorious murders in 1811, had been guilty of the crimes. Frances promised she would look into it. The conversation then turned to the Professor's boxing academy, and by degrees and as more beer was fetched and consumed, he was invited to demonstrate his strength by lifting Jeb Smith using one arm, something he accomplished with ease. Further demonstrations followed, such as the space available would allow, and then Mr Smith treated everyone to a tune on the penny whistle, after which someone sent out for more beer. Frances had never been partial to beer, and was not sure afterwards how she had managed to consume so much of it, but it was very refreshing.

It was time to leave, and as the Professor went to find a cab, Mr Smith tapped Sarah on the arm and said, 'He'll do.'

Chapter Ten

When the morning newspapers arrived, it was with some trepidation that Frances opened them to read the reports of the inquest into the body found at 2 Linfield Gardens. They were even worse than she had imagined.

Inquests that were considered to be of minor importance were usually gathered together in a single column under one heading, but Dobree's had been granted its own space, with headlines such as 'Lancelot Dobree Mysterious Death' and 'Well Known Philanthropist Found Dead'. After describing all that could be gleaned from anonymous informants in the police force, the newspapers had gone on to draw attention to Frances' presence in court and speculate that she was acting for Mr Dobree's family, which naturally suggested that it was a case of murder. The rumours that Miss Doughty had retired from her detective work were premature, they declared, claiming that she was even now looking into a whole host of hideous crimes and arrests were imminently expected. More worryingly, one paper suggested that her energy and logical brain could mean only one thing, that she was not, after all, female, but a man cunningly disguised so as to delude criminals into imagining that she was no threat.

The *Bayswater Chronicle* was, thanks to Mr Gillan, more restrained. While making much of the horrible appearance of the rat-eaten corpse, it had concentrated on the almost magical and inexplicable means by which Lancelot Dobree had vanished from the Lodge room, and the role of the intrepid Miss Doughty, whose clever investigations had led to the discovery of the body when the Kensington police had failed. Frances wondered what Inspector Payne would make of that.

She decided to go out about her more humdrum business before any more reporters could assemble. As she departed she saw that there were two police constables in the street, which gave her some comfort. Returning home after a quiet afternoon staring at parish records, Frances had just enjoyed a well-deserved pot of tea with a slice of one of Sarah's excellent and generously sized jam tarts when she received another visit from Inspector Payne.

He declined to take a seat and strode around the parlour, flinty-eyed, before turning on Frances with a hard stare. 'Miss Doughty, can you advise me when and where you last saw Mr Albert Munro of Munro & Son House agents? He is the "Son" of the enterprise, the gentleman who showed you the property in Linfield Gardens.'

Despite the warmth of the room, Frances felt suddenly chilly. It was the kind of question that never boded well, and there was something in her visitor's manner that told her he brought bad news. 'Don't tell me he is missing, now?'

'Just answer the question.'

'You were there, Inspector. I last saw Mr Munro three days ago, when Mr Dobree's body was found. I have not seen him since.'

Payne nodded. He didn't look inclined to dispute her reply. 'Yesterday afternoon Mr Munro was called away from his office after receiving a message from a prospective lessee who wished to view some properties. He went out taking three sets of keys, and did not return. The office assumed that he had gone home after seeing the client. In fact, he had not. Mr Munro occupies a separate bachelor apartment in his father's house, and therefore when Mr Munro senior retired for the night, he was not aware that his son had not come home. It was only when Mr Munro junior did not appear at the breakfast table this morning that his father became aware that something might be amiss. After enquiries were made at the office and with friends, with no result, the houses the son had gone to were searched. All three were furnished properties of quality, all had been burgled, and in one of them Mr Munro was found dead. Although the inquest has yet to be held there can be little doubt that he was murdered.'

A whirlwind of thoughts entered Frances' head. Even though the man was hardly known to her, there was shock and sorrow at the news, but also the miserable feeling that she was unable, however hard she tried, to escape involvement with murder. She asked herself why she had ever consented to help Mr Fiske, but of course she knew the answer. 'Do you think that Mr Munro's murder is connected with the death of Mr Dobree?'

'We don't know. Unfortunately, it has not yet been possible to interview Mr Munro senior, who is, as you might imagine, in a state of distress.'

Frances picked up her notebook. 'I did have a brief conversation with Mr Munro junior before you arrived.' She turned through the pages. 'Here it is. He told me that the only person he had shown around the Linfield Gardens property was a Mr Johnstone.'

Payne nodded. 'Yes, the office has a record of that and we have spoken to Mr Johnstone. He did not return for another look. Something about dry rot.'

'But Mr Munro also said that there was another enquiry, from a young man who did not leave his name and who promised that he would arrange for a viewing but did not.'

'Now that we didn't know,' said Payne. 'I don't suppose you have a description?'

'I'm afraid not.'

'Well someone else in the office might remember him. Mr Fiske tells me you are to be at the resumed inquest on Mr Dobree.'

'At his request. He was very anxious that I attend in order to give my observations, and I will, but only as a favour to him. Are any members of Mr Dobree's family to give evidence?'

Payne narrowed his eyes. 'Inevitably. Are they of interest to you?'

Frances wished she could have taken back her question. 'They did not attend the first hearing.'

'No, they sent a solicitor to watch the proceedings for them. Junior man. But I expect the big guns will be out next time. Mr Marsden.' He smirked. 'Friend of yours, I've been told.'

'Oh dear,' said Frances.

Henry Marsden had long been one of the leading solicitors in Bayswater and, following the sudden and spectacular fall from grace of his chief rival Mr Rawsthorne, considered himself to be unassailably the most important solicitor and one of the most respected citizens in the district. He had never restrained himself from belittling and pouring scorn on all of Frances' successes and trumpeting his delight at her failures. There was nothing personal in his dislike, it was simply that Frances was intruding into an area of endeavour for which he believed women were unfit. Had she been a dutiful wife and mother, he would have tolerated her.

Matters had recently taken a curious turn when Timothy Wheelock, formerly Mr Rawsthorne's confidential clerk, a young man with his inky fingers in most of the underhand activities in Bayswater, had narrowly escaped a criminal prosecution and gone to employ his very peculiar talents in the office of Mr Marsden. During Mr Wheelock's brief period in police custody Frances had performed a professional service for him, retrieving some papers he had hidden away. She had only agreed to carry out this unsavoury task in order to obtain some material that related to her own family affairs. While Marsden knew about her action, there were two important circumstances of which he was unaware. Frances had refused to accept any payment from Mr Wheelock, and as a result he regarded himself in her debt. It was a debt she hoped never to have to call in but it was there, all the same. She also knew that some of the papers, which were now in a private deposit box to which only Wheelock held the key, could either control or destroy Mr Marsden. Given a choice in the matter, Frances never wished to see either of these two individuals again, but she had a horrible feeling that this wish was unlikely to be granted.

The next day was a Sunday, when Frances liked to use the cool quiet of St Stephen's church for contemplation. She prayed for those she had lost in the last months, not without wondering, as she would no doubt do to her dying day, if there was anything she could have done to prevent those deaths. On this Sunday she also prayed for the souls of the recently deceased Mr Dobree and young Mr Munro.

The question continuing to torment her mind was whether she had done the right thing in agreeing to help Mr Fiske. At the time it had seemed like the right thing to do, but then how often had she been dangerously misled by her curiosity? The best she could hope for from the resumed inquest was that the final verdict would be that death had occurred from natural causes, Dobree having suffered a catastrophe of the brain that had led him to wander by chance to the place where he had been found. Almost as the thought crossed her mind she realised how absurd it was. There was clear deliberation, probably careful planning, in what he had done and possibly also in where he had gone. The jury, however, might not choose to see things in the way she did, and be willing to come to a verdict that caused the least upset to the family. Frances had read numerous inquest reports and seen many an obvious suicide declared, against all the evidence, to be an accident for exactly that reason, but of course in such cases there was no criminal to be brought to justice.

Was she really hoping for a wrong verdict to save her own feelings? If it was murder, then that was what must be found. A killer must be made to suffer the penalty decreed by law. She wondered if the Salter family might want to engage her help in the investigation. She would refuse, not only because she had sworn to no longer deal with criminal cases, but also because it would almost certainly involve an encounter with Vernon Salter, her natural father, the man who had cruelly deserted the woman who had borne his children in pursuit of a fortune. The more she thought about him the less inclined she was ever to endure a meeting with him.

CHAPTER ELEVEN

As Frances and Sarah descended from their cab outside the handsome Italianate edifice of Kensington Town Hall she saw two men standing outside. While it was apparent that they were acquainted with each other, it was obvious from their demeanour that it was a situation that gave neither of them any pleasure. One was the sour-faced solicitor Mr Marsden, the other she had never before seen, but a glance told her at once who he was. He was in his mid-forties and very tall, well over six feet in height, and of a willowy thinness. His features were not so very like those of Frances that he would immediately have been taken to be her father, but had the two of them stood side by side, something she intended should never happen, the resemblance would have been apparent to anyone who cared to look for it. She lowered the veil on her bonnet, and she and Sarah slipped quickly past the two men into the building.

A heavily veiled lady in deep mourning was taking a slow turn around the foyer as if waiting for someone. Her carriage was regal, her walk measured, the head set proudly on firmly squared shoulders. A young gentleman of the press, seizing his opportunity, approached her, notebook in hand. 'Excuse me, but you wouldn't be Mrs Salter by any chance?'

The lady turned to stare at him. Even through her veil she must have had a piercing look. 'If you don't leave this instant, I shall call the police and have you removed,' she said. The voice was one of quiet authority that did not expect any denial. The young man backed away.

As Dr Diplock had anticipated, the room set aside for the inquest was filled to capacity with interested persons, and this suited Frances very well as she hoped to be able to vanish in the crowd. Apart from Marsden and the Salters she saw numerous pressmen, Inspector Payne, members of the Literati Lodge, and other gentlemen who she thought must be Dobree's brethren in Mulberry Lodge.

Sitting quietly to one side but looking about him very intently was a young man whose face was adorned with an enormous set of Dundreary whiskers, and whom Frances at once recognised. Arthur Miggs was, or liked to think of himself as an author. He published trite and syrupy verses as well as romantic melodramas under the *nom de plume* Augustus Mellifloe. Frances was no great judge of literature but she had attempted to read one of his novels, *The Divine Heart of Lady Mabelle*, and it had evoked in her a strong desire to slap the heroine until she came to her senses. The presence of Mr Miggs at the inquest was both worrying and no surprise. He had once been a candidate for admission to the Literati, but had been enraged by a witheringly harsh review in the *Bayswater Chronicle* of his slim volume of poetry, *Mes Petites Chansonettes*. The piece, although published under the byline of Mr Fiske, had actually been penned by his less forgiving wife. As a result, Miggs, feeling deeply insulted by what he believed to be wholly unwarranted criticism, not only withdrew his candidacy but also became a violent and intractable opponent of freemasonry. The fraternity, he would tell anyone with the patience to listen, was a secret society of disreputable men, cloaking traitorous plots under a mask of charity. During the recent spate of Face-slasher murders he had deluged the newspapers with letters suggesting that the series of inexplicable killings were all part of a Masonic plot, and he must have been bitterly disappointed to discover that this was not the case. He was undoubtedly attending the inquest in order to accumulate ammunition for a new campaign.

The proceedings began with the enquiry into the death of Albert Munro, aged thirty-four, unmarried, a property agent who had been found dead in an empty house on the firm's books. He had been called away, apparently by a prospective client, after receiving a note that he had taken with him. To spare the father, who was in frail health, the body had been identified by his uncle Anthony. The deceased had been in good health, and the cause of death was an injury to the back of the head, which could not have been accidental, especially since it appeared that he had been struck more than once. These multiple blows had made it difficult to arrive at any conclusion concerning the attacker from the appearance and direction of the injury. The note was nowhere to be found and it was assumed that it had been removed by the killer. Some money, keys and a gold watch had been stolen from the body, as well as valuable ornaments and pictures with which the property, a superior class of furnished rental, had been much provided.

Dr Diplock advised the jury that even if they believed that the person who had struck the blows had intended to do no more than knock the victim unconscious, the case was still, in view of the intent to do harm, considered to be one of murder. The jury, after brief consultation, had no difficulty in returning a verdict of murder by a person or persons unknown. Since the other properties to which Munro had carried the keys had also been robbed, Dr Diplock offered the theory that there might be a gang operating, luring people to empty houses where they could carry out their crimes unobserved. He suggested that property agents might wish to take that into account when accompanying clients they did not know.

After a short interlude, the resumed inquest on Lancelot Dobree was duly opened. Inspector Payne described the action taken by the police, which had involved more than a hundred interviews and visits to all the properties in the area. Everyone who had been in the Duke of Sussex Tavern on the night of Lancelot Dobree's disappearance had been spoken to and no one recalled having seen him after he entered the Lodge room. The end result was that no more information had emerged as to Dobree's movements after his disappearance, or how he had met his death. The owner of the empty lodging house, a lady of advanced years who lived with her daughter in Sussex, still had her own copies of the keys in her possession, which she kept in a box under her bed and had lent them to no one.

'That's a miserable-looking character,' muttered Sarah as Payne tucked his notebook into his pocket and headed back to his seat.

'Perhaps he has something to be miserable about,' replied Frances.

Sarah grunted. 'Well, I don't trust him.'

Dr Northrop stepped up to deliver his report. 'I have completed my examination of the body of Lancelot Dobree, and I am in no doubt that the cause of death was a single blow to the back of the head that fractured the skull and caused substantial bleeding in the brain. He would have become unconscious immediately after the blow, and death would have ensued very soon afterwards. I made a careful search of the location in which the body was found, and there was no object nearby or even in the house which could have caused that injury. Also, in my opinion it is impossible for the injury to have occurred by accident. Mr Dobree was struck by something like a hammer or maul, which created a distinctively shaped fracture, and the weapon was then removed from the scene. It is also now clear that as I suspected the fatal attack occurred outside the fuel store and the body was placed there afterwards, in all probability for concealment. The blow would not have caused a lot of external bleeding. There was blood matted in his hair and some on his collar and cravat. I found a few drops on the paving of the yard, but there was nothing to say exactly where the attack took place. I have no hesitation in stating that the intention of his attacker was at the very least to disable his victim, and quite possibly to kill him.'

'Were you able to determine anything about the attacker from the weight and position of the blow?' asked Diplock.

'Yes, I believe that the attacker was either male or a strong female, but more probably male. He would have been right handed and taller than the deceased.'

'How tall was the deceased?'

'Five feet seven inches.'

'Have you been able to determine the time of death?'

'Based on my examination of the stomach contents, and information about his last meal, I would estimate that he died not long after he was last seen alive.'

Dr Northrop returned to his seat.

The next witness was the architect Mr Herman, who testified that Lancelot Dobree had been interested in purchasing a property for conversion into a school. He confirmed that he had not been told the address of the property Dobree wanted him to see, and neither he nor any of his employees had previously visited the house where the body was found. He did not know of any business dealings that might have led to the attack or any enemies Dobree might have had.

An elderly gentleman who crept slowly to his place on a walking stick was Mr Westvale, a friend of Lancelot Dobree for many years and Master of Mulberry Lodge. He could only reiterate the good opinion of others, and confirm that he knew of no reason why anyone would want to harm the deceased.

As he shuffled back to his place Frances was deep in thought. She was more than ever convinced that Dobree had not been the victim of a chance street robbery or his killer would not have taken the trouble to hide the body. Dobree might have been lured to the location of his murder by his killer, perhaps on the pretext that he would be shown over the property. That still didn't explain how Dobree had managed to leave the Lodge room, why if he had a meeting he had not advised anyone of it, how either Dobree or his killer had obtained access to the building without the house agents or owner being aware of it, and also where he had been planning to go that night that had required him to pack a change of linen and toilet articles. The late Mr Munro was not a suspect as he had not been a tall man, but there must be many individuals in Dobree's circle of friends and acquaintances who would fit the portrait of his killer.

With great gentleness Dr Diplock asked if he might question Mrs Salter, and she was offered a chair and a glass of water, the first of which she availed herself of, while the second she left perched on the coroner's table, untasted. She did not raise her veil.

'Mrs Salter, I will make this as brief as possible,' began Diplock. 'Did your father tell you where he was intending to go after the meeting of the Lodge?'

The voice was crisp, firm, assured. 'He did not.'

'Did he ever mention to you his plans to found a charity school?'

'Yes. It was to be named in memory of my mother and I was to be patroness. That is all the information I have.'

'Can you think of anyone who might have meant any harm to your father?'

'No. He was greatly liked and admired by all who knew him.'

Diplock glanced at the jury but they indicated with a shake of the head that they did not wish to trouble the witness further. Dr Diplock advised that he had no further questions and called Vernon Salter to give evidence.

As Vernon Salter unfolded his long body from his chair, there was a certain amount of whispering in the room. Frances gazed on the face of the man who was almost certainly her natural father, the man who had lured her mother away from her husband and children and then abandoned her for an heiress. Revolted by his treachery she tried to find it in herself to hate him, but somehow she could not. The grief she had felt when she had discovered her history had wound itself into her body and mind, strangling any other emotion.

He stood quietly by the coroner's table, his discomfort palpable.

'Mr Salter, I understand you have been travelling on business – when did you return?'

'Late last night.'

'Where were you last Monday night?'

'I was staying at the cottage in Berkshire which is owned by my wife's family. I left the following morning.'

'Do you have a witness to confirm that?'

'No, I was there alone.'

As he spoke, Frances saw Inspector Payne's posture change. He had been studying a bundle of papers and began to pay particular and close attention to one of them. Then he raised his head and subjected Vernon Salter to a stare of considerable intensity. After a brief pause he wrote something in his notebook, tore out the page, and handed it to the coroner's officer, indicating that it should be passed to Dr Diplock.

'What do you know about Mr Dobree's interest in founding a school?' continued the coroner.

'He mentioned the plan to me and asked if I would be willing to oversee the renovation work. I said I would. But he never told me what property he had in mind, neither have I viewed a property or had any keys.'

And now, thought Frances, of the two men who might have been able to confirm or deny that statement, the Munros, one was dead, the other too ill to be questioned. She saw the jury-men glancing at each other. Were they thinking as she did, that the murders of Lancelot Dobree and Albert Munro could be connected?

'Do you know of anyone who might have borne ill will to your father-in-law? Or someone who might have benefited by his death?'

'No. He was a very well-liked and highly respected man. I have not seen his will but I understand that the bulk of his property is divided between a trust for the grandchildren, to charity, and to my wife. I do not and have never expected to benefit in any great material way from my father-in-law's death.'

Vernon Salter returned to his seat, and the coroner paused to study the note passed to him by Inspector Payne. Whatever the contents of the note, it obliged him to give it extended considera-tion. He then called the next witness, the deceased's manservant Mr Jeffs, to give evidence as to the circumstances of his master's absence from home.

Jeffs came forward with his accustomed calm dignity. 'Mr Dobree advised me that he was to attend a Lodge meeting in the afternoon, but would not dine or return home that night. He said that he was attending to some private business but told me nothing further; neither did he say where he was intending to spend the night. However, he did say that he would send a telegram to advise when he could be expected home. I packed his overnight bag myself. Nothing was missing from it when it was returned to me.'

'Did you receive a telegram from Mr Dobree?'

'I did not.'

'Was this unusual behaviour on Mr Dobree's part?'

'To be absent from home without saying where he was bound? Yes. I have never known him do such a thing before. But his instructions were clear and of course I did not question them or ask for further information.'

'Mr Jeffs, can you advise the court what action was taken when you were notified by Mr Fiske that your master was missing from the Lodge room?'

'I consulted Mrs Salter on her return home, and I was instructed to dispatch a telegram to Mrs Barrett, who manages the cottage in

Berkshire. In due course we received a reply confirming that Mr Dobree was not at the cottage, neither had she received advance notice that he would be there.'

'When a member of the family wishes to stay in the cottage is the housekeeper always informed of this?'

'Yes. Mrs Barrett does not occupy the cottage herself but lives very close by and therefore needs to be advised when she is required to make it ready for occupation.'

'Please tell the court what occurred next.'

'It was decided to wait for a telegram from Mr Dobree, but since he did not have his overnight bag with him, it was thought he might change his mind and return that night, so one of the maids was instructed to wait up for him. I should mention that not only is the house locked at night but also very securely bolted. I retired to my bed, but not long afterwards I was alerted by the maid, who said that she had heard someone trying to enter the house by the back door. She knew it could not have been the master, as he would have gone to the front door. Even if he had mislaid his keys, he would have rung for a servant to let him in. I investigated and while any would-be intruder was no longer there it was clear that someone had attempted to gain entry using either a key or some other implement. The door, which I had locked myself, was now unlocked, but the bolts had held, and the criminal must have realised that his attempts would not be rewarded and run away. Naturally a constable was summoned, but there was nothing to see. Since Mr Dobree had already said that he would be away from home that night, I suppose no importance was then attached to his absence. We made sure to have a servant guarding the house for the rest of the night, and the following day we made further enquiries with friends and acquaintances of Mr Dobree in case anyone knew of his whereabouts.'

'Did you assume that someone had obtained Mr Dobree's house keys?'

'We didn't know what to think.'

'Were the keys distinctive? If a stranger had found them in the street would he have known which house they belonged to?'

'There was a leather fob, stamped with the words "Mulberry House". It is a well-known residence in Kensington.'

'I see. What was your next action?'

'The following night, when no communication had been received from Mr Dobree, and Mrs Barrett confirmed by telegram that he had still not come to the cottage, we alerted the police.'

Dr Diplock once again perused the note provided by Inspector Payne. 'Mr Jeffs, did Mrs Barrett mention Mr Salter's presence at the cottage?'

'She did not.'

'Did you ask her if he was there?'

'No.'

'Thank you, you may stand down. I would like to recall Inspector Payne.'

Payne approached the coroner once more.

'Inspector, in your own words please let me know the result of the enquiries made by the Berkshire police.'

The Inspector consulted his papers, but not before directing a brief and hostile stare at Vernon Salter. 'When the police were alerted to the deceased's disappearance I was advised that there was a family cottage in Berkshire, and it was very possible that Mr Dobree might be found there. I accordingly telegraphed the Berkshire police who contacted the housekeeper. I have here a copy of the report we were sent, which confirms that not only was Mr Dobree not at the cottage, but that no member of the family had stayed there for some weeks.' There were gasps in the courtroom and all eyes now turned to Vernon Salter. Frances could hardly bear to look, but forced herself to do so. Salter had gone pale. He was a poor liar and was having a hard time dealing with the consequences of being found out. Payne handed a paper to Dr Diplock who studied it and handed it back. 'Thank you Inspector, that will be sufficient. Please stand down. I now wish to recall Mr Salter.' There was a busy murmur of comment in the room, which was soon hushed as everyone waited to hear what the witness would say.

Vernon Salter, looking like a hunted and cornered animal, got to his feet and once again prepared to be questioned. Dr Diplock gazed at him with an unreadable expression. 'Mr Salter, you stated earlier in response to my question that last Monday, the day of Mr Dobree's death, you were staying at the family cottage. The court has been provided with information that indicates that this was not the case. I suggest therefore that you might like to reconsider your earlier reply.'

Salter hesitated, tried to say something and stumbled over his words. 'I am – very sorry – truly I am – I may have been confused – I have been travelling on business and – sometimes I can find it fatiguing – and – and …' a nervous gulp, 'to be perfectly honest I do not think I can tell you where I was that night.'

Dr Diplock raised his eyebrows. There was muttered conversation amongst the onlookers and he was obliged to call for quiet. 'Very well, Mr Salter, but you would be best advised to examine your memory for that information, as it may well be needed.'

To Vernon Salter's immense relief he was permitted to resume his place but not without many suspicious glances being directed at him. Frances doubted that his testimony was as he claimed, a simple error. It seemed far more likely to be a deliberate lie, which raised the question – had he lied about anything else? Who knew what such a rogue might be capable of? Supposing he had had keys to the lodging house after all, and had invited Lancelot Dobree to inspect the property? The only risk was being observed but that was not a great risk in the evening quiet of Linfield Gardens. And this creature, she reminded herself, was her father. The mere idea made her feel unwell.

To everyone's surprise, the next witness called was Mr Marsden. Frances bent her head, hoping that her veil would conceal her features. Even if he did recognise her she thought he would probably put her presence at the inquest down to a love of snooping. As Marsden took his place he glanced around the room, taking in those present. It was a prideful sneering look, too acutely conscious of his own cleverness and the respect that he believed he commanded.

'Mr Marsden, how long have you been acquainted with Lancelot Dobree?'

'I have acted as his solicitor for more than twenty years, and my father acted for him many years before that when I was a junior partner.'

'Where and when did you last see him?'

'At my office, two weeks before his death.'

'What do you know of Mr Dobree's plans to found a school?'

'He mentioned it, but only in a general way, saying that he was looking for a suitable property and of course I agreed to act for him in any purchase. He did not, however, indicate which if any properties he was interested in.'

'Did he tell you about the journey he was intending to make last Monday night after the Lodge meeting?'

'Not specifically, but I know that there was something that deeply troubled him and his plan may well have been in connection with that.'

'Did he reveal what was troubling him?'

'He did not discuss it in any great detail, since he was unwilling for personal reasons to divulge too much, even to me, but he indicated that his concerns related to the behaviour of his son-in-law, Mr Salter.'

There was a marked intake of breath in the room, and some whispers, quickly stifled. Frances found herself starting to tremble, and Sarah clasped her arm firmly.

'I should explain that I was involved in drawing up the marriage agreement between Mr Salter and the Dobree family. It is my opinion that the terms of the agreement are of some significance to this court. Mr Dobree was anxious that his daughter would not fall victim to a fortune hunter, and in this arrangement her personal fortune was therefore carefully secured to her use under the administration of her father. Mr Salter received a marriage portion to enable him to start up in business and an annuity, the capital remaining in the possession of his father-in-law, but no more. There was, however, a provision that should Mr Salter ever be made bankrupt, be convicted of a crime, or fail to honour his marriage vows, then the annuity would cease, the loan would be returned to the family and the couple would separate. Under Mr Dobree's will Mr Salter was due to receive the cottage, and the bonds which produced the annuity were to pass into his possession, but only if he had met the requirements of the marriage contract. Mr Salter is not a wealthy man, and should Mr Dobree's suspicions have proved correct he would have been a very poor one.'

'And the deceased gave you no clue as to the precise nature of these suspicions?'

'He did not. But he was determined to make enquiries to discover if there was any truth in the matter. There were several issues at stake; the happiness of his daughter, the honour of his family and the standing of his Lodge. His suspicions were further aroused by the fact that Mr Salter had recently requested an amendment to the marriage contract that would have granted him an increase in the annuity, something my client was unwilling to condone. I suggested to Mr Dobree that he should consider employing a detective to look into Mr Salter's activities; I know of one or two competent men I could recommend; but he believed it was too sensitive an issue to reveal to a stranger, and he declined. He said he would look into the matter personally.'

Mr Marsden returned to his seat and Frances desperately hoped that he had not noticed her presence in the crowded room. She dared not now look at Vernon Salter. Consumed with her own thoughts she barely heard Dr Diplock give his final advice to the jury, after which they elected to retire to an adjoining room to consider their verdict. They were absent for what seemed like an age but was probably about twenty minutes. Frances was glad to have Sarah by her side, solid and comforting, and knowing exactly when no words were necessary.

At long last the jurymen returned and took their places, then their spokesman rose to address the court. 'We find unanimously that Mr Lancelot Dobree was murdered. Although the perpetrator is unknown, we believe that very grave suspicion should be attached to his son-in-law Mr Vernon Salter.' He sat down. Frances could hardly have felt worse.

What followed was inevitable. Inspector Payne summoned a constable and asked Vernon Salter to accompany him to the police station. He was not at that stage actually under arrest, but it was clear that he was about to undergo some very searching questions.

As the chattering crowds left the room, Mr Fiske approached Frances. Barely able to speak, she shook her head. 'I'm sorry,' she said, 'but the answer is no. Please, I mean it, no.' She hurried away under Sarah's protective wing before he could say a word.

Chapter Twelve

arah took Frances home as quickly as possible, and although it was early in the day insisted that she swallow a medicinal dose of brandy. Tea naturally followed with thick slices of sponge cake, which had been intended for later but which Sarah now felt Frances needed as an urgent restorative.

Nothing was said about the inquest, and when she had eaten, Frances went to deal with some correspondence. It was hard trying to put that morning's events out of her mind but she did her best. From time to time, the picture reappeared before her eyes of Vernon Salter being removed from the inquest court by the police. She wondered if he was simply an evil man, or callous, or just weak-willed. Perhaps he was all three. She feared that somewhere within her were the seeds of this wickedness, and that one day perhaps even she would abandon all she had ever thought she believed in and commit murder.

There were no appointments for that afternoon, and Sarah proposed that she should make a nice supper for later and invite Professor Pounder to join them. Frances readily agreed to this plan and Sarah went down to the kitchen.

When the doorbell rang Frances took no notice, assuming, and rather hoping, that the visitor was not for her. She was disappointed, however, when the maid knocked on her door. 'If you please, Miss, there's a Mrs Salter to see you and I don't think she's the type who'll take no for an answer.'

Frances sighed. 'Very well. Show her up.'

Many of the people who came to consult Frances arrived in a state of agitation, others who were more composed and finding themselves in the unaccustomed position of approaching a private detective looked about them for evidence of bad taste in their surroundings. Alicia Salter was in neither category. Her posture was that of icy emotionless calm, and she took no notice at all of her surroundings, as if it would have been beneath her even to turn her head and glance at them. Her mourning gown was heavy, with the shine of bombazine and silk, sculpted with elaborate features like a work of architecture, and she was veiled in deepest black behind which there was only a hint of a face and none of her expression.

Frances, facing the woman for whom her father had deserted her mother, nevertheless adhered to the formality of the occasion. Alicia Salter, she felt certain, must be quite unaware of her husband's former transgressions. If her visitor had thought for a moment that the detective she was consulting was her husband's natural daughter she would surely never have come. 'Mrs Salter, I wish to offer my deepest condolences at your sad loss. I never met your father, but I am aware that he was a man who had earned the highest respect in society.'

The lady inclined her head in acknowledgement of the sentiments, but did not speak.

'How might I assist you?' Frances indicated the visitors' chair, and Mrs Salter availed herself of it, slowly and with grace. Frances took the chair opposite. 'Would you like a glass of water?'

'Thank you, no, I do not consume the unboiled product of the London taps.' The veil was lifted and Frances saw the face of a woman in her fifties, plump and rounded, although not to excess, eyes of a piercing intensity, brows set high and proud, her mouth a firm line of determination. 'I am here at the recommendation of Mr Fiske, who has interested himself in this horrible business. I believe you attended the inquest this morning.'

'I did, at Mr Fiske's request.'

'He has told me of the work you carried out for him, and unlike so many of his sex he does not underestimate the value of the female mind.'

Having met Mrs Fiske, a lady of intelligence who commanded her household and family like a schoolmistress ordering her pupils, Frances thought that her husband was most unlikely to do so.

'I have come to engage your services regarding the ludicrous travesty of justice that we witnessed today.'

'I am very sorry, but I no longer involve myself in criminal cases. When I agreed to help Mr Fiske, all I knew was that your father was missing, and I assumed that he had either been called away on urgent business, or had been taken ill or suffered an accident. Once the coroner's jury delivered its verdict I could no longer continue to act in the matter, and I so informed Mr Fiske.'

Mrs Salter was unperturbed by this information. 'I don't think you understand the position. My husband,' she wielded the word pridefully like a staff of office, 'is innocent of any wrongdoing. Of that I am quite certain. A monstrous creature has killed my father and now walks free. Worse than that, it is very clear that the police fully intend to charge my husband with this abominable crime, and because they think they have their man, they are not troubling themselves to look for the real culprit.'

'That is a terrible situation, I agree; but I hope you don't expect me to investigate a murder. I cannot undertake such a task.'

'No, but what you can do is gather information to exonerate my husband. Then the police will recognise that they have made a mistake and pursue the real criminal. Did you not free an inno-cent man last year? One who was about to be hanged? I recall that there was a great fuss about it.'

Frances never made any great claims for her successes; she left that dubious task to the newspapers. 'That was not my work alone.'

Mrs Salter made a dismissive gesture. 'Do not trouble me with false modesty. I will hear no protest. You are engaged for the pur-pose I have described, for which you will be very well paid. Mr Fiske recommends you and moreover my husband, for reasons that I do not quite understand, says that you are the only detective to whom he will speak. So it is settled. I have already told that unpleasant Inspector that you will go to the police station imme-diately for a private interview.'

Frances was appalled. She knew she could refuse to do what had already been arranged for her. If she did not wish to interview Vernon Salter, no one could kidnap her and force her to do so. Losing the goodwill of both Mrs Salter and Mr Fiske was some-thing she could survive. She had already earned the distrust and contempt of Inspector Payne, and not arriving for the appoint-ment would damage that situation very little.

She opened her mouth to tell Mrs Salter that she would not and could not be coerced into taking this commission. Most of all she recoiled at the prospect of facing Vernon Salter, who could not have been unaware that he was in all probability her natural father. It was her curiosity that made her pause. Here at last was an opportunity to finally establish the truth behind her mother's desertion of her family and her father's abandonment of Rosetta; an opportunity that would not on the surface appear to have anything to do with her past, but came under another guise. And supposing Vernon Salter was innocent of the murder? To discover that would allay her worst fears. With regret she realised that it was a chance she could not miss. 'Very well, I will go,' she said.

Alicia Salter was used to having her own way and there was barely a blink of satisfaction. She took a card from her reticule and dropped it on the table. 'Mr Jeffs will attend to all financial matters.'

A new thought occurred to Frances, the involvement of Mr Marsden, who would take enormous pleasure in obstructing her at every turn. 'Will your solicitor also be making enquiries on your husband's behalf?'

Alicia Dobree's expression froze into a mask of fury. 'I hold Mr Marsden fully responsible for my husband's current plight. I do not trust him and no longer employ him. He will learn to regret his meddling. I have been recommended a Mr Kingsley and will meet with him today.'

Frances gave Mrs Salter her card, a plain item by contrast with the fine quality of the one she had received. Frances kept her cards in a little silver box, a gift on the occasion of her twenty-first birthday from her friend Cedric Garton. Alicia's eyes wandered to the box, which was tastefully decorated and engraved. She said nothing, but she looked at it greedily, as if wondering why it should not be hers.

Alicia Salter had departed by the time Sarah returned to tackle Frances on the question of turnips or potatoes. She saw at once that something was wrong, and Frances did not hesitate to tell her what had transpired, worried that she would be told she had made the wrong decision. Sarah merely nodded. 'It'll be for the best to get it out in the open. Even if he is a murderer, what if he was hanged and you never got to ask him what you want to know? You'd never be at peace.'

Frances acknowledged the wisdom of this observation, and prepared to go out.

'I'll come with you if you want.'

Frances put on a plain cape and her bonnet with the light veil. 'If you don't mind, I'll go alone.' Sarah didn't argue.

CHAPTER THIRTEEN

The journey gave her time to reflect on what lay ahead. She must be strong and firm and treat the interview principally as a matter of business. Since, however, it was most probably the only time she would ever speak to Vernon Salter, she must make the most of the opportunity and learn what she could about the man who was her father.

When Frances arrived at Kensington police station, she found when she gave her name at the desk that she was expected. The sergeant gave her a strange look, indeed many of those waiting for attention gave her similar looks since a respectable, modestly dressed woman was not a common sight in such a location, but she had long ago learned to ignore such curiosity. Even Kensington had its poor and distressed; argumentative types who had grown courageous on drink; sad, faded women who had abandoned all hope in life and clung like drowning creatures to bad men and dirty children, the smirking youths with quick fingers and belligerent girls whose trade was all too obvious. Frances, standing quietly in that company, exhibiting a calm she did not feel, was, she thought, like a smooth rock battered by a turbulent sea.

She had only to wait a short while before Inspector Payne came to meet her. 'A word first,' he said, and with as much courtesy as he could muster, which was not a great deal, conducted her to his office. The walls were ringed about with shelves stuffed with folders of papers and boxes whose ill-fitting lids revealed bulging contents. The desk was piled on either side with more fat folders bound with tape. Every item, Frances noted with surprised approval, was clearly labelled, and the only loose papers were laid neatly on the desk with a pen, ink, blotter and pencil to one side.

'So this is the position,' said Payne, when they were seated. 'We have Vernon Salter in custody and we think he is the man who murdered his father-in-law with a hammer and then threw him to the rats. He denies it of course, but he either can't or won't suggest to us where he might have been on the night of the crime. But he wants to talk to you.' His eyes narrowed with suspicion. 'Now why should that be?'

'According to Mrs Salter, who called on me today and practically ordered me to come here, I have a reputation for saving innocent men from being hanged,' said Frances, drily.

'Have you had any dealings with the family before?'

'No, but their acquaintance Mr Fiske was once a client of mine.'

Payne gave this some thought. He did not look wholly convinced by that explanation, but appeared to acknowledge that it was the best one he was likely to receive. He made a note on one of his papers then tapped thoughtfully on the desk with the pencil.

'Have you been here before?'

'No.'

He gazed at her as if trying to recall something, then shook his head and stood up. 'Come with me.' Frances followed him out of the office. 'We'll put you in the interview room. I won't show a lady into the cells because I don't approve of it.' Frances refrained from telling him that she had interviewed clients in the cells at Paddington Green before. 'But I don't like you being alone with him. He's a dangerous man.'

'Not if he is innocent,' Frances reminded him. 'You may post a constable outside the door and if Mr Salter attempts to murder me I promise I will call for assistance.'

'He won't try that,' said Payne, confidently.

'Inspector, may I ask if you have traced the cabdriver who arrived to convey Mr Dobree on the night he disappeared?'

'Of course we have, but there was nothing to learn. He was hired by Dobree, but not told where he was to go. So we're none the wiser.'

Frances was shown into a small room, which was bare apart from a heavy table and two chairs. She sat and waited. A minute or so later Vernon Salter was brought to her by a constable. He was handcuffed, and as he sat facing Frances one wrist was freed and the empty cuff secured to a leg of the table. He had the good grace to look embarrassed. Despite his angular features, the sharp chin and prominent jawline and cheekbones, his eyes were disarmingly gentle.

The constable straightened up. 'You sure about this, Miss?'

'Yes, please leave us,' said Frances.

The constable shrugged and left the room, shutting the door. He remained visible through the window standing outside.

Frances took out her notebook and pencil and placed them on the table, trying to stop her hands from trembling.

There was a brief silence. Salter shifted awkwardly in his chair. 'I have been wanting to meet you for so long, but I never thought it would be like this,' he said.

'Nor I. But to business. What do you wish to tell me?'

It was a rebuff and he knew it. He took a deep breath. 'I did not murder my father-in-law. I have never meant him any harm.'

'So you say. But you lied at the inquest about where you were on the night of his death.'

'Yes, that was foolish, but when I was questioned I didn't realise that the police had been to the cottage or that the housekeeper had been there during the time I said I had been staying there.'

'I do not enjoy being lied to. I can do nothing for you until you tell me the truth, and perhaps not even then.'

'I understand. Believe me, I have committed no crime. I was not in London on that day, but if I am to tell you the truth, I must ask that it remains a secret between the two of us.'

Frances was puzzled. 'Are you saying that you have an alibi for the murder but you don't want it known?'

'Yes.'

'Even at the cost of your life?'

He looked alarmed. 'I am praying that it won't come to that.'

'Mr Salter —'

'Can you not call me "Father"?' he pleaded.

Her voice was as sharp as his was soft. 'No, I cannot. The man I knew as my father was the man who brought me up. Now tell me, where were you? I am guessing that this is something to do with the terms of your marriage contract. You have told me you have not committed a crime, and I feel sure that you were not trying to avoid a bankruptcy order, as it would have been very hard to conceal that. So I am left with one conclusion. You were with a mistress. Is her reputation worth your life?'

'I was with your mother,' he said.

Frances was momentarily speechless, and lost her grip on the pencil, which clattered to the table top. A host of questions crowded into her mind. 'Where is she?' she said at last.

'That I can't say unless you agree to help me in confidence. She is in delicate health, and needs a better climate than London provides. My income is not great but I can just afford to maintain her as well as pay for the schooling of our son, Cornelius. Oh, I have adhered to the terms of the marriage contract. Rosetta is not my mistress; since I married we have been no more than loving friends, but I doubt that anyone would believe that. Imagine the consequences should Alicia learn that I meet privately with Rosetta. I would lose my income, and be unable to pay for Rosetta's care or Cornelius' education. Recently the school has demanded higher fees, which makes it doubly hard for me.'

'Is that why you asked your father-in-law for an increase in the annuity?'

'Yes. But you can see why I need to be cleared of this charge without my connection with Rosetta being revealed. Can you help me?'

Frances thought deeply. When she had learned of Vernon's marriage to Alicia it had never occurred to her that he had continued to support or even see her mother. But was he telling the truth? A man might say much to save his life. 'Before we go on, I need you to tell me the whole story of why my mother deserted her family and why you then deserted her and married another. And I will need some proof. I have been lied to more times than I care to mention.'

He looked mortified. 'There was no desertion on either side — is that what you were told?'

'No,' she replied harshly. 'I was told that my mother was dead. I did not discover otherwise until two years ago.'

He groaned. 'How could anyone do such a thing?'

'I suppose my family didn't want me to find her. But you can't deny that she deserted her husband and children.'

Vernon shook his head. 'It wasn't like that. When William Doughty found that Rosetta and I were meeting in secret he cast her out. She begged to be allowed to visit her children but he refused. He also refused to divorce her, so we were unable to marry.

There was a separation, but the law was cruel, and she was denied all contact with her children while he won the right not to maintain her. When she became distracted with grief he threatened to have her put in an asylum. We only narrowly avoided that.'

Frances reflected that from the age of three, when her mother had vanished from her life, Rosetta's name had hardly ever been mentioned. There had never been a portrait of her on display, and none had been found amongst William's effects. Frances had been led to assume that no portrait had ever been taken, and that Rosetta had not been talked of because to do so would arouse insupportable grief, but supposing that was not the case? Supposing the emotions being concealed were shame, anger and a sense of betrayal?

'I know that in 1865, the year after my brother Cornelius was born, you left my mother and married Alicia Dobree.'

He nodded. 'I can see what that must seem like to you.'

Frances gave him a hard look.

He tried to lower his head into both hands, but was prevented by being shackled to the table leg. The handcuffs had chafed his wrists but he didn't seem to notice. He had long fingers like hers, a tall, inelegant form, like hers, and the face was far too like hers. 'Rosetta was never in good health after the birth of the twins, especially when our daughter died. I did what I could. I found work as an assistant in a jeweller's shop. But we knew that while we might manage to live, Rosetta needed better care than I could afford, and we could never give our son the education he ought to have. One day I was sent by my employer to take a tray of rings to the home of Lancelot Dobree. He wanted to purchase one as a birthday gift for Alicia and asked me to show them to her so she could make a selection. She took a long time looking at the rings and said that she could not decide and I should return the following day with another tray. I did so. But on that second occasion she was again unable to make her choice. My employer thought it was my fault, he told me to be more flattering to the lady, so I was. She asked me to help her try on the rings, to advise her on what best matched her complexion. My visits took longer, and she insisted I stay for refreshment. After the fourth or fifth tray it dawned upon me that Alicia was less interested in the rings than the man who brought them. Lancelot asked to see me privately, and told me that his daughter wanted me as her husband. And believe me, Alicia has always got what she wanted, from the day she was born.'

'She must have had suitors before.'

'She did. But Alicia is not the easiest person and Lancelot has always been blind to her faults. He sought to protect her from fortune hunters and in doing so placed restrictions in the marriage settlement. Her hand would only have been sought by a man violently in love or so desperate for money that just a little might save him.'

'And you were the latter?'

'I was. I talked to Rosetta. I was afraid of losing her. She gave me permission to marry. With the annuity and the income from my new business I was able to rent a place for her and our son away from London with fresh air and sunlight, where she could regain her health. She is able to do a little fine needlework and I supply the rest of their needs. I visit as often as I can. She goes under the name of Mrs Martin, and it is given out that she is my widowed sister, but people draw other conclusions of course.'

'Inevitably.'

'I am sure that I am not what Lancelot might have wanted in a son-in-law, but I was what Alicia wanted and more to the point when we met she was a spinster of thirty-seven and he was anxious for grandchildren. There are three. So you have a half-brother and two half-sisters in addition to your full brother Cornelius. I am pleased to say that he is doing well. A son to be proud of; he is studying for the law.'

'Did my mother never try to see me in all these years?'

'No. She has always feared that you would be ashamed of her. Our plan, our hope, is that one day, when Cornelius is a man of law, Rosetta and I may be together. Our union would be sanctified if not by law, then by love. I will repay every penny that Lancelot gave me so we would no longer be beholden to the Dobrees.'

He appeared to be sincere, but Frances still could not accept what she was being told. 'Mr Salter, forgive me for saying this, but I have only your word that all of this is true. I have met many plausible scoundrels and some of them have been murderers. At the very least let me have my mother's address so that I may write to her, and ask if she will permit a visit. I will honour your request to maintain this secret, but it may be necessary one day to reveal it to save your life.'

'I am not sure that it would. Even if I did say that I was with Rosetta on the night my father-in-law was killed, who would believe the word of an adulteress, who lives off the allowance I give her? She would be shamed and my son declared illegitimate and denied an education, and I would still be hanged.'

'There are no witnesses to your visit?'

'None as far as I am aware.'

'Let me have the address. I will write to my mother. If she can confirm your story then I will do my best for you. Of course she may decide to come forward and provide you with an alibi, and there is nothing I can do to stop her.' Frances handed him her notebook and pencil, and he wrote. 'She will have read in the newspapers about your father-in-law.'

'Yes, she has.'

'But she will know nothing yet of this development.'

'I would rather she did not. I cannot bear the thought of her learning of it in the sensational press. The shock would be a terrible thing.'

He pushed the notebook back to her. In it he had written an address in Brighton. 'Then I will do my best to prepare and reassure her,' Frances promised. 'But there will be rent to pay. Food and fuel. Who knows how long you will be in custody?'

'She has sufficient resources for a month. Please tell her to think only of herself and our son. She knows of your fame and will trust you to set things right.'

That of course was what Frances was partly afraid of. But in other ways her mood was lifted. If Vernon Salter's story was true then she was not as she had thought, the daughter of two people whose chief legacy had been a tainted character, but she was a child of love. And love was all she had ever really craved.

CHAPTER FOURTEEN

When Frances Doughty thought about love, which she could not prevent herself from doing more often than she suspected was good for her, she wondered what it might be like to have her heart and mind so stirred by another person that she could not bear to be parted from him. She had met men who had amused and charmed her, and whose company she enjoyed, but was there one amongst them who could be the companion of her soul, and who might feel the same about her?

In the last year a series of stories had been published by a Mr W. Grove extolling the achievements of a lady detective called Miss Dauntless, undoubtedly an admiring caricature of herself. Sarah had once declared that these were little more than love letters, although Frances had refused to believe it.

In one such adventure the daring Miss Dauntless had attended a ball, where she had been the dance partner of a devoted swain who wore a dark cloak and a Venetian mask. Not long afterwards came the catastrophic night on which the Bayswater Face-slasher had claimed a final victim, and had at last been arrested. Frances had so very nearly met her death, but a man had rescued her, a man in a dark cloak and Venetian mask, who had given the name W. Grove. He was tall and strong and commanding, and when he knew she was safe and unharmed, he had clasped her in his arms in a way no man had done before, and it had been intoxicating. During that heady encounter Frances had breathed in the scent of a gentleman's soap, and later, with the expert assistance of her friend Cedric she had identified it. In the drawer where she kept her linen there was a bar of Gentleman's Premium Ivory Cleansing Soap still in its wrapper. An expensive product, it was not in common use. Sometimes she took it out and inhaled the aroma. When

she had done so, she usually felt the necessity of spending some
time swinging her exercise clubs.

Frances worded her letter to her mother with care, since there
were things, particularly her continued relationship with Vernon
Salter, that Rosetta might not wish to be written about openly.

'Dear Mother,' she began, and paused for a few moments to see
how those words looked on the page, words that she had never
imagined she would ever write, before continuing;

> I cannot express what pleasure it gives me to be able to write to
> you at last. You have long been in my thoughts, and I had feared
> that we might never meet, but now I am filled with hope.
>
>   I must prepare you for news that will cause you some dis-
> quiet. Your brother is presently under suspicion in a certain
> matter for which he has been detained. I am doing my best to
> ensure that he is cleared of all blame and freed. Therefore, I beg
> you to be calm whatever the newspapers might say. I will let
> you know the instant all is resolved.
>
>   I have met with him and he has advised me of the events
> which led to your current situation, however, for my better
> assurance, I wish to hear of this in your own words, and eagerly
> await your reply to this letter,
>
> Your loving daughter,
> Frances

Neither Rosetta nor Vernon knew this but Frances did have in her
possession a letter her mother had written to William Doughty
many years before, begging to be allowed to see her children
before their lives were severed. It was a great relief therefore when
she received a reply in what was undoubtedly the same hand.

In an outpouring of emotion Rosetta expressed her great joy
at being able to correspond with Frances and her immense pride
in her daughter, whose career she had followed in the newspapers
with trepidation and wonder. She had been upset to learn that her

'brother' was suspected of anything dishonourable, but was fully confident that Frances would quickly resolve the terrible misunderstanding. He had over the years been a tower of strength to both her and her son, and she would be lost without his many acts of kindness.

These revelations brought Frances a new peace and clarity. She was not after all the damaged person she had imagined herself to be, constantly fighting to keep at bay any bad impulses she had inherited. This led to other considerations. Was she, as she had been thinking, really unfit to be a detective? Had she been precipitate in abandoning a successful calling? There was only one way to find out. Since the police believed that they had the killer of Lancelot Dobree in custody, they were presumably not looking elsewhere but simply accumulating evidence to be presented at his committal for trial. Two years ago, William Doughty, who she had then believed to be her father, had been suspected of killing a customer of his chemists shop by making a fatal error in a prescription. It was his plight that had first launched her into the world of detection. Now, with so much more experience of that profession, she resolved to perform the same duty for her natural father.

Frances could not, however, think of embarking on the case without first discussing it with Sarah. Her companion had always warned her against getting involved in cases of murder, something that seemed to happen whether she tried to avoid it or not. On this occasion, however, Sarah simply listened to her friend's explanation and nodded. 'You don't think it's unwise?' asked Frances.

'Wise or unwise, it's your father and he needs your help,' said Sarah. 'I know you decided to stop chasing criminals after what happened last year, but I can see you miss it. You've been dull these few months. Not that you didn't need to be, I think you did, but now that's done you have to get on and be true to yourself.'

Frances smiled with relief.

'Now tell me what wants doing.'

Together, Frances and Sarah made a list of all the people they felt should be interviewed. It was a very long list, since it included all members of both the Literati and Mulberry Lodges, members of the Dobree household, the staff and customers of the Duke of Sussex Tavern who had been there on the night Lancelot Dobree disappeared, any former or current business associates of the dead man, anyone who had recently visited the house where the body had been found and the new solicitor, Mr Kingsley. Frances also reluctantly added the name of Mr Marsden, who, if Alicia Salter had given him his marching orders, might be stinging enough to provide some useful information.

It was never like this for Miss Dauntless, thought Frances dispiritedly as she studied the list of names. Miss Dauntless scaled roofs and climbed through windows. She chased villains by bicycle or on horseback, and had once, with the aid of her burly assistant Sally, wrestled one to the ground, handcuffed him and delivered him to the police. It was only a matter of time before she fought a duel. She never had to interview a hundred or more potential witnesses.

Chapter Fifteen

s Frances began the lengthy task of writing letters requesting interviews, a note arrived from the solicitor, Mr Kingsley, no doubt at the behest of Alicia Salter, to say that Vernon Salter was to appear before the magistrates on the following day. Frances had little stomach for watching the proceedings and it was decided that she would pursue her enquiries while Sarah went to the court.

Frances returned to Kensington, arranging to meet Sarah at the tavern once the magistrates' hearing was concluded. Apart from the question of who might have wanted to kill Lancelot Dobree, there were three purely practical mysteries to be solved – how had Dobree managed to leave the Lodge room, how had he left the tavern without being seen, and how had he entered the empty house?

Understandably, there was a notice on the office door of Munro & Son advising that the business was closed due to bereavement, but when she peered through the window she saw two gentlemen inside, neither of whom she recognised. She ventured a knock on the door.

One of the men within looked up then turned away, as if hoping that she would leave, but she knocked again and wearily he rose to his feet and unfastened the door. He was aged about sixty and rather portly, his grey hair like the wavy edge of an underbaked piecrust around his bare scalp. Frances gave him no time to protest that the business was closed. 'I am sorry to trouble you at this sad time, but this is not a business enquiry. I have come about the recent death of Lancelot Dobree.'

She provided her card, which he studied with a frown. 'I thought the son-in-law had been arrested?'

'He has, but the family feels that the police have been precipitate and have asked me to look into the matter. I only wish to speak with you for a few minutes.'

He hesitated.

'May I have your name sir?'

'Anthony Munro. I am the younger brother of Mr Jacob Munro, the owner.'

'May I offer you my sincere condolences,' said Frances. 'When I was here last your nephew very kindly showed me and my associates around the property in Linfield Gardens. I know you must feel his loss most terribly.'

Realisation came. 'You are the detective lady who found Dobree's body?'

'I am.'

He gave a heavy sigh. 'Well, you had better come in, I don't suppose it will make much difference. I am just here to complete a few transactions and then the business will be sold. My brother has retired. He hasn't the heart for it now, and I don't blame him.'

As Frances entered she saw that the man with whom Munro was in conference was an elderly gentleman, one of those thin persons like an insect so dried up that it was impossible to say what age he might be. There was an impression about him of a man of substance who did not like to spend it on fripperies. His clothes were of sound quality but old, his hair hung in long white wisps about a face lined with meanness, but he wore a thick gold watch chain from which there hung a row of guineas, like a travelling bank. Hands encased in gloves of black leather were curled about the head of a stout walking stick. The desk at which he sat was covered with documents which, judging by the many stamps and signatures with which they were adorned, were legal in nature, together with a sheaf of papers describing properties held on the firm's books.

It was then that Frances saw the third man in the shop, a man in grey who seemed to melt into the shadows as if he was not there. He held a notepad and a pencil, and a leather document case was balanced on his lap. He was neither tall nor short, nor fat nor thin, nor old nor young, nor anything except most probably a clerk.

'I am sorry, Mr Johnstone,' said Mr Munro, addressing the elderly man, 'but if you would be so kind as to take some moments to study these papers, I will deal with the lady's enquiry as soon as possible.'

'Oh,' said Frances to the customer, 'are you the gentleman who Mr Munro the younger showed around number 2 Linfield Gardens some weeks ago?'

Johnstone stared at her in an unfriendly manner. 'I am,' he growled. 'What of it?'

'Then I would like to speak to you, too.' Frances offered her card. 'I am acting for Mr Vernon Salter. I was one of the persons who discovered the body of his father-in-law, Lancelot Dobree.'

Johnstone stared at the card and grimaced. 'Women detectives. Whatever next!'

'Miss Doughty has enjoyed some singular successes,' observed Munro.

Johnstone looked dubious but he didn't seem disinclined to talk to Frances. She sat down facing him, sensing that he would comply if only out of curiosity.

'Have you decided to buy the property?'

Johnstone gave a derisive laugh – probably from his general demeanour the only kind he knew. 'Only a fool would buy it at that price! Dry rot! Too much time and money before I saw a penny in rent!'

'Mr Johnstone is here to purchase the business,' explained Munro, gently.

'If I want to!' snapped that gentleman. 'Nothing in writing yet.'

Frances descended to flattery. 'You have a keen eye for a property.'

'That I do.'

'Did you know that Lancelot Dobree was interested in the house?'

'No. Never met the man.'

'When Mr Munro junior showed you the property, did he take the set of keys that was kept here?'

'I expect he did, yes.'

'You don't have any keys to the house?'

'No. Why should I?'

'And the two of you entered by the front door?'

'Of course.'

'Did you see all the house?'

Another derisive laugh. 'I saw enough to know not to buy it at the asking price.'

'The owner,' explained Mr Munro to Frances, 'is a very stubborn lady and has determined on a price that is quite unrealistic. My brother tried to persuade her to reduce her demands but she will not.'

'Who is this lady?' asked Frances.

'A Mrs Collins. She lives in the country with her family. The house has been empty for two months now.'

Frances turned back to Johnstone. 'During your tour of the property did you enter the yard and examine the fuel store?'

'I saw the yard, but I'd made my mind up by then so I didn't pay much attention to it.'

'So you saw nothing to cast any light on how Mr Dobree might have entered the premises? It seems he didn't have the bunch of keys held by this office.'

Johnstone shrugged impatiently. 'I've no more to tell you.' He tugged at his watch chain and examined an antique timepiece resembling a large gold turnip. 'If that is all, I'll bid you good-day.' He got to his feet and turned to Munro. 'I'll take the papers and call tomorrow.' He nodded at the silent clerk, who put away his notebook and pencil, straightened the pile of documents and put them in the leather case which he tucked under one arm. Johnstone stuffed one hand deep into his pocket and plying the stick energetically with the other, marched rapidly away with the clerk at his heels.

Mr Munro sighed unhappily and sat down. 'I really don't know how I can help you, Miss Doughty. I was not here when Mr Johnstone toured the house or on the day Lancelot Dobree died there. I have my own business to attend to, and only call in here once a week. My brother might know more but he cannot be interviewed at present. He is very distraught. Poor Albert was his only son.'

'Perhaps you could let me know when he might consent to see me. I know that there were further enquiries about the property, and there was a young man who said he would arrange a viewing but did not return. Do you know if he left his name?'

'I will take a look at the records and write you a note if I find anything. Do you really think the police have made a mistake?'

'I do.'

Mr Munro shuddered. 'How horrible. Then none of us are safe.'

Frances' next call was to the Duke of Sussex Tavern. She knew that in another class of establishment some inferences might be drawn from the appearance of a single woman, and took care to enter the more genteel lounge bar. She was relieved to find Mr Neilson at the bar counter.

'Troubled times,' said Neilson, with a shake of the head. 'I for one won't believe it of the son-in-law.'

'I too believe he is innocent and I am acting on his behalf. There are two theories about the death of Mr Dobree. Either he was lured to the place he was killed by an enemy we currently know nothing about, or he left the Lodge room for another reason, and it was chance that he met his death. What I don't understand is how his body came to be where it was found.'

'I wish I could enlighten you, but it is a mystery to all who knew him. And now we have poor young Munro being so savagely killed.'

'Did you know him?'

'Only as a customer, he sometimes came in for luncheon, or for a beer at the end of the day.'

'Perhaps other members of your staff here might have seen something on the night Mr Dobree was killed? Can you tell me who was here that night?'

'Let me consult my book.'

Mr Neilson's perusals showed that there were five men who staffed the tavern, as well as a cook, a maid who helped in the kitchen, served meals and did light cleaning, a scullery maid, and a charlady who did the rough work. Of those persons, only the charlady had not been in the tavern on the night Lancelot Dobree disappeared. The senior barman, Mr MacNulty, had been supervising the premises while his employer had been officiating as Tyler. MacNulty and the two other barmen, Tetlow and Adams, never left the bar rooms during the whole time the meeting was in progress. None of them had seen Dobree after he went upstairs for the meeting. The other two men, Capper and Spevin, had been working in the storeroom and the cellar. Both were sure that Dobree had not entered that part of the premises. Frances thought, however, that given the nature of the work undertaken by all five men, there might well have been times when their attention was on their work and someone who was determined to slip past them might have done so. None of the employees, confirmed Neilson, had a key to the back door. Only MacNulty had access to the safe where the copy was kept, but he was adamant that he had not left the bar during the meeting and the two barmen agreed.

Once again Frances took a walk around the storeroom. It was roughly square in shape and all the shelving was around the perimeter, so there was nowhere that Capper could have been working where he would have been unable to see someone walk past, nevertheless, if his back had simply been turned, a man who had gone down the back staircase from the Lodge room on the first floor and walked very quietly might just have slipped past without him noticing. From there Dobree would have been able to pass along the corridor into the public bar and, if his luck held, not be seen in the crowds. None of this would have been possible however if Dobree had not first been able to leave the Lodge room. Neither did it explain how he had got into the yard and why he had gone there.

Frances had no wish to sit in either bar room alone, so Mr Neilson kindly permitted her to use the office to sit and write her notes. She was pondering the unanswered questions when Sarah arrived and sought her out.

'I suppose Mr Salter was committed for trial,' said Frances resignedly.

'Not a bit of it. Released without charge.'

'Really?' said Frances, in astonishment. 'Well I am delighted of course, but how was that achieved? Inspector Payne seemed very determined.'

'Oh he wasn't happy at all. It was the new solicitor Kingsley who pulled the rabbit out of the hat. You remember how at the inquest Salter said that at the time of the murder he had been staying at the family cottage, but the housekeeper had already told the police he wasn't there.'

'Of course we know where he was and why he lied about it.'

'So we do.'

A thought, half alarming, half exciting, crossed her mind. 'Don't tell me my mother come to court and gave him an alibi?'

Sarah shook her head. 'It was Mrs Barrett, the housekeeper of the cottage. Said she had made a mistake and he was there after all. Not only that but she said he had arrived that afternoon at four o'clock and stayed till next morning. So he has a complete alibi for when Mr Dobree disappeared and was likely killed. The magistrate asked her how come when she got the telegram from London asking if Dobree was there, she didn't mention it to Mr Salter? She said it was because she wasn't expecting to see Mr Dobree that night so she didn't think anything was wrong. Said that when Mr Salter or Mr Dobree wanted to stay she always got a note the day before as she needed to air the cottage, and Mr Dobree never sent her one that time. She lives about five min-utes' walk away. By the time she got the second telegram from the family Mr Salter had already left.'

'Did the magistrate ask if Mr Salter sent her a note about his plan to use the cottage?'

Sarah chuckled. 'Yes, you could see he wasn't too impressed about her changing her story. She said she was sure she had got a note, but she had lost it.'

'But of course her tale is all lies.'

'Oh yes, and there's money passed hands, I've no doubt of it. I wouldn't mind betting that it was Mrs Salter who told her new solicitor Mr Kingsley to pay the housekeeper to lie to the magis-trates. From the look on his face Payne knows it too, but he also knows he can't prove it.'

'So we still don't know where Mr Dobree intended to go that night. I wonder what will happen now? Mrs Salter engaged me to find information to free her husband, and now he is free. I have the impression that those who know him do not consider him guilty of murder so his reputation with his friends has not been sullied. But he is a man of business, too. There will always be those who will suspect him. He will have to live with that for the rest of his life unless the real killer is found.' Frances rose to her feet. 'I had better find out what they intend me to do.'

'What if they want you to find out who killed Mr Dobree?' Sarah asked.

'That of course is a police matter, but we all know of cases where a suspect is freed and the police decide to look no further. They think they had the right man, and will always be waiting and watching for him to give himself away.'

'I'll tell you who else was unhappy – Mr Miggs. He was there in court hoping to see a Freemason charged with murder. That would have suited him right down to the ground. Very disappointed he was!'

Chapter Sixteen

W hen Frances and Sarah arrived on the doorstep of the Kensington home of Vernon and Alicia Salter they found the doorbell hung with a cascade of black crape tied with ribbon, a stern warning to the casual caller that this was a house of mourning and idle enquiries were therefore discouraged. Frances rang the bell, and a maid opened the door. She was a stout girl, with a plain face that was not improved by a look that suggested it would take more than a simple enquiry to achieve entry to the house. 'May I know your business please?'

'Miss Frances Doughty and Miss Smith,' said Frances presenting her card. 'We are employed by Mrs Salter on important private business.'

Their names were known to the maid, that much was clear, but there was a curious twist to the corner of her mouth like a barely suppressed smirk. 'Please come in and wait and you will be attended to shortly.'

They were ushered into a wide hallway resplendent with oil paintings, the glow of many gilded lamps reflecting from polished tables. One of the portraits, its frame draped in black, was of Lancelot Dobree. It was hard, thought Frances, as she paused to gaze upon the painted features, to assess personality from such a representation, which only showed the image the subject wished the world to see. The work was undated, but she thought that it had probably been painted when he was still active in business. He had been a well set up man, with a suggestion of controlled strength and vigour in his form and pose, his mature years only serving to indicate solid respectability. His hair, which was thick and abundant and very little receded from a broad forehead, was dark grey, with side whiskers to match, the mouth firm, the eyes clear and blue. The impression was one of geniality and confidence. He was wearing a signet ring very like the one Frances had noticed was worn by Mr Fiske, and she realised the device it bore must be a Masonic emblem. His hand rested on a table on which were a number of items of Masonic significance, as well as a classical statue draped in a swathe of silken fabric. Behind the seated figure was a scroll bearing the words, 'Charity, Brotherhood, Truth'.

The visitors were not permitted to remain in the hallway long, for on the maid's return they were quickly conducted into what appeared to be a small reception room. 'Kindly wait here,' said the servant, and departed.

'You have not met Mr Salter, but I think you will find him a quiet, gentle person,' said Frances. 'Unless he is adept at deception, I really don't think he is capable of murder.'

Sarah did not comment but looked as if she needed to be convinced. 'I wonder what they'll ask you to do now? It's far from over, but they might not know that.'

'I agree. Mr Salter has been freed on perjured testimony. Such a fragile structure can crumble without warning and I think Inspector Payne is attacking it even as we stand here.'

Their wait lasted no more than five minutes, but when the door opened it admitted the Dobree manservant, Mr Jeffs, who approached them with dignity, his face cold and impassive as a statue. He was carrying an envelope, which he handed to Frances. 'Miss Doughty, Mr and Mrs Salter wish to express their grateful thanks for all that you have done, and confirm that under the circumstances your services will no longer be required. I think you will find the enclosed cheque very generous indeed.'

'I see,' said Frances, thoughtfully. She put the envelope into her reticule without looking at it. 'Might I have the opportunity of a few moments interview with Mr and Mrs Salter?'

'That will not be possible. Allow me to show you out,' said Mr Jeffs, holding the door of the reception room open for them, the formal politeness of his manner concealing that they had effectively just been ordered to leave.

'You are too kind,' Frances replied. Sarah raised a quizzical eyebrow, but Frances allowed herself to be shown out without protest.

Moments later she and Sarah stood on the pavement.

'Well!' said Sarah. 'What now?'

Frances opened the envelope and took a few seconds to appreciate the amount written on the cheque. 'To the bank,' she said. 'I need to pay this in at once.' They hailed a passing cab and climbed aboard. 'If all my clients paid me so much for a day's work, I would soon become a lady of leisure.'

Sarah looked dubious. 'You'll never be a lady of leisure.'

'I suppose not. But you do see what this means? Mrs Salter, who is undoubtedly the commanding force in this, is afraid to employ me further. She is concerned that if I continue my investigations I will be able to prove that she arranged for the bribing of a witness to give false testimony at a magistrates' court.'

'Do you think Mr Salter has told his wife the truth of the matter?'

'I don't know. To do so would reassure her that he is innocent, but it would also raise suspicions of infidelity. Since I do not know the lady well, I am unsure whether murder or a mistress looms larger in her catalogue of crimes. Neither do I know whether Mr Salter told his wife or his new solicitor that he revealed to me where he was on the night of Mr Dobree's death.'

'If he did, they'll know that you know the housekeeper's new story was a lie. They might think you suspect it in any case.'

'Which makes me a dangerous person to be silenced.'

Sarah said nothing but clenched her large fists.

'They think that my silence can be purchased, but the truth is, I have no interest in uncovering their schemes, which would be far more damaging to Mr Salter. I have interviewed his wife only once, but I judge her to be a lady who arranges the world as she would wish it to be. Her husband's presence at the cottage that evening has become the truth and Mrs Salter will choose to believe it. She may have persuaded herself that her father was killed in a street robbery and is not troubling herself over the inconvenient details that engage my mind. Whatever the damage to her husband's reputation she believes her wealth will smooth it over, and of course she may be right.'

'So that is an end of the case?'

'It seems so. I was asked to find a missing man, which I did. I was asked to exonerate Mr Salter and that has taken place. There is nothing more for me to do. The murder of Lancelot Dobree is now a matter for the police, and not me.'

'Hmm,' said Sarah.

Once the cheque was safely banked, Frances wrote another letter to her mother.

> Dear Mother, I hope you are continuing well.
>
> You will be overjoyed to hear that all the difficulties your brother has lately experienced have now been happily resolved. The result has been a great relief to everyone concerned.
>
> I do hope that when my current business is completed you will permit me to pay you a visit. I can understand why you have been reluctant to see me, but I cannot find it in myself to blame you for following the dictates of your heart. The past is past and I now believe that all differences can be mended.
> Your loving daughter,
> Frances

Frances sealed the letter wondering why love should be so complicated and difficult.

That afternoon saw a greater than usual number of clients coming to Frances' door. Rumours that she was again investigating crimes had brought a train of hopefuls. There had been a recent outbreak of petty thefts in the vicinity; jewellery and watches taken from homes and hotel rooms, and this had prompted several visitors, but Frances said she could do no more than ask her agents to look for the stolen items in the pawnbrokers.

Tom and his 'men' often saw and noted suspicious behaviour in the streets, and they already had their eye on a slippery character who, it was alleged, took pleasure from going up to women and attacking their clothing with scissors. His latest victim, outraged at the cutting of a flounce from a favourite gown, wanted the man stopped, since his depredations had defied even the efforts of her dressmaker to restore, and the garment was ruined. Frances wrote to Tom, saying that the man, of whom they now had a good description, should, if seen, be followed carefully to discover where he lived, but not approached, and then reported to the police.

More seriously, there were unhappy women looking for a separation from their husbands, or even, for the more desperate, a divorce. A new law enacted in 1878 enabled a wife to obtain a separation if her husband had been convicted of assaulting her, the main difficulty being proof, since such crimes usually happened behind closed doors. Even if witnessed, it was often hard to get someone to testify on behalf of the wife, since the husband could discourage witnesses with threats or bribes. Sarah was adept at giving frightened women the resolve to report assaults to the police, getting them to make statements while their bruises were still fresh and swollen. A face marked in several colours and with wounds at different stages of healing would demonstrate the persistent nature of the cruelty. Once the wife had found the courage to speak out, Sarah found that reluctant witnesses could be persuaded to talk.

As Frances interviewed her new clients and determined how their appeals could be dealt with, she reflected that solving their problems was a far more rewarding occupation than drawing up family trees to satisfy a client's vanity, or scouring the newspapers to make notes of rival tradesmen's claims. She was busier than she had been for a very long time, and she found she liked it.

Frances Doughty, lady detective, was back in business.

CHAPTER SEVENTEEN

On the following morning, much to her surprise, Frances received a visit from Vernon Salter. She was tempted to ask him how he had obtained permission from his wife to leave the house, but refrained. He made a stumbling apology for the manner in which she had been dismissed the previous day, but she waved it aside. 'I assume that Mrs Salter wishes the accusation against you to be forgotten as soon as possible.'

'She has forgotten it already, but I think she is the only person who can. Alicia believes that once she has put something out of her mind, it no longer exists.'

Frances was alone, since her assistant had gone out to strike terror into the hearts of erring men. She had been busy planning her own cases but now she put her papers aside and freshened the teapot. There was enough hot water for two more cups, and Salter gulped the tea gratefully.

'Are you able to explain the housekeeper's sudden change of story? Or is that better not discussed?' Frances asked. If there was more than a hint of sarcasm in her voice he appeared not to notice it.

'Mrs Barrett has been a loyal servant for many years, and I can only assume it was that loyalty that prompted her new testimony. But I am not sure if it was a good or bad thing. I have been freed of course, but it might have been better if I had been tried and acquitted, then I could not have been tried again. Inspector Payne made it very clear to me when I was released that he still suspects I was involved in my father-in-law's murder and will be watching me carefully. Even if he accepts that I have an alibi for the crime itself, and I don't think he does, he might still believe that I have lawless associates who acted for me. He is biding his time, and means to arrest me again as soon as he sees his chance. But I can assure you, I know nothing at all about it.' He glanced longingly at the teapot, but it was empty.

'Shall I ring for more tea?' asked Frances.

'No, please don't trouble yourself. I hardly know what I want or should do. Would you believe they questioned me about my father's silversmith's tools? They seemed to think I still had them, but of course they were all sold years ago.' Frances poured him a glass of water from the carafe. He looked as though he needed it.

'I assume that you do not wish to engage me to discover the real murderer?'

He almost choked on his drink. 'Oh, I would never ask you to do such a dangerous thing! But would you be prepared to find out what further enquiries the police are making about me? And listen for any rumours or gossip that might not come to my ears?'

'Of course. After all I was engaged to gather information in your defence, and will gladly continue to discover anything that might assist you further.'

'Alicia says she is sure that the real murderer will be found soon, although she does not say how, since she does not trust the police. Frances …,' he paused, 'may I call you that?'

She took a deep breath. There were no reasonable grounds for her to object. 'You may.'

He gave a smile of grateful relief. 'Thank you. If I am to live under this cloud we must keep our connection secret; I would not have you damaged by it. The same is true of your brother Cornelius. But think of my other dear children! When I was arrested we had to take them out of school and send them to the country with tutors, but that is hardly satisfactory. The police have questioned my friends, my business associates, and my brethren in Mulberry Lodge. They know nothing against me – there is nothing to know – but it is far too easy to sow the seeds of doubt.'

'I do understand. I will go and see Inspector Payne; he may be willing to tell me something.' Frances didn't say so, but she doubted it, although she knew she had to try.

'And I must go to see Rosetta. I have written to tell her my good news but I know her mind will not be at rest until she has seen me.'

'Do you spend a great deal of time away from home?'

Vernon looked embarrassed. 'Truth to tell, Alicia and I have nothing in common except the children. She has her own circle of friends and amusements, and I have a separate life.'

'Was she very close to her father? I have detected few signs of grief in her.'

'That is her manner. Do not mistake apparent coldness for lack of feeling. The firmer her speech and actions the more she feels.'

'One thing I should investigate is the reason why your father-in-law suspected you of an action he clearly deplored. It might go some way to explaining his movements that night, and lead the police to his murderer.'

He emptied the water glass and shook his head. 'I wish I could enlighten you, but I can't.'

'What would you say were his main concerns? The things he might have taken risks for?'

'Alicia, his grandchildren, his charities, his Lodge. Alicia was always first. Lancelot, within the confines of the law, of course, would have done whatever she wanted, her happiness was all to him.'

'The foundation of his suspicions may well be the conditions of the marriage contract, which mentioned the consequences of infidelity, bankruptcy and crime. When we last spoke you assured me that you were innocent of all three.'

'That is correct.'

'But your father-in-law might have thought otherwise. He mentioned but did not describe his concerns to Mr Marsden, but he does not seem to have asked anyone to help him establish the truth behind his suspicions. Why do you think that was?'

Salter was thoughtful. 'From what I know of my father-in-law, I can only suppose that he wanted any enquiries to be as discreet as possible, hoping that he would ultimately find that his suspicions were unfounded. He would have been most distressed to have inadvertently spread rumours that would have upset Alicia only to find there was no truth in them. So whatever it was, he kept it to himself.'

'Unfortunately we know nothing of what steps he took or was about to take in pursuit of information.'

He gave a despairing sigh. 'Nothing at all.'

'Did he ask you any questions recently – questions which might have seemed unremarkable at the time, but if we examine them, they might reveal what was on his mind? I suppose it is hard to remember what might have been a very casual conversation.'

'He never asked me about my relations with Alicia. He knew what they were. About a week ago he asked how my business was. I told him it was doing well.'

'He didn't offer you a loan?'

'No.'

'He didn't agree to an increase in the annuity?'

'No.'

'Had he suspected impending bankruptcy, might he have assisted you financially?'

'I suppose he might have done, but he didn't, and in any case, I was not about to go bankrupt. I may do so in future, of course,' he added mournfully.

'From what you say, Mr Dobree most probably did not suspect either marital difficulties or bankruptcy. So we are left with one last condition of the contract. Might he have suspected you of something criminal?'

'He might. I don't know what.'

'Because I can't help thinking that all the secret creeping about and walking through locked doors suggests that he was looking into some criminal activity. Whether this has anything to do with you, we can't know, unless Mr Marsden knows something he isn't telling us.'

'Alicia sent a very firm letter to Mr Marsden,' said Salter in a tone that suggested this was a fate he would not have wished on any man.

'I doubt that he will share anything with me, but I suppose I will have to try. Mr Marsden may be passing on material to your new solicitor, Mr Kingsley, but he is not likely to speak to me either. Your father-in-law must have kept papers and correspondence at home.'

'He did, but after the will was read the executors called and took everything away. Or so I understand. I was in police custody at the time.'

'Who are the executors?'

'Members of Mulberry Lodge, I believe.'

'Have you seen the will?'

'No. Alicia and I are due to meet Mr Kingsley and the executors soon to discuss it.'

'Find out as much as you can for me. If you can secure your father-in-law's papers once the executors are done, they may contain some clues.' He nodded.

Frances pondered the problem for some time. 'Tell me about your business,' she said.

'I buy and sell items of silver. I'm no great expert, but I know enough to see a good bargain and I know what price to pay. I have customers – collectors – who tell me what they are looking for. I go to sales – bankrupt estates, house clearances and similar. I buy mainly small pieces such as tableware. I don't have a shop; I hire part of the strong room of a business called Kensington Silver. They often buy from me, but I also visit other businesses. My papers are all kept in a study at home. I've no secrets.'

He suddenly frowned and looked thoughtful.

'What have you recalled?'

'About three months ago I was at a sale of a deceased gentleman's effects and purchased a snuffbox and some other items, a sauceboat, teaspoons and a cream jug. Not long afterwards I saw a list of items that had been stolen and suspected that the snuffbox I had bought was amongst them. I took it to the police and they confirmed that it was. Of course I had documents to show I had bought the lot in good faith. I told the police as much as I knew and I heard no more of the matter.'

'Did you mention this to your father-in-law?'

'I think I did; in fact, yes, I am sure I did. I remember saying how relieved I was that my papers were in order.'

'I assume that the items your father-in-law wore or carried on the night of his death, the things that could have identified him immediately, have not been found? If they had the police would have asked someone to look at them and confirm they are his.'

'I have heard nothing about it, so I suppose not.'

'Please describe to me what these things would have been?'

'There was his apron – it was white leather edged with blue silk, decorated with three silver set squares, and two sets of silver tassels. A light blue collar made of silk, with a set square attached to it. Two breast jewels on coloured ribbons. He also wore a signet ring with a set square and compasses in gold on blue enamel.'

'Did you know your father-in-law had a slight defect in one foot?'

'No, I'm not sure anyone would have known other than his shoemaker and manservant.' He gazed at Frances with ill-concealed pride. 'I am so relieved you have agreed to help me!'

Frances was not yet willing to adopt a daughterly manner. 'I will do what I can. But since I have been politely shown the door to your house, or perhaps I ought to say your wife's house, how am I to contact you if I need to?'

He smiled ruefully and handed her a card with the words V. Salter, Fine Silver, and a post office box number.

With no great expectation of success, Frances went to Kensington police station and asked to see Inspector Payne. She had to wait in the station for an hour, where she was stared at and occasionally jostled by the less honest and more desperate of Kensington's inhabitants, but at last he appeared and ushered her into an interview room. He did not look pleased to see her, but then he never looked pleased about anything. Frances sat down, but Payne did not trouble himself to do so.

'Is this about the Dobree case?' he snapped.

'It is, but as yet I have no further information. I must advise you, however, that I was recently engaged by Mrs Salter to gather evidence to assist in her husband's defence against the charge of murder. Although he has since been cleared of the crime, I am making further enquiries to help repair the damage to his reputation.'

'Was it down to you that Salter's housekeeper changed her story?'

'No, that was as much a surprise to me as it was to you, but I am glad of it, as it means that an innocent man will not be tried for murder. There has, however, been the inevitable effect on his public and business standing and also consequences for the children of the family. I have come to ask you if you are confident that the real killer will be found soon. Have you made good progress?'

'I am not about to reveal anything to you about police work. All I can tell you is that we are continuing our enquiries.'

'The various things that Lancelot Dobree was known to wear or carry about his person – have they been found?'

'They have not, but we are checking all possible locations.'

'Do you have a suspect?'

It was clearly one demand too many. 'Miss Doughty,' said Payne irritably, 'I need to explain something to you. It is the police who ask the questions, not the other way about.'

Frances could not resist a smile. 'I have been told that many times. But we are not enemies or even rivals. We both want the murderer to be caught. And if I do stumble across anything that you might find useful, I will of course let you know.'

He looked sceptical. 'That is very kind of you. Now, unless you have something to tell me, I had better get on with some proper work.'

Frances had no alternative but to leave, but she paused and faced him one last time. 'Inspector, please be open with me. Do you still consider Vernon Salter to be a suspect in the murder of Lancelot Dobree?'

'I am not ruling anyone out. That is all I have to say.'

CHAPTER EIGHTEEN

As Vernon Salter had feared, he was still, despite everything, a suspect. Frances, who had ceased making her enquiries when paid off by Alicia Salter, was now obliged to resume them. She had been about to question the staff of the tavern who had been present on the night of Lancelot Dobree's disappearance, and that was to be her next step.

As Frances reached the tavern she saw some boys running up and down the High Street distributing pamphlets, and had no sooner descended from her cab when one of the publications was thrust into her hand. She had expected it to be either a moral tract, an advertisement for hair oil or a diatribe against the government, but it turned out to be something closer to home. Not only that but on reading the first few lines she recognised the high moral tone of the author who had signed himself 'One Who Loves Justice'. She put it in her bag for later detailed perusal, knowing that she would find it unpleasant reading.

When Frances explained what she wanted to Mr Neilson, he readily agreed, acknowledging that the combined memories of his staff might provide a clue as to the fate of Lancelot Dobree. He hesitated to speak ill of any of them, but his comments as Frances made her list gave her some interesting insights. This done, the little office was made available to her and she sat at the desk with her notebook and pencil while the staff members were sent in one by one.

The first to arrive was Mrs Robson, the cook. Aged about forty she had supervised the tavern kitchens for some five years, and had the unstinting good opinion of her employer. Her family consisted of two daughters in service and a husband who suffered from a mysterious illness that rendered him incapable of work. Her responsibilities were to consult with the bar manager Mr MacNulty regarding what food was to be ordered and dishes served, and prepare luncheons and dinners with the assistance of the general maid, Minnie, who she was training up to be a cook, and the scullery maid Lizzie whose position in life was unlikely to advance beyond her present status. To Mrs Robson's recollection, the night of Mr Dobree's disappearance had begun like any other on which a Lodge met at the tavern and the gentlemen stopped to dine. The kitchen had been advised in advance of the numbers and their requirements, and it was confirmed that all the gentlemen but one were to dine that evening. She had been working in the kitchen all the time, and had seen nothing of importance. Lizzie and Minnie had been there too, working under her direction, and both young women had gone back and forth to the dining room taking dinners to tables and clearing plates. The only other staff member she had seen was Mr Capper, who delivered new stock to the pantry.

Lizzie, who Frances interviewed next, was a nervous girl of about twenty, with the bony leanness and reddened hands that spoke of a young life mainly spent in peeling vegetables, scrubbing floors and scouring plates and pans. All her family were in service. She agreed that Mrs Robson had not left the kitchen between the hours of five o'clock and the end of dinner service. She herself had been continuously busy and noticed nothing of any significance.

Minnie was a robust and capable-looking girl of about twenty-five, who told Frances that she was always very busy throughout the dinner service, and the night of Mr Dobree's disappearance was no exception. She had not, as far as she could recall, seen Mrs Robson leave the kitchen during that time. When waiting at table she had overheard some conversation amongst the Masonic gentlemen about Mr Dobree, who had left unexpectedly early. All the diners had been mystified as to the reason, and they were discussing what to do with the property he had left behind.

'Are you looking for the murderer of Mr Munro?' asked Minnie, suddenly.

'No, but if you have any information which might lead to the criminal, do let me know.'

'I don't, I just thought it was a shame as he was so young. He often used to come in for a pie or ham and potatoes at luncheon, and he had a very pleasant manner with him.'

'Did he eat alone?'

'Sometimes, although he and Mr Weber – the manager of the confectioner's shop – often sat at the same table; they seemed to be very friendly.'

'What kind of things did they talk about?'

'Oh business usually; how good or bad things were. The price of houses, things like that.'

'Did Mr Munro ever mention Mr Dobree or the house at 2 Linfield Gardens?'

'Not that I heard.'

Mr MacNulty, the bar manager, was a short round man of about fifty-five who confirmed that he had worked at the tavern for fifteen years, and at other establishments for twenty years before that. The implication in his tone of voice was that this commendable record of service entitled him to be not only respected as a valued employee but above any suspicion of underhand activity. MacNulty readily confirmed that he was the only man apart from Mr Neilson who had keys to the safe, keys that he kept secured to his person, adding that in all his time at the tavern nothing had ever gone missing from the safe. The back door of the building, the one that led directly out into the alley, was always locked except when deliveries were coming in. On those occasions, either Mr Neilson unlocked the door with his own key, or if Mr Neilson was not available, MacNulty unlocked it with the spare key held in the safe. The door was always relocked immediately once the deliveries were in. On the day that Dobree had disappeared there had been an afternoon delivery and it was MacNulty who had unlocked the door.

'And did you keep the keys in your possession all the time the door was open?'

'I did, yes.'

'Did you supervise the delivery?'

'Yes, it only takes a few minutes to bring the stock in, then I locked up, went back to the bar and left Capper and Spevin to deal with the rest.'

'What time was the delivery?'

'About half past four, perhaps a bit after.'

'How long did it take to bring everything in?'

'No more than ten minutes.'

'Do you remember Mr Dobree arriving for the Lodge meeting?'

'Not specifically, but he was there that night. The men gathered for a social talk in the lounge bar before the meeting as was usual, and I know he was with them, then they went up to the Lodge room.'

'And he went with them?'

'I expect so.'

'Did you notice anything unusual in his manner?'

'No.'

'Did you see him again that evening?'

MacNulty thought hard and shook his head. 'I've been asked about this a dozen times. I don't remember seeing Dobree again that night, although if I had done I don't suppose I'd have taken special note of it. I do remember his friends being very concerned about him and after the meeting they did ask me if I had seen him. I told them at the time that I hadn't.'

'Did Mr Dobree ever ask to borrow any of the tavern keys?'

MacNulty looked startled by the question. 'No, never. In fact, I have never been asked that by anyone, whether customers or staff.'

'You were in one or other of the bar rooms all the time during the meeting?'

'I was. After all, Mr Neilson was busy guarding the Lodge room with his sword, so I had to be here keeping a double eye on everything.'

'Was there any reason not to trust the bar men to work in your absence?'

MacNulty bristled at the suggestion. 'Not at all, they are very efficient, but I know my duty. I am Mr Neilson's eyes when he is not here. He is very particular about that.'

'And Mr Tetlow and Mr Adams; they didn't leave the bar area during the time when the Lodge meeting was in progress?'

'Not that I saw. I don't believe so, they were very busy.'

'They didn't leave to fetch stock?'

'No, young Capper brought in the new stock.'

Mr Tetlow was next, the man who had greeted Frances on her first visit to the tavern with Mr Fiske. He was a smart fellow in his late twenties who had worked at the tavern for four years, and although he didn't say it outright, his manner revealed that he considered himself as next in seniority to Mr MacNulty. There was something a little arrogant about Tetlow, who insinuated that MacNulty, whatever he might like to think, was a man past his best; not active enough, not sharp enough, who might be well advised to make way for a younger man. Neilson had told Frances that Tetlow's parents managed a beer shop in Chiswick, and the son, wanting to improve himself, didn't like to admit to his humble origins. Tetlow confirmed that he, Adams and MacNulty had been fully occupied with customers during the Lodge meeting and he had not seen Dobree at all after he had left the bar for the Lodge room or noticed anything unusual in his manner.

Adams, a twenty-one year old, had worked at the tavern for a year. He was the son of a carrier whose business made the stock deliveries and had helped his father before making the change to bar work. He told essentially the same story as MacNulty and Tetlow. 'I know Mr Dobree by sight, of course, he comes here for the meetings of Mulberry Lodge. He was here that night you're asking about, I remember being asked where he had gone, though I hadn't seen him go. I saw him arrive with Mr Brassington, and he talked with the other gentlemen before they went upstairs.'

'Did he seem troubled in any way?'

Adams thought about this. 'Not troubled, exactly. I did wonder if he had indigestion or something like it. Just the expression on his face. And he did go to the convenience, and when he came back he looked out of sorts, so I wondered if he'd been a bit unwell in the waterworks department, if you'll excuse my saying it.'

Frances wondered about this while she waited for the next man to arrive. This was the first suggestion that Dobree had been anything other than in good health. Had he been in fear of a serious illness, one that had led to him taking a risky and precipitate course of action? There had been no mention of this in the postmortem report, but then faced with a man who had obviously been killed by a blow to the head the examiner might not have looked much further.

Capper, who was twenty-six, had been employed at the tavern for about two years, and divided his time between the storeroom and cellar with occasional bar work and waiting on tables. He arrived with a guarded air. 'I've already said all I had to say to the police,' he said as soon as he sat down. Frances looked at her notes and saw that Capper was the son of a rug-maker and he and Spevin shared the basic accommodation in the attic.

'It shouldn't take long to repeat it to me,' said Frances. 'On the day Mr Dobree disappeared, did you and Mr Spevin take in a delivery of stock at the back of the tavern?'

He looked surprised at the question. 'Yes, like usual.'

'Who unlocked the back door?'

'Mr MacNulty.'

'You don't have a key?'

'No, only Neilson and MacNulty have a key.'

'Are you sure that Mr MacNulty relocked the door when the stock had been delivered?'

'Yes, he's very careful about that. Don't want all sorts wandering in.'

'Then you and Mr Spevin worked on dealing with the delivery?'

'Yes.'

'But you weren't in each other's sight all the time?'

'No, well after we moved the stock in, Spevin had his cellar work to do.'

'And while you were working you didn't see Mr Lancelot Dobree?'

Capper gave a short laugh. 'What, in the storeroom? Customers don't come in there, especially gents like that.'

'Just supposing someone, a customer, had gone down the corridor to the convenience, lost his way and found himself in the storeroom while you were there, could he have done that without your noticing?'

Capper stared at Frances. 'Well that's a funny idea. Why would anyone do that?'

'It's just a theory. Mr Dobree for example, on the night he left the Lodge room, he might have come down the back stairs and then gone through the storeroom and walked out of the tavern that way, since the back door was locked.'

Capper combed a hand through his hair thoughtfully. 'If he was quick and very quiet, I suppose he just might have done. But I didn't see him.'

'But you weren't in the storeroom all the time while the Lodge meeting was in progress?'

'No, I was there some of the time, but I was also back and forth taking what was needed to the bars and pantry.'

'Do you think there would have been time enough in your periods of absence for someone to slip through the storeroom?'

'Yes, I suppose so.'

'What time did you finish your work with the stock?'

'I'm not sure. It was after five o'clock.'

'Was the Lodge meeting still in progress?'

'It might have been. I went up to my room and had a wash and brush up because I was going to help serve dinner later.'

Spevin was a lanky youth in his twenties with a confident manner and watchful eyes. He said he had worked at 'the Duke's' for six months, where he was largely engaged in the heavy labour, general repairs and other menial tasks. He seemed sharp enough, but appeared to have no ambition to do anything more demanding. He didn't like bar work, and he didn't wait on tables apart from collecting empty plates and glasses. According to Neilson's comments, Spevin was supporting a widowed mother, since his father had been killed falling from a ladder when putting up a shop sign. Perhaps some awkwardness or lack of caution was a family trait, since Spevin had a reputation for clumsiness. His pay had twice been docked for dropped glassware, and Capper had been ordered to keep an eye on him.

Spevin readily supported Capper's story. He had been in the cellar, alone, at the time of the Lodge meeting. If anyone else had entered he could not have missed it, he would have heard a footfall on the steps. Once his work there was done, and Frances had the impression that Spevin was not one to hurry about his business, he had been sent to the printers to collect some new menu cards. This was shortly before six o'clock. By the time he returned, the meeting was over and the tavern was in a state of consternation over Dobree's disappearance.

When Spevin had left, Frances read through her notes and considered what she had learned. Mr Neilson arrived, looking hopeful.

'I'm afraid I still don't know how Mr Dobree managed to leave the Lodge room without alerting everyone inside, but if he left by the back stairs, he could have gone through the storeroom at a time when Mr Capper was absent taking supplies to the bar or pantry. I am sure he had a good reason for doing so, but what it was I could only guess at. He then managed to leave the tavern without anyone seeing him. Perhaps he just mingled with the crowds in the public bar. He had the opportunity to go and get his hat and coat and bag, but he didn't. And he would have been wearing his regalia, unless he had removed the things himself, and put them somewhere. Perhaps he hid them in the storeroom?'

'It's possible,' admitted Neilson. 'I suppose another search is in order. I'll see to it.'

Mr MacNulty returned to the office just then, to get the key to open up the dining room for the day so that Minnie could renew the flower arrangements, and Neilson took the opportunity to give him instructions for a meticulous search of the premises. Running a public house was constant hard work, and while neither man relished the idea, both accepted the additional task as one of the burdens they had to bear.

Frances thanked Mr Neilson. Her next visit was to the confectioner's shop next door, first pausing to look in the window at the display of fine breads and cakes. Sarah was an excellent hand in the kitchen and her pastries were the best Frances had ever tasted, nevertheless the decorated fancies in the window were tempting. Frances told herself that she would stand a better chance of getting information from the manager, Mr Weber, if she bought some of the products – at least it was a very good excuse to do so.

There were two lady assistants in the shop, both well turned out, with clean white caps and spotless aprons. The number of customers present, all in agonies of decision over what to buy, augured well for the quality of the merchandise. Frances had to wait to be served, which only increased her anticipation. She had been intending to buy a slice of fruit loaf, but by the time she reached the front of the queue this had translated into half a dozen lemon tartlets.

'I would like to speak to Mr Weber,' she said as she paid for her purchase.

The assistant looked concerned. 'Oh, Madam, I do hope there is nothing wrong.'

'Not at all.' Frances presented her card. 'It is nothing to do with the bakery. I would just like to ask him a few questions about a friend of his.'

There was a short wait while the assistant went into the office, and the other customers looked sharply at Frances because she was the reason for the delay in their getting their cakes. The gentleman who returned with the assistant, looking at the card with a worried expression, was in his mid-forties, and with a white apron covering his suit. He looked as if the suit was his preferred garment, the apron quickly thrown on to provide his credentials as a master baker.

'Miss Doughty,' he said. 'How may I help you?'

'I would like to speak to you about the late Mr Albert Munro,' said Frances. 'I understand he was a friend of yours?'

Mr Weber looked quite alarmed. 'Well — er — in a manner of speaking I suppose he was. He purchased cakes here and we sometimes ate luncheon together at the tavern.' He paused, hoping that this information would suffice, and when it was clear that it did not, sighed in resignation. 'Come into the office, and we can talk there.'

The office was small but tidily kept, and Frances took a seat. There were family portraits on the wall, which was a nice touch. All the individuals depicted were large, cheerful, comfortable-looking persons wearing voluminous aprons and proudly carrying baskets laden with bread and cakes. There were also several framed diplomas for excellence in pastry making. Mr Weber was not quite as comfortable as his ancestors, but this was a scheme in development, judging by a napkin-covered dish on the desk, which emitted a warm sugary fragrance. 'I was wondering if in any of the conversations you had with Mr Munro he said anything that could cast some light on what happened to Mr Dobree.'

'Not that I can recall,' said Weber. 'We tended to talk about general trade matters, as men do.'

'Did he say anything about the house at number 2 Linfield Gardens?'

'That's the property which backs onto the alley where the tavern and our premises have their rear exits?'

'It is. It is also where Mr Dobree's body was found.'

Weber nodded. 'Yes, he did tell me about that. The old lady it belongs to was one of our customers. Lived there all alone except for one maidservant, as old as she was. The maid used to come round here once a week to see if there was stale bread and cake that could be bought cheaply. Then one week she didn't come. Turned out she'd dropped dead. Then the lady's family came and took her away and I heard she was selling the house. Munro said that if the lady had been not in her right mind then the family would have sold it for her, but she was sharp as a pin and very obstinate. Wanted a price no one would pay because she'd let the place rot. Munro reckoned it would stay empty until the owner died and the heirs sold it.'

'Did he mention anyone who had come asking about the house?'

Weber shook his head. 'I think he said there had been some enquiries but he didn't expect it to sell.' Weber paused. 'Oh, wait, he did mention that Dobree had shown an interest in the house, but hadn't viewed it yet.'

'When did you last see Mr Munro?'

'About a week before …' Weber's lip trembled and he took a folded handkerchief from his pocket and pressed it to one eye. 'That was such a nasty cruel thing. I liked Munro. I still can't believe it. You don't know who it was?'

'I'm afraid not.' Frances left him to his thoughts.

Chapter Nineteen

Frances boarded a cab for home, and read the pamphlet she had been given. The work, entitled 'The Brotherhood of the Wicked', was as bad as she had anticipated.

The horrible murder of Lancelot Dobree has set all London talking. Justice must be done, but this author fears that it may never be done, as the secret fraternity protects its own. It is well known that the police force, especially amongst the senior ranks, is riddled with freemasonry, as is our justice system. Together they conspire to ensure that no brother Mason can be convicted of a crime. I say nothing as to the guilt or innocence of the man who has just been released and cleared of suspicion. That issue will one day be decided in a higher court, one that cannot be suborned. No, I speak only of the interests that led to that position.

We must ask ourselves what business Mr Dobree was pursuing which was so urgent that he left the Lodge in the middle of its diabolical rituals? Was he perhaps disgusted by the practices of the Literati? Or was he bent on some secret Masonic business of his own, business that he was anxious should not be revealed even to his closest associates? Had he all these years been concealing something unspeakable under a mask of charity? It would be well if all Mr Dobree's private affairs were thoroughly investigated, but where can we find an independent uncorrupted body of men to do so? Sadly, such a body does not exist, as the evil of freemasonry spreads its tendrils throughout all areas of public and professional life.

As to his killer, I do not feel we have to look any further than amongst his own unsavoury associates. The only questions now are whether the murderer was an Ancient or a Modern, and was the weapon of choice the rough or the smooth ashlar?

'This is without a doubt the work of Mr Miggs,' observed Frances when she showed the pamphlet to Sarah. 'I am afraid that he does not take well to literary criticism. He cannot recognise that his own moralistic and sentimental outpourings are tiresome and without merit, and sees conspiracies everywhere which deny him the success he thinks he deserves.'

Frances had placed the purchased tartlets on a plate, and Sarah, after eyeing them suspiciously, was obliged to admit that they looked very good, there being only one way to consolidate that impression. They had eaten two each, washed down with a liberal supply of tea.

'These Masons, it's like a Friendly Society?' asked Sarah, brushing pastry crumbs from the pamphlet.

'Yes, or a gentleman's club, or benevolent association. They have meetings, and dine together and collect funds for charity. Mr Neilson is quite adamant that if a fellow Mason has committed a crime his brethren are expected to report him to the authorities, not cover up his guilt, as Mr Miggs seems to believe.'

'They won't like this paper, then. Are Masons all men?'

'They are. I notice that Mr Miggs nowhere suggests that lady detectives should look into what so infuriates him, not that he would think such a task is suited to us. And who knows but a lady might be a Mason's wife or mother or sister? I, of course, am tainted forever in Mr Miggs' estimation by the fact that I have been employed by Mr Fiske. I only hope Mr Fiske doesn't expect me to do something about this. Mr Miggs cannot be reasoned with; he may have just steered clear of a potential libel charge, and any opposition will simply add fuel to his fire and draw more attention to his message. Perhaps that is what he is hoping for. If Mr Fiske does come to see me I will advise him to do nothing unless he can substantiate criminal charges.'

'Miggs makes such a noise about his own character I wouldn't be surprised if he was hiding something he wouldn't want found out,' said Sarah, with a significant look.

'That is possible, but if he has been indiscreet in the past and has since put all sin behind him then it would be churlish to expose him now and I am sure Mr Fiske wouldn't want to do that.'

'Perhaps Miggs is still sinning. He might have a whole harem of fancy women.'

Frances and Sarah thought about that for a moment then shook their heads. 'In any case he is an author,' Frances pointed out, 'he can't afford such luxuries.'

Sarah nodded agreement and studied the pamphlet again. 'What's an ashlar?'

'It's a stone. They have them in the Lodge. A rough one is supposed to symbolise someone without learning and experience, and the smooth one is the man after he has been educated. And the Ancients and Moderns were two rival groups of Freemasons who united quite some years ago. If my notes are correct, the Moderns are older than the Ancients, but I'm not sure why.'

'So Mr Miggs knows something of what he is talking about?'

'Well he was a candidate for the Literati before Mrs Fiske wrote that review of his poems. I expect he had meetings with some of the members and they told him about the rituals.'

Sarah tapped the pamphlet with a stubby finger, as if prodding the author. 'He's careful not to own up to it, but it's his work alright. I know the way he goes on. Still, we ought to get proof. If you don't mind, I'll take this and have a word with the printer.'

Sarah, Frances was well aware, was adept at getting information from printers. In this case the firm only needed to be reminded that they had printed something which was designed to insult and even libel some of the most prominent and respected men in London for the desired information to be readily forthcoming. The one mystery that had so far resisted all her enquiries was the real name of Mr W. Grove, author of the Miss Dauntless stories, since the printer had been supplied with no information of note. Frances might have given the printer a letter to pass to Mr Grove, but what would she say? As soon as the idea came to mind, she found herself blushing.

'I'll make another pot of tea,' said Sarah, and left Frances to her thoughts.

By the time her companion had returned, Frances had managed to turn her mind to business. 'While I am waiting for Mr Fiske to arrive and engage me to undertake the impossible task of making Mr Miggs a more sensible man, I have more important things to think of, although I am sorry to say that Mr Miggs is in a way involved. It is clear to me and to Mr Salter that the police still suspect him of killing his father-in-law, and he has asked me to keep an eye on the situation for him. He is anxious about the effects of this continuing suspicion not only on his own reputation but on his business and his children.'

'Not on his marriage?' asked Sarah, although it was less of a query than a statement.

'I don't think his is much of a marriage, but I am not sure he minds. If it was not for Mr Miggs I would be hoping that before long the whispers against Mr Salter would cease for lack of evidence, and new things will arise to occupy the gossips; and of course there is always the chance that Inspector Payne will find the real killer. But Mr Miggs is working hard to ensure that the matter stays in the public mind. This pamphlet may only be the beginning. He has probably written to the newspapers as well. Even if Mr Salter is exonerated there will always remain those who will never be convinced of it. You know how the public likes plots.'

'You're not off chasing murderers again?' Sarah poured more tea and took another lemon tart.

'Well no, not exactly. I mean it would do no harm and possibly quite a lot of good if I was to bend my thoughts to the situation, and then if I had some useful ideas I could suggest them to the police.' Frances helped herself to the last of the tartlets, telling herself that its richness supplied much needed nourishment to a detective's busy brain. She then brought a large sheet of paper and a pencil to the table, a clear sign that she meant serious business, as she anticipated filling more space than might be available in the leaves of her notebook. 'I am going to make a list of all the things I don't yet know.' Frances gazed apprehensively at the empty page. 'Your suggestions would be very welcome.'

Sarah nodded. 'How did Lancelot Dobree get to where he was found?'

'We can divide that into a number of questions. How did he leave the Lodge room? How did he leave the tavern unseen? Where was he killed? How did he enter the house?'

'Had he ever left a meeting like that before?'

'You're right,' said Frances. 'That is an important question. He was after all only a guest at the Literati meeting – but he was a member of Mulberry Lodge which holds its meetings in the same room. So he was familiar with the room. And of course the next question – why did he leave? Where was he intending to go? Did he meet his killer by accident or design? If he went without his coat and hat it does seem to be unplanned. Could it have been as a result of something he saw and heard during or shortly before the meeting?' Her pencil raced across the paper.

'Did the way he behave have anything to do with Mr Salter?' suggested Sarah. 'I know you think Dobree had no good reason for whatever he suspected but it would have affected what he did.'

'True.'

'Why did the killer take the Masonic things? What happened to them? Nothing has turned up.'

'They would have been hard to dispose of without drawing attention to the killer. Perhaps he thought it would prevent or delay identification, although why that was important we don't know. He might have hoped the body wouldn't be found for some time. But it does suggest that he didn't plan to commit murder or he would have made better arrangements to dispose of the body – perhaps taken it further away. I suppose it was a kind of organised panic – he took some steps but not enough.'

'Did the killer return to the house afterwards?'

'I didn't see any sign of it – but then when I went there I was looking for Mr Dobree, injured or ill. I didn't know there had been a crime, and then just as the body was found the police arrived and took charge.'

'You need to go back, then.'

'Yes, I think I do.'

'How much do we know about the house?'

'It is owned by an elderly lady who neglected it and wants a bigger price than anyone wants to pay. Both Mr Johnstone, who rents properties in the area, and Mr Herman the architect thought it a poor purchase at the asking price. There has only been one actual viewer that we know about, Mr Johnstone, but there was another enquirer who never returned, and we don't have a name or description. Unfortunately, the man who could have told us more about him is now dead.'

'Strange that.'

'Yes, very.'

'Are the two murders connected?'

'Both men were killed in an empty house that was on the company books, both were killed by a blow on the head from behind, most probably with a hammer. We know that Munro was lured to the place where he died, but despite the fact that it might have been premeditated, there was no attempt to hide the body or conceal his identity.'

'Was it him they meant to kill? There are three men called Munro. Or didn't they mind?'

'There have been no other similar murders in the area or I would have read about them in the newspapers. But have there been any attacks that were failed attempts?'

'And where was Lancelot Dobree planning to travel to that night? Somewhere close enough for a cab ride? Or was he going up to get the train?'

'Not a short distance, or a place where he could get food, as he ordered some to take with him.'

Frances looked down at the sheet of paper. It was full.

CHAPTER TWENTY

As Frances perused the correspondence pages of next morning's newspapers she reflected that if Mr Miggs brought as much talent to the composition of his poetry and fiction as he did to irate letters and sarcastic pamphlets he would be far more readable, but his poems were full of posies and his novels were hymns to impossible virtue, and could never be interesting. A man who opened his *Ode to a Rose Petal* with the line 'A rose, I ween, is but a flow'r' could not in Frances' estimation have anything of value to impart.

Miggs, writing to the newspapers under the name 'Quis Custodiet', nevertheless revealed his true identity through the determined thrust of his argument and petty obsession, but was sensible enough to realise the significant difference between what was publishable in a national newspaper and libel. He had been careful to allude only in the most general terms to the recent murder of Lancelot Dobree and the unexpected outcome of the magistrates' hearing, without actually saying that he believed that a guilty man had been freed. The implications were, however, clear to any moderately perceptive reader. Both the murdered man and the suspect were, Miggs pointed out, members of a certain suspiciously secretive organisation whose business, he felt, should be subjected to a close scrutiny. This was something that should have been carried out many years ago except that those who might have been entrusted to do so were also members. Who, he demanded to know, guarded the guards?

An advertisement in the Bayswater newspapers revealed that Miggs, under his poet's *nom de plume* Augustus Mellifloe, had recently hired Westbourne Hall for an evening in which he would recite his own work, an over-ambitious project since the hall held several hundred persons and Frances did not think Bayswater held that many citizens requiring a cure for insomnia. He was,

continued the advertisement, about to favour the world of literature with a second volume of poetry, this one entitled *Les Fleurs de
Virtu*. Frances suspected that the world of literature was not holding its collective breath with anticipation.

The papers also included a worrying announcement exhort-
ing Bayswater women to join the newly formed Ladies
League Against Female Suffrage, an organisation founded by
a Mrs Cholmondeleyson, presumably, thought Frances, someone with too much idle time and too little brain. While Mrs
Cholmondeleyson had every right not to want the vote herself,
she did not, thought Frances, who was impatient to exercise the
eagerly anticipated franchise, have any business denying it to
others. A public meeting was planned to attract influential ladies
to the cause, with refreshments provided. Frances was a member
of the Bayswater Women's Suffrage Society, whose vigorous leaders, devoted companions Miss Gilbert and Miss John, regarded
her as a radiant example to womankind and often persuaded her
to address gatherings and attend rallies. She feared that the ladies
might decide to mount a demonstration at the anti-suffrage meeting, since they had already shown a tendency to veer wildly from
peaceful protest to dangerous dissent with very little warning.
Diminutive Miss John was enough of a threat with her sharp little
bodkin, and after recent events Frances could only hope that Miss
Gilbert had persuaded her companion to dispose of her gun.

With so many areas to investigate Frances and Sarah reviewed
the list of necessary enquiries and divided tasks. Sarah, after
enquiring about the pamphlet at the printers, was to visit Mr
Fiske to ask him if he could recall any incident either just before
or during the meeting that could have induced Dobree to leave
the room on the spur of the moment. She was also to obtain from
him a letter of introduction to Mr Westvale, Master of Mulberry
Lodge, who might have his own insights into the character and
concerns of Lancelot Dobree.

Frances returned to Munro & Son with the intention of
obtaining the keys to number 2 Linfield Gardens and viewing it
in more detail than she had before.

The office was open for business but as soon as Frances
entered she could see that it was different. At a front desk sat a

miserable-looking clerk, and further back, but not so far that he could not see all that went on, was Mr Johnstone, in conference with his grey-suited assistant.

'What can I do for you, Miss?' asked the clerk, looking up from an appointment book without enthusiasm.

'I would like to view a property,' said Frances. 'Is Mr Munro not here?'

'Mr Jacob Munro is retired from business, Mr Anthony Munro is not available, and Mr Albert Munro is deceased,' said the clerk. 'Which property might you be interested in?'

'The lodging house, number 2 Linfield Gardens.'

The clerk took a large bound ledger from a shelf and began to leaf through it, but before he could respond Mr Johnstone had left his desk and arrived in the front office, moving along smartly and brandishing his black walking cane, which in his hand was not so much a support as a weapon. 'I remember you,' he grunted. 'You're not a customer, you're that detective and you don't want to buy or rent, you've just come prying about.'

'Yes, I am engaged in an enquiry relating to the death of Mr Lancelot Dobree and I would like to look around the property where his body was found.'

'It's been sold,' said Johnstone curtly. 'The new owner has the keys.'

'That is very surprising,' said Frances, as the clerk with a puzzled expression leafed through the ledger, but seemed not to find what he was looking for. 'I thought the seller was asking too high a price.'

Johnstone suddenly prodded the clerk with his cane, making him jump back, then he lunged at the ledger and snapped it shut. 'She was, but I informed her that finding a murdered man with his face eaten by rats in her property might make it hard to dispose of. She took my point and lowered her price. It was sold this morning.'

'Who is the new owner?'

'We never divulge that information. Is there another property you wish to view?'

'No.'

'Then I bid you good day.'

The clerk, looking surprisingly unruffled, as if this was a normal incident in his working day, restored the ledger to its shelf then returned to his perch and the appointment book, showing no inclination to address Frances further. Frances strongly suspected that Johnstone had seized the opportunity offered by the murder to acquire the property at a bargain price, and she would not be permitted to enter it. No one, however, could prevent her from taking another look at the exterior of the house, which was as she remembered it, including the fact that the front door and back gate were still locked. Miss Dauntless, she reflected, would not have stood helplessly in the alleyway. Miss Dauntless would have arrayed herself in stout boots and breeches, roped herself up like a member of the Alpine Club and made nothing of that high wall. Miss Dauntless might have clasped the gallant and dashing Mr W. Grove in a warm embrace, and not allowed him to disappear into the night. The more Frances thought about it the more she dreaded to think what that daring lady might have done. The best she could do was to engage Tom Smith's army of messengers and detectives to watch the house for her and see if they could discover anything useful.

Frances returned to the Duke of Sussex Tavern and spoke to Mr Neilson, who confirmed that the search for the missing regalia had been conducted without success. 'I can assure you no one could have hidden a pin here without my finding it.'

'I would like to interview the members of the Literati who were present when Mr Dobree disappeared. That would include the gentlemen who were not in the Lodge room. What is the best way to achieve this? When will they next be meeting?'

'That will not be for another two weeks, but we could arrange for a Lodge of Instruction, which our members would be expected to attend. I shall ask Mr Fiske to issue the necessary summons, and let you know when we have a suitable date.'

'That would be very convenient, thank you,' said Frances, relieved that she was saved the labour of visiting all the members individually. 'What is a Lodge of Instruction?'

'It is not a meeting proper, but a gathering to rehearse our ritual.'

Frances had an idea and was about to make another request, but decided to say nothing just yet. Some things were better left unspoken until the last minute.

Back in Bayswater, Frances ascended the stairs to the business premises occupied by Sarah's juvenile relative Tom Smith. She found Tom and Ratty in conference over steaming mugs of cocoa, determining how jobs were to be allocated amongst their battalion of runners who dashed nimbly up and down the stairs at regular intervals. Tom's most urgent current concern, according to Sarah, was to try and look older than his years in order to secure more important clients than might have come to a youth who was hardly fourteen. Ratty was probably only a year older but had grown so many inches in recent months that he could well pass for seventeen or more, and Tom kept giving him envious glances, as height was the one thing that money could not buy.

After the usual greetings and offers of refreshment, which included some irregularly shaped cakes that Frances decided not to deprive them of, they settled down to business. 'There is a house I would like watching,' Frances explained, supplying the address.

Ratty and Tom exchanged knowing glances. 'That's where the Masonical gent was found dead,' said Ratty. 'You was there, I 'eard.'

'I was,' said Frances, 'but the house has just been sold and I am unable to discover to whom, although I suspect that a Mr Johnstone who lets properties in the district has acquired it cheaply because of its notoriety.'

'That's a good wheeze,' said Tom approvingly. 'When I wanter buy a property I shall look in the papers for news've where dead bodies 'ave been found so the 'ouse can be got cheap.' Tom, who had been earning well and living frugally, had been getting Sarah to invest his profits for him, and Frances thought it might not be too long before that idea was put into effect. He would probably own half a street of houses by the time he reached his majority.

'So what is it you wanter know?' asked Ratty.

'I need descriptions of who goes in and out. Find out as much as you can about them. I was hoping to get the keys and look around in case there was anything I missed the last time I was there, but the agent was most unhelpful. If you can establish for certain who the owner is, I might be able to arrange a viewing.'

'You don't want one've my lads to go in?' asked Tom.

'Shouldn't be too tricky, old 'ouses never are,' added Ratty.

Frances hesitated but declined. 'That would be against the law, and I couldn't possibly ask you to do it or condone it if you did. You could end up in prison.'

'We wouldn't break anythin',' protested Ratty.

'I should hope not.'

'Only a winder might be left open by accident.'

'That's still trespass.'

'And our poor little cat could've climbed in an' got itself trapped, an' we'd 'ave to go in an' get it back, or it might die,' added Tom, with an expression of deep melancholy.

'You haven't got a cat.'

'No, but we could get one.'

Frances gave in. 'Very well. These are your instructions. Your task is to observe, no more. You must break nothing and remove nothing. If you do enter the premises you must have a reasonable excuse for doing so. It is well known that I employ your services to find missing pets, so if you are caught you could well be believed if you claim that you were hoping to find a trapped animal. It would still be trespass but if you don't commit another offence then I doubt that any action would be taken against you. Do you agree?'

They nodded.

Once her business with Tom and Ratty was completed Frances had only to descend the stairs to the ground-floor offices of the Bayswater Design and Display Company whose directors, generally known to their friends as Chas and Barstie, were energetic young men determined to establish themselves as pillars of the best Bayswater society. Alert to every secret whisper concerning the commercial world of West London, their knowledge was such that they were able to provide Frances with insights that she could have obtained in no other way. She often thought that the little commissions she sought from them were undertaken not so much for the fee, but as a welcome diversion from their more humdrum daily endeavours. The young clerk in the outer office knew her by sight and jumped up to greet her politely. 'Good morning, Miss Doughty! If you'll wait one moment I'll let the gentlemen know you're here.'

Frances waited, reflecting that it was some weeks since she had engaged the two directors to assist her on a criminal investigation. Recently they had done no more for her than check on the bona fides and finances of men who had applied for business partnerships, or sought the hand in marriage of a valued and valuable daughter.

The clerk returned very soon and conducted her to the office, where the two directors sat facing each other across their desks. As usual, Barstie's was crowded but tidy while Chas was content to work in a small portion of the available space surrounded by a debris of used teacups, cake wrappers, smears of jam, scattered coins and disorganised piles of paper. The fact that a charlady tidied and cleaned the office regularly only made the situation more remarkable.

They greeted her warmly. 'It is our great pleasure to receive a visit from you,' said Chas, climbing to his feet and offering Frances a chair. 'And how delightful to see you in such good health! I trust you are now fully restored?'

She could well understand his concern. Following the last desperate act of the Bayswater Face-slasher and her own narrow brush with death, Frances had not left the house or received visitors for some while, and when she had finally emerged it was as a wraith of her former self, even paler and thinner than usual. Only Sarah's constant care had prevented her from fading away altogether.

'Thank you, I am greatly recovered.'

'I am pleased to hear it. Refreshments will appear in a mere moment. No arguments. We insist!' The young clerk was dispatched to the kitchen. 'And we have some good news to share, don't we Barstie?'

'We do,' said Barstie, looking less enthusiastic than his partner.

'Barstie has finally won the heart and hand of a lady, the one who has lived in his hopes for so long.'

'Her father has consented to the engagement,' said Barstie. 'A very long engagement,' he added dejectedly.

'I am sure the time will pass very quickly as you labour to prove yourself a worthy son-in-law,' said Frances in what she hoped was a reassuring manner.

'There will be an announcement in the newspapers very soon, and a little supper to celebrate the betrothal,' said Chas. 'You will of course receive an invitation.'

'I am honoured.' Frances did not ask Chas if he was any closer to marital bliss. He had once hinted jovially that she interested him, but that was before he had prospered and she had been made poor after her father's money was lost. He now looked to brighter horizons, preferably involving fortunes in securities and land.

'But tell us, to what circumstance do we attribute this visit?' asked Chas as the tea tray arrived. 'How may we be of service?'

'I have a confession to make,' said Frances. 'I may have been somewhat precipitate in giving up my criminal investigations. I had my reasons for it at the time, but now I find myself looking at a puzzle I cannot resist trying to solve.'

'You have our complete attention,' said Chas with a grin.

'You will have read about the murder of Lancelot Dobree.'

Both partners exhibited alarm. 'We have indeed. You are not looking into that, surely?'

'Although Mr Salter has been cleared of suspicion, he fears that for some, particularly his business friends, his reputation will always be in doubt. He has therefore engaged me to collect information to exonerate him in the eyes of the world.'

'Would that not involve finding the real murderer?' asked Barstie with a worried expression.

'At this stage, perhaps not. All that may be required is to show that there might have been a motive other than the one suggested at the inquest. The police are still convinced that Mr Salter is guilty and are watching him, waiting for him to make a slip so they can arrest him again. They may be pursuing other suspects, of course, and if I can uncover more information which leads to the guilty man, then all I need do is hand it to the police.'

'Ah, very sensible,' said Barstie, and Chas looked relieved.

'There may be something in Mr Dobree's professional life or his charity work that could have led to him being lured to his death. He may have had rivals, enemies. He might have a hidden past. Or perhaps he was on some private business of his own which turned sour.'

Chas nodded understandingly. 'All good men have enemies,' he said. 'Leave it with us. We will find out what we can about both Mr Dobree and Mr Salter.'

Chapter Twenty-One

Frances was not anticipating a visit to solicitor Mr Marsden with any pleasure, but knew that that caustic necessity had to be carried out as soon as possible. Mr Marsden's office occupied the corner site linking Westbourne Grove with Hatherley Grove. The outer office was polished to a cruel shine, and she had the impression that if anything had been found dusty or out of place by the proprietor then the repercussions would have been severe indeed. The employees were smartly dressed, they moved smartly and all had a little fear behind their eyes.

Frances presented her card to a young man, saying that she would like to see Mr Marsden if that was possible or make an appointment to see him very soon if it was not. The young man studied the card and when he saw her name he raised his eyebrows then looked at her hard. He did not trouble himself to enquire as to the nature of her business, and this, she felt sure from his manner, was because he already knew.

'If you would be so kind as to wait for a moment,' he said, and hurried away before she could reply. Frances waited. Whether or not she would see Mr Marsden she did not know, but she was sure she would not be offered tea and cake.

After a short wait the young man returned. 'If you could step this way, Mr Wheelock will speak to you,' he said.

Frances hesitated, then reluctantly complied. Mr Wheelock might be the best she could achieve in this unfriendly place. She felt some curiosity as to how well matched he was with his new employer. He had once been trusted by his former master, Mr Rawsthorne, who was still, due to the complexity of his affairs, awaiting trial. Wheelock's office at Rawsthorne's had been a grubby nest formed from the accumulated scraps of paper he liked to collect. These were things tossed idly away by others, or even consigned as they thought to consuming fire, but rescued by the clerk's busy fingers, and held safe against a time when he might use them to his advantage. Frances suspected that Mr Marsden would not tolerate such a cave of crumpled treasures on his premises and so it proved. Mr Wheelock's new domain was a small room dominated by high wooden cabinets, all looking impenetrable, and shelves of card boxes. The desk held an imposing pile of paperwork and a fine array of ink and pens. The clerk himself had, under the demanding eye of his new principal, treated himself to a suit of dark clothes, and there had even been some effort to scrub away the worst of the ink that stained his hands and mouth, although some fresh marks about his lips revealed that he had not abandoned his habit of sucking pens.

Wheelock grinned at Frances as she entered, revealing blue and red blotches on his teeth. 'Well, Miss Doughty, up to your old tricks again?'

He didn't bother to offer her a seat so she sat down uninvited. 'Is Mr Marsden not available?'

'Not to you, no.'

'I'm surprised you agreed to see me.'

'So would he be. Right now, if he should ask, I am busy telling you that you are to leave and never return and we can offer you no assistance either in the Dobree case or any other. So we won't be talking for long, and you won't be back.'

'I understand.'

He took a card from his pocket and dropped it on the desk. 'Private office, for private business,' he said.

Frances picked it up. It read 'T. Wheelock', and gave an address, an apartment in a nearby lodging house. She had no desire to visit him in what was presumably his home, but did not say so. 'What I intended to ask Mr Marsden was what Mr Dobree said to him about the suspicions he had concerning Mr Salter. If I could find out more, then it might give me a clue as to why Mr Dobree suddenly left the Lodge room, and who he was meeting.'

'So you're working for the Salters?'

'Mr Salter has convinced me that he is innocent of any wrongdoing, and he is concerned that the police still believe him to be guilty and are not pursuing other possible suspects.'

'Then you'll know that Mr Marsden is no longer acting for the family. Mrs Salter hates him particularly.'

'I'm not surprised after what he said at the inquest.'

Wheelock grinned again. 'I'll let you into a little secret. Surprising what you can find when you go poking around in old papers. Many years ago Mr Marsden was a young ambitious solicitor in a small practice. Not out of the top drawer nor even the one next down, and therefore looking for an advantageous marriage. So he set his sights on Miss Dobree as she was then, daughter of the senior partner's best client. Her father was in favour of the match, but the lady wasn't. It was soon afterwards that she met Mr Salter and decided that he was just what she wanted. Mr Marsden wasn't too pleased to see his prize slipping away. He looked into Salter's family and found out that his father had been a bankrupt. And then there was all that funny business over the partner.'

Frances was aware that the silversmith business of Vernon Salter's father, Bernard, had collapsed in 1858 after his partner had absconded with money and valuables, but decided not to reveal the extent of her knowledge to Mr Wheelock. 'Funny business?'

'I expect Mr Salter didn't care to mention that.'

'Perhaps he thought it not relevant to my current enquiry.'

'Do you?'

'I don't know unless you tell me.'

He sucked his teeth noisily. 'Well it seems that Mr Bernard Salter and his partner George Cullum weren't on the best of terms. Neighbours used to hear them arguing. Not a good sign for men of business where there are a lot of valuables about, money owed, money owing.'

'Do you know what they argued about?'

'According to Salter, the business hadn't been doing so well; that was in the bad old days before Mr Whiteley made his mark and Westbourne Grove was known as "Bankruptcy Avenue". Mr Cullum thought he had the answer – dealing in stolen goods. He thought they could make quick profits out of it and get themselves out of trouble, but Mr Salter wasn't having any of it. He told Cullum that if that was what he was thinking of, they shouldn't be in business together. But Cullum wouldn't have come out of it so well; he was the junior man, and all the property was in Salter's name. Next thing, the man was gone, and cash funds and silver missing.'

'Was he ever found?'

'No, never seen again.'

'And the silver?'

'No. He was careful to take nothing traceable. Must have been melted down long ago. But you can see how Dobree was thinking. Bankruptcy, partnered with a criminal, not a good sign.'

'That was Mr Salter's father – it's no reflection on him.'

'And there was a rumour that Vernon Salter was running about with a married woman.'

'Oh!' said Frances, shocked that her family shame was so widely reported.

'Didn't know about that, did you?' he sneered.

'You said it was only a rumour. And in any case, many men are – a little wild when they are young, and settle down to being good husbands once married. So I attach no weight to that story. But I expect Mr Dobree did, and Mr Marsden might well have made things seem worse than they were.'

'It was Marsden who proposed the terms of the marriage settlement. I reckon he thought Salter wouldn't agree to them and then the wedding would be off. But to his surprise the man agreed. All these years Marsden has been looking for a way of getting his revenge. Not that he still has hopes of Mrs Salter, no, he just wants revenge.'

'And I suppose with his client dead he really had little to lose by speaking up at the inquest.'

'Exactly. So there we have it. And I don't know what it was Dobree told Marsden, only that there's nothing in writing.'

'Were they great friends?'

'No, ever since Marsden was disappointed of the charming Miss Dobree, it was strictly business between them.'

'They didn't meet socially?'

'Not that I know of.'

'Is Marsden a Freemason?'

'What, and give his money away to charity?' said Wheelock scornfully.

'And the two last met about two weeks before the murder? Not since?'

'Not that I know of.'

'What can you tell me about that meeting?'

'From the papers they ordered to be brought it was to do with charities and property. I didn't see Dobree arrive, but I saw him leave. He was usually in good spirits, but that day he was not a happy man.'

'If Mr Marsden knew more than he said at the inquest regarding Mr Dobree's concerns, he would have told the police. But they have brought no charges against Mr Salter so it might have been nothing.'

'Nothing provable. Which is why he hasn't gone public; he doesn't want an action for slander.'

'As far as I am concerned, it is not a question of what is true or provable, only what Lancelot Dobree believed or suspected, which might have prompted his actions. And of course his behaviour that night might not have been concerned with his son-in-law at all but something else, something he felt compelled to act upon himself, something he could reveal to no one.'

Frances reflected on the one awkward incident in Vernon's recent past, his purchase of a stolen snuffbox, but in that case he had done the right thing, exactly what his father-in-law would have approved of, taken the item to the police. There was no reason for Dobree to find that suspicious, rather the opposite, unless there was something else, something she was not being told.

CHAPTER TWENTY-TWO

There was a note from Miss Gilbert and Miss John await-ing Frances on her return home, referring her to the local newspaper and saying that an urgent meeting was required. There was hardly time for Frances to dispose of a light supper before the ladies arrived. Miss Gilbert, large and buxom, burst in like a storm of passionate activity, with diminutive and deceptively meek Miss John peering from under a cloud of grey curls travel-ling in her wake.

Miss Gilbert was not so much clutching as brandishing a rolled copy of the *Bayswater Chronicle*, as if she would have liked to bela-bour the annoying Mrs Cholmondeleyson with it. 'Outrageous! The dreadful woman has taken leave of her senses and means to have us all made slaves to men!'

'She has been married three times,' said Miss John, with a shiver of distaste. 'Just imagine that!'

Frances could hardly imagine being married once.

'And the worst of it is,' Miss Gilbert went on, 'she is beyond reproach in every aspect of her life. She has eight children, all of whom have married well, and they are either professional gentle-men or domestic angels. None of her husbands died in suspicious circumstances, and all left her wealthier than she was before. So she parades herself as the very model of what a lady should be, holds that the things she concerns herself with are those all women should espouse, and declares that those she shuns are outside our legitimate sphere. And, of course, people listen to her and take note.'

'Every improvement has had its opposition,' said Frances. 'That is human nature. Consider the printing press, or the steam engine. Opposition leads to open debate, and that can only be a good thing. The more people talk about it the more the idea spreads.'

Miss Gilbert was not comforted by this observation. 'I can understand menfolk wanting to deny women the vote, or any voice at all in public matters, but really, what are we to do when women turn against their own? It is all very well for Mrs Cholmondeleyson with her servants and her carriages to say that she doesn't need to think about what Parliament decrees, and imagines that she speaks for the majority.'

'Has she published a statement of her beliefs and intentions?' asked Frances.

'Not yet, but it is bound to follow. As you see, she is holding a meeting at Westbourne Hall very soon, and all are welcome. I intend to go and shout her down, and we would like you to join us.' Miss Gilbert's triumphant smile indicated her confidence that Frances would agree.

'Might I suggest a different approach?' said Frances, who had no great wish to be arrested for disorderly behaviour.

'Of course,' said Miss Gilbert, 'we always appreciate your advice.'

'I think we ought to attend, but with the intention of discovering what they have to say, what they mean to do and how much support they have. If we simply cause a disturbance and are turned out of the hall, then we will learn nothing to our advantage. Only when we have the facts can we decide what if anything we need to do. Oh, and I think it would be unwise to carry anything that might be construed as a weapon.'

Miss John looked understandably disappointed.

Sarah, who arrived home with a letter of introduction to Mr Westvale of Mulberry Lodge, reported that Mr Fiske had not been able to recall anything else of importance, and was extremely agitated as someone had shown him a copy of Mr Miggs' pamphlet. Like Frances, he was in no doubt as to the authorship, and Sarah's visit to the printers had confirmed that their suspicions were correct. 'Is there nothing to be done about this nuisance!' Fiske had exclaimed. 'I have taken legal advice, but he has been too careful and avoided a charge. If I took him to court I would be wasting my money, and what is worse, bringing him more prominently into the public mind. He is the Cinna the Poet of our age, only there is no mob to tear him for his bad verses.'

'Mr Fiske told me that Cinna was a bad poet who was murdered in a play,' Sarah explained.

'Then we must wish Mr Miggs the best of health, or there will be more trouble,' said Frances. She dispatched a note to Mr Westvale and was pleased to receive an early reply making an appointment for the following day.

Mr Westvale lived in very comfortable circumstances, his long connection with the silk industry apparent from the lustrous yet tasteful furnishings with which he surrounded himself. Frances was conducted to his study where his role in freemasonry was proudly displayed, a large oil portrait showing him arrayed in full regalia, with apron, collar and breast jewels. On that evidence, he had been handsome in his middle years, but age had shrunk him, and his face was like a withered fruit. Nevertheless, his hair and beard were faultlessly groomed and he was every bit as debonair in his manner and clothing as his younger self.

He greeted her with cordial respect, although there was a shadow of sadness behind his eyes. 'It is my great pleasure to meet you Miss Doughty. Mr Fiske speaks very highly of you, and I am sure we are all most grateful to you for ridding our streets of that dreadful murderer, and at such danger to yourself.'

'I often feel that the newspapers tell too dramatic a story,' said Frances.

'You are too modest. I sense a determination in you; a need to discover the truth and ensure that justice is done. That is not always easy, and yet it is a challenge you accept again and again. I did think from what I had read in the papers that you had abandoned that endeavour.'

'I had, but I made an exception to help Mr Fiske, and now I believe I will go on with my former career, one in which I can do some good in the world.'

Westvale smiled his approval. 'How may I help you? I am as anxious as anyone to see Lancelot Dobree's murderer brought to justice, and I cannot believe that Salter was involved.'

'How long have you known them?'

'Dobree I first met some twenty-five years ago, through mutual trading interests. He was an honourable and charitable man, directed by prudence. We were both members of the Mercer's Guild and I asked him to join Mulberry Lodge. He progressed through the Lodge offices, and was a past Master. Salter did not join us at once, as he was unsure if his business, which involves considerable travelling, would allow him to be a useful member, but he did eventually join. He is currently Inner Guard.'

'This is a hard question I know, but are you aware of anything questionable in Mr Dobree's life that could have led to his murder?'

Westvale smiled gently. 'I promise you, Miss Doughty, unless we have all been thoroughly hoodwinked these many years, there is nothing of that kind.'

'Mr Marsden told the inquest that Mr Dobree was concerned about something, although he did not say what, and this may well have informed his behaviour, even if his worries were unfounded. Mr Fiske has confirmed to me that he thought Mr Dobree had something on his mind. This may have led him to leave the Lodge during the meeting and could well have been connected with his plans to go away. Can you enlighten me at all?'

Westvale gave the question very intense thought. 'There is no doubt in my mind that Dobree was a troubled man. In the last weeks of his life there was a heavy burden weighing on him. The last time I saw him was about a week before his death, at the last meeting of Mulberry Lodge he attended. I asked him what was troubling him; I thought at first that it was an issue with his health and asked if he was well, and he assured me that his health remained strong and that no member of his family was indisposed. I knew of course that he was retired from business, so it was clear that it could not be that. He saw what I was thinking and told me that he was not in any financial difficulties. Finally he spoke to me in confidence as a friend, a confidence I only break now that he is no more, and in the hopes of finding his murderer. He said that he suspected a serious irregularity regarding a brother Mason, but he could not act upon it or reveal it to another person until he was certain of his facts. The consequences of acting before he was certain could be catastrophic if he was wrong.'

'Catastrophic to whom? Himself? His family? His charities? The Lodge?'

Westvale smiled. 'A very good question. He didn't say. I advised him to consider employing a detective, but he said he didn't want to involve anyone else. I could see, however, that the suggestion had set him thinking, so it is possible that despite this, he might have done so. At any rate he had no more to say on the subject, at least nothing that he would tell me.'

Exploring the inner thoughts of a deceased man was hard, but Frances wondered if the next topic discussed by the two friends would reveal something; a thought that might have emerged from the earlier one. 'Was that the end of your conversation or did it go on? What else did you talk about?'

Westvale leaned forward and balanced his chin on his hands. 'I think we went on to discuss his forthcoming visit to the Literati. I don't think there was anything of moment he had to convey, merely that he was due to be a guest.'

'Had he visited the Literati before?'

'I'm not sure he had. It is a fairly recently formed Lodge. They use the same Lodge room as Mulberry.'

'He didn't reveal where he planned to go after the meeting?'

'No.'

'In all the years that you and he have been members of Mulberry Lodge, has he ever left a meeting while it was in progress?'

'Never. I am certain of it. He did not do so when I was present, and if he had done such an extraordinary thing during a meeting I did not attend I would have been sure to be told of it.'

'But if it was dark he might have slipped out and come back without anyone knowing?'

Westvale shook his head. 'I don't see how. In any case, the period of darkness is not in all our ceremonies.'

'Yes, Mr Fiske told me it only occurs during a raising. But there must have been such ceremonies in Mulberry Lodge?'

'Oh yes, and we have records of them and who attended and in what capacity. But Dobree, as an officer of Mulberry Lodge, would have been participating in the ritual. He would have been fully occupied and would not have had the opportunity to go out unnoticed.'

'I see, whereas as a guest of the Literati he was not so occupied, and could have slipped out unseen?'

Westvale permitted himself a smile. 'Leaving aside the question of the locked, guarded and tyled doors, yes.'

'Do you or any members of the Mulberry Lodge have keys to any of the external tavern doors – the ones that lead into the High Street, Linfield Gardens or the alleyway, Linfield Walk?'

'I am quite sure none of us do. Mr Neilson is very careful and vigilant. You will find nothing slipshod in his arrangements.'

CHAPTER TWENTY-THREE

Frances was deep in thought all the way home. Dobree's discussion with Westvale about his visit to the Literati might have been intended to move the subject away from something he felt uncomfortable talking about, or, more interestingly, it could have followed from his hidden thoughts. Had it just occurred to Dobree that the specific circumstances of the Literati meeting gave him an opportunity he would not have had in his own Lodge? The chance, at a time when there would have been witnesses to his being present during a Lodge meeting, to be in quite another place? Westvale had suggested to Dobree that he hire a detective, something that he felt unwilling to do, and Marsden had mentioned something similar. Perhaps, thought Frances, Dobree had decided to act as a detective himself, as she had once done. If so, it seemed probable that he had only intended to be out of the room for a few minutes, just during the period of darkness, enough time to meet secretly with someone, or listen in on a conversation, and then return without anyone being any the wiser. She recalled the fact that the Literati included a ritual known as an address, which Mulberry did not. The period of covering darkness in the Literati Lodge was therefore longer than in Mulberry.

Given that Dobree was without hat or coat, he cannot have intended to leave the building for long, if at all. Which still left the question of where he had been killed and how he had got to the place where his body had been found. Frances was beginning to wonder if Dobree could have done what he did without the collusion of another person, someone he had hired, perhaps, not so much to investigate sensitive secrets but to help him achieve what might have seemed impossible alone.

❧

On her return, Frances found a Mrs Maxwell waiting for a consultation, and such was the client's distress that it was some while before she was able to explain the reason for her visit. It transpired that her cat, Fluff, a devoted companion and confidante for many years, had vanished one afternoon after being permitted to snooze in her garden in a patch of rare winter sunshine. There was no cat like Fluff, she declared, none more loyal, or with a sweeter purr or softer coat. She felt sure that Fluff, who was in the last season of a cat's life, and whose eyesight had been failing, had wandered away and been trapped in some outhouse or stable somewhere, and was in danger of starving to death. She had advertised in the newspapers without result, but now appealed to Miss Doughty's wondrous ability to find lost pets. Mrs Maxwell had an oval locket with a miniature of the adored feline, and a watercolour portrait she had painted herself. On this evidence, Fluff was a plump and sleepily contented animal, with white fur in downy profusion, attractively streaked and spotted in dark grey, and tiny blue eyes sunk deeply into a pudgy face. There was a glitter in those ailing eyes which suggested that Fluff would despise anything that came within scenting distance that was not handing her a dish of food. Whatever Frances thought of pets, she knew better than to say anything other than what a beautiful creature the missing darling must be.

Mrs Maxwell had scarcely departed, leaving a trail of teardrops as she went, when Tom and Ratty arrived looking pleased with themselves. Frances was hoping that they had identified the miscreant who had earned himself the soubriquet 'the Bayswater Gown-slasher' but apart from some near misses no progress had been made. The subject of their visit was 2 Linfield Gardens.

'Watched the place all day, nothing doin', no one goin' in or out,' said Tom. 'I've got men still there, lookin'. But it's locked up, tight as a trap.'

'Well, keep up the work,' said Frances. 'Sooner or later the new owner or his agent will go in and then I might be able to take a look. I only wish I knew what I was looking for.'

Tom and Ratty glanced at each other and grinned.

Frances was not sure she liked those grins. 'What have you done?'

'We got over the wall into the yard,' said Tom.

'How did you manage that? I hope you weren't seen.'

'No spyin' eyes about. I stood on Ratty's shoulders, peeked over, nothin' much to see but I thought I could scramble over the wall. Once I was in, there was enough wood an' old bricks lyin' about, so I made a pile, stood on it an' 'elped Ratty get over.'

'So we 'ad a look about,' Ratty went on, 'dint touch nothin' like you said, so it was just accidental like that we found the stuff.'

'Stuff?'

'Things what someone might wanter steal. Dint know what some of 'em rightly was. There was silky and shiny stuff, an' a ring, an' things that looked like medals, and there was other stuff too but we thought we oughtn't to touch any of it.'

'Where was all this? I hope you didn't break into the house?'

'No we never went in,' said Tom. 'I saw some little bits've the outer walling of the 'ouse that 'ad fallen down, an' I thought there might be some reason for it. It looked solid enough, but when I tapped on it with a stick I 'eard it was 'ollow underneath. So I called Ratty over an' we found some bricks were loose. Well we reckoned they was like that for some reason, so we worked on 'em and it wasn't 'ard to get two bricks out. It was a bit too dark to see exac'ly what was there, but it looked like some kind of 'idden treasure so we got more bricks out to see better and when we saw all the shiny stuff we thought the best thing to do was cover it all up again and come and tell you about it.'

'You did the right thing,' said Frances. 'And now we must all go and tell Inspector Payne of the Kensington police.'

Tom and Ratty exchanged worried looks.

'I will advise him that you were working for me, looking for a missing animal, and take full responsibility for anything you have done. I doubt that he will question it. In fact, I have a new commission for you, a Mrs Maxwell, whose cat, Fluff, has wandered away. Fluff is the best cat in the world and Mrs Maxwell is very anxious for her safe return.' Frances handed over the picture.

'No 'urry then,' said Tom. 'It could live off its own fat for a fortnight.'

'Now then, both of you, I will take you to Kensington to see Inspector Payne.'

'Do we 'ave to?' snarled Ratty.

'I know you don't like the police, but it will be better for you if you tell them what you have found and not hide anything. In any case, you will be demonstrating your superior detecting skills.'

'I tole Ratty 'e oughter apply for copperin',' said Tom, 'but 'e won't 'ave it.'

Ratty scowled.

CHAPTER TWENTY-FOUR

At Kensington police station Frances took the lead and informed the desk sergeant that the boys she had employed to search for a missing pet had stumbled by chance on what she thought were the items missing from the corpse of Lancelot Dobree. There was an immediate flurry of action and they did not have to wait long before Payne appeared and beckoned them into his office.

'Were you present at this discovery?' he asked Frances, sinking wearily into his chair.

'No, but I take responsibility for the actions of my agents. In this case both are minors and do not have parents to guide them, so I saw it as my duty to accompany them here.'

'I am sure you did,' he said drily. 'But I want to hear it in their words, not yours. You, young man,' he nodded at Ratty, 'what's your name?'

Ratty's head had sunk inside his collar like a tortoise drawing its head under its shell. 'Ratty,' he muttered. 'I calls myself Jonsmif if I goes to give evydence.'

'Well that's a good start.'

'Ratty is very observant and has provided valuable information to the police in a number of cases,' said Frances.

Payne ignored her and pointed to Tom. 'And you?'

'I'm Tom Smith, of "Tom Smith's Men". Ratty 'ere is one of my best men. We both work for Miss Doughty.'

Payne studied the nervously cowering Ratty for a moment. 'Alright, Tom Smith, tell me all about it.'

Tom was not far into his description when Payne sat up straight and took a keen interest. He jotted a few notes. 'We'll go along now and you can show me what you found. How did you get into the premises?'

'We shinned over the wall,' said Tom. 'As soon as we 'eard the poor little lost puss cryin' for its mother.' He displayed the picture of Fluff. 'I mean we couldn't leave it to die now could we?'

Payne gave a heavy sigh. 'Of course not.'

'I believe the property has been sold since the body was found,' said Frances. 'Mr Johnstone, the man who last viewed it, has bought the business of Munro & Son, so he might be able to tell you who has the keys.'

'Then let's take a look,' said Payne, rising to his feet. On the way out of the station he signalled to a constable to accompany him. 'We won't be needing you, Miss Doughty, you can run along home now.'

'I beg to differ. I must accompany the boys in the capacity of guardian and advisor.'

'Are you usually this hard to shake off?'

Frances smiled, and Tom and Ratty laughed.

Payne disdained the idea of a cab and strode hard towards the High Street, somewhat disconcerted to find that Frances, with her youth, energy and long legs, was easily able despite the weight of her skirts to keep pace with him. Frances was taller than most men, but Payne was about an inch or two taller than she, or would have been if he had not been so hunched with irritation.

At last he reduced his pace, then stopped and turned to face her. 'Are you still working for the Salters?'

'Yes, with the understanding that should I discover anything of interest you will be informed at once.'

'Very generous. Now be honest with me, you're here as a detective, not to take care of these two who are obviously more than able to take care of themselves.'

There was no point in denial. 'I am, yes. I want to take another look at the house but was refused the keys by Mr Johnstone, who said he has sold it and wouldn't reveal to whom. I suspect that he bought it himself, getting it at a cheap price after the murder.'

'And what do you hope to find in the house?'

'I'm not sure; anything I might have missed on my first visit when I was simply hoping to find Mr Dobree alive.'

Payne grunted and walked on.

At the house agent's Mr Johnstone had still not troubled himself to replace the sign of Munro & Son, perhaps on the grounds that it was an unnecessary expense. Payne strode in and found the proprietor in conference with his assistant. 'Now then, Mr Johnstone, you're an honest tradesman and I know you wouldn't want to fall foul of the police. So just let me have the keys to number 2 Linfield Gardens.'

'What do you want with them?' growled Johnstone. 'I thought you'd finished tramping around the place.'

'Well we had, but now we want to tramp around it again.'

Johnstone responded with a sour grimace, then nodded to his shadowy assistant, who rose from his desk and went into the back office. He returned with a set of keys, which he handed to Payne.

'And much good it will do you!' said Johnstone ungraciously. 'Watch your step, the place is riddled with dry rot. If you fall through and kill yourself it won't be my fault!'

Payne turned and walked out without another word.

For the second time, Frances entered the lodging house, but this time she was not looking for an injured man. Quite what she was looking for she did not know. Payne, too, was staring keenly around him as he passed through the bare, dark and acrid-smelling rooms, although he had undoubtedly been back there more recently than she. As far as Frances was aware nothing was different from her first visit and if Payne had noticed anything he gave no sign of it. In the yard, however, it was clear that there had been considerable activity as much of the detritus on the ground had been moved, probably during the police search. The large heap of old planks that had once lain against the boundary wall had been dismantled, thoroughly explored and scattered. Frances noticed the sturdy pile of wood and bricks that Tom had constructed to give him enough extra height to help Ratty scramble over. The wall itself, she saw, on a closer examination than she had given it previously, was uneven enough to provide footholds for a determined climber. Miss Dauntless could certainly have scaled it. Frances lifted the latch of the door to the fuel store, finding the mechanism so rusted and stiff that it could be left in a raised position and not fall back. The interior had been swept clean apart from a residue of gritty coal and stones. The other outhouse with a badly rotted door and damaged lock she confirmed was a grimy malodorous privy.

'So let's see what you discovered,' said Payne.

Ratty and Tom set to, and as they worked it was clear that the hiding place had been an effective one, since the bricks had fitted almost exactly. In the dingy yard space an uneven crack in the already dilapidated wall would not have been especially noticeable. The constable assisted, and Frances and Payne watched. At last Frances said, 'That was not the work of a moment. I am sure that whoever killed Mr Dobree must have known that that space was there, and used it.'

Payne nodded. 'We'll need to talk to the former owner again, but she may know nothing. I think she once took in lodgers, so that space could have been carved out by anyone at any time.'

'Here we are!' said the constable, pulling out the last brick.

Payne crouched down for a look, then he reached in and drew out what Frances recognised as a Masonic apron of the kind described by Vernon Salter as the one worn by Lancelot Dobree. He handed it to the constable, and removed other items; a collar and what looked like shiny medals, a gentleman's ring, a leather pocketbook and a small jewellery box. He flipped open the lid of the box, raised his eyebrows, and snapped the lid shut again. 'Quite a little treasure trove,' he said. 'No gold plates but you can't have everything.'

'Is that Lancelot Dobree's property?' asked Frances.

'Looks like it.' Payne leafed through the pocketbook, which was empty. 'I'll get it to Mr Westvale, he ought to know.' He paused, and added, 'Thank you, Miss Doughty, for your prompt action in informing the police. There's many a private investigator who wouldn't have been as quick, or as honest. But I don't have to tell you to be careful and not go running about getting yourself in danger, I expect you've been warned about it before.'

'I have. Inspector Sharrock of Paddington Green makes very sure of that.'

'And as for you two,' Payne turned to Tom and Ratty, 'smart work. I hope you find your cat.' The two boys looked relieved.

Frances and the two policemen returned to the office of Munro & Son, and it was obvious even beneath Johnstone's usual unfriendly exterior that he was thunderstruck by news of the discovery. 'What villains!' he exclaimed, waving a leather-gloved fist. 'A man is not safe in his own house!'

'So it is yours?'

'As of yesterday, yes. I was due to make an inspection today before you came and took away my keys.'

'You knew nothing about the hiding place?'

'Why would I? I had only been there once before with that young fellow who was killed. He didn't know of it, or if he did he never told me. Can I have my keys back now?'

'I'm afraid not. I need to get a team of men in there for a very thorough search. If you have another set you must give me those, too. You can have them back when it's done.'

Johnstone scowled with annoyance but accepted the situation.

'I think,' said Frances once she, Payne and the constable were in the street again, 'that Tom and Ratty have shown that even for someone without keys, it is possible for active young men to climb over that wall without difficulty if there are two helping each other.'

'True,' said Payne, 'and once in the yard they are secure from observation. The space could well have been used by thieves and vagrants. The old lady and her maid might have known nothing about it.'

Frances was trying to picture in her mind the yard as it had been when she first saw it, and realised that when the planks had lain in their original position, while appearing to have been casually thrown to one side, they could have facilitated someone climbing over the wall into the alley. Perhaps they had been very carefully placed. If Lancelot Dobree had not had the keys to the house, could he have scaled the wall from the outside, even with assistance? If he had succeeded could he have done so without injury? He would surely have suffered some grazes, and there had been no mention of any at the inquest.

The idea of a man of more than seventy attempting such a thing while wearing his Masonic regalia seemed ridiculous. If on the other hand he had been killed outside the wall then it would have been a considerable task for his killer or killers to get his body over the wall, and again, it would have left some marks on the body. It followed that when Dobree entered the yard, whether alive or dead at the time, he had done so through a doorway, either the back gate from the alley, or after being brought through the house.

'Have you discovered anything more about the murder of Mr Munro?' Frances asked.

Payne looked annoyed at being questioned again, but seemed a little more willing to be forthcoming in view of her recent help. 'We don't have the culprit, if that is what you mean.'

'You don't think there was a personal motive?'

'No. He seems to have had no enemies. Respectable family and friends.'

'Then it was robbery? I suppose he was lured to an empty house on purpose. I am hoping it is not some new fashion that criminals will start to follow.'

'We've thought of that. The police have warned all house agents in the area to be on their guard. They're not to go to any property alone with someone they don't know.'

'But surely if the motive was robbery the murderer didn't need to kill him?'

'He thought he did. This was no street thief. Street thieves snatch bags and watches and run away, usually so fast that the victim never gets a good look at the robber. Some hit from behind and the victim never sees them at all, but Munro must have seen his attacker if he met him in the property and then he was struck on the head when his back was turned. Then ...' Payne paused. 'This will come out at the resumed inquest, so I suppose it's no harm to tell you now – the medical examiner believes that a second and possibly a third blow was struck when the man was lying face down on the floor. Someone wanted to be sure that he was dead.'

'What was he carrying that was so valuable?'

'Keys, cash, a gold watch. By the time he was found and we knew what keys he had had on him, the house he was in and two other empty houses had been robbed. All under cover of darkness. The thieves knew what they were looking for, empty houses offered to be let furnished and ready to move in to. High-class properties, with enough portable trinkets to tempt a burglar, but too secure to get into without attracting attention. They made a nice haul in one night. And men have been killed for far less.'

'Was Mr Munro's own house robbed, like the attempt made on Mr Dobree's?'

'No. He had his own house keys, but unlike Dobree, nothing on them to say where he lived.'

'So you don't think Mr Munro's murder was connected with that of Mr Dobree?'

'I haven't discarded any theories yet. Now if you've done questioning me …'

'Just one more.'

He rolled his eyes. 'Go on, then.'

'Did Mr Marsden tell you what it was that Mr Dobree confided in him?'

'No. Oh I asked him, but he just said that he had already told us all he knew at the inquest. He's a close one.' With that Payne hurried away before Frances could ask any more questions.

When Frances returned home she sat down to write to Vernon Salter. She had never addressed a letter to him before, and debated with herself as to how she should address him. 'Dear Father' she could not bring herself to write. 'Dear Mr Salter' seemed a little strange. Ultimately she wrote:

Dear Sir,

I am pleased to inform you that some effects that appear to be those of your father-in-law have been found. Inspector Payne has them and is taking them to Mr Westvale for identification but I think you should see them also. Once you have done so, I would like to speak with you.

Yours faithfully,

Frances Doughty

CHAPTER TWENTY-FIVE

Westbourne Hall was an architectural jewel set in the otherwise more commercial strand of the Grove, where Bayswater business flourished, creating what many regarded as the Regent Street of West London. Built in 1861, the hall's white pillars and arches were embellished with sculpted foliage, fruit and flowers, and to emphasise the cultural significance of the building, there were busts of the great writers and artists of history, presided over with expressions of stern satisfaction by the Queen and her late much-lamented consort.

The building was frequently used for meetings, lectures and musical and literary entertainment of a more refined nature than the popular theatre, although its hiring for political assemblies had been restricted after an election meeting in 1880 had ended in an undignified fracas. The lessees no doubt assumed that a gathering of anti-suffrage notables would not be concluded with flying furniture, and Frances certainly hoped so.

Frances had wondered if she and Sarah ought to be veiled in view of their known pro-suffrage sympathies, but reflected that in Bayswater the arrival of a tall thin lady accompanied by a shorter wide lady would convey only one meaning to anyone who saw them. The meeting was open to all, both men and women, since the organisers supposed that many men would approve of the withholding of suffrage from their womenfolk and add their voices to the argument. Sarah had asked Professor Pounder to accompany them, as his height, calmness in the midst of mayhem, and impressive muscularity would be an advantage if anyone objected to their attending. He would also be an additional pair of eyes on the behaviour of Miss Gilbert and Miss John, whose taste for havoc had been given extra relish after taking part in the hue and cry that had culminated in the arrest of the Filleter. Miss Gilbert arrived with a firm aggressive stare as if daring anyone to try and eject her from the hall, but to her surprise and noticeable disappointment, she was welcomed in warmly. Miss John merely looked surprised, and her eyes flickered about to assess possible threats from the gathering, more in hope than anxiety.

'It is obvious that they know who we are,' said Miss Gilbert, with some satisfaction. 'Perhaps they suppose that we have come about to their point of view.'

'There's newspapermen here,' said Sarah, with a tilt of her head towards a small group of young men standing at the back with notebooks at the ready. 'All they're waiting for is a fight to break out and then it will be the talk of Bayswater that the suffrage ladies are just the sort that shouldn't have the vote.'

'As if I cared what people thought,' said Miss Gilbert scornfully.

'Some of us must write and some of us must fight,' added Miss John, with an impish twinkle in her eye that left no one in any doubt as to what she perceived to be her role. 'Either way, we will not be ignored, all the way on our path to victory.'

To Frances' surprise, her good friend Cedric Garton was also in attendance, although he was quick to point out as he greeted them that he was as ardent a supporter of women's right to vote as anyone in Bayswater, only he had heard that there was also to be a poetry reading and he adored a fine poet.

Frances had met Cedric under unusual circumstances during her first murder investigation. She was not then a professional detective and had obtained an interview by masquerading as a gentleman of the press, wearing a suit of clothes that had once belonged to her late brother, and was therefore an indifferent fit. Although enjoying the freedom of movement this attire had afforded her, she was well aware of the potential embarrassment, not to mention prosecution that might follow, if she was ever discovered in public wearing such a costume. She had therefore only committed this dangerous act on one subsequent occasion in order to visit a private mortuary that refused to admit female visitors. For this escapade she had purchased a better fitting suit and Cedric had coached her on how to stand and walk convincingly. Frances had never been tempted to adopt male attire again, even though Cedric had said with an extravagant sigh what a handsome boy she made.

They took their seats as the hall gradually filled. Many of the ladies, some of whom had brought their husbands, were extremely prosperous in appearance. In their fashionable gowns, furs and jewels they resembled travelling exhibitions displaying the financial success of their spouses, and looked supremely satisfied with their position in life. These were women who could want for nothing better and were more than willing to accept that men were best suited to have control of those troublesome worldly matters.

There was a sudden great burst of noise as a lady swept in and immediately received enthusiastic greetings and congratulations. This was the renowned Mrs Cholmondeleyson, who was instantly in full command of everything that happened in the hall. Her dimensions were substantial, a feature that was assisted by her gown, in deep blue velvet with a metallic sheen that encased her like her own private horseless steam coach as she walked, the long skirts heavy enough to sweep aside anyone who opposed her wishes. As a young woman she must have been very attractive, with bright eyes and a delicate pointed chin. Now aged about sixty, her eyes still glowed and the chin still came to a charming point, but all was luxuriously cushioned with excess flesh.

Mrs Cholmondeleyson progressed regally through the hall and took a place of honour on the stage, directing the display of the banners one of which ran the whole width of the platform and was flanked by two which hung vertically. The wide banner merely announced in large letters 'Ladies League Against Female Suffrage', embellished at each end with what appeared to be the chosen emblem of the movement, a pink rose, symbol of peerless English womanhood. One of the side banners depicted a virtuous-looking woman surrounded by a brood of beautiful children and receiving the admiring glance of her substantial husband. The motto here was 'A woman's place is in her home and not the polling-booth'. The other banner showed a woman clad in Grecian draperies and crowned with flowers holding a sign saying 'The women of Britain do not want votes'.

'Oh my dear Lord!' exclaimed Cedric suddenly, as another figure mounted the stage. This was the energetic form of Arthur Miggs, also known as Augustus Mellifloe, Bayswater's own poetic muse. Trim Mr Miggs looked smugly pleased with himself, in so far as it was possible to detect this under his Dundreary whiskers. 'I thought we were to hear poetry,' groaned Cedric. 'It seems I was mistaken.'

'Mrs Fiske doesn't look too pleased,' said Sarah.

Frances saw Mrs Fiske sitting not far from her party, the lady's usually dignified demeanour marred by a thunderous frown. 'Let us hope he does not read anything of his own composition, or if he does, that the lady does not have a supply of rotten fruit with her.'

The ladies who joined Miggs and Mrs Cholmondeleyson on the platform were not known to Frances but all looked to be members of what some referred to as 'Bayswater gentry', persons of quality in the district who believed that they were the leaders of society, and whose duty it was to ensure that others thought so too.

Once the room was called to order there were some hundred persons seated, which was far fewer than usually attended meetings of the Bayswater Women's Suffrage Society, but it was still an impressive gathering and none of those on the stage appeared disappointed.

Mrs Cholmondeleyson rose to address the hall, and there was an immediate anticipatory hush. 'Ladies and gentlemen, it gives me great pleasure to see so many of you here today. Our numbers may be small, and you might think that this means we have little support for our views, but such is not the case. In fact, I am convinced that the great majority of women do not want the vote. If it were given to them, many would have no desire to use it, unless to do so on the advice of their husbands. You can easily see the fault in that arrangement – married men would then be accorded two votes, when surely each man ought only to have one?

'Now we all know that there are a few individuals who, although they have the franchise, are incompetent to vote due to age and infirmity. Do we really mean to add to those numbers by giving the vote to women who by their nature, inclination and education, are ignorant of politics? If the majority of persons were entitled to vote on matters they simply did not understand, what would be the result? I dread to think. Sensible women, who know their proper place in life, should refuse to vote at all.'

'What rubbish!' said Miss Gilbert, a little too audibly, and a few heads turned towards her.

'Hush, my dear,' whispered Miss John, 'we must hear all she has to say before we can decide what to do.' Her hands closed tightly on her reticule, which usually held the tools of her embroidery, a collection of sharp little implements she would not hesitate to use on troublesome men.

'This so-called boon, which if we do not oppose it will be forced upon us, will, it should be understood, come at a great price,' continued Mrs Cholmondeleyson. 'I very much doubt that these suffragists have paid any thought to what rights and privileges women will lose if they are given the vote? It would be a disaster not only for all women, but also for the country at large. Surely political decisions are best left to men? We rely on the knowledge that only they possess or can acquire. Of course women can influence questions of politics, but it is by a gentle, indirect influence that is both appropriate to our situation and most highly valued. Were women granted further powers, they might even demand to enter Parliament, and then the government of this country would come to confusion and collapse altogether.'

She paused to allow this dreadful prophecy to enter the hearts of those present. Some of the men were nodding vigorously.

'What will our next action be? To begin with, we will publish a manifesto putting forward our contentions. I know that all persons of education will read it and wholeheartedly agree. We will then gather a petition, which we will place before Parliament. You might ask why we consider this to be necessary. The answer is simple. In recent years there has been agitation by a noisy minority of women who are demanding to be given the vote. I see some of those women in this hall here today,' – at this, many of those present stared about them as if it was possible to identify these monstrous females by appearance alone – 'and I can only hope that when they have heard what I have to say they will see the common sense of my arguments. The fact is that this minority of women do not represent the views either of society at large or the female sex, but the noise they make and the energy they bring to their arguments have convinced some that they do. By contrast the vast majority of women who do not want the vote and have no desire to take part in the political life of this country, are by their very feminine natures, reluctant to come forward into any kind of public prominence. That is their preference, and I understand it, of course, but I regret to say that if right is to be done, then it will be necessary for this diffident majority to exercise their voices. I will now ask my friends on the platform to address you regarding our campaign.'

Mrs Cholmondeleyson proceeded to introduce the next speaker, who rose to polite applause, and began to outline the manifesto that would soon be published, urging all listeners to purchase and distribute copies.

'Well this is all nonsense, is it not?' said Miss Gilbert, fortunately in a whisper.

'Of course it is,' replied Frances, 'but I can understand some of the reasons behind their thinking. Ladies such as they want to retain their privileges and little think of others less fortunate than themselves, who have none. As things stand now, even if women were offered the vote, it is doubtful that it would be given to other than a few at the pinnacle of society. The goal, surely, is for all women to exercise the vote as men do, and to achieve that I think we must first improve women's education. Better schools for all, more women doctors and chemists, women admitted to professions that are currently closed to them. Once women play a greater role in society than they do at present the absurdity of denying them the vote will be so apparent that the change will be welcomed.'

'That is all very well, but it will take many years for that to come about,' protested Miss John.

'I fear so, but it may be better to wait for the right time than make the change too soon.'

'I would take the opinion of a sensible woman over a university man any day,' said Cedric, 'but then, I am not as other men.'

Another speech followed, describing the spheres of life which were believed to be appropriate for women and which should give them more than enough influence in the world without them troubling their heads about politics.

Mrs Cholmondeleyson rose again to thank the other speakers, and assured all present that the petition would be available for signature very soon. 'And now,' she went on, 'I have a very special treat for you. Mr Augustus Mellifloe will, in honour of our campaign, read one of his delightful poems.'

Miggs rose to thank her with a saccharine smile, and produced a sheaf of paper from which all could see it was a very long poem. There was restrained applause.

He coughed politely to clear his throat and took a sip of water, the greater to increase anticipation in his audience, then spoke:

'Ode to a Rose Petal.

A rose, I ween, is but a flow'r
What sweeter sight? I sigh.
I dream of it in reverie,
I see it with mine eye.'

Frances looked around but there was no easy avenue of escape. 'Don't worry,' she consoled Cedric, who was muttering imprecations under his breath, 'I see that they are putting out the tea urns so we will soon have some refreshment.'

'Oh, I will need a stronger restorative after this.'

The poem rambled on, and some forty stanzas later no one in the hall was in any doubt that the author was very fond of roses, and indeed could conceive of no greater happiness on earth than contemplating said flower, although his claim that the sight of a fallen petal had moved him to paroxysms of grief did seem a little unconvincing.

Mrs Cholmondeleyson expressed her grateful thanks to Mr Miggs, with apparent sincerity, and after brief applause everyone made a sedate rush for the tea.

Frances had just secured her cup when she was approached by Mrs Fiske. 'Miss Doughty, I had not expected to see you here. I rather thought you and your friends were devoted suffragists.'

'It is always wise to listen to other viewpoints,' said Frances. 'My feeling is that at present we should be working to improve the education of women and then in time, the vote will naturally follow.'

'Mrs Cholmondeleyson sees nothing natural in it,' observed Mrs Fiske, 'but I suppose that as a woman in a man's sphere you might.' She paused and sipped her tea. 'On that subject, I have heard conflicting reports. One moment you have abandoned your career as a detective and the next you are engaged by my husband in the Dobree case.'

'He made his appeal most earnestly,' said Frances. 'I could not refuse.'

'Well, I am glad of it. You may not know this, but Alicia Salter and I are old friends.'

Frances recalled the marriage certificate of Vernon and Alicia, which she had obtained when investigating the history of her family. One of the witnesses had been a Miss Edith White whom she had never traced. Mrs Fiske's Christian name was Edith, and it now looked as if that question at least had been answered.

'So you will excuse me for asking if her husband has now been exonerated of all blame?' Mrs Fiske continued.

'His complete innocence of any crime has been proven to my satisfaction,' said Frances. 'But the police remain watchful, and I fear that his reputation may remain under a cloud until the real culprit is caught.'

Mrs Fiske looked concerned. 'I do hope that is soon. Alicia is very devoted to her husband and can think no ill of him, but she did confide in me before the wedding that her father was unhappy about the attachment, due to the unfortunate events in the Salter family.'

'You mean his father's bankruptcy? But that was surely no one's fault except the partner?'

'Who has never been found,' said Mrs Fiske meaningfully. 'Oh, this is not gossip of my invention. Mr Dobree had a very long talk with Alicia before he would consent to a marriage settlement, especially after Mr Marsden exposed the truth.'

Frances scented interesting revelations. 'Perhaps you could enlighten me as to what you mean by "the truth"?'

'You must know the story Mr Bernard Salter told the police after his partner disappeared?'

'Yes, that they had argued after Mr Cullum wanted to deal in stolen goods, and Mr Salter refused. Then Cullum absconded after stealing money and silver.'

Mrs Fiske looked about her cautiously. 'Let us stand to one side where we cannot be overheard.' Frances followed her to the side of the hall, away from the clusters of tea-drinking ladies. 'As to any of these facts, we have only Mr Bernard Salter's word. The police, however, had another theory. They believed that Mr Cullum was not a thief, and it was Salter's own incompetence that resulted in the failure of the business. It was that that was the subject of their quarrel.'

'Then where is Mr Cullum?'

'Where indeed?' said Mrs Fiske. 'He has quite disappeared. When a man vanishes after a bitter quarrel with another man, what is one to think?'

Frances suddenly understood what was being implied, and was astounded. 'The police thought Mr Salter murdered him?'

'Not necessarily Mr Bernard Salter, he was only one of three suspects. The others were his son, Mr Vernon Salter, and an associate of theirs, James Felter.'

That last name was familiar to Frances, but she said nothing.

'I only met Mr Felter once, he was best man at Alicia's wedding,' added Mrs Fiske.

'Then I would like to speak to him. Do you know where he can be found?'

'I am afraid not. It seems he has not been seen for several years.'

When Frances had first seen the name James Felter in the newspaper report on the Salter/Dobree wedding, she had tried to locate him without success. All she had learned from the trade directories was that he was no longer resident in Bayswater; neither had she found any record of his marriage or death. She tantalised herself with the idea that he might hold information which lay at the root of the distrust that had attached itself to Vernon Salter, and there were secrets which she must unearth from deep in the past in order to clear her father's name.

CHAPTER TWENTY-SIX

Chas and Barstie had a report to make on the Dobree and Salter businesses, and Frances was happy to invite them to sample Sarah's new apple turnovers in front of a roaring fire. There was something robust and honest about Sarah's baking which Frances preferred to the sweet delicacy of the purchased lemon tarts.

'Not a lot to say,' said Chas, biting into the pastry, which sparkled and crunched with powdered sugar. 'Mr Dobree was a silk mercer who effectively retired from business at the age of seventy. That was five years ago. His business was sold as a going concern and made a substantial profit. This was partly invested and partly applied to charitable purposes. His main interests are the West Kensington School, the Paddington Widows and Orphans Trust, and the Josiah Finchbourne Home for Destitute and Distressed Children.

'Vernon Salter, well you know about his background. I have to say, if he is making a lot of illicit money he is hiding it very efficiently. But I doubt it. He's in business in a small way, buying and selling, doing well enough, travels a great deal. No great reputation in the business world. And importantly we have found no evidence of any wrongdoing of either man. Neither of them lost any funds in the crash of the Bayswater Bank.'

This information accorded with Frances' impression of Vernon Salter, that he was not a great financial or criminal brain and was just getting by in his chosen profession. 'Do you know anything about Mr Munro senior or Mr Johnstone who bought up Munro's business?'

'Munro's is a business of longstanding in the area. Reputable. As for Johnstone, if ever money made a man miserable he's the one! Doesn't trust banks, does all his business in cash. Won't spend a copper coin unless he has to. Clever, but not educated. Can't read or write. Has a man, Kennard he's called, who does all his paper-work for him. Reputed to be very rich, but who knows.'

'You must have heard about the bankruptcy of Mr Salter's late father.'

Chas and Barstie glanced at each other. 'Oh that was many years ago,' said Barstie. 'How did you come to hear of it?'

'It was mentioned to me quite recently. The partner, George Cullum, stole money and silver and ran away. There was a friend of the family, James Felter. If you should hear anything of either of them I would like to know it.'

Next morning, Frances and Sarah were perusing the newspapers when they received a visit from Vernon Salter. He looked weary, and thanked them profusely for the work they had done on his behalf. He brought a gift, wrapped carefully in paper. It was a framed photograph and although Frances did not recall the subject she did not need to ask her name. The lady in the picture, a tasteful arrangement of flowers on a pedestal by her side, was seated in composed fashion, her expression calm but wistful, a faded beauty in her face. Once she must have glowed like a ripe peach in the sun, the eyes dancing with merriment. Now, with her youthful-ness and so much of her joy a thing of the past, all that remained was the hope of achieving some measure of contentment.

'Rosetta wanted you to have it,' said Salter.

Frances was for a moment overcome with emotion. Tears sud-denly welled in her eyes and spilled down her cheeks. She took a handkerchief from her pocket and pressed it to her face. 'When was this taken?'

'Only last week. Do you have a portrait of yourself? Rosetta would so like to have one.'

'No, but I shall sit for one, of course.' Frances placed the portrait on the mantelshelf, where it was accorded a prominent position. 'Please,' she said, 'you will be more comfortable by the fire.'

Sarah raised her eyebrows but said nothing. Clients, unless they were actually ill, were always asked to sit in the straight-backed chairs at the little table. The young detective, by offering her visitor such a place, had demonstrated that he was less a client than a friend. Sarah remained at the table, studying the newspapers with one eye while keeping the other on Frances, who sat facing the father she had never known.

'Yesterday,' he began, 'Mr Kingsley and the executors came to read Lancelot's will. There were no surprises; all was as Mr Marsden had said. The house and its contents are left in trust to the children until their majority, with Alicia granted right of occupation for life. Alicia and the executors are joint trustees. There were substantial annuities to Alicia and the children and a small annuity and the cottage to me. Then there were large sums to charities, including the projected founding of a school. I was assured that there was no reason why the will should not be proved, and the property distributed under its terms. All the same ...' he trailed off with a doubtful shake of the head.

'Yes?'

'They could not say when this might occur, and I gained the impression that they were imposing a deliberate delay in case any further suspicion might attach to me.'

'Have you been able to see the items found at number 2 Linfield Gardens?'

'Yes, Inspector Payne brought them for us to look at. That is, myself, Alicia and Jeffs. We all agreed that the apron, collar, breast jewels and gentleman's ring were without doubt those worn by Lancelot, and the Inspector said that Mr Westvale was also sure of it. The pocketbook was empty but it was stamped with Lancelot's initials, and there could be no doubt that it was the one he had carried. His keys were missing, but we think the murderer had taken them to try and burgle the house. I doubt they will be recovered but in any case, we have had the locks changed and new keys made. There was one other item, a small box containing a lady's ring, gold, set with an emerald. Alicia said that it was hers, but since it no longer fitted Lancelot had told her he would take it to be enlarged, which explained why he had it with him.' There was a long silence during which he wrung his hands distractedly. 'The thing is, neither I nor Alicia had ever seen that ring before! I feel sure that Jeffs hadn't either, although he was careful to say nothing about it. I tried to talk to Alicia after the Inspector had gone, but she refused to discuss it. In her mind not only is the ring hers but it always has been.'

'Have the items now been returned to you?'

'No, the police are still holding them, and I don't know when we will get them back. We are hoping that the body will be released for burial soon.'

'Perhaps Mrs Salter took the view that the ring must have been purchased by her father as a gift which he had not yet presented to her.'

He shook his head. 'Alicia never wears green, and in any case Lancelot would have consulted her before he bought such a thing, to be sure it was to her taste. And it is hardly suitable for the girls. I am sorry to say that there is only one conclusion I can draw. Lancelot must have had a mistress. How scandalous that might turn out to be for a man of his reputation, I really don't know. And Inspector Payne is no fool. He knew that Alicia was lying; I saw it in his face. He must be trying to trace the origins of the ring now.'

'It is well known that many men who are accounted respectable have mistresses, and as long as they do not advertise the fact and do not neglect their lawful families, no great disapprobation attaches to them. Your father-in-law was a widower and might have felt lonely and in need of female company.'

'True, and I don't think any of us, family or brethren, would have objected to his having a respectable lady friend of appropriate years whose company cheered him. That is the reason I am concerned about his secrecy.'

'I understand. When I next see Inspector Payne I will make a note of anything he might say on the subject. Of course this does add another possible reason for your father-in-law's unusual behaviour that evening. Perhaps his sudden absence from the Lodge room or his planned journey, or both, could have been connected with a personal matter and had nothing at all to do with any suspicions he might have had about you.'

Salter took very little cheer from this. 'That is possible. I can't imagine what he might have believed about me.'

'He never knew about my mother?'

'No. We did think at first about representing her to Lancelot as my widowed sister, but I am glad we didn't. That lie serves us in

Brighton, but in London Mr Marsden's spies would have found it out very quickly. She was so ill – any further upset and I would have lost her.' His voice shook.

'You have told me all the truth of your affairs?'

'I have.'

'The only time you ever received a stolen item was the snuffbox you bought in good faith?'

'As far as I know, yes.'

'Can you tell me about the sale where it was purchased? Who was the owner?'

'A Mr Riley of Regent's Park. He was quite elderly and passed away some months ago. Having no heirs, his will directed that all his property should be sold and the proceeds given to charity. He had been a collector of silver in a small way for a number of years. I purchased several items of tableware, and the snuffbox interested me because of its attractive oval shape. I thought I would easily be able to find a buyer. I happened to mention it to one of the directors of Kensington Silver and he said that he thought he had seen something like it on a list of stolen goods. You can imagine how I felt when he produced the list and there it was, maker's stamp, hallmark and all. It was the same item. How and when Mr Riley had obtained it I don't know, but I had no alternative but to take it to the police.'

'Did the police suspect you of involvement in the theft? It seems very unlikely.'

'No, I simply provided them with all the information in my possession, showed them the documents relating to the purchase, and that was an end of the matter. They thanked me,' he added drily. 'I have heard no more about it since.'

Frances made some notes. 'Well, I need to look at every possible avenue, so I shall see what Inspector Payne can tell me. He has been rather more helpful since I led him to the place where your father-in-law's effects were found.'

'I am glad of it. He has not been so friendly to me.'

Frances stirred the fire while she thought about the next subject she wished to discuss. 'I spoke to Mrs Fiske recently.'

'Ah, yes, Alicia's friend.'

'She told me that your father-in-law had been making enquiries about you before the wedding, and in particular that the police had some doubts about your father's partner, Mr George Cullum.'

'Doubts? There could hardly be any doubts. The man did not repay the trust my father had placed in him. He was a criminal.'

'He has not been seen since his disappearance?'

'I have not seen him, and neither had my father. We assumed that he had fled abroad with the proceeds of his theft. I am sure that what he took from the business was only a part of what he carried away. He must have had a cache of stolen goods.'

'What kind of stolen goods?'

'From what my father said, Cullum had acquired small items of jewellery, easy to transport and hide. He never saw them, but it was these that Cullum wanted him to deal in.'

'The police suspected that Cullum's disappearance was for more sinister reasons. They thought he had been murdered.'

'Oh? Well, that wouldn't be surprising. If a man mixes with criminals he runs a risk. Some of those gangs care nothing for the lives of others. They will murder each other in the blink of an eye if one of them takes more than his share or talks to the police.'

'The main suspects, it seems, were you, your father and a Mr James Felter, who was a business associate I believe.'

Salter stared at her, dumbstruck.

'What can you tell me about Mr Felter?'

Salter found his voice again with difficulty. 'He is the son of one of my father's oldest friends; I have known him since childhood. He was best man at my wedding. I would say he is the very last man to commit an act of violence.'

'Where does he currently live?'

'Switzerland, he has a business there. We correspond from time to time. The police questioned all of us after the robbery, but it was never suggested that anyone had done away with Cullum. Of course, someone might have done so since then, although James did once tell me he thought he had seen the man sneaking about.'

'When and where?'

'It must have been just before he went abroad. About five years ago. But it was years since Cullum was last seen and James said he had changed – older, greyer. To be truthful, I thought he was mis-taken. The man was going into a house somewhere in Shepherd's

Bush. Why would Cullum still be in London when he is a wanted man?'

'Did Mr Felter tell the police what he had seen?'

'He might have done. I suggested he should, but when I queried what he told me he began to have second thoughts.'

'If we could find Mr Cullum, it would remove another reason for the police to be suspicious of you.'

'I would hope so.'

'This is what I would like you to do. Try to remember as much as you can about him, his age and appearance, his likes and dislikes, his business dealings, his family, his friends – write it all down and then let me know, and I will see what I can do.'

'Very well.' Salter gave a strange little smile. 'You are so much like Rosetta. Not in looks, but in your way of thinking and expressing yourself. She confessed to me once that she felt as if William Doughty was trying to stifle her, not allowing her to be the woman she could be. They were children when they met, and betrothed when she was twenty. Her father had encouraged the connection, but before the date for the wedding was set she had begun to see that she might have made a mistake. But she had no choice. She thought afterwards that Doughty had seen her wavering and had pressed her into a foolish indiscretion to maintain his hold over her. The marriage took place six months before your older brother was born. Rosetta has an intellectual life, an enquiring mind; she reads and she learns. When I talk to you, it is like talking to her.'

When their visitor had gone, Sarah gave Frances a veiled look. 'Now I'm not saying anything against Mr Salter, who I am sure is as honest as the day is long, but if Mr Dobree already had his worries, there's things that might have made them worse.' She tapped a finger at the newspaper. 'There's all these sneak thieves around, some of them very audacious – getting into the fancy hotels and taking silver and gold off dressing tables; finding out when families are from home and breaking into houses. They climb walls, they climb up drainpipes, they cut out windowpanes and squeeze through. They take small valuables, snuffboxes, watches, jewellery and the like that they can put in their pockets and carry off.'

'I have read the reports, but surely Mr Dobree can't have imagined for a moment that his own son-in-law was involved. Besides, he handed the snuffbox to the police.'

'Maybe it was too risky for him. Couldn't sell it or get it melted down without attracting the wrong kind of attention. So he gives it in, and gets a reputation as an honest man. Bills of sale can be forged.'

'Is that what you think?'

'No, but it might be what Dobree thought. Perhaps it's what the police think.'

'I can understand the police being suspicious, but why would Mr Dobree think such a thing? Mr Salter has been married to his daughter for almost seventeen years —'

'You get less than that for manslaughter.'

'And as far as we know he has never given him any reason to think badly of him. Why suddenly now?'

'Didn't he say his son's school wanted more money?'

'That's true – but you're not suggesting that he has started burgling houses or receiving stolen goods to pay for it?'

'He asked his father-in-law for a bigger allowance.'

'He did. That could have aroused suspicion. Well, maybe I will know more when I have spoken to Inspector Payne.'

CHAPTER TWENTY-SEVEN

Some time later Frances sat facing Inspector Payne across his laden but tidy desk. He didn't look pleased to see her and she felt far from pleased to see him, nevertheless the question had to be tackled.

'Inspector, you must recall the occasion some months ago when Mr Vernon Salter handed in a snuffbox which he had bought at auction and which he later found to have been stolen?'

'Yes, of course.'

'After that incident did you have any enquiries about it from Mr Dobree?'

'Dobree?' Payne was clearly surprised. 'No, why should it concern him?'

'Mr Salter assures me that after he handed in the snuffbox he was never suspected of having anything to do with its theft. He had full proof that he bought it in good faith in the ordinary way of business.'

'That is correct, yes.'

'What I am trying to establish is not so much the truth of the situation, which I think is evident, but what Mr Dobree believed, which might have been very different and led him to behave in the way he did. You recall what Mr Marsden said at the inquest. I am wondering if Mr Dobree, not having the full facts, thought that his son-in-law might have been involved in the recent robberies, and had decided to dispose of an item he was unable to sell without attracting attention.'

'Well that's a new one,' said Payne. 'Do you have any evidence that that was what he thought?'

'No, none.'

'Well, if Dobree did think that, it's a pity he didn't come and ask about it. That snuffbox was part of a collection that the seller had had in his possession for more than twenty years. So it was nothing to do with any of the recent crimes. It was stolen from a manor house in Sussex sometime in the late fifties. The interesting thing is that when we looked at the auction catalogue we found some other items in the sale that were all part of the same haul. How the deceased gentleman acquired them, we don't know, as there was no paperwork to say.'

'So the fact that Mr Salter bought that snuffbox wasn't a coincidence – other buyers would have acquired items which were stolen in the same robbery?'

'They did, only they weren't so smart off the mark about handing them in as Mr Salter.'

'Of course Mr Dobree wouldn't have known about that.'

'The only man who might tell you what he thought is Mr Marsden. I've spoken to him, but he keeps things close.'

'Mr Marsden would not tell me the time of day. He disapproves of me.' Payne gave a sudden twist of a grin, quickly quelled. 'I suppose you haven't traced the thieves?' she continued.

'Not much chance of that now. Although there's a good chance they've gone away for other crimes.'

'Might one of them have been Mr George Cullum?'

'Cullum?' Payne looked surprised. 'Now there's a name I've not heard in a while.'

'He might have changed it after ruining Mr Salter's father. Has he ever been found?'

'Not that I know of.' Payne leaned forward, rested his chin on his hands, and stared at her. 'You seem very interested in this business, Miss Doughty.'

'It is my profession. I am a detective.'

'Oh it's more than that, I can see you're particularly keen to get it sorted out. Not close to the family are you?'

'I had never met any member of that family before Mr Dobree's death.'

'Really?' He rose from his chair. 'Wait there.' Payne left the room and after a few moments returned with a small dark blue jewellery box. 'Do you recognise this?'

'Is it the item you found amongst Mr Dobree's effects?'

'It is.' He opened the box and showed Frances the emerald ring. 'Have you seen this before?'

'No.'

'You're sure of it?'

'I think I would remember.'

He took the ring from the box. 'Ladies ring, very nice, small size, suit a slim lady.'

'Perhaps it is Mrs Salter's, I am told she has claimed it.'

'Mrs Salter is not slim.'

'I expect she was, once. I understand that Mr Dobree was having it enlarged for her.'

'Is that what Mr Salter told you? Because I don't believe one word of it. Here, try it for size.'

'Me?'

'Yes. Just to show what kind of finger it would fit.'

Frances hesitated, then took the offered ring and slipped it onto her finger. For some reason she put it onto the ring finger of her left hand.

'A perfect fit. Could have been made for you.'

Frances found herself blushing and quickly took off the ring and handed it back.

'You see we've traced the jeweller who sold it. Mainly hard work and shoe leather, with a little luck thrown in. The buyer was a gentleman of advanced years who declined to give his name. He was accompanied by a female taller than himself, who, although veiled, was clearly much younger than he and with slim fingers. The ring was a little too large for her and so it was made smaller to fit. The gentleman came to collect it when the work was done.'

'When was this?'

'About a week before Mr Dobree was killed.'

'And do you believe the buyer was Mr Dobree?'

'The description fits. We think he might have been carrying the ring on the day of his death because he was on his way to an assignation with the young person. What can you tell me about that?'

'Nothing at all. Why do you think I would —' Frances stopped short. 'You surely don't imagine —' but Inspector Payne clearly did imagine. Frances controlled her annoyance. 'I appreciate that you have to ask these questions, Inspector, but I can assure you that I have never in my life met Mr Lancelot Dobree.'

Payne folded his arms and gave her a cynical look.

'Just because I practice a profession usually thought to be the preserve of men, it does not make me into an immoral woman. I have never had an assignation with Lancelot Dobree or indeed any gentleman.'

The look remained cynical.

Frances, increasingly furious, rose to her feet. 'And I am prepared to sue anyone who suggests otherwise.' She made for the door, then rounded on him so sharply he was startled. 'Which jeweller was this?' she demanded.

'Solomon Finewax & Sons, Portobello Road,' he said, then regretted speaking almost as soon as the words were out.

'Thank you.' She walked out.

Chapter Twenty-Eight

Frances was still simmering with anger when she told Sarah about the conversation. 'If nothing else, I need to clear my name of Inspector Payne's vile allegations. But if I can discover something about the young woman for whom the ring was intended, I might be able to trace her and learn more about Mr Dobree.'

'Perhaps he confided his worries and secrets to her,' hinted Sarah. 'Men can get very confiding under certain circumstances.'

'I believe I can guess your meaning. Well, I shall visit the jeweller concerned and see if there is anything to learn.'

'Hard work getting into the mind of a dead man.'

Frances wondered if she would ever understand men, dead or living. 'I would still like to know more about that stolen snuffbox. We know now that Mr Salter can have had nothing to do with it, but what did it lead Mr Dobree to believe? Did he think it was stolen recently? And if he did, why?'

Sarah nodded. 'Leave that to me. I've got a separation case to sort out before anyone gets killed, and then I'll find out about that box.'

The business of Solomon Finewax & Sons was not, even to Frances' inexperienced eye, one of the grander jewellers in London. While advertised as providers of fine jewellery, she gathered from the contents of its windows that its primary trade was that of pawnbroker, repairs, and the sale of second-hand adornments. The gentleman behind the counter was of venerable appearance, with two sets of spectacles, one on his nose, and one on his forehead, and a magnifying device on a chain about his neck. He peered at Frances over the first set of spectacles. A lifetime of experience in the jewellery trade was in his eyes as he judged that she was not there for a transaction of any great value.

'Good morning, how may I help you?'

Frances presented her card. 'I am a detective making enquiries concerning a ring purchased here recently.'

'Would this be the emerald solitaire? The police have already been here to enquire about it. I believe that no questions attach to the item itself.'

'That is so; I am trying to trace the purchaser.'

'Hmm, I am not sure that is possible. Let me look at our books.'

He brought a large ledger from under the counter, and changed spectacles. 'Yes, it was sold a month ago to a gentleman who did not give his name and paid in banknotes. I made the sale myself. There was a lady accompanying him, and she tried on the ring but it was too large. We agreed to make the adjustments and a week later he called again and took away the ring.'

'Was it in a dark blue box?'

'It was.'

'Could you describe the gentleman to me?'

'Elderly, but active. Well dressed. There was nothing distinctive about his features or apparel.'

'Did he wear any jewellery of note? A Masonic ring, perhaps?'

Mr Finewax smiled. 'I would have noticed such a thing, and he did not.'

Frances still carried the drawing of Mr Dobree that Inspector Payne had given her, and handed it to Mr Finewax. 'Could this be the man?'

He studied the portrait at a number of distances. 'This is the same picture the police showed me. It's possible.'

'Can you describe the woman?'

He paused. 'She was rather more decorative and fashionable in her apparel than the gentleman. She wore a veil so I did not see her face clearly but I had the distinct impression that she was very much younger than he. She laughed a great deal.'

'Laughed?'

'Oh yes, quite loudly. She found everything he said to be most entertaining. I could be mistaken, although I rarely am about such things, but she struck me as being a female of a certain type.'

'You didn't think that she might be a relation?'

'Most definitely not. She was of quite another class. Her clothes were expensive but not of the most refined taste. To be very blunt, if you will excuse me, I took this to be a romantic assignation in which money was to change hands, one which the gentleman concerned might have wished to conceal from his family and friends.'

Had the gentleman been Lancelot Dobree, thought Frances, she might have expected him to remove something like a distinctive Masonic ring when meeting with such a companion.

'You have not seen either the gentleman or his friend since?'

'Not the gentleman, but I might have seen his friend. I believe I once saw her entering a hotel not far from here. It is called the Portobello London. She might well have been going there to meet the gentleman, or indeed another gentleman entirely. I should warn you that it is an establishment, so I have heard, where friends who wish to meet in private can do so in comfort with no questions being asked about the propriety of the arrangement. A respectable female who knew its character would never be seen there.'

'I see,' said Frances. 'I am afraid that my enquiries do require me to interview this person. I suppose there is nothing distinctive you can recall about her dress or appearance that might help me to discover her?'

'The only thing I have a note of is her ring size.' He paused to consider. 'I do remember she was taller than the gentleman and her walking dress was the colour of burgundy, and very extensively trimmed with fur. Rather too much in that way I thought.'

'Thank you,' said Frances.

'I will keep the card, if I may. A lady detective is a new idea to me, but I can see that if one wishes to make enquiries about jewellery she may be just the thing. A lady sees the jewel and the man, alas, sees only the price.'

The Portobello London Hotel had a narrow frontage which was neither discreet nor inviting, and did no more than inform the passer-by that it was a hotel that one could enter or not as one pleased. Just inside the entrance was a large man in a commissionaire's uniform. He said nothing to Frances as she walked past him, but his eyes followed her, and he seemed to be weighing up what kind of woman she was. The foyer was dimly lit, and Frances could well imagine that couples who were not married would find it convenient to be in a place where their faces might be in shadow. There was a curved wooden counter behind which a young man stood, his dull expression undergoing no noticeable change when Frances appeared. He was pale, like a plant that had never known the light, with short blond curls and slightly protuberant grey eyes.

'Good afternoon Miss, which room would you be wanting?'

'I am not here to see a room,' said Frances, presenting her card. 'I wish to make enquiries about one of your patrons.'

He stared at her card as if it was taking a long time for him to read it. 'Hmm,' he grunted. 'Well I can't help you whoever you are. We don't give out information about our guests here, and especially not to detectives.'

'There is no legal action being contemplated against either the lady or the gentleman she accompanied. It is not a case of divorce or separation. I am not working for a solicitor. It is another matter entirely. All I wish to do is speak to the lady.'

'So you say,' said the man, throwing the card on the counter in front of him. 'But how do I know you are telling the truth? We have a very select clientele here and we don't want to lose customers by blabbing about who was here and when. So you had better go, before I ask Mr Burns here to conduct you from the premises.' He nodded at the large uniformed man, who squared his shoulders, quite unnecessarily, Frances thought.

'I understand,' she said. 'Good-day.' She turned and left, but did not trouble to pick up the card.

Frances decided to engage the services of Tom Smith's Men to watch the hotel. If they saw a young female with a burgundy colour walking dress elaborately trimmed with fur, they were to follow her discreetly as she left the hotel, learn all they could without alerting her or asking questions and then report back to Frances.

'We know that place,' said Tom. 'It's for when respectable people want to do things that aren't respectable without anyone knowin'; I've run messages back and forth from there enough times. Lot's've people go there but no one ever admits to it. Not surprised the clerk wun't tell you anythin'.'

'Won't 'ave t' stay outside long if we see 'er goin' in,' said Ratty. 'That type meets friends fer the arternoon, so the gent c'n go back ter 'is wife at night, all 'spectable like, 'n then 'e tells 'er 'ow 'e's bin workin' 'ard.'

Frances gazed at the boys, unhappy at how knowledgeable they had become of the cruder aspects of life in so short a time.

CHAPTER TWENTY-NINE

Unexpectedly, the next morning brought Bayswater's favourite poet, Mr Arthur Miggs, to Frances' door. She and Sarah exchanged glances of astonishment as his name was announced. He had doubtless read the press reports of the meeting of the Ladies League Against Female Suffrage, which included faithful renditions of the principal speeches, but if that had prompted his action, why he should want to consult Frances was a mystery.

Frances had been relieved to see that the newspapers had not mentioned her presence at the event but the correspondent of the *Chronicle*, while careful to report on the proceedings without taking sides, had been less than kind to Mr Miggs:

Since the emblem of the movement is the English rose, the author who extravagantly dubs himself Augustus Mellifloe, although his real name is the far humbler Miggs, having composed a poem of forty stanzas in which he expresses his inconsolable grief at the fall of a single petal, has taken it upon himself to be the male figurehead of that movement. He would, however, have been well advised not to treat the company with the full rendition of his work. One stanza was more than enough, five was already far too much, ten invited boredom, at number twenty the audience looked ready to flee the hall and more than that roused this correspondent into a near murderous rage.

'Whatever he wants cannot be good,' said Frances. 'He means only trouble to the Literati and what he imagines I should do for him I do not know, but I shall refuse any request.'

'Will you send him away?'

'No, better to find out what he wants.' Frances nodded to the maid. 'Please show him up.'

Sarah, who had been about to go out in pursuit of the snuffbox mystery, decided to remain, and ground a large fist into a meaty palm. 'As long as he doesn't mean to read us any of his poems,' she snarled.

A minute later Mr Miggs appeared. His manner in private mirrored that in his public appearances since he was for every second of the day fully aware of the image he wished to present. Frances wondered if he was the same when alone and suspected that he might be even more so, since his faultless deportment could not have come without much practice and preening in front of a mirror. She knew many men who prided themselves on good grooming, which was something the female eye always appreciated, but Miggs wished to demonstrate to the world that he was also impeccable in both character and taste.

He was carrying a copy of the *Chronicle* and stared at Frances as if she was a nasty insect. He had never forgiven her for disrupting a protest meeting he had once called, and he knew that she had acted for Mr Fiske. She could only be an enemy.

Her formal greeting of 'Good morning' was returned with cold ill will.

'Really Miss Doughty, must you poke your nose into every matter of concern in Bayswater? Must you despise everything that is moral and good and espouse all that is degenerate?'

'Please explain why you are here,' said Frances. 'I doubt that you wish to engage my services as a detective.'

He gave a snort of contempt. 'I did hope from recent reports that you had given up that mad idea, but no, that was clearly an untruth. It seems that nothing is safe from you.' He waved the rolled up paper at her. 'Do you deny that you wrote this scurrilous article about the meeting? You were there with your questionable companions, I saw you!'

'I have never written anything for the *Chronicle*,' said Frances.

He wrenched the paper open and stabbed an angry finger at the article. 'Even if I accept that assurance, which I am far from doing, I am convinced that you must know the identity of the author! You move in some very dubious circles; you mix with

Freemasons, pugilists and criminals, and men and women who scarcely seem to know what sex they are. I am sure that one of your associates is responsible for this outrage!'

'Do you mean to say,' asked Frances, 'that only someone of depraved sensibilities would despise your work?'

'I mean that exactly! I am one of London's premier authors; my poems and novels are admired and acclaimed everywhere! My name is on everyone's lips! My elegiac work *Oh Daisy Sweete!* has been discussed in the most elegant and refined salons. This article,' he threw the paper down on the table in disgust, 'is not merely an attack on my authorship but on myself, my honour, my very soul!'

'I can see that you are upset,' said Frances calmly, 'but I really cannot offer any assistance. I did not write the article, nor do I know who did. If you wish to sue the *Chronicle* you are of course at liberty to do so, but an opinion is merely an opinion, and you might be better advised not to pursue the matter.'

For a moment Frances enjoyed a mental picture of Mr Miggs in a court of law facing the editor of the *Chronicle* and being obliged to recite his *Ode to a Rose Petal* in support of his case to a grim-faced jury.

'Tell your associates that I intend to find the culprit and make him pay!' said Miggs. 'When I am hailed as the premier literary figure of Britain someone will regret that insult!'

He snatched up the paper and stormed out.

Frances was about to write to Mr Neilson as she was eager to interview the members of the Literati, but her plans were prevented by the receipt of a telegram.

'Come to Brighton at once. V.'

There was no need to provide the address, the name of the sender or the reason for the urgency. 'Do you want me to come with you?' asked Sarah.

'Thank you, but I need you here to continue the work, and you have your own cases to pursue.'

Sarah knew better than to argue.

Frances had no idea how long she would be needed but quickly packed a few necessaries, and departed.

As the train sped her to her destination she was lost in thought. Her mind was consumed with the fear that her mother's health had taken a serious turn for the worse and now, as she stood on the brink of a reunion, that longed-for outcome would be snatched away. She tried to distract herself by thinking of the mysteries that were crowding in on her – the curious actions of Lancelot Dobree – his murder – the savage killing of Albert Munro – the disappearance of Bernard Salter's partner George Cullum – the stolen snuffbox – the emerald ring – were these all quite separate, or were they in some way connected? The only thing she felt sure of was that it would improve Vernon Salter's standing with the police if she could allay the old suspicions as to his past.

Brighton was clear and cold, the sky a vivid light blue, the air sharp, the wind snatching at everything it could. The streets were quiet and all had a clean, fresh look that London lacked. This was the winter season, when the carriage classes came to enjoy the kind of sumptuous gatherings to which Frances would never be invited. A cab brought her to a lodging house not far from the seafront. She was pleased to see that it was clean and respectable looking, with well-scrubbed steps and neat curtains. A maid in a crisp white apron answered the door, and nodded at once as Frances said she had come to see Mrs Martin. At least, thought Frances with profound relief, her mother was still alive.

Frances was shown up to a set of apartments on the second floor, and was encouraged by the sharp scent of polish and lack of dust, which showed that while the accommodation was simple, it was well maintained. Vernon met her at the door, his pleasure at seeing her slightly softening his anxiety.

'How is my mother?' asked Frances, as he conducted her to a seat at the fireside. The parlour was warm and comfortably if plainly furnished. On the mantelpiece was a portrait which made her breath catch in her throat; Rosetta, much younger, seated on a couch, with her arm around a small boy beside her and a baby on her lap. The boy was undoubtedly Frances' brother Frederick, who had so sadly passed away in 1879 and the baby could only be Frances herself. She could not resist taking a closer look and wondering how happy that time had been.

'She looks on it every day,' said Vernon. 'I have seen her kiss and caress it a thousand times.' He sighed. 'She collapsed last night, soon after receiving a visitor. I was sent for, and a doctor came and said that her heart is very weak and she needs rest. I have engaged a nurse to sit with her. All we can do is pray that in time she will regain her strength.'

'May I see her?'

'She has been sleeping, but I will see if she is awake now.' He rose and went into the next room, then after a few moments he returned and nodded. 'Yes, you may come in. I have told her that you are here and she is very happy to see you, but please, no excitement, she needs calm.'

'Of course.' As Frances approached the door she felt a fluttering in her chest, as if a bird had been hiding there and was about to take wing. She paused for a moment to compose herself, then went in. The room was dim and there was a gentle fire providing enough warmth for the invalid, while the window was open sufficiently to admit fresh air. There was little of the inevitable bad odour of the sick-room, showing how well it was attended to, and any mild unpleasantness that might have lingered was modified by the scent of laundered sheets and a sprinkling of lavender. A small table held the expected medicines, tonic mixtures from the chemist and some brandy and water.

The nurse who had been sitting by the patient occupied with some needlework, rose up as she entered. 'If you please, Miss, the patient is doing well, and has had a nice sleep and a little broth.'

'Thank you,' said Frances, and the nurse moved to a chair by the window so she could take a seat.

Rosetta lay propped up on pillows, a coverlet drawn almost to her chin. Her eyes were moist, and she smiled weakly, extending a pale hand. Frances sat beside the bed and took the proffered hand. The skin was warm and very dry. 'Frances.' The lips moved and the voice hardly sounded. 'Can you forgive me?'

'All is forgiven,' said Frances. 'All. Please don't tire yourself. I am happy just to sit by your side.'

Salter drew up another chair and sat by her. 'How long can you stay?'

'As long as I am needed. I can send to London for anything more I might require.'

'I am expecting Cornelius here, soon. Your brother. Oh there is no doubt about it, he looks so like you. We are very proud of him. He studies hard and will be a man of law one day.'

Rosetta smiled her agreement.

There were questions Frances wanted to ask, but this was not the time or place. The nurse brought them all some tea, and Rosetta managed a little bread soaked in broth before she drifted into sleep again and Frances and her father crept from the room.

'I do so look forward to the conversations we will have when my mother has regained her health,' said Frances. 'But tell me, how did her illness come about? You said there was a visitor?'

'Yes, the maid said it was a man she had never seen before, but he was most insistent and asked for Rosetta by the name of Mrs Martin. I believe Rosetta consented to see him thinking that he had brought a message from me, but instead he must have said something to distress her. After a few minutes he called the maid, saying that Rosetta had fainted and he could not revive her. Then he fled. I dare not question Rosetta about the interview in case it brings on another collapse.'

'I will ring for the maid and ask her about the man.'

The maid arrived promptly and listened carefully to Frances' questions. 'I have never seen the man before, not here or anywhere else. He was about forty years of age, and dressed very plain, with a moustache but no beard or side whiskers. His hair was dark and he had uncommonly thick eyebrows. He did not carry anything or bring a calling card. I asked him his name and he said it was Green, but I am sure it was not as he had a foreign accent.'

'Could you describe the accent? French? German?'

'Neither. He spoke good English, but it was like a foreigner would speak it. He asked to see Mrs Martin, saying it was urgent. He said he had come down from London on purpose to see her. I asked the reason for his visit but he said it was confidential. I went up and asked Mrs Martin if she would see the gentleman and she said she would, so I showed him up. I returned to my duties, but only a few minutes later he rang for me very insistently and I went up and found Mrs Martin lying on the floor in a fainting state. He told me she had been suddenly taken ill and next moment he had gone. I sent for help at once.'

'And I am most grateful for your quick action which might have saved her life,' said Vernon.

Once the maid had departed Frances said, 'I fear that the interview provoked or hastened the attack, and the visitor left suddenly because he thought he would be blamed. I wonder if this could be connected with the police and their suspicions of you. Perhaps the man was a plain-clothes detective.'

They had little time to consider the matter before the maid knocked again. 'If you please, there is an Inspector Payne here asking to see Miss Doughty.'

CHAPTER THIRTY

'How does he know you are here?' asked Salter, when the maid had been sent to show the Inspector up to the apartment.

'I think I can guess,' said Frances, grimly. 'The man who came here must have been a plain-clothes policeman sent by Inspector Payne as part of his continued enquiries into your past. I wonder how much he knows or what he has guessed? Well, I intend to give him a piece of my mind.'

'I think I know better than to try and dissuade you. Do you wish me to stay here?'

'You may go and sit with Mother if you wish. I have faced worse than Inspector Payne.'

Salter favoured her with a look of quiet paternal pride before he left the room.

Inspector Payne was shown in and looked around him. 'Good morning, Miss Doughty. I must say this is all very cosy.'

'I suppose you have come to gloat on your handiwork?' she snapped.

He had been about to sit down, but paused and stared at her instead. 'I beg your pardon?'

'A lady is lying dangerously ill because of your actions. I hope you don't mean to disturb her, because if you try I shall do everything in my power to prevent it.'

He looked puzzled. 'I am sorry, but I don't understand your meaning.'

'I am talking of the man you sent here to question Mrs Martin. He had hardly been here a few minutes before she collapsed, and she has been confined to her bed ever since, hardly able to move or speak. We hope she may live but that is far from certain.' Frances realised that it was impossible for her to keep the emotion out of her voice, either the anger or the distress.

'Miss Doughty, I can assure you that I have not sent any man here to ask questions, although I can guess who that man was and his purpose.'

'Oh? Then tell me.'

He drew up a chair and warmed himself by the fire, and she sat and faced him. 'Did he have a foreign accent and call himself Green?'

'He did.'

'Then he was not a policeman but a private detective.'

'In whose employ?'

'That he will not reveal, although one might hazard a guess. But he has been extremely diligent, and uncovered some very interesting information. Realising that what he had found was of importance to a police enquiry he was good enough to pass it on. As we have discussed, although Mr Vernon Salter was provided with an alibi for the night of Lancelot Dobree's murder and released from custody, he remained under suspicion. After all, a man may have an alibi while employing others to do his work for him. But I always had my doubts about the housekeeper's sudden change of story, and this has been confirmed. We now know, through the enquiries of the energetic Mr Green, that Mr Salter was not staying in the country cottage that night, in fact he was here, in the company of his mistress.'

Frances opened her mouth to protest at Rosetta being described in that way, but thought better of it and was silent.

'I have had a word with the housekeeper and she is now prepared to admit that she might have made a mistake when giving evidence before the magistrates, as she was feeling unwell that day. Of course I can understand given the terms of his marriage contract why Mr Salter wanted to keep his location secret. If his connection with Mrs Martin had become known it would have meant penury for them both, and, considering her delicate state of health, even more serious consequences.' He paused and gave Frances a searching look. 'But I think you already know all this. Mr Green suspected that Mrs Martin was not the lady's real name, and that she was not, as her landlady had been informed, Mr Salter's widowed sister. Mr Salter does have a sister but she is unmarried and does not live in Brighton. She did, however, have her own story to tell, and this led Mr Green to the conclusion that Mrs Martin is in fact Mrs Rosetta Doughty. She is your mother, is she not?'

It was a challenge but Frances had no intention of being shaken by it. 'She is. And I should tell you that Mr Salter has assured me that he has not contravened the terms of his marriage contract. He and my mother are merely friends.'

'Whatever they may be now, that was not always the case, was it? And even if he is telling the truth, would his father-in-law have believed it? There was one thing that Mr Green never uncovered, but then he had never met you. I have been wondering for some time why your face was familiar to me; it was as if I had met you before, although I knew I had not. Now it all becomes clear. Mr Vernon Salter is your father.'

He clearly expected her to protest, but she saw no point in denial. 'I believe that to be the case, although I have only recently learned of it.'

'You see, when a man is murdered and we don't have the suspect red-handed, the first question I ask is who had the motive? Mr Salter and Mrs Doughty both had motive to put an end to Mr Dobree's enquiries. Neither was in London at the time of Dobree's death and in the case of Mrs Doughty I do not think she had the strength to commit the crime. You, on the other hand, were in London and had motive.'

For one brief moment Frances thought the Inspector was joking with her, but saw almost immediately that he was deadly serious. 'That is ridiculous.'

'And yet here you are. I paid a visit to your home to interview you and your lady companion advised me that you had gone away but could not provide me with an address. But you had left the telegram in sight suggesting that you had gone to Brighton, and through the hard work of Mr Green I knew exactly where to come. Miss Smith was unable to give you an alibi for the night of Mr Dobree's murder and she was sensible enough not to lie to me. That night she and her fancy man were attending an exhibition of pugilism, while you had decided to remain at home. So she and Professor Pounder have excellent alibis, but you do not.'

'I was at home all that evening. I have never met Mr Dobree and certainly had no wish to kill him or anyone else for that matter.'

'You may have to convince a jury of that.'

'If you are trying to frighten me you are not succeeding. And now I must ask you to leave.'

He rose to his feet. 'Of course, I will go at once. But you will be coming with me.'

'What do you mean?'

'Well, I can't have you running off, can I? So you are to accompany me to the station for further questioning.'

She hesitated but saw it would be futile to argue. 'Very well, the sooner this is resolved the better. I would like to send a telegram first, to ask Miss Smith to notify my solicitor to be at the police station to advise me. I do not think you can deny me that right.'

Payne agreed, and Frances went to say farewell to her mother. Rosetta was awake and smiled weakly as Frances kissed her brow.

'Is there anything I can do?' asked Salter when Frances explained that she needed to return to London with the Inspector.

'Just look after Mother, and keep me informed.'

The train journey promised to be silent, especially as Payne occupied himself with his notebook and a newspaper, but as Frances sat opposite him deep in thought she realised she had the opportunity to explore another avenue.

'I was told recently that Mr James Felter, a business associate of Bernard Salter, claimed to have seen George Cullum in Shepherd's Bush about five years ago. Did he ever report that to the police?'

'I don't know.'

'Then I would be grateful if you could examine your papers on the case and see if he ever did make a report and if it was followed up.'

He rubbed his hand across his eyes. 'Why do I always feel that I am the one being questioned?'

Frances smiled.

Frances' solicitor Edward Bramley was waiting at the police station when she and the Inspector arrived. Sarah was there, too, her face darkly furrowed with concern. 'What's going on?' she demanded.

'Really, it's nothing,' said Frances soothingly. 'Thank you for fetching Mr Bramley.'

Bramley stared at Frances quizzically over his spectacles. She was not his usual kind of client, and he had only been acting for her for a few months following the dreadful circumstances that had befallen her previous solicitor. He was, thought Frances, neither astute to the point of sharp dealing, nor did his work give rise to suspicions of laxity. He did his business with commendable care and attention to detail and that was quite sufficient for her needs. 'How might I advise you, Miss Doughty?' he asked, looking about him. 'Is this concerning a client of yours?'

'Come this way,' said Payne. 'Not you, Miss,' he added to Sarah.

Frances hoped that he would not insist on Sarah leaving, but she simply grunted and sat down to wait, and Payne seemed content with that.

They took their seats in the interview room. 'It is concerning myself,' Frances explained to Mr Bramley. 'The Inspector believes that I am capable of murder.'

'Good heavens! I am sure he is mistaken.'

As to whether or not she was capable of murder Frances could not tell, and she simply said, 'I assure you I am innocent of any crime.'

Inspector Payne faced them across the desk and opened a file of papers. 'Not so long ago, Miss Doughty, you put an announcement in the newspapers to advise that you would no longer be taking on any cases where a crime was involved. Very commendable. But recently you have interested yourself deeply in the murder of Lancelot Dobree. I wondered from the start if your interest was more personal than professional and so it appears.'

Mr Bramley raised his eyebrows and glanced at Frances but she said nothing.

'So, Miss Doughty, for our records, I would like the answers to some questions. To begin with, is Mr Vernon Salter your natural father?'

'I believe that to be the case.'

'And the lady living in Brighton under the name of Mrs Martin, the lady who Mr Salter visits regularly, her real name is Mrs Rosetta Doughty and she is your mother?'

'Yes.'

'Are you aware of the terms of the marriage contract between Mr Salter and his wife?'

'I first learned of the existence of that contract at the inquest hearing on Mr Dobree.'

'You father did not tell you of it?'

'My first ever meeting with him was here, after the inquest.'

'But you do agree that he has flouted the terms of the contract?'

'I do not. He has assured me that he and my mother, who has been in poor health for many years, have known each other only as affectionate friends since his marriage. I can see that others might have placed a different interpretation on his behaviour.'

'If their connection had become known the consequences for both your parents would have been very serious?'

'That is possible, had they not been believed.'

'And from what Mr Marsden has told us, Mr Dobree harboured his suspicions, and could well have discovered enough to make your father a beggar and send your mother to an early grave.'

This was not a question, and Frances said nothing.

'But that fate might have been avoided by the death of Mr Dobree.'

Still Frances was silent.

Inspector Payne consulted his papers again. 'I have been making some enquiries about you with other police stations and they have some interesting stories to tell about your activities in the last two years. It seems that there is hardly anything you will not dare to do; in fact, you are a regular Miss Dauntless. I think that you did know about the threat to your parents, and decided to do something about it, after making sure that neither of them could be under suspicion. You didn't reckon with the housekeeper at the cottage having visited the premises on the day in question and being able to give the lie to Mr Salter's alibi, however, you soon squared that, didn't you? The plan was to lure Mr Dobree to an empty house and murder him. What inducements you offered him we can't yet know, but maybe you said you could reveal something damaging concerning Mr Salter. Perhaps Mr Salter told you about his father-in-law's plans to buy a premises and after making enquiries you found one that would suit your purpose, a house that was likely in view of the exorbitant price demanded to remain empty for some time. I know that a young man came to Munro & Son to ask about the property, a young man who has yet to be identified, but I also believe that you have in the past dressed as a man during the course of your enquiries. I spoke to an Inspector at Kilburn who told me he suspected as much. And there is a suit of man's clothes in your wardrobe far too small for Miss Smith, although it would fit you. Do you know what I think? I think you visited Munro's disguised as a man, and stole or otherwise obtained the keys to the house. I don't know how Mr Dobree was able to slip out of the Lodge room for a secret meeting – perhaps you managed that, too, but you met him in the house, killed him, and hid his body in the shed. I wouldn't usually suspect a young woman of a crime like that, but maybe you are one of those mannish females. Tall, active, a member of the suffragist movement, in possession of a set of wooden clubs that could be dangerous weapons in the right hands.'

'This is pure imagination,' said Frances.

'Of course you couldn't have the man missing and the will not proved, that would have made things hard for your father, so next minute along comes the famous detective Miss Doughty and the body is found.'

'I was engaged by Mr Fiske to find Mr Dobree, as you know.'

'Well, even if you had not been, I am sure you would have wormed your way into the case somehow. Then, of course, your boy agents, who claim they are searching for a missing cat, find, behind what appeared to be a solid wall, the hiding place for Mr Dobree's regalia, together with a lady's emerald ring. Do you have anything to say about that?'

'Yes. I am sorry to say that Mrs Maxwell's cat is still missing.'

'Were the police supposed to think that the ring was the property of Mr Dobree? That he had crept out for an assignation with a female friend? Did you or your agents plant it there to add confusion to the mystery? Is it your ring? It certainly fitted you.'

'I had nothing to do with that.'

'And then we have the strange event where the housekeeper changed her story very conveniently for Mr Salter. It must have been very upsetting when you killed Mr Dobree and your own father was suspected. Did you persuade her? Did you pay her off?'

Frances hoped fervently that the police did not decide to take a look at her bank account and see the large cheque she had received from the Salters.

'Inspector,' interrupted Mr Bramley. 'It strikes me that what you have is a great deal of supposition and not one particle of proof. I believe that your purpose today is to try and frighten Miss Doughty into making a confession, without which you would not be able to proceed against her. Miss Doughty is, however, wholly innocent of any wrongdoing, and you are fishing in the dark. I cannot imagine that you intend to make a charge on no evidence whatsoever, and if you have now come to an end of your interview I suggest that Miss Doughty should be allowed to depart.'

Payne looked displeased. 'I have yet to ask about the murder of Mr Munro.'

'That was the day after the inquest was it not?' asked Frances, thankful that she had been asked to go with Sarah and Professor Pounder to meet the Smith family.

'It was.'

'Then you will find that I can account for my movements all that day.'

'In that case, I will need a statement from you naming any witnesses.'

'You shall have it.'

There was a knock on the door of the interview room, and a constable looked in. 'Sorry to interrupt you sir, but Inspector Sharrock of Paddington Green is here, concerning Miss Doughty.'

From Payne's expression this was the very last man he wished to arrive. 'Very well, I'll see him in my office.' He pushed a sheet of paper and a pencil across the desk. 'A statement about your movements on Saturday.' He strode out.

Frances picked up the paper and began to write.

'Inspector Sharrock?' queried Bramley.

'We have worked on quite a number of cases together.' It was not an entirely accurate description but it would serve. She and

Sharrock had not so much collaborated as tackled the same cases separately with the Inspector issuing furious warnings about the dangers of her meddling in work more appropriate to men. She knew, however, that he had a kind heart underneath an often abrasive exterior and took an almost paternal interest in her welfare. It must have been at Sarah's request that he had come.

Bramley looked surprised but did not enquire further. 'Do you have many witnesses to your movements on the day of Mr Munro's murder?'

'Yes, several.' Frances listed the names. 'I don't know why Inspector Payne is suggesting that I am involved. The police believe that Mr Munro was killed by a member of a gang who stole his keys and used them to burgle furnished properties. There is no reason to doubt this.'

Frances had completed and signed her statement when Payne strode back into the room with a face like a squeezed lemon. He picked up the document, glanced at it and threw it down on the desk. 'Very well, you can go, but make sure of this, I will be watching you very carefully from now on!'

Frances and Mr Bramley left before he could change his mind. 'I don't think that was an empty threat,' confided Mr Bramley.

CHAPTER THIRTY-ONE

Inspector Sharrock was waiting for them with Sarah. 'So what have you been up to this time?' he demanded. 'You told me you'd given up all that detective work.'

'I had,' said Frances, 'but perhaps I made that decision too soon.'

He uttered a groan of despair. 'Oh no, I knew it was too good to be true. Well I've spoken to Payne and he's agreed to let you off for now. He always thinks the worst of women since his lady love ran off the day before their wedding with a man who passes forged cheques.'

'That must have been very upsetting for him,' said Bramley.

'He's not a bad sort.' Sharrock gave a meaningful glance at Frances, who responded with an angry stare. Sharrock's preferred method of putting a stop to her detective career was finding her a husband, and he was constantly suggesting the names of any single men of his acquaintance however remote their suitability. The main qualification appeared to be that they were not known criminals.

'Maybe not, but he took his time poking around our apartment looking for hidden weapons,' growled Sarah.

Sharrock gave her a look as if to say that Sarah needed no weapons, hidden or otherwise. He was thoughtful on the way back to Bayswater, but before he left the cab he said, 'The lad who calls himself Ratty – you're quite sure he doesn't know his real name?'

'So I believe.'

'Only – I've had an idea. Let me think some more, and I might have an answer. If I'm right, he won't like it, but he ought to know.'

After they had left the Inspector outside Paddington Green station, the cab continued on its way. 'I didn't wish to say this before either of the policemen,' ventured Mr Bramley, 'but if there is anything you feel you need to advise me of, please do so now.'

'Inspector Payne's suspicions are quite unfounded,' Frances reassured him. 'However, I listened to his speculations with some interest as there are some observations which might have some merit. The suggestion that the young man who made enquiries at Munro & Son might have been able to obtain the keys to the lodging house, for example. That would explain how Mr Dobree got inside – his killer unlocked it, and Mr Dobree simply walked in, though why I do not as yet know. I am glad that Mr Salter is no longer suspected of having actually killed his father-in-law, although the Inspector seems unwilling to admit that he is entirely innocent in the affair, and now clutches at the straw that he had an accomplice.'

Mr Bramley seemed relieved at Frances' calm comments; at least he appeared disinclined to pursue that line of questioning.

'What Sharrock said about Ratty,' began Sarah, once Bramley had left them, 'I hope it don't mean his ma and pa are in prison, or hanged. There's some things it's best not to know.'

'I think Inspector Sharrock sees Ratty as a boy who has some promise in making his way in life. But maybe there is some blot that will hold him back if it is not rubbed away. It might pain him, but in the end I hope he will be thankful for it. I am sure the Inspector would never mean him harm.'

The between stairs maid had a general instruction that if Tom or Ratty were to arrive in the absence of Frances and Sarah they were to be shown up to the apartment and requested to wait. It was not surprising therefore to find Tom making himself at home, with fresh coals piled on the parlour fire, to which he was offering a muffin on the end of a toasting fork. The butter dish was open on the table, but as far as Frances was concerned he was welcome to make free with it if he brought her interesting news.

'Arternoon!' he said cheerily, sniffing the aroma of the crisp delicacy with great appreciation. 'Got any jam?'

Once Tom's requirements had been attended to, he produced from his pocket a photographic card illustrating a young woman by the name of Lorna Lee, posed so as to emphasise a fine bust and a tumble of long hair. She was, according to the card, 'London's favourite songbird.'

'That's 'er,' he said. 'Sings at the Portobello Playhouse of Varieties, two shows daily, one at three o'clock and the other at eight. All sorts there; dancers, jugglers, comedians, performin' dog, band, 'n everythin', an' there's Miss Lee on the poster outside, all prettified, kickin' up 'er 'eels and showin' off 'er ankles.'

'And this is the lady who was given the emerald ring?'

'Seems she 'as another business between performances. I saw 'er goin' into the Portobello 'Otel, bonnet 'ad a veil, but she was wearin' a nice walkin' dress, dark red, an' all trimmed out in fur. Then soon arter that a gent goes sneakin' in, with a muffler round 'is face so 'e won't be recognised. They was only there an 'our or so, 'cos she 'ad to do the evenin' turn dint she? Then she comes out, an' off she goes up the road, an' I follers 'er and she goes inter the theatre, by the stage door. Takes 'er veil up as she goes in, so I sees 'er face. That's when I sees the poster an' I know 'er name. I bought a little posy and sent it up to 'er askin' for 'er picture an' she sent me this.'

'Thank you, that is very useful.'

Sarah stared at the picture, suspicion written all over her face. 'You want me to go and see the woman? I don't mind.' Frances took her meaning. The main danger in such an interview was to her reputation.

'We will question her together,' said Frances, preparing to write a note. 'A respectable teashop would be a suitable location.'

'Yes, she'll want something for her trouble. That sort always does.'

Sarah had been far from idle during Frances' absence in Brighton, and had made a number of discoveries regarding the stolen snuff-box that Vernon Salter had purchased and handed to the police, making copious notes in her bold handwriting regarding material she had gleaned from the newspapers. She had also gone to the auctioneers who had sold the silver collection that was part of the late Mr Riley's estate, and obtained a spare copy of the catalogue. Once Tom had departed she and Frances studied the new information.

In 1857 there had been a series of burglaries, all of substantial houses in the counties of Sussex, Kent and Essex, which were believed to be the work of the same gang. The men, and there were three of them, were desperadoes of the worst kind, quick to inflict any amount of violence to achieve their ends. All three were armed with guns and coshes. The burglary carried out at Hayworth Hill Manor had been particularly brutal. A servant had been threatened with a gun and then coshed so savagely that when found he had at first been taken for dead. While making their escape, the men had been spotted by a local constable, who on trying to apprehend them was callously shot dead. The police had felt sure they knew the identities of the men, but the villains had gone to ground, and their associates were too afraid or simply unwilling to say where they might be found. In 1858 two of the men were arrested for another offence and identified. They were tried for the murder of the policeman and hanged, but not before asserting that it was their missing associate, David Dunne, who had actually fired the fatal shot.

'Has Dunne ever been found?' asked Frances.

'Not that I know of. He might have changed his name, of course; he could be in prison for some other crime.'

The newspapers had published a list of the stolen valuables, and comparing this with the sales catalogue, there were several items in the collection of the late Mr Riley which could well have been a part of that haul. 'None of this was stolen from the business of Benjamin Salter by his partner,' observed Frances. 'Cullum was said to have taken money and bullion. Of course, that is only according to Mr Salter. Supposing he or his partner had become involved in dealing in stolen goods. The items wouldn't have been entered in the company books, and Salter wouldn't have reported them missing when Mr Cullum disappeared. In the meantime, Mr Riley, being a keen collector, might have bought them either from the thieves or any intermediary they used.'

'Unless Mr Riley was actually Mr Dunne.'

'Is that possible?'

'It could be.' Sarah tapped her notes. 'He was about the right age. And he didn't show up till after Dunne's friends were hanged.'

'And decided to lead a respectable life?' Frances was doubtful.

'Without attracting any suspicion to himself. He knew he'd get a rope round his neck if he did.'

'So it is still possible that Mr Bernard Salter could have been involved in passing on the stolen items.'

'Or his son,' Sarah reminded her. 'I know you don't want to suspect him, but you can't rule him out just because he's family.'

'I wish I could, but you're right. Of course if he had helped his father in some underhand business I would hope that he has put all that behind him now.'

'And then there's Mr Cullum. Is he still around? Perhaps the late Mr Riley wasn't Dunne but Cullum? That would explain how he was seen in London a few years ago.'

'It would. Well loath as Inspector Payne might be to accept any advice from me, I will write to him and suggest that he might look into Mr Riley's antecedents. He will no doubt decline to reply.'

CHAPTER THIRTY-TWO

The tea shop which was chosen by Miss Lorna Lee was not far from the theatre, and while smart and clean was patronised by a louder and more jovial crowd than similar establishments in Bayswater. It specialised in generous amounts of hot tea, and sandwiches and pastries in sufficient quantity to serve as a meal rather than simply an afternoon treat.

Miss Lorna Lee, London's favourite songbird, was a woman of more mature charms than she might have liked to admit, but able through the dextrous application of paint to convey the impression of blushing youth combined with a hint of worldly experience. She was trim of waist but with a fine bust and hips and this exaggerated effect drew interested glances as she paraded her form into the tea shop, moving like a dancer, so that she could be admired from every point of view.

'I am quite intrigued by your letter,' said Miss Lee, arranging herself carefully on her chair to show herself to the best advantage. 'I have never met a lady detective before and now I am meeting two. It sounds like a very interesting profession. I should mention, however, that there are certain confidences I am unwilling to break.'

'I understand,' said Frances. 'But I do hope that you may be able to help me, as a man is suspected of a terrible crime which he did not commit and his reputation is threatened.'

'Ah, yes, gentlemen's reputations. I know all about those.' Miss Lee studied the menu card. 'Well, now, what shall we have? I do like a nice fruit tart.'

'Might I ask if you ever received a gift from a gentleman of a ring set with an emerald? A ring that had to be made smaller to fit your finger? It was purchased from Mr Solomon Finewax.'

Miss Lee was astonished, then suspicious. 'What do you know about that? Have you got it?'

'The police found it together with some other property which was taken from the body of a murdered man.'

The songstress uttered a gasp of dramatic proportions. 'Oh my word!'

A waitress arrived and Frances ordered tea and fruit tart with sandwiches, bread and butter and madeira cake. 'Perhaps to begin with you might like to tell me about the gentleman who bought the ring for you.'

Miss Lee took a handkerchief from her reticule and made a great performance of dabbing her eyes without actually touching them. 'Oh the poor man. Well he was a very nice old gent, that's for sure. At least – you said he had the ring?'

'It does seem like it, yes.'

'Well I never.' The handkerchief disappeared whence it had come. 'All right, I'll tell you all about him, but there's not much to tell. These fancy gents in the high life, they never give their real name to their special friends. It's all "call me Sammy" or "call me Jimmy". This gent, he liked me to call him Joe.'

'Can you describe him?'

'Smart dressed, quite old, but still with a bit of fire in him if you know what I mean. Still with his own hair, side whiskers, no beard.'

Frances produced the drawing of Lancelot Dobree. 'Is this he?'

'That isn't a bad likeness. So he wants to take me to the hotel so we can have a little private dinner. Just the two of us. He's bought me this ring, but it had to be made smaller and he got it from the jewellers and met me at the hotel. So then we went to our room where we had dinner. That was when it was stolen.'

'Were you not wearing the ring at dinner?'

'I tried it on and it fitted nice, but I took it off and laid it aside before we started our dinner.'

A laden tray arrived with all that was necessary for a nourishing repast and Miss Lee began to pile sandwiches and pastries onto her plate.

'Why did you remove the ring before dinner?' asked Frances.

Miss Lee smiled, and Frances felt Sarah's foot nudge her ankle.

'Oh. I think I understand.' Frances quickly helped herself to bread and butter to cover her confusion.

'And Joe he had a nice gold watch which he took off before – you know.'

'Dinner,' said Sarah.

'Exactly,' beamed Miss Lee, biting hungrily into a fruit tart. She dabbed her lips with a napkin. 'Well we had a very merry time, so if a thief had crept in through a window and taken our jewellery we might well not have noticed it.'

'How long were you at dinner?' asked Sarah.

'It must have been half an hour. Elderly gentleman can take much longer than the young ones over their dinner, but then they appreciate it more. So then Joe goes to get his watch and says, "Oh here's a nice thing, my watch and your ring have been stolen!" And of course he didn't want to report it and get the police involved. But he promised he would buy me another ring as good as the one that was taken.'

'Did he buy you another?' asked Frances.

'No, in fact I never saw him again. That was when I started to wonder. Suppose he was a cheat and only pretended to find the things stolen. So you say he was killed?'

'He was, yes.'

'I am sorry, of course, but perhaps he cheated a lady once too often. I don't suppose the police would let me have my ring back?'

'Only if you can prove ownership. I think you should go to the police and identify the ring. Mr Finewax should be able to help, as he can testify both to the sale and making the alteration.'

Frances suddenly found she had little appetite for what the tea shop had to offer, not that it was not appetising, but because she saw that this recent revelation gave a quite different picture of Mr Lancelot Dobree from the one accepted by his friends. Not only did he consort with women of a certain character, something that might have been excused in a lonely man, but also there was the accusation of tawdry cheating which was in many ways far worse. She was going to have to tread very carefully indeed.

On her return home, Frances found a letter waiting for her from Vernon Salter. To the best of his recollection, at the time of George

Cullum's disappearance in 1857 he had been between thirty-five and forty years of age. If Cullum was still alive then he would, Frances calculated, now be in his early sixties. Salter didn't know when or where Cullum had been born. He had never met any member of Cullum's family but knew that he was married with young children. Cullum had been of average height and proportions, with light brown hair and whiskers and no distinguishing features. He was left handed, both as a silversmith and with a pen. While the general description of Cullum was too vague to be useful, and his appearance could have changed over the years, the one thing Frances knew he could not alter was being left-handed, and determined that in future she would look very carefully for handedness in all the men of the right age she encountered.

Salter wrote that his father had never really liked Cullum but the man was highly skilled in his craft, and supervised the workshop. Although they often described themselves as partners the arrangement had never been legally formalised, although that possibility had been discussed. The lease of the property was in Bernard Salter's sole name, and Cullum had wanted to buy a share of the business.

Regarding Cullum's disappearance, Salter had searched his memory for the events that had immediately preceded it. About two months before Cullum had disappeared he had been taken ill, at least that was the import of a letter received from Cullum's wife. Although there was some inconvenience in unexpectedly losing the work of an experienced man, Bernard Salter had been somewhat relieved. His son was young but he had been learning the trade and was able to take over some of Cullum's less demanding work. Father and son had had an earnest discussion, since Bernard Salter now wanted to take on his son as a full partner. When Cullum unexpectedly returned, he was secretive about the nature of his illness and said he did not wish to go back to the toil of silversmithing. The Salters weren't sure that Cullum had been ill at all, and suspected that his absence was actually a cover for some illegal business he had been conducting.

Bernard Salter and Cullum had a meeting. Salter suggested that if Cullum was too ill to work he could retire, and offered to make a severance payment. Cullum took this with very bad grace. He proposed instead that the business could be made more profitable if they dealt in stolen goods, and that that side of the business should be turned over to him. The shop with its legitimate trade would be the perfect front. Salter, angered and insulted by this, refused, and the two men had argued. Two days later Cullum vanished.

Frances made a quick search of her collection of West London street directories, which soon revealed that Cullum's name had disappeared after the last one that had been printed before he himself was gone.

Next morning Frances visited Somerset House to see the records of the Registrar General, where she had better fortune. A George Cullum had married in the parish of Paddington in 1852. She ordered a copy of the certificate. The birth registers showed three possible children of the marriage; a son, John, born in 1854, a daughter Eliza in 1856 and a son, Harold, in 1858. In 1858 there were two Cullum deaths, Jane and Harold. Frances wondered if this was the abandoned wife and the last-born. Further searches through the books did not reveal either marriages or deaths for John and Eliza Cullum. Frances wasn't sure if she could trace these individuals, but if she could then they might be able to clarify the fate of their father.

Once home, Frances brought out her growing collection of local newspapers and studied the copies for the last two months. She was especially looking for burglaries that had been concentrated in West London, and found a large number reported but not solved. A recent editorial in the *Chronicle* mentioned that the incidence of such crimes had increased of late. These numbers, thought Frances, would be swelled by losses from dubious hotels like the Portobello, which might not have been reported to the police. Could one person be responsible, or several, or could it be the actions of a gang?

The afternoon brought good news about other cases. Sarah, on behalf of the client with the unknown admirer, had made an assignation by dropping a note to the mysterious would-be lover in the same location where he had left his note for the lady. An appointment had been made in Hyde Park and the young gentleman who arrived was surprised to find that the person who met him was not the object of his affections. He was, it transpired, painfully shy, with a dreadful stammer, and having seen the maiden from afar was unable to gather the courage to approach her. Sarah decided to make careful checks on his credentials, and if he appeared honest would ask the client if she would agree to a chaperoned meeting.

The truanting schoolboy had been followed by Ratty, and his secret destination discovered. A tall youth, he had claimed to be eighteen and had been admitted as a student to life-drawing classes, where he was making a study of the female form. Frances decided to consign him to the mercy of his no doubt furious mother.

Chapter Thirty-Three

Frances began to put together what she knew concerning recent events. A man had made enquiries at Munro & Son about empty properties and, so Inspector Payne thought, had obtained the keys to number 2 Linfield Gardens. He could well have been the man who lured Lancelot Dobree to his death. Why he should have chosen that time and place remained a mystery, as did the means of Dobree leaving the Lodge room. If Dobree had had an innocent associate who had assisted him, this person had not come forward, possibly because he or she feared being accused of involvement in the crime. Dobree had been trying to gather information about his son-in-law either alone or through a private investigator or both. The stolen snuffbox might have suggested to him that Salter was involved in the recent thefts. Perhaps Dobree had been lured from his meeting with a promise of secret intelligence. And was the murder of Mr Munro junior connected with the death of Dobree, or simply a coincidence?

'Is it so easy to steal keys from the house agent's office?' asked Sarah. 'They can't be that careless.'

Frances cast her mind back to her visits to Munro's. 'The keys are kept in the back office. When young Mr Munro went to get them, his father was working there.'

'And if someone took them, they'd have to put them back. All without anyone seeing or suspecting anything. But Munro's didn't only have the key to the yard?'

'No, the front and back doors as well, all on the same bunch.'

'Well there you are, then,' said Sarah. 'All that stolen stuff; why was it in a hole in the wall? Why not under the floorboards in the house? There's something not right.'

Frances could only agree. At least she now had a description of the man who had called on her mother – Mr Green – and hoped to locate and speak to him. If he had been employed by Lancelot

Dobree, the detective could well hold the clue to what had been troubling the dead man and give some insight into the murder. Frances studied the Kensington newspapers and local trade directories to see if there might be a private investigator called Green, and soon found what she wanted in the small advertisements. 'Peter Green, Private Investigator, for expert Confidential Enquiries. Divorce, Watching suspected persons, Missing friends. Secrecy guaranteed. As recommended by solicitors.' There was an office address in Kensington.

'You're not to go alone,' said Sarah, sternly. 'He might be a murderer.'

'Then you will be by my side to protect me.'

'One thing we don't have is a description of the man who called at Munro's about the house. The only man who spoke to him is dead.'

'True, but if Mr Munro senior was in the back office at the time, he might have taken note of a caller. I wonder if he is well enough to be questioned? I will write to his brother and ask.'

Frances was interested in the idea of a private investigator who actually had an office address, something to which she did not think she could ever aspire, and in Kensington no less, although in the event it turned out to be in a backwater of that district, far from the fashionable parts. The houses were divided into offices of small solicitors and property agents, and Green and Co. was on the first floor of a building whose ground floor was a dowdy purveyor of furniture and porcelain.

A small outer office was guarded by a short, round, grey-haired woman who asked tersely in a thickly accented voice if they had an appointment with Mr Green. Frances was not to be deterred so easily. 'We do not, but we are willing to wait until he is available.' They sat down. From time to time there was the echo of footsteps on the stairs, and messengers went back and forth with notes, some of which the lady clerk stared at before handing on another note; other missives were important enough to be taken into the adjoining office where presumably Mr Green was holding court.

It all looked a little drab and cheap, but then Frances supposed that someone coming to engage a private investigator was not concerned with the decor and the man himself might not wish to expend more than necessary on his workaday surroundings. Voices emanating from the inner office told Frances that a client was there, and eventually there was the sound of chairs scraping on a wooden floor, and the door opened. The client who emerged was a lady, heavily veiled, and she hurried out without a sideways glance. Showing her out was a plain-dressed man of about forty with thick eyebrows.

'Mr Green,' said the clerk, getting to her feet and offering Frances' card, 'Miss Doughty and Miss Smith have come to see you. Are you available now, or shall I make an appointment?'

Green looked at the card without a hint of surprise. 'Ah, I thought you might call before long. Well, do come in ladies. I am at your service.' He spoke the English of an Englishman, but his accent was a diluted version of the clerk's, who Frances was beginning to think must be his mother.

He stood aside for them to enter.

'Please do take a seat. What can I do for you?'

The inner office was simply furnished but tidy and clean. He brought forward two well-worn chairs, designed for solidity rather than comfort.

'You know who I am, of course,' said Frances.

He smiled. 'I could hardly fail to know.'

'And you are the man who recently called on Mrs Martin in Brighton, which resulted in her terrible collapse.'

The smile vanished to be replaced with an expression of regret. 'That was very unfortunate. Please reassure me that she has recovered from her faint.'

Frances did not spare him. 'It was not a faint, Mr Green, she has a weak heart. She is now very ill. She might have died.'

He paused for a long while. 'I am extremely sorry to hear it. It is not unknown for ladies to faint away under questioning and I really thought it was nothing more, but I did summon assistance at once. Had I known the lady was in delicate health I might have acted differently, but I was unaware of the position.'

'Can you advise me of the nature of your enquiries?'

'No, Miss Doughty, and I am surprised that you should ask me such a thing. I am sure that if someone other than the police came to you and demanded confidential information then you would not reveal what you were sworn not to.'

'You went to the police about your enquiries in Brighton.'

'I did not. They came to me. I'm sure I don't have to tell you that they were looking into a criminal case, and the information I had uncovered was of importance.'

Frances was puzzled. 'Then how did the police learn of your activities?'

'I don't believe I am at liberty to answer that question.'

'If it was not for the fact that your client is deceased I might imagine that it was he who went to the police.'

Mr Green was silent but Frances could see that her comment had surprised him.

'Are you able to tell me for whom you are now acting? Who instructed you to interview Mrs Martin?'

'I think you can easily guess that I am not prepared to name my client.'

It was all perfectly friendly and business-like, but Frances could see that she would learn no more from him. The visit raised several new questions. Who had alerted the police to Green's enquiries? After Dobree's death had another man been instructed to continue on his behalf? It could not be Marsden so perhaps it was Alicia Salter's new solicitor, Kingsley.

Frances didn't know if it was relevant, but she was always interested in secrets that people were unwilling to divulge. Once home, she wrote to Tom and Ratty asking if a watch could be kept on Mr Green's office to see if anyone went in whom they recognised.

CHAPTER THIRTY-FOUR

A note arrived from Mr Anthony Munro, uncle of the murdered Albert Munro.

Dear Miss Doughty,

Thank you for your recent letter. I am very grateful that you have been kind enough not to trouble my unfortunate brother directly. He has, as I am sure you must realise, been in extremely fragile health since my poor nephew was so cruelly taken from us, and matters have not been helped by the enquiries necessarily made by the police. I am sorry to report that the dreadful crime remains unsolved. If you are able to bring any insight to these terrible events, I believe it might allow my brother a little peace. I have spoken to Jacob and he has agreed to see you as long as I am present at the interview. I am sure I don't have to appeal to you not to distress him. He will be at home at 10 a.m. next Monday.

No sooner had Frances replied confirming the appointment then she received a note from Mr Neilson. The brethren of the Literati would be meeting at the Duke of Sussex Tavern at 5 p.m. on Monday for a Lodge of Instruction. All those who had been present on the night of Lancelot Dobree's disappearance would be there and all had agreed to be interviewed.

On Monday morning Frances presented herself at the house of mourning. The door was hung with a wreath and inside all was dark and dreary. The maid wore a black crape ribbon on her cap, and anything that might have been considered bright and cheerful was draped in deepest black. Mr Anthony Munro greeted her quietly with solemn eyes before conducting her to a little drawing room.

'It is really very kind of Mr Munro to agree to see me,' said Frances. 'I will do my best not to upset him. How is he?'

'Very low, and he will never again be the man he was,' said the unhappy brother. 'Albert was his only son, and the business was all for him; everything was for him. His life is empty now; nothing will ever replace that hope for the future or bring him any comfort. And to think it was such a cruel thing to do, all for money. But tell me, what do you hope to learn?'

'A young man came to visit the shop to make enquiries about the property where Mr Dobree's body was found. I was hoping your brother might be able to describe him.'

Anthony Munro nodded. 'I think the police might already have mentioned him but I am not sure if there is anything to be learned. Still, come with me and we will see if there is any more Jacob can remember.'

Virtually the only light in the drawing room came from the soft flicker of a coal fire that did little to warm the atmosphere. As Frances stood in the doorway, her eyes growing accustomed to the dimness, she was able to pick out items of furniture standing like wooden tombstones, and festoons of dark silk foliage occluding mirrors and pictures. The stricken father, who had aged many years since Frances last saw him, sat in an armchair by the fire, his knees covered by a blanket. On a small table beside him were a candlestick, the candle unlit, and a glass of water. A bible lay on his lap, closed, his hands resting on it, but he did not look at the book, his gaze seemed far away, beyond the interior of the room, but seeing nothing. As Frances entered, he raised his head slowly.

'Jacob, this is Miss Doughty. You remember she was to call and speak to you?'

'Oh. Yes. Have they caught the man?'

'Not yet, I am afraid,' said Frances. 'But I am hopeful that the criminal will be brought to justice.'

He nodded and gestured vaguely for her to sit down. Frances sat in an armchair facing the bereaved father, and Mr Anthony Munro also sat, quiet and watchful.

'Mr Munro, I wanted to ask you about number 2 Linfield Gardens.'

He sighed. 'Ah, I always knew that property would be troublesome. The owner was so obstinate about price, I thought we would never sell it.'

'Did you have many enquiries?'

He shook his head. 'Very few. Even from the outside it could be seen that it was in a very poor state. I think most buyers took a look but decided not to ask further.'

'But you did have an enquirer who came into the office — a young man, I believe.'

He thought carefully and nodded. 'Yes.'

'I was hoping you might be able to describe him.'

'Oh? I thought I had done this already?'

'I am sure you have. Maybe now you might be able to remember a little more?'

He lifted the water glass with a shaking hand and took a small sip, then carefully replaced it on the table. Frances noticed that he used his right hand. 'I didn't see him very closely. I was in the back office. It was Albert who spoke to him. I do remember thinking at the time that he was very young to be thinking of buying such a property.'

'What did you judge his age to be?'

'It's hard to say. No more than twenty-five.'

'Perhaps he was a man of substance?' Frances asked, but Munro shook his head.

'No, not judging from his clothes — in fact, I doubted if he was asking on his own behalf, I thought perhaps he was a servant on an errand for his master. That was Albert's impression, too. I'm sorry I can't tell you any more.'

'Please don't worry, what you have said has been very helpful.' Frances reflected that this visitor, given his age, could not have been Mr Green. 'Did you see him again?'

Munro looked vague, and there was a long silence and his brother appeared anxious. 'Jacob — perhaps you should rest now?'

'Rest?' exclaimed Munro bitterly. 'What good is rest to me? I do nothing but rest. No, I was thinking. Yes, he did come to make a second enquiry about the house. He wanted to know if it had been sold. He was hardly there for a minute. Albert told him that it had not and that the seller refused to move over the price. Then he simply went away. I spoke to Albert about it afterwards. There was something not right about that man. I know when someone is a serious buyer and when he isn't, and that one wasn't.'

'He did not leave a name? Had he been to your office before?'

'He left no name, and was a stranger to us both.'

'He didn't borrow the keys to the house?'

'No.'

'Could he have stolen them?'

'No. He had no opportunity to do so.'

'Were there any other enquirers?'

'Mr Lancelot Dobree, now he was a serious client – he was going to come back with Mr Herman, his architect, to look it over, but – but he didn't. And then there was Mr Johnstone; I think he was the only man to take a look inside, but it was too high a price for him. Albert showed him round —' he gulped suddenly and tears started in his eyes.

Anthony Munro rose to his feet. 'I think that we had better end here,' he said, anxiously.

It was clear that the stricken man could not go on, and Frances did not insist, but quickly thanked him for his time and departed. Munro saw her to the door. 'I hope that interview was helpful to you,' he said, with the unspoken implication that it had to have been worth the upset to his brother.

'Yes, thank you, I have learned much that was new to me. I do wish your brother the very best for his future health. If he should recall anything more, any small detail, do please let me know. Sometimes the very smallest clues can trap a criminal.'

Frances thought carefully all the way home. There had been three enquirers about the house, two serious ones from Dobree and Johnstone, and two from the same unidentified young man who had not seemed like a genuine buyer.

Frances wished she could know what the police knew, but it seemed very unlikely that Inspector Payne would tell her anything. She, on the other hand, could tell him what she knew whether he wanted to hear it or not, and whether it made him suspect her of involvement or not. She wrote a letter.

Chapter Thirty-Five

L ater that day, Frances went to the Duke of Sussex Tavern, where the brethren of the Literati were gathering for their Lodge of Instruction. She brought the list of names supplied by Mr Fiske, and checked that everyone she wanted to see was there. The gentlemen gathered in the lounge bar and Frances was introduced to the Master of the Lodge, Mr Brassington, a tall hearty gentleman of about sixty with a large beard and merry eyes.

'Delighted to make your acquaintance,' said Mr Brassington. 'Mr Neilson has kindly made his office available for the interviews, which I trust will not take too long as we have our usual business in hand. Where would you like to start?'

'If you don't mind,' ventured Frances, 'I have had an idea that will give me a clearer impression of what occurred on the night in question, the precise course of events, and where each individual was positioned throughout. Would it be possible for the Lodge members to re-enact the ceremony, only with myself standing in the place of Lancelot Dobree?'

There was a stunned silence as the gentlemen looked at each other and then at Mr Brassington. Several looked as though they were about to swallow their own beards. One or two smiled, and not a few began to laugh.

'Oh that is quite impossible,' advised Mr Brassington. 'Our rituals are only open to men.'

'I agree,' said Mr Fiske, 'and it is with some regret that I do so, since I believe that it is essential to discover the truth behind the cruel death of a brother Mason. Is there not some common ground?'

'I would have thought,' said a diminutive gentleman with a serious expression, who had been introduced as Mr Chappell, Director of Ceremonies, 'that we would have been better advised to employ an investigator who is also a Freemason. Or at the very least a man, who would be a suitable candidate for membership.'

'I am afraid I do not know of a private detective who is a Freemason,' Mr Fiske pointed out. 'And how long might it take to discover one, I can't imagine. Even if I found a suitable candidate to attend such a ceremony he would have to be initiated, passed and raised. You know how long that takes. I should also point out that many private detectives are former police officers who have left the force under a cloud. Do you wish to employ such a person? He would certainly not be acceptable to the Lodge. Miss Doughty is not only an excellent detective, but she is known for her discretion. You might object to Miss Doughty because she is a female, but on no other grounds.'

'Might I suggest something,' said Frances. All eyes turned to her. 'Is it possible to proceed through the ceremony just providing a sufficient description of what took place but without actually performing any part which is closed to me?'

The brethren turned to their Master for guidance. Mr Brassington gave the question some thought. 'I think it would be best if Miss Doughty retires to the office for a few minutes while we discuss her suggestion.'

Frances thanked him, and the gentlemen sat down for a conference, their thoughts assisted by glasses of the landlord's finest beer. Ten minutes later, Mr Fiske called her back to the lounge bar.

'It is our decision,' said Mr Brassington, 'that it is possible with due care, to go through the evening's ceremonies without revealing any secrets that a lady, or indeed anyone not of our fraternity, ought not to have.'

'So long as the ceremony proceeds in the same manner as the original and everyone is placed where they were before, I am content,' said Frances.

The gentleman looked relieved if a little apprehensive.

'Then let us begin. Assume that I am now Lancelot Dobree, I will be arriving at the tavern at about – when?'

'Some time after four o'clock, with me,' said Mr Brassington. 'Half past, perhaps.'

'Mr Chappell, when did you arrive and check that the room was in order?'

'It was about quarter past four.'

'Were Mr Brassington and Mr Dobree here when you arrived?'

'No, but they came not long afterwards.'

'Could I ask you to check the Lodge room as you did on that occasion?'

Chappell, after glancing at Brassington who nodded, departed about his duties.

'I assume that Mr Chappell will obtain the key from the office and unlock the Lodge room by its front door?'

'Yes, he will,' said Brassington. 'It won't take more than two or three minutes. He keeps the key in his pocket until the ceremony is over. In the meantime, the other gentlemen remain here and engage in conversation.'

'Then let us all be seated,' said Frances.

Everyone sat, although there was a distinct lack of conversation and none of the gentlemen were at their ease.

Mr Chappell returned. 'Do you now have the key to the front door of the Lodge room in your pocket?' Frances asked him.

'I do, and I confirm that the room is in order and properly secured.'

'Do you have the key to the back door?'

'No, that is not required, but I did try the door as I always do, and I am certain it is locked.' He looked about him, and as everyone else was sitting he did so too.

Frances turned to Mr Brassington. 'And once Mr Chappell took his place you were all here all the time until it was time for the meeting to begin?'

Brassington gave this some thought. 'Well, not exactly. Some of the gentlemen would have gone to fetch a drink from the barman, and others would have attended to their personal comfort.'

'So you were not all seated here all of the time?'

'No, there would have been the usual to-ing and fro-ing.'

'Did Mr Dobree go to the bar?'

'He did not. He was my guest, and I purchased a drink for him.'

'Did he attend to his comfort?'

Brassington frowned. 'I expect so. It's not something one takes special note of.'

'Where did Mr Dobree sit when he was in the lounge bar?'

'I really can't be sure.'

'Perhaps he sat by you?'

'Yes, I think he did.'

'Could you go to the bar and fetch your guest a drink?'

'Oh! Yes of course!' Brassington sprang to his feet. 'Mineral water?'

'Yes please.'

Brassington went up to the bar and Frances quickly took the opportunity to leave the lounge and pass into the public bar. Ignoring the startled glances of the customers at the sight of a lone young female, she made her stride more purposeful and looked neither to right nor left, but entered the corridor. There were some yells after her, 'Oi! Miss!' as if she was about to commit the unthinkable act of wandering into the gentleman's convenience, or getting lost in the storerooms or cellar. She wondered if Wellington would pursue her, but the huge dog seemed to understand that he was a guardian of the night only, and did no more than utter a warning growl. Frances knew that when she retraced her steps she would be greeted with the ribald amusement of the drinkers, as it would be assumed that she had made an embarrassing mistake, and so it proved, but she kept her steps firm and her face impassive. When she returned to the lounge bar the bartender was busy and she was back in her seat before Brassington had delivered her drink. Silence reigned until glasses were emptied, and Frances took the opportunity of watching to check if any of the men present were left-handed. There was only one, who was far too young to be Cullum. Frances stood up. 'Shall we assume now that it is time for the ceremony to begin?'

Mr Brassington rose. 'Gentlemen, and er – lady – let us make ready.'

The brethren obediently left their chairs and mounted the stairs to the anteroom. Here coats and hats were removed and placed on the rails provided. Mr Neilson brought a chair to the door of the Lodge room. He explained to Frances that at a Lodge of Instruction the brethren did not wear regalia, and the door was not tyled, but on this occasion as she wished to know where members had been positioned during the last meeting attended by Dobree, he would act as Tyler.

'Now,' Brassington told Frances, 'all the members other than the officers enter the Lodge room and are seated. A guest usually goes in with the man who invited him, but in this case Brother Dobree was my guest, and so he went in with the other brethren. So you can go through now, and will be shown where Dobree was sitting.'

'So where he sat was his own choice?'

'It was, yes.'

The gentlemen, with cautious looks at Frances, entered the room, and she went with them. She was conducted to a seat on the row to the right of the Master's chair; the last seat on the end of the row, on the side of the room nearest to the back door. If she had wanted to leave by the back door, it was the shortest possible route, and she would not have had to walk in front of anyone else.

The officers then entered and processed around the room, before going to their stations. Mr Brassington took the Master's chair and the two Wardens occupied their positions. Mr Fiske and another gentleman who was the treasurer sat at the secretary's table near the front entrance. The Inner Guard, Mr Manley, having established that all except Mr Neilson were within, bolted the door and sat beside it.

'For the information of Miss Doughty,' began Mr Brassington, 'the first part of the proceedings was to open the Lodge. At this point all members were in the room. On the night of the meeting when Mr Dobree was present, I duly opened the Lodge, and then the acting secretary read the minutes of the previous meeting for approval.'

'Please let me know the subject of those minutes,' asked Frances, hoping to gain a valuable clue as to any information that might have provoked Lancelot Dobree's unusual behaviour.

'Of course. The minutes recorded the business of the last meeting and there was a report of the indisposition of a brother Mason, and a fund being set up to provide new books for one of the schools we support. Finally there were apologies from those not present. During the reading I clearly observed Brother Dobree in the Lodge room, and I feel sure that he was where Miss Doughty is now.

We then proceeded with the ceremony. After this the Almoner reported that our indisposed brother was on the road to recovery, but would not be able to resume his duties as Lodge secretary and

Brother Fiske had kindly agreed to act as secretary. The treasurer then reported on the amounts raised by the book fund, and the acting secretary provided the proposed date on which the brethren will entertain their ladies to a dinner. I then closed the Lodge.'

Frances thought that Mr Miggs would have been very disappointed to discover that the business of the Lodge was so mundane, although he would probably have concluded that any plans the Literati might have had to overthrow the government and kidnap the Queen would not have been formally minuted.

'So Mr Dobree was in the room before the ceremony began?'

'Yes.'

'Please describe the ceremony.'

'I first requested that all First Degree members should retire, and opened the Lodge in the Second Degree. Brother Dobree naturally remained.'

Several of the gentlemen rose and respectfully made for the door, which Mr Manley unbolted to permit them to leave. 'Where will these gentlemen go?' asked Frances.

'They will retire to the lounge bar. On that night they would have first divested themselves of their regalia. The next business of the evening was to test the candidate, Brother Alsopp, to ensure that he was ready for the ceremony of raising.' Brassington indicated the gentleman in question, a cheerful-looking individual with a sandy moustache, and eyes like a puppy. 'Before this took place the other members in the Second Degree were asked to leave.'

At this point several more members rose and left. 'As you might anticipate, they will join their brethren in the lounge bar. There were questions and answers which, of course, I cannot go into now, and then Brother Alsopp retired from the room.'

Mr Alsopp was conducted to the door guarded by Mr Manley. The door was opened and he left the Lodge. Once again the door was bolted.

'Where was Mr Alsopp while he waited?' Frances asked.

'He was outside being prepared by Mr Neilson.'

Frances looked around and counted twelve gentlemen present, including the Master and his officers. Those of the brethren not at an officer's station were seated in chairs around the perimeter.

'The next step,' explained Brassington, 'is to open the Lodge in the Third Degree and prepare it for the ceremony.'

'Mr Brassington, can you advise how long this procedure would have taken from first entering the Lodge to the start of the ceremony?'

'About thirty minutes.'

'And the lights were lit all the time, and Mr Dobree was present?'

'Yes. He could not have left the room by either exit without our noticing. All brethren were seated in their appropriate places. The Tyler, having prepared the candidate, knocked on the door to let us know that he was ready. And this, Miss Doughty, is when the lights were extinguished.'

The Lodge officers moved about the room turning down all the lamps, and there remained only the soft flicker of a candle beside the Master's chair. Frances was aware of some movement as the brethren took their positions.

'The Inner Guard was directed to see who sought admission and he opened the door.' Mr Manley duly opened the door. As he did so, a shaft of light entered from the corridor.

'Once the Inner Guard was satisfied that the candidate was properly prepared he was admitted and the ceremony proceeded,' Brassington continued.

The candidate entered – he was clearly silhouetted against the light. The door was closed and once again the room was dark. Although Frances was aware that it would have been possible to see a fair amount of activity even by candlelight, it was obvious to her that all eyes would at that time have been on Mr Allsopp.

'At this point,' said Mr Brassington, 'we all rose to say a prayer, and the ceremony, of which I cannot divulge the details, proceeded.'

Every man in the Lodge room who was not already standing rose to his feet, and Frances did so, too. She was aware only of shadowy figures moving about the room with slow deliberation.

It was now very clear to Frances that any attempt to leave surreptitiously by the front door of the Lodge would be bound to fail. Even if Dobree had managed to walk to the door unnoticed by all those whose paths he would have crossed, even if the

Inner Guard had colluded with his scheme, and not challenged him but unbolted the door, the light that flowed into the room on the opening of the entrance would have alerted the brethren that something unexpected was taking place. When the door had been opened to allow the First and Second Degree men to leave, and later the candidate, the Lodge room had been lit and no one had seen Dobree trying to make a surreptitious exit. Surely Mr Neilson, on guard with his sword, would have noticed if the guest had slipped away? That only left the back door, yet both it and the ground-floor exit had been locked.

Cautiously, Frances left her seat and crept over to the back door. She was able to do so silently, without passing in front of anyone else, and had already availed herself of the key during her earlier brief walk down the corridor. She now tried her best to open the door, but so dim was the light that she was unable to accurately place the key in the lock, with the result that a metallic scraping noise was apparent before the key even went in.

'I believe our guest is attempting to leave the Lodge,' observed Mr Brassington, and she could tell from his voice that he was smiling.

'I had to see if it was possible,' said Frances, returning to her seat. Of course, she reflected, she only had Mr Chappell's word that the back door was locked at all.

Everyone was then asked to stand again. 'In this part of the ceremony,' said Mr Brassington, 'the candidate takes his sacred oath, a pledge of brotherhood, honour and respect. The next part is rather lengthy and I do not propose to go into it in detail, in view of our lady guest.

'I next requested Worshipful Brother Fiske to perform the address. For the benefit of Miss Doughty I should mention that this is not performed in all Lodges, but Brother Fiske is very proficient in it and Brother Dobree was especially interested in seeing it since it is not a feature of the ritual in Mulberry Lodge. In fact,' Brassington paused, 'I recall something now. Shortly before the address commenced I glanced across at where Dobree had been sitting and I noticed that he had gone from his seat. I assumed he had moved to obtain a better view.'

'Then I had better move,' said Frances, rising. 'Where did he go?'

'I really don't know. All I could see was that the chair where he had been sitting was empty.'

Frances looked about the shadowy room. Her eyes were getting used to the darkness and she could easily see the forms of the seated men. 'Did anyone see him move? Does anyone recall Mr Dobree coming to sit by him?'

There was some discussion, but no gentleman in the Lodge recalled Lancelot Dobree either walking in front of him or moving to another place.

'Then it would appear,' said Frances, 'that Mr Dobree left the Lodge before Mr Fiske spoke.'

'I really don't know what to make of that,' said Mr Brassington, mystified.

'Please go on.'

Mr Fiske rose, went to stand beside Mr Alsopp, and took a small hand bell from his pocket. 'At this juncture I performed the address. Of course, with Miss Doughty in attendance I cannot speak the words, but I will carry out the procedure.'

There was an interval of about five minutes during which Mr Fiske walked about Mr Alsopp, ringing the hand bell at intervals. Mr Fiske then returned to his seat.

'There are a few more parts of the ceremony in which I entrusted Mr Alsopp with the secrets of his degree, after which he briefly retired from the Lodge room,' said Brassington. 'The lights were then re-lit.'

As the Lodge room was once again bathed in light, Frances looked about her. 'Mr Brassington, am I correct that Mr Dobree was never at any point called upon to take part in the ceremony?'

'That is correct. He was here as a guest, and simply observed.'

'Did you notice him being here when the lights were re-lit?'

'No, but there was a part of the ceremony still remaining in which I was principally involved, and I simply didn't look. I naturally assumed that he was here. After that part of the proceedings the junior members of the Lodge were re-admitted, the rest of the business was conducted and then I closed the Lodge.'

'Could he have slipped out when the junior members returned?'

'I very much doubt it. He would have had to walk past Mr Manley and Mr Neilson. It was when the officers of the Lodge prepared to file out that I looked around for Dobree and saw that he wasn't there. We searched high and low, but he was nowhere to be found.'

'At the time when you realised Mr Dobree was missing, which of the Lodge members had actually left the Lodge room?'

'None, and we are all sure that he was present at the start.'

Frances realised she had a great deal to think about.

'And now,' said Mr Brassington, 'we may draw the formal part of the evening to a close and retire to the lounge bar. Miss Doughty, have you seen all that you require to see?'

'I believe so.'

Mr Chappell coughed gently. 'I think you need to return a key.'

CHAPTER THIRTY-SIX

'Unless I have been seriously misled,' said Frances as she discussed the events with Sarah, 'Mr Dobree was undoubtedly in the Lodge room at the start of the ceremony and was not there at the end. I do not see how he could have left unnoticed by any exit while the lights were on.'

'You said there were times when some of the men left and came back. Might he have slipped out then?'

'Someone would have remarked if the guest had suddenly walked out part way through the proceedings. I spoke to the men concerned and they all swear that Dobree did not leave when the front door of the Lodge was open. Mr Neilson and Mr Manley are also certain. The only time he could have left unnoticed is when the lights were out. And if he did, he could not have gone out through the front door which was guarded and would have let the light in.'

'So he used the back door, which was locked, and made a squeak when it opened.'

'The only time the squeak would not have been heard was when Mr Fiske was ringing his bell. It was my theory that Mr Dobree had used that noise to cover his exit, but now it seems that by then he had already gone. I can't believe there has been some plot in which all the members of the Lodge were involved. However, if Mr Dobree left by the back door unnoticed while the lights were out, there is only one way he could have done so. Despite what Mr Chappell says, the door must already have been unlocked. I have tried it myself and if one is careful, opening the unlocked door can be done very quietly.'

'In that case it was unlocked that night specially; just so Mr Dobree could go out. He couldn't rely on Mr Chappell being careless.'

'Mr Chappell might have been his accomplice,' said Frances. 'Mr Dobree might have told him of his plans and asked Mr Chappell to unlock the back door for him. So it was Chappell who locked it again afterwards. If so, he is not admitting it. He could easily have relocked it during the search without anyone noticing.'

'Or,' Sarah pointed out, 'it could have been unlocked by one of the men who left the room early. Any one of them might have slipped away, saying he was going to the gentleman's convenience, got the key and opened the door.'

'But according to Mr Neilson very few men even knew where the keys were concealed. Dobree didn't. If he had done, Dobree might have unlocked the door himself after Mr Chappell checked it but before the meeting began; but then why did he relock it? He didn't take any of his possessions with him, so he must have intended to come back in unnoticed the same way he went out. To relock the door only increased the risk of being heard. He would have known it was almost never used and thought he could relock it any time he liked when no one was about. Remember his own Lodge, Mulberry, uses the same premises. And then he had to put the key back in place and leave the tavern, all without being seen by anyone. The tavern was busy that evening and he was a well-known figure there. It is astonishing that he was not seen in either bar.'

'He didn't know any magic tricks, did he?' asked Sarah. 'I mean things with bits of thread and wire and false doors and mirrors and lock picks hidden up his sleeve?'

'If he was in the habit of entertaining his friends after dinner with a display of conjuring no one has mentioned it,' said Frances. For a moment she toyed with the idea of someone entering the Lodge room in a wig to impersonate Dobree and then removing the wig under cover of darkness. If it had been a room full of strangers that might have been plausible but he was in the company of men who knew him well. She dismissed the idea.

'We still don't know why he went,' added Sarah.

Next morning Frances returned to Somerset House to collect the marriage certificate she had ordered. It confirmed what she had thought, that George Cullum's wife had been called Jane. It seemed probable that she was the Jane Cullum who had died in 1858. Who, then, had cared for the two Cullum children, John and Eliza, after their father's disappearance? Mrs Cullum, Frances noticed, was formerly Jane Capper, a surname that sounded familiar. Leafing through her notes Frances saw that one of the employees of the tavern whom she had interviewed was John Capper, the young man who had been working in the store-room at the time of Lancelot Dobree's disappearance. Could he be related to Jane Cullum? Capper was about twenty-five, and Frances looked through the birth directories but found no births of a John Capper at the appropriate time. It was possible that he had been born in Scotland, since Somerset House held only the records for England and Wales, but Frances had a more interest-ing thought. Could John Capper actually be John Cullum, son of the missing George, using his mother's maiden name because of his father's disgrace? The Bayswater directory yielded details of a family called Capper in Bayswater who were rug makers, the trade Frances had been told was that of Capper's father. She made a note of the address before returning to the tavern.

John Capper, assisted by the maid, Minnie, was waiting on tables during the busy luncheon period. Many of those present were tradesmen or professional gentlemen from the immediate area. Mr Weber of the bakery was sitting alone staring miserably into a pint glass, while in a corner, also alone and merging into the shadows, was Kennard, Mr Johnstone's grey-suited amanuensis.

Capper recognised Frances. 'You want Mr Neilson?' he asked.

'I will have a glass of lemonade and the roast mutton,' said Frances. 'And once you are free, I would like to talk to you.'

'I've got nothing more to tell you about Dobree.'

'That isn't what I want to ask about.'

His eyes narrowed. 'What then?'

'Do you have a rest from your duties when the luncheons have been served? If not, I will ask Mr Neilson to allow you a few minutes.'

He made no reply, but moved away.

Frances half expected him not to return at all, but once she had completed her meal, and the tables had been cleared, he did. 'Mr Neilson says we can talk in the office.'

Once there, Capper flung himself into a chair, and Frances occupied Mr Neilson's seat.

'Well?' said Capper uneasily.

'I want to know if you are related to a Jane Capper. The Jane Capper who married George Cullum.'

Capper abruptly slumped forward, hid his face in his hands and groaned. 'Oh no! I've been dreading this ever since you came here. I've heard what you're like. You wouldn't ask if you didn't know already. I could try lying, like I've been lying most of my life, but that wouldn't do me any good, would it? You know, or you'll find out.'

Frances said nothing, but allowed him to recover some composure.

He looked up at her earnestly. 'Look, you won't say anything, will you? I mean there's those that think if the family is bad then all of them are bad. I don't know what Mr Neilson would say if he knew. And then me and Minnie we want to get married when we've saved up enough. We want to open a little tea-shop.'

'Tell me what there is to know,' said Frances.

He leaned back and sighed. 'Yes, my mother was Jane Capper when she married Cullum. I've got a sister, Eliza. Mother was expecting again when my father ran off. She died when my brother was born, and the baby died soon after. Then our aunt Lottie Capper, mother's sister, she looked after us, and we took her name. I was about four at the time, and Eliza was two, so we didn't think about it then, but later on, Aunt Lottie told us about our father. She said that the family never wanted my mother to marry him. They always knew there was something wrong about him, but he was a clever type, educated, had a good business, and she thought he could give her and any children a comfortable life. But she was wrong. He was a brute and a criminal.' He raked his hands through his hair. 'Why do you want to know all this?'

'I have been told that when your father disappeared several people were suspected of having killed him. It's a suspicion that lingers today. But I have also heard rumours that he might still be alive. I want to know if at any time since he disappeared he has made contact with his family.'

'Well if he tried to see my aunt she never said so.'

'Might I speak to your aunt?'

'She died two years ago.'

'Has your father tried to contact you or your sister?'

'Not as far as I know.'

'And you haven't seen him since you were four?'

'That's right.'

'So if you did encounter your father now you wouldn't know him?'

'No.'

'Has any member of your family – any friend or associate of his who might know and recognise him – seen him since his disappearance?'

Capper shook his head. 'You won't tell, will you?'

Frances well understood the fears that came from a doubtful heritage. 'I have no reason to tell Mr Neilson, but you must be prepared. The truth may come out one day.'

Frances hoped that the Capper family of Bayswater might hold a clue, but when later that day she visited the address she found that they had moved away and no one knew where they had gone. She engaged Tom and Ratty to discover if any carriers had been hired to help them move their effects.

Chapter Thirty-Seven

rances and Sarah had barely settled to their supper when the maid with a highly nervous look announced that Inspector Payne had arrived and was demanding to see Frances. 'Shall I show him up?'

'Please do so,' said Frances. As the maid scurried away Frances added. 'He will come in whether I say yes or no.' She often worried what Mrs Embleton, her patient landlady, made of the frequent visits of the police to her door. That source of disquiet had calmed since the ground-floor apartment had been vacated and taken by Professor Pounder, who Mrs Embleton liked to think of as a solid line of defence against any unwanted intrusion. There only remained the retiring top-floor tenant, a lady who was so rarely seen that Frances wondered if someone should go up and check if she was still alive.

Payne appeared in moments, brushing quickly past the maid and striding into the parlour.

'Inspector, what brings you here so soon after your last visit?' asked Frances politely. 'Are there any of my personal effects you have neglected to search? Surely not. This must be a social call. Please sit down, our cocoa is freshly made if you would like a cup, and there is bread and butter.'

He looked harassed and unwilling to accept hospitality, but after a brief hesitation took a seat and nodded. Sarah poured the drink and he gulped it down and wiped his mouth with the back of his hand, then helped himself to two large slices of bread and butter. Frances realised he had probably been too busy to eat for some while. 'Thank you,' he said reluctantly when the food had disappeared, something he achieved with remarkable speed. 'Now then, I want you to tell me everything you know about Mr Harry Abbott.'

Frances searched her memory. 'I'm afraid I don't know anyone of that name.'

'Oh no? And I suppose you'll tell me you've never been to the Portobello Hotel? Don't try to deny it.' Payne pulled one of Frances' business cards from his pocket and tossed it onto the table. 'This was behind the front desk. Regular visitor there, are you?'

Frances bridled at the implication behind his words, but retained her calm. 'I have been there once, in connection with some enquiries. I was there for a few minutes only, in the foyer, and on that occasion I supplied my card. I have never stayed there, I can assure you.'

'What date was that?'

Frances looked in her notebook, and told him the date.

'Who did you speak to while you were there?'

'The young gentleman behind the desk. He was extremely unhelpful and didn't give me his name.'

'Tall, was he? Blond hair, funny eyes?'

'Yes.' Frances paused. 'Is he Mr Harry Abbott? The only other person I saw there was the doorman, who I did not speak to, but he was called Burns.'

'And what was your enquiry concerning?'

'The emerald ring found amongst Mr Dobree's effects. It was last seen at that hotel.'

'Ah. Now I see. Have you spoken to a Miss Lorna Lee?'

'Yes. I told her to go and see you.'

He nodded. 'She did and claimed the ring as hers. We're making enquiries about that. Seems like Mr Dobree was not as respectable as he liked to make out.'

'Miss Lee said that the gentleman she dined with gave her the ring, but she removed it before —'

'Before they dined? Yes, that's what she told us.'

'Exactly. And then the ring and her friend's watch were found to be missing. She wondered if he had abstracted the ring himself as an excuse not to give it to her and then claimed it had been stolen.'

'So she said. Not at all a nice thing to do. Even to her sort. But there's things go on at that place we can never fathom, and of course no one wants to talk about it and hardly anyone admits they have even been there. So, tell me, have you seen Mr Abbott since your visit?'

'As I have said, I have been there only the once.'

'But you might have seen him later – you might have taken tea with him, or gone for a walk, or simply passed him in the street?'

'I have not to my knowledge seen him since. If I do chance to, I will let you know where and when. I assume he is not at his place of work or his home?'

'Same place. He has a room at the hotel. Two days ago he didn't appear at the desk and when the other staff looked in his room he wasn't there. Nothing disturbed, all his things left behind. No message and none of his friends or family have seen him. Do you know anything about that?'

'No.'

'The hotel people weren't all that bothered, but his mother was, and told the police. Hotel management weren't too happy when we turned up, but that can't be helped. We had a look around his room and do you know what we found?'

'I have no idea.'

'Stolen goods. Trinkets. Watches. We think Mr Abbott went into people's rooms using a pass key either while they were sleeping or having their dinner or whatever they call it, and stole things. The guests were led to believe it was someone breaking in and most never reported anything as missing as they didn't want their husbands or wives to know where they'd been.'

'Do you think Mr Abbott stole the emerald ring?'

'That's one of the first things we will ask when we find him. But how it came to be where it was, we don't know. It's the same ring all right; the jeweller, Mr Finewax, has identified it as the one he sold and altered.' Payne shrugged. 'I doubt that Mr Abbott was the only thief about.'

Frances poured more cocoa. 'Did you receive my message?'

'Oh yes, well we get letters all the time from the public with information and theories. Some of it useful. Only some. Last year with the Face-slasher business we got sacks-full, mainly from wives denouncing their husbands. A few from husbands saying that the slasher was not Jack but Jill. Anyhow, we know the truth now.'

'I have been trying to find out how the stolen snuff box that Mr Salter bought in all innocence and very commendably handed in to you could have been acquired by the late Mr Riley. Perhaps Riley was not his real name? Could he have been Mr David Dunne, the man from the Hayworth Hill Manor robbery and killing who was never arrested?'

Payne leaned back in his chair and appeared to be giving the question intense consideration. 'In my opinion, no,' he said at last. 'There are two reasons. First of all, types like Dunne don't simply go straight and lead blameless lives. Even when they get old – if they do – and can't get up to their youthful tricks, they find another way of breaking the law. Mr Riley, as far as we can see, was as straight as they come. The second reason is that David Dunne was killed in a fight outside a beer shop not long after his friends were hanged.'

Frances ignored the note of heavy sarcasm in his last comment. 'I see. Well, that is one line of enquiry I need not pursue. But Mr Dunne and his gang – how did they dispose of the stolen items?'

'They had a number of contacts, men with different specialities, and requirements. These characters, the men who deal in stolen jewellery, are not crude criminals, they often have a respectable man's knowledge, they know what to look for and how much it's worth. Some of them have a proper business with a shop window to hide the shady one. Like Bernard Salter and his partner George Cullum.'

'Mr Salter had no hand in any dealings in stolen goods.'

'So he said.'

'Could Dunne and his gang have sold the silver to Cullum who sold it to Riley? Or the late Mr Riley might have been Mr Cullum.'

Payne hesitated and Frances saw that he had at least been considering this. 'Riley was born abroad and came to settle in London in 1859.'

Frances smiled. 'So he said.'

Payne grunted. 'Well, that's as may be. It would suit you, wouldn't it? All the witnesses dead?'

'It would not. I want answers and I can't get them from dead men. And I want you to stop treating Mr Vernon Salter as a criminal.'

Payne gave a humourless laugh. 'Well that's a tall order.' He gulped the last of his cocoa. 'Thanks for that, it was very welcome.' He stood up. 'And don't go leaving London again. I can see that I'll be back.'

CHAPTER THIRTY-EIGHT

Frances had not expected to hear from Lorna Lee again, so next morning she was surprised to receive a heavily perfumed note asking if she might come to tea in the little establishment by the theatre. There was a subtle inference in the wording of the note that this was more than just a social event, and by attending Frances might learn something of interest.

Sarah had gone to take one of her regular calisthenics classes at Professor Pounder's academy. She specialised in exercises conducted with the aid of a staff generally known as a 'wand' and Frances had seen demonstrations carried out with the feminine grace appropriate to that appellation. In Sarah's hands, the staff appeared more menacing and she usually referred to it as 'the big stick'. No one sought to contradict her.

Frances, not feeling the need to carry a stick, big or otherwise, dared to meet with Miss Lee alone. She began to regret that decision when shown to the table reserved by Miss Lee and saw that she was also to enjoy the company of a gentleman. That individual was a courteous type, very reserved, and smiled a great deal. His hair was very little receded, and grey with a flush of light brown that must have come from a dye bottle. He rose politely to his feet as Frances approached, revealing a notable want of stature, and though his manner was friendly, there was a wariness about him, like that of a man who had something to conceal.

'I would like to introduce my very particular friend who is a great patron of the theatre, Joe. Joe, please meet Miss Doughty, the best detective in all London.'

'Charmed, I am sure,' said Joe.

'Likewise,' said Frances.

'We have already ordered refreshments for three,' said Miss Lee, 'so we will be very comfortable and pleasant here.'

'Hot tea on a cold day is such a wonderful thing,' said Joe.

'It certainly is,' said Frances. She recalled that Miss Lee liked to entertain many gentlemen who gave names like Jimmy or Joe, or Bill, and that the buyer of the emerald ring had been a Joe. Perhaps Miss Lee's most ardent admirers were gentlemen of a certain age since this particular Joe, despite his auburn locks, looked to be well in his seventies, judging by the evidence that time had carved on his face. She could not tell what his occupation might be or have been, except that his garments were of the best quality and freshly tended. He wore a hothouse flower in his buttonhole, and Miss Lee was in possession of a posy, undoubtedly a recent tribute.

The refreshments were brought to table, and involved a three-tier cake stand, each level of which was laden with sandwiches, tartlets and slices of cake. It was hearty rather than delicate, but then so was Miss Lee.

'The last time Miss Doughty and I met here we had a very interesting conversation about the emerald ring,' said Miss Lee, piling sandwiches onto her plate. She smiled. 'The dance does give me such an appetite, but then the theatrical life takes all one's energy and encourages slenderness. Since our discussion, I have visited the police station in the company of Mr Finewax and the police are now satisfied as to my ownership of the ring, and have promised to return it once it is no longer evidence. So that at least is settled. However, I had believed that the kind gentleman who made me such a generous gift was deceased. I was led to believe this because I had not seen Joe in some while, and Miss Doughty told me the ring had been found amongst the effects of a dead man. You cannot imagine the dreadful upset I experienced. But now, it seems it was all a mistake.'

Joe smiled and nodded. 'Yes, I was called away quite suddenly, and the note I sent to Miss Lee informing her of that fact must have been lost.'

'Then you are the purchaser of the ring?' said Frances. She still had the sketch of Lancelot Dobree in her reticule, and brought it out. 'I had thought it was this gentleman.'

Miss Lee studied it. 'That is the portrait you showed me before. There is a likeness, only I think Joe is handsomer!'

'How very kind,' said Joe. He patted his hair and Frances observed that he used his right hand. 'Yes, it was indeed I who bought the ring, but that is not a fact I wish to be known by everyone. I am sure, Miss Doughty, that in your profession you understand these things better than most. But since I am told that a murder is involved, I did not feel I could stay silent.'

'That is very good of you,' said Frances, 'I promise I will be discreet. Might I ask some questions about the day the ring was stolen?'

'Please do, I will answer whatever I can.' There was a pause for refreshment as Frances readied her notebook and pencil.

'Do you recall who was on duty at the reception desk of the hotel?'

Joe thought about this. 'It is not always the same man, so I can't be sure.'

'Oh, I am,' said Miss Lee. 'There's a very saucy fellow – he gave me a look, one of those looks, you know,' Frances didn't know but pretended she did, 'which I didn't like at all.'

'Can you describe him?'

'Oh well he's young and quite tall, with light hair and bulgy eyes. Not handsome. The other man who is sometimes on duty is shorter and very serious looking with spectacles. Much more polite.'

Frances concluded that the desk had been manned that day by the missing Mr Abbott. 'Did you show him the emerald ring or mention it?'

'No, of course not. Joe had it in his pocket and then later on he put it on my finger.'

'But you took it off before you dined?'

'Yes, well, I didn't want it to slip off. Wouldn't do to lose it in the soup.' She gave a little trill of laughter, which was only stifled by the application of cake.

Frances turned to the gentleman. 'Mr – er —'

He smiled. 'Joe, just call me Joe.'

'Yes. Mr Joe, I believe that your watch was stolen at the same time?'

'It was, yes.'

'Was either item reported as stolen, or even lost?'

Mr Joe had the courtesy to look embarrassed. 'The thing is,' he explained diffidently, 'my friendship with Miss Lee is a very private matter. My – family wouldn't understand it. I didn't feel I wanted to make an official report.'

Frances, feeling sure that the word 'wife' could in the interests of greater accuracy be substituted for 'family', asked, 'Did you take any action at all to recover the watch and ring?'

'Yes, well, once we knew the items were missing, I went to the reception desk and told the man there what had happened.'

'The tall man or the one with spectacles?'

'It was the tall man.'

'What did he say?'

'He said that there had been a number of incidents recently which the management thought was due to thieves using a stolen pass key. The hotel was going to get all the locks changed. The police did know about it, but he suggested I report to them directly. Of course I didn't, and I think he knew I wouldn't. He asked me to provide my card so he could let me know if the stolen things were found. He said thieves sometimes hid them away until the fuss died down and they might turn up in time.'

'Did you give him your card?'

'I did. He promised not to reveal that I had been to the hotel. I have a card with a business address. I deal in furniture.'

'Fine furniture,' said Miss Lee.

'I assume you heard no more.'

Mr Joe hesitated. 'Well, as a matter of fact …'

'You did?'

'Yes, I received a note a few days later saying that my watch had been found. I'm wondering now if it would have been difficult to sell or pawn because of the engraving inside. I was told that I could get it back for a price. Well, it was an heirloom and my – family – expected me to wear it. I had already explained its absence by saying that it was being repaired. I suspect that some of the price I was asked to pay involved purchasing silence about where it had been stolen. The note suggested a meeting in Hyde Park after dark. I went, and the transaction was made.'

'With whom?'

'I'm not sure. He had a muffler around his face and said very little.'

'Could it have been the tall young man at the hotel?'

Mr Joe paused. 'He was about the right height. Yes, it could have been him, but I wouldn't like to swear to it.'

'When did this happen?'

'About four days ago.'

'Because the young man who is called Harry Abbott hasn't been seen for two days. Do you know anything about it?'

'No, and I haven't seen him recently.'

Miss Lee ate the last sandwich and signalled to the waiter. Joe smiled indulgently.

Frances realised that she had on the slenderest of evidence assumed that the man who bought the emerald ring for Miss Lorna Lee had been Lancelot Dobree. Unless the meeting with Mr Joe had been an elaborate masquerade, it now appeared that she had been mistaken. Just because the ring and the items taken from Dobree's corpse had all been found in the same location, it did not necessarily mean that the ring had ever been in his possession. The discovery was a source of some relief, because she had not looked forward to the possibility that she would have to advise Vernon Salter of unsavoury details of his father-in-law's activities. As for 'Mr Joe', he would have to run his risks and take his chances.

New questions now arose. How had a ring stolen from a dubious hotel on the Portobello Road found its way into a hole in the wall of an abandoned lodging house in Kensington? And was there any kind of a connection with Lancelot Dobree?

CHAPTER THIRTY-NINE

Frances was left with the impression that there were a great many circumstances that might not appear to be connected but were, while others that would seem to be connected were not. And even if she could identify the connections, would they prove to be of any importance? In the past she had drawn out charts or diagrams to help her understand events, and where and when they had taken place, which sometimes answered the questions of how and why. Now she felt she needed to do so again, but what would be the shape of the diagram? It appeared in her imagination to be a large wheel, with spokes pointing to some central place, and cross connections like a spider's web. But who or what was the spider?

The analogy pleased her. Lancelot Dobree was most unlikely to be the spider; she thought he was merely an unlucky fly who had by chance stumbled into the web, which had proved fatal. The threads that held the web together were financial, and involved the theft and sale of fine silverware and jewellery, trades with which Dobree had no personal connection. Even his son-in-law was a very minor dealer and not an especially wealthy representative of that trade.

The only connection that Frances could think of between Dobree and a crime was the discovery of a stolen ring in the house he had been intending to buy – a house which he had never even entered until the day of his death.

Frances took a large sheet of wrapping paper and at its centre drew a square. In the square she wrote '2 Linfield Gardens'. On the edge of the paper she put another square and in it wrote 'Portobello Hotel'. She drew a line between the two. Along the line she wrote 'emerald ring'. At the other edge she drew a circle and in it wrote 'Lancelot Dobree'. She drew a line between the circle and the square and along it wrote 'interested in buying'.

There were other connections to the house: Mr Munro senior and Mr Munro junior, the house agents; Mrs Collins, the original owner; Mr Johnstone, who had recently bought the property; and the unknown man who had made enquiries about it and not returned. Everyone who had made enquiries about the house and its original owner were therefore connected to the house agents. Frances drew another square and in it wrote 'Duke of Sussex Tavern'. This was connected to Lancelot Dobree and Munro junior, Munro's lunchtime companion Mr Weber, and Mr Johnstone's shadowy assistant Mr Kennard, who were all customers. It was also connected to Dobree's architect friend Mr Herman, who was connected to the lodging house as he had advised Dobree about it. Another square was labelled 'Literati' and connected to the tavern as a meeting place. The only connection between the tavern and the lodging house was their proximity.

Thus far the only stolen jewellery involved was the emerald ring, but there was one other connection. Frances drew lines connecting the tavern with its employees, and from the name of John Capper she drew another line, to the missing Cullum. Cullum was connected to Vernon Salter who was connected to Dobree. But did this mean anything? Frances didn't even know if Cullum was alive, and his last known criminal activity was twenty-four years ago.

Frances stared at the diagram and wondered who might make sense of such a tangle. It was all very confusing. Had she got it wrong? Was there a web at all, and if so, was it she who was trapped in it, like another helpless fly?

She took a second sheet of paper and made a list of addresses. These were all the locations in which thefts of valuables had taken place in the last few months. They included the Portobello Hotel, the house where Mr Munro junior had been killed, and the properties that had been burgled with keys stolen from his body, and Lancelot Dobree's home and the tavern where there had been attempted break-ins. Careful scouring of the newspapers enabled her to extract some other addresses, hotels from which jewels had been stolen and burglaries from private houses. There were twelve locations, all in the Paddington, Kensington and Bayswater area. More than ever she became convinced that there was a gang in operation, a gang whose activities connected all these places. Had Harry Abbott been a member of the gang, or had he worked alone? If a lone wolf, he might have wandered into the territory of a gang who thought that they ought to have all the pickings. If in a gang, he might have fallen foul of his criminal confederates. His abrupt disappearance without taking his possessions and cache of stolen goods suggested either that he had left the hotel in fear and in a very great hurry, or he had been abducted while away from his home, and was most probably dead.

A carriage drew up outside the house and Frances peered out of the window, wondering if it was a new client. Since word had spread over Bayswater that she was taking on criminal cases again, new clients, especially those with domestic issues they preferred to put before a sympathetic female, had been arriving with increasing frequency. It was taxing, since the Dobree case was already occupying much of her time, but she felt she had nothing to complain about. She saw Mr Anthony Munro step down from the carriage, and to her surprise he carefully assisted the descent of his older brother Jacob. Both men approached her door, Jacob shuffling slowly at his brother's side.

Frances was impatient with curiosity until the maid announced them, and did her best to ensure that the parlour was comfortable, adding a cushion to the armchair, putting a small table by its side with water and a glass, and mending the fire with fresh coal.

Jacob was panting a little as the two men arrived at the door, and Frances greeted them and watched carefully as the older man was guided to the armchair. Anthony Munro, relieved that his charge had been safely delivered, faced Frances across the little round table.

'I do hope you are both in good health,' said Frances politely, although in the case of Mr Jacob she felt some anxiety.

Anthony Munro sighed and glanced at his brother. 'We can only hope that in time the pain of our loss will recede in some measure, but it has been hard thus far. To be honest, I don't know if it is a good or bad thing that poor Albert never married. A wife and children would have imposed a duty of care on the family but they would also have given Jacob something to think about beyond his own grief. I have been trying to distract him and today was the first time I was able to persuade him to leave the house, just for a drive. And as we talked, he recalled something. I don't know if it has any significance.'

'Well, let me see.' Frances rose and went to sit opposite Jacob. The fire was hissing and popping with little sparks jumping up. Frances was obliged to check that the guard was secure but her visitor seemed oblivious to any danger. 'Mr Munro, I believe you wanted to tell me something?'

'Ah, yes. I'm not sure why I didn't think of it before. Of course it might mean nothing. It was something my poor boy said to me. It was on the day he went with you and the other gentlemen to the property where the body of Mr Dobree was found. When he returned to the office he asked if the key to the yard gate was there, but it wasn't and I hadn't seen it.'

'What key was this? I thought all the keys to the property were on the bunch kept at the office?'

'No, there was one other, a spare key to the back gate. It was a rusty thing, never used, and hung on a hook in the yard by the side of the gate. But it was no longer there.'

'I see.' Frances pondered this. She could not recall having seen such a key on either visit, but had it been a rusty object it might not have been readily visible against the dirty walling. She wondered if it was even possible to determine when it had gone missing. 'Mr Munro, did you yourself visit the property when your office began to act for the seller?'

'Yes, I did. Last November. The owner's son showed it to me. The key was there then. I was told it was used to unlock the back gate for the coal man.'

'And between then and the day the key was found to be missing, the only visit to the property was when your son accompanied Mr Johnstone for a viewing?'

'It was the only viewing. I asked the owner to reduce her price but she was very stubborn. The result was that the only people who asked to see the property were Mr Johnstone, who declined to buy at the asking price, and Mr Dobree, who had yet to view it at the time of his death.'

'Do you know if the key to the gate was still there when your son showed Mr Johnstone the property?'

'As far as I know it was. Albert was very meticulous and would certainly have made quite sure that all was locked and bolted before he left. Oh … he did go back there once. I remember now. He was worried about the possibility of dry rot and looked over it again.'

'That was after Mr Johnstone was shown around?'

'Yes, a day or two afterwards, and he never mentioned a missing key.'

Frances had a new thought. 'Is it possible that you or your son might have lent a set of house keys to a trusted person – a valued customer, a professional man who was known to you, and not accompanied them on the visit?'

Munro thought hard about this. 'It is possible, yes. I myself didn't lend the keys to anyone but Albert might have done so under the circumstances you suggest.'

'Might he have lent them to Mr Dobree?'

'We would certainly have trusted him to borrow the keys. Dobree was very interested in the property. He had viewed the outside several times, and unlike others had not been deterred by its appearance.'

'Would he have lent them to an architect such as Mr Dobree's friend, Mr Herman?'

'Oh yes, I have known him for many years.'

So, thought Frances, Dobree or another man could have toured the property unaccompanied and without risk of being observed, abstracted the key to the gate, and left the inner bolt open. This would only have admitted someone to the yard, but it was a yard with a compartment in which a stolen emerald ring had been found, a yard where a body had been left to be devoured by rats. Making a copy of a bunch of keys might have aroused suspicion, and involved a third party, but whoever took what appeared to be an old neglected key must have thought its absence would not be noticed.

Frances tried to think back to her first visit to the property. Had the key been there when she entered the yard? She didn't know. Everyone present had been anxiously searching for a missing and possibly ill or injured man, and once the body was found that had occupied all their attention. 'But you would never have lent the keys to the young man who came to enquire, since he was not known to you?'

'No. He was not a serious buyer. I don't know what his business was. Albert told me he saw him again, lurking about in the street, and was sure he was up to no good.'

'When was this?'

'Oh, did I not say? It must have been the day after Dobree's body was found. Albert recognised him and asked him if he was still interested in the property but the fellow became quite alarmed and took to his heels.'

Chapter Forty

Old Mr Munro soon tired, and Frances was pleased to see him safely taken home by his brother. She hardly had time to think about what she had learned when Ratty arrived and was soon warming himself before the fire.

'Well I found Mr Capper, just the way you thought,' said Ratty. 'Went round askin' all the carriers and carters and found one who remembered takin' 'em to their new 'ome, which was out Camden way. Then I went round all the rug makers in Camden and found 'im. 'E weren't all that 'appy ter be found. I tole 'im I was wantin' ter know what 'e knew about Mr Cullum, and when I said the name 'e went white as a ghost. Took some time ter convince 'im that I weren't workin' for Cullum.'

'If he thought you were working for him then he must think Cullum is still alive,' said Frances.

'I fink 'e knows it,' said Ratty.

'Do you think he would be willing to come and see me and tell me what he knows?'

Ratty shook his head. 'Nah, that I'm sure of. Capper said 'e'd never talk ter a detective or walk inter a police station. I fink 'e's scared that Cullum would get ter know of it. No, these were 'is terms. 'E said 'e would tell me what 'e knew face ter face, but in return I was never ter come near 'im again.'

'And did he tell you?'

''E did, an' very interestin' it was too. Got it all up 'ere,' Ratty tapped the side of his head. His introduction to the arts of reading and writing had been recent and he had developed an excellent memory that served him well.

'Is he related to Jane Capper?'

'Yes, 'e's the brother. An' 'is sister Lottie looked after the Cullum children after the mother died.'

'What did he have to say about Mr Cullum?'

'Never trusted the man and dint want 'is sister to marry 'im. But she were determined, an' 'e couldn't make her change 'er mind.'

'What does he know about the arguments with Mr Salter and the disappearance?'

'Well, accordin' to 'is sister, Cullum got in with a bad lot and wanted to drag Salter inter it as well, ter make money off stolen jewels, but Salter wasn't 'avin' any 'v it. An' then Salter wanted 'im out 'v the business altogether.'

'That was after his illness? Did you find out about that?'

Ratty grinned. 'Cullum were never ill, that were just a story.'

'You mean he was away committing burglaries? I believe Mr Salter suspected as much.'

'Naw, 'e never did that kind 'v stuff, but 'e did take some silver off a man 'e shouldn't 'v crossed. Name 'v David Dunne. When Dunne found out 'e'd been cheated 'e found Cullum an' shot 'im.'

'He was shot?' Frances exclaimed.

'Oh yeah, that Dunne, 'e were a real bad 'un, 'e dint care what 'e did.'

'So Cullum wasn't ill but injured. Where was he shot? Is there a scar?'

'D'no. Any'ow, Capper thinks that Cullum is still around, an' 'e don't mean ter take any risks. Cullum don't ferget wrongs, and 'e don't fergive. 'E don't do the dirty work 'imself, though, 'e gets others ter do it for 'im. Capper thinks Cullum 'ad David Dunne killed. That why 'e's so scared.'

'Dunne was killed about a year after Cullum went missing.'

'Yeah. P'raps it took 'im that long ter find 'im.'

'Does Capper know that Cullum is alive? Has he actually seen Cullum himself or is he just guessing? Is that the reason he moved away?'

''E wun't tell me no more. But I fink there's fings 'e knows an' is not tellin', 'cos 'e knows what c'd 'appen if 'e does.'

Frances decided it was high time she found out more about the death of David Dunne. Early next morning, she paid a visit to the offices of the *Bayswater Chronicle*, where so much of her researches took place. Mr Gillan was just about to leave but delayed his departure to speak to Frances. 'Now you can't deny that you're back doing your detective work,' he said. 'Is there a story in that?'

'Perhaps, but I'd rather you held your fire until there is more to know.'

'You always say that,' he grumbled.

'And don't you get a better story by waiting a while? If there is anything sensational to print, then I promise it will be yours.'

'I suppose I shall have to be happy with that,' he sighed. 'But at least give me a hint of what you're about. It's the murder of Lancelot Dobree, isn't it? Your footprints are all over that one.'

'The reason I am here is to find out more about a man called David Dunne.'

Gillan looked puzzled for a moment. 'Dunne? That was the jewel robber, wasn't it? Nasty piece of work. But that was a good few years ago. Isn't he dead?'

'That is what I'm interested in finding out. There must be reports of his death. It was after the Hayworth Hill Manor robbery in 1857.'

'That was a big case, I remember. Wasn't there a policeman shot and killed? We're bound to have a file on it. Wait there, I'll see what I can find.'

Frances sat down at a desk. All around her were men, and a few women too, bent over their desks, writing and sketching. Some had copies of the daily papers open in front of them and were busy compiling snippets of news into smaller pieces, some were going through correspondence, others were working on columns of advertising. All was happening at a fierce pace, for news faded faster than flowers, soon losing its shine and savour. In a day, it would be old and stale and would have to be cast away and replenished.

Gillan returned with a folder and put it on the desk in front of Frances. 'That's what we have. I need to go out now; just leave this on the desk when you're finished, and I hope to hear more.' He winked and hurried away.

Frances opened the folder and found a selection of cuttings taken from both daily and local newspapers. Although the robbery had taken place in Sussex, it had attracted the attention of the London papers because there had been early rumours of the involvement of a gang operating from a base in Shepherd's Bush. In 1857, three men had broken into Hayworth Hill Manor House and threatened the servants with revolvers before coshing a footman, holding the elderly owners at gunpoint, and stuffing family silver and jewellery into sacks. After leaving the house, the sight of men carrying heavy sacks had attracted the attention of a policeman, who blew his whistle for assistance and, despite having revolvers waved at him, gave chase. Frances could only wonder at how an unarmed constable was expected to tackle three men with revolvers, but that was what this young man had attempted to do, and he was shot to death for his bravery. Although the robbers had worn masks, they were known villains, and the few details of their clothing that the victims were able to describe soon suggested to the police whom the trio might be. Two of the men were arrested, but David Dunne, thought to be the worst of the three, had vanished. None of the stolen silver and jewellery was found apart from a ring that one of the men had given to his sweetheart and was identified as part of the haul. Both eventually confessed, but denied having shot the policeman. That, they said, was the work of Dunne. The court was not impressed by this claim. All three had gone out armed; all three were prepared to use their weapons. Which one of the three had actually done so was not of any moment; they were all equally guilty. Dunne's two associates were, despite loud protests, found guilty of murder and sentenced to hang. They went to their deaths with curses in their throats.

There were reports in the newspapers about police searches for David Dunne, but he continued to elude capture. A year after the robbery, however, he was found stabbed to death in an alleyway beside a beer house of decidedly unsavoury reputation in Notting Hill. Inspector Payne had spoken of a brawl but he had been mistaken. Either that or all those present in the beer house that night had either been looking the other way or suffered a dreadful lapse of memory. No one recalled a fight, or even an altercation. No one remembered Dunne or anyone resembling Dunne being in the beer house. The inquest had been adjourned to find more witnesses, but when it reconvened all they could bring was a child who claimed to have seen Dunne, or someone resembling him, weaving drunkenly out of the beer house in great good humour accompanied by another man. The two had disappeared into the alleyway together. Under further questioning, however, the child became confused about the date on which this incident had taken place and his testimony was discounted. The jury found that David Dunne had been murdered by a person or persons unknown. The newspapers assumed that Dunne had been trying to sell some of his stolen goods in the beer house, and been accompanied to a secret location to complete the transaction only to be killed and robbed. The coroner observed that should the staff and customers of the beer house ever retrieve their memories they might be able to tell a better story.

That was the last cutting in the folder.

CHAPTER FORTY-ONE

Was Cullum still alive, and if so, was he the spider at the centre of the web? More to the point, who was he? All Frances knew was that he was in his sixties, knowledgeable about silver, was left handed, and had an old injury from a shooting. There was more than one reason to find him, since it would remove all suspicion from the Salter family concerning his disappearance, trap a killer and remove a dangerous man from society. Could she do all this? There was a time when Frances felt she could do almost anything. Then came a time when she thought she was of no use at all. That was passing, and she was left with the conclusion that nothing would be achieved without trying.

Frances returned to Kensington with a host of unanswered questions. She took another look at the property at 2 Linfield Gardens, hoping to see it in the way Lancelot Dobree must have done, eyeing the detail as if she was a potential buyer. As she gazed up at the front, with its rotting window frames and crumbling brickwork, the door opened and Mr Johnstone emerged, tucking his walking stick under his arm in order to pull the door shut behind him. It was the right hand, she observed, that both plied the walking stick and closed the door. Frances thought he might see her, but he turned away and walked up Linfield Gardens away from the High Street. She continued her tour around the property, noticing the condition of the back wall, its powdery mortar leaving deep gaps between the bricks, then moving on into the alleyway. All was quiet, with only the occasional passer-by across the end of the alley. The high small windows of the warehouse at the end of the cobbled way afforded no reasonable view; in fact, gazing up at the rear of the tavern premises, she could see that there was only one window which looked directly out across the lodging house yard, the small one on the upper landing of the tavern.

Frances went into the tavern and once again astonished the patrons of the public bar, some of whom had seen her before and started muttering amongst themselves. This time she mounted the back staircase, and at the top of the stairs she stood and looked out of the little window. It was the only possible location from which one might view anything that took place secretly in the yard.

As she stood there she heard a clatter from below and a charwoman with a bucket and mop began wielding a brush on the stairs. Frances waited for her to reach the landing and greeted her.

'I think you're lost, Miss,' said the charlady.

'Oh, I came up here to admire the view,' said Frances.

'Really?' said the woman dubiously, eyeing Frances up and down and concluding that the young lady was probably an eccentric.

'Your window here is so beautifully clean, one can look out and see such a long way. Tell me, does anyone else come up here to look?'

'I wouldn't know, Miss. Oh, there was an old gent up here once. I came up here to do the stairs and he was standing where you are now, just looking out.'

'Do you know his name?'

'No, but he's one of those Masonic gents. You see them here quite a lot.'

Frances showed her the sketch of Lancelot Dobree. 'Was that the man?'

'Could be. Why?'

'Do you know what day you saw him?'

'Oh, I don't remember! No wait, I tell a lie. It was the day before my Susan went into labour. I had to get my sister to come and clean while I took care of the baby. Let me think.' There was a long pause for thought until the charlady came up with the date. It was a week before Lancelot Dobree's death, the last time he had attended a meeting of Mulberry Lodge.

'Did he say why he was looking out?'

She scratched her head. 'Now I think about it he said something about wanting to buy the house over the way.' She peered out of the window and pointed to the yard of 2 Linfield Gardens. 'That one. Then he tried the door to the room, the one where the

Masonic gents meet, only it was locked up, like it always is. I said "You won't get back down that way, you'll have to use the stairs".'

'"Isn't there a key?" he said. I says "Yes there is, but you'll have to ask Mr Neilson about it because he keeps it." And he says "Thank you I will." And I says "You know you've got some rivals. Same time as you gents have your meetings in that there room, there's other gents meeting in the yard across the way." I don't think he liked that idea because he gave me a very funny look.'

'What do the gents in the yard do?'

'Oh I don't know, because they're in the dark.'

'How long have they been meeting there?'

'Only since the old lady moved out.'

And now Frances thought she knew a little more. Because of Dobree's interest in the property he must have inadvertently seen something while viewing its exterior that had led him to believe that the empty house was being used for criminal purposes. How he had connected that with his son-in-law she couldn't say, but it seemed that he had, and in view of Vernon Salter's possible involvement he had decided not to go to the police but check for himself whether or not it was true before making any damaging accusations. This was not, she felt sure, because of any desire to protect his son-in-law from prosecution, or even out of any affection for him, but because he did not want to take any action that would distress his daughter without being absolutely certain of his ground. Not only had he found the only vantage point from which he could spy on the activities in the yard, he had also discovered when those activities occurred.

Frances returned downstairs and located Mr Neilson at his desk. He looked up hopefully. 'I'm sorry to disturb you, but I would like you to cast your mind back to the day of the last meeting of Mulberry Lodge which Mr Dobree attended.'

'I'll do my best.'

'Did he by any chance ask to borrow the Lodge room keys?'

'No, I would have remembered something like that and told you.'

'He didn't ask you where you kept the keys?'

'No. We did have a conversation, but it never touched on that subject.'

'What was the subject?'

'Improvements to the Lodge. More comfortable seating for our elderly brethren. He offered to make a donation.'

'Where and when did that conversation take place?'

'Here. Before the Lodge meeting.'

'Did anyone come into the office while you were speaking?'

'Possibly. I don't exactly recall.'

Frances knew better than to prod him for memories. In any case, she thought she had the answer.

CHAPTER FORTY-TWO

In the midst of all this uncertainty Frances was pleased to find some activity that assisted her thought. That afternoon she went to Professor Pounder's academy to take part in the class taught by Miss Harrison. Her instructor was small, lean and dark with sharp little eyes and shoulders that never tired. She almost never spoke during the classes. She strode out to face the group of ladies, holding her clubs, then, with one clasped in each hand she would take a breath, stare straight ahead as if fixing her gaze so far distant it appeared to reach India, and raise her arms to begin the exercises, which the class members were expected to imitate. They began slowly, raising, lowering, swinging, rotating, small movements which gradually progressed, becoming larger until all the class swung their clubs like the turning of great wheels.

It was, as had been explained to Frances when she first began, an activity that could be practised by all, wooden clubs of various sizes and weights for ladies, and larger heavier ones for men. The rhythm helped calm the mind, the exercises promoted flexibility of wrists, elbows and shoulders, and expanded the chest, strengthening the action of the lungs. Ladies were usually advised to wear a loose chemise with light or even no lacing, to gain the best advantage. The first few classes Frances had attended she had found the movements harder to do than they looked and was grateful to be allowed to start slowly as a beginner as she had more than once struck herself on the ear. With practice, she gained in confidence, and the exercise became more natural and instinctive. At home there was room for some of the smaller, gentler swings. Frances was too sensible to carry the clubs about openly, and had sewn a deep pocket inside her cloak where they could easily be concealed.

Following her conversation with the charlady at the tavern, Frances swung the clubs and allowed her mind to explore what she had learned. It seemed very probable that Lancelot Dobree, when visiting the tavern for a meeting of Mulberry Lodge, had taken the opportunity to look over the outside of the building he wished to purchase. It was possible that when doing so, something had come to his attention that suggested the yard was being used as a meeting place by a criminal gang. Frances recalled that when she had stood in the alleyway outside the yard gate she had been able to view the upper window of the tavern, the only place from which the yard could be overlooked. Anyone, customer or staff, could have had access to that window. Had Dobree seen someone there? Perhaps a member of the gang acting as lookout? Was that why he had mounted the back stairs to check the view for himself? In doing so he had learned that meetings of criminals took place at the same time as those of the Lodge.

Dobree ought to have taken his suspicions to the police, but he did not, he decided to make his own enquiries, and for some reason Frances still could not understand, Dobree suspected his own son-in-law of colluding with the gang. Perhaps he thought Vernon Salter was the man at the window, using his visits to the Lodge to conceal a darker purpose, although it was unlikely that a distant view through thick glass would have been clear enough to positively identify him.

Dobree, she thought, was most probably the man who had hired Mr Green to follow his son-in-law, but he had not confided his real suspicions to family or friends, with the sole exception of his solicitor Henry Marsden. The more Frances thought about it the stranger this seemed. Why would Dobree tell Marsden and not a close friend? Marsden had claimed that Dobree had told him only that he had unsettling concerns about Vernon Salter, but his client had not gone on to engage him to look into them.

Frances was finding Marsden's story increasingly unconvincing. What was he omitting? She was reminded of what Wheelock had revealed. Marsden had good reason to resent the man who had married the fortune he had had his eye on. He had designed the marriage contract hoping it would put an end to the marriage plans, but had succeeded only in preventing Vernon Salter having access to the Dobree fortune. Would the solicitor lose any chance at the inquest of getting his final revenge? Frances didn't think so.

If he had information that could destroy Vernon Salter, he might have kept silent at the behest of his client, but after Dobree's death there was no restraint. He would have told all. Marsden's incomplete account at the inquest didn't make any sense.

Dobree, she recalled, had only started to display unsettled behaviour after the last time he saw Marsden, two weeks before his death. A week later he had been seen spying on the yard from the upper window of the tavern. She could imagine Dobree becoming suspicious, watching the house for unusual goings on, and afterwards confiding in Marsden, but when he had looked out over the yard, he hadn't seen Marsden for a week, and didn't see him again before his death. Somehow events just seemed to be the wrong way around.

When realisation came, Frances almost lost her rhythm and it was only by good fortune that she didn't strike herself on the back of the head. She would never be able to prove it, but all was explicable if Marsden had lied to the inquest and Dobree had never told his solicitor that he suspected his son-in-law. It had been the other way about. Supposing Marsden had commented to Dobree about the number of jewel robberies that had taken place in the Kensington area recently and hinted that Vernon might, given the doubts about his family background, have been involved? Dobree had followed up the suspicions planted in his mind by Marsden, and stumbled across something that had led to his death.

Perhaps Marsden had assumed that Dobree would simply employ someone to keep a watch on his son-in-law and not take any personal action. In doing so he had misjudged his client's devotion to his daughter, which had led him to keep his worst suspicions to himself, and undertake his own enquiries. Frances was so angry that she could barely concentrate, and it was lucky that the class was almost at an end.

It was dark as she left the academy, and she hailed a cab. Despite the expenditure of energy, she felt stronger, and not at all weary, and had to quell a wholly unwise temptation to visit Mr Marsden with her Indian clubs and explain to him the error of his ways. As soon as she reached home, she would sit down and commit all her thoughts to paper.

The street was deserted as she stepped down from the cab, but as she headed towards her front door, key in hand, she heard a slight movement behind her, the faint scrape of a boot on the path, and turned to see a tall figure who must have been concealed behind a hedge. To her astonishment the man who stood before her was none other than Harry Abbott, the young man from the desk of the Portobello Hotel, who had been missing, thought dead, for several days. The light of the nearby gas lamp illuminated his face. He was dishevelled, wild-eyed and panting, his arms folded tightly across his body. One side of his face and jaw were badly bruised, his lips cut and crusted in dried blood, the nose swollen into an ugly, shapeless protuberance.

'Mr Abbott!' she exclaimed. 'Whatever has happened to you? Do you need help?'

He uttered a wrenching sob. 'It wasn't my idea! But I've got to do it.'

She was about to ask him what it was he had to do, when he unfolded his arms and she saw that he held a hammer in his right hand.

Even if she could have outrun him there was nowhere to go. She was trapped in the area in front of the house, surrounded by a wall, hedges and the gate. She could not get past him into the street, and there was no time to get indoors. To turn her back would have been fatal, and a shout for help would be useless and far too late. She tried to remain calm. 'You don't have to do this,' she said, as evenly as possible. 'I can see you are hurt. Why don't you put down the hammer, come inside and have your injuries tended?'

He shook his head. 'No, no choice,' he lamented.

'Of course you have a choice. I don't know what has driven you to this, but if you can't tell me, and won't let me help you, then go now, go home, and I promise that I will say nothing about it.'

He gulped. 'You'll say nothing, Miss Doughty. That's the whole idea.' He took a deep breath, raised the hammer and ran at her.

There had been enough time as they spoke for Frances, under the cover of her cloak, to slip a club from her pocket, and now she swung it at him as hard as she could. There was a loud crack like the sound of willow on leather as the wood contacted Harry

Abbott's head. His knees buckled, but Frances never even saw him slump to the ground. She turned and ran up the front steps, and with trembling fingers that could barely hold the key unlocked the front door and almost fell into the hallway, pushing the door shut behind her with immense relief. Her detective work had put her in danger before, and on those occasions she had been unable to save herself, relying on the stout arms of Sarah or the commanding speed of Mr W. Grove, but this was the first time she had faced death alone. She hurried up the stairs, and to her surprise saw Sarah and Inspector Payne coming down to meet her.

'We heard something,' said Sarah.

'And there's a man lying on your front path,' added Payne, as if this was an eventuality he found unsurprising.

'It's Mr Abbott,' said Frances. 'Harry Abbott, the missing man. He accosted me just now and tried to kill me.'

'Are you hurt?' demanded Sarah.

'No, I don't think so. He had a hammer, he tried to hit me with it, he said that it was something he had to do. I had the clubs with me, so I struck him.'

Mrs Embleton appeared from her apartment below stairs. 'Is there something the matter?' she asked, peering up at them nervously.

'No need to worry yourself,' said Payne. 'There was a disturbance in the street. I am an Inspector of police and I will deal with it. You just go back downstairs, now.'

The landlady hesitated and then with a doubtful glance at Frances reluctantly retired.

'Miss Smith, you take Miss Doughty up to your rooms and I'll see what's what.'

Sarah nodded. She took Frances by the elbow, removed the club from her hands – until then Frances hadn't even realised that she was still holding it – and accompanied her up the stairs. The parlour was cosy and comforting in the soft firelight, and Sarah, with a gentle firmness, guided Frances to an armchair and fetched a glass of brandy.

Frances hardly tasted it as it went down. 'I hit him,' she said, 'with the club. I don't know how much he is hurt. But he was already bruised about the face. I think someone beat him and made him try to kill me.'

'I always knew the exercises would come in useful,' said Sarah, as a blast from a police whistle sounded outside. She looked at the end of the club and frowned. 'Well, you did the right thing. Do you want another brandy?'

'No, I think the Inspector will want to question me and I need a clear head. Did you hear what happened?'

'No voices, just a bang.' Sarah drew the curtains and peered out of the window.

'What can you see?'

'I think the man's still down, Inspector Payne's looking him over.'

'I know it sounds strange but I really hope I didn't hurt him too much. He looked so desperate.'

'Constables are running up, now,' said Sarah. 'Payne's giving orders. I expect they'll wheel Abbott off in an ambulance.' There was a long pause as she continued to look.

'What have you seen?' asked Frances.

'Just more police coming up. Payne will let us know what's going on soon enough.'

Frances felt strangely calm, which was worrying as she thought it might presage a breakdown, but as each moment passed she thought she might come through it. 'It's very peculiar,' she said, 'but I didn't feel afraid. I suppose I didn't have time to think, I just did what I had to. It was he who was afraid. I thought I could calm him by talking, and I did try, but he didn't think he had a choice.'

'Best not to think about it,' said Sarah.

'Why was the Inspector here?' asked Frances.

'More questions. He didn't say what about.'

It was some while before Inspector Payne knocked on the door and was shown up. He fixed Frances with a heavy stare, then sat down and took out his notebook. 'Now then, before we go any further I want you to repeat what you said to me earlier.'

'Yes, well, Mr Abbott approached me from behind, I think he had been hiding behind the hedges just in front of the house, waiting for me. I heard a noise and turned around and he was in a very agitated state and said he was going to do something and then I saw he had a hammer.'

'Which hand was the hammer in?'

Frances thought for a moment. 'His right hand. I tried to calm him down, but he raised the hammer and came forward to hit me with it. But I had the Indian clubs with me and hit him with one. I must have knocked him unconscious. I hope he isn't hurt too badly. But he was afraid; he had been beaten. Someone made him do it. Ask him, he'll tell you.'

'I'm not asking him anything – no one will. He's dead, Miss Doughty. You killed him.'

It was a few moments before the words had any meaning. 'No ... are you sure?'

Sarah came up and squeezed Frances' shoulder, and feeling that steadying pressure she realised the reason for her companion's recent silence as she gazed out on the scene; she must have seen the body being removed.

'No doubt about it,' said Payne.

'Well, I am very sorry to know that,' said Frances. 'But if I had not defended myself, I would be dead. I did try to persuade him not to attack me.'

Payne leaned back and folded his arms. 'Do you know why I was out there so long?'

'Doing what was necessary I suppose.'

'I was looking for that hammer you said he had. Because there wasn't a hammer in his hand or on the ground. I got three constables shining their lanterns about, but there's nothing to be seen. No water troughs, no drains nearby, nowhere it could have gone. There was no hammer. So it's beginning to look as if you made it up. Which means that you attacked an unarmed man with your club, a weapon which you have been training to use for some while, striking him a violent blow on the forehead which stove in his skull and killed him on the spot.' Payne shook his head. 'If it was up to me I'd ban those classes and ban women carrying clubs about the street.'

'Well it isn't up to you,' said Sarah, rather more sharply than was advisable in addressing an officer of the law. 'There's men out there think it's a sport to beat women with their fists. If we can save our own lives with clubs and sticks then that's what we need to be prepared to do.'

'Only that wasn't what Miss Doughty did, was it?' Payne rose to his feet and addressed Frances. 'Miss Doughty, it is my duty to take you into custody on suspicion of murdering Harry Abbott. Please accompany me to Paddington Green station, where I shall hand you over to the officers there with the advice that you should be formally charged.'

CHAPTER FORTY-THREE

Frances knew better than to argue. The calm of quiet resignation settled on her, and she put a restraining hand on Sarah's arm. 'Sarah, I am content to go. I am sure that when daylight comes the hammer will be found and then I will be released. In the meantime, could you advise Mr Bramley of what has happened.'

Payne seized the club and looked at the head which, Frances now saw, was smeared with blood and hair. 'Evidence,' he said, tucking it under his arm. 'So, are you coming quietly or do I have to cuff you?'

'I have no intention of making a fuss,' said Frances.

'Where's the other one? I know there's two.'

Frances took the second club from her pocket and handed it over. He stared at it as if expecting to find evidence of a previous killing, but was disappointed.

'Any more weapons about? Knives in your pockets? Guns in your bag?'

She shook her head.

'Miss Smith, I would be obliged if you could open Miss Doughty's cloak and demonstrate that there is nothing hidden underneath.'

Frances nodded assent and with considerable ill will Sarah complied.

Payne nodded. 'There's a cab waiting.'

As Frances left she noticed with very little surprise that a constable had been posted outside her door to ensure that she did not make a dash for freedom. Abbott's body had already been removed. While she had no great wish to see it, had he still lain there it would have helped her to understand what had just happened. As it was, it was hard for her to believe he was actually dead. She, Payne and the constable climbed aboard the cab, which drew away smartly.

'Inspector, why did you come to see me this evening?'

'No questions! In fact, don't even speak!'

Frances had a whole battery of questions, about Harry Abbott, about David Dunne, about George Cullum, about Riley, and she also wanted to tell him her conclusions concerning Lancelot Dobree and Mr Marsden, but she remained silent.

At Paddington Green she was delivered to the desk where the astonished sergeant booked her in and handed her over to a constable who conducted her to a cell. Frances had visited clients here before, but this was the first time she had herself been a prisoner. She wrapped her cloak closely about her and sat on the wooden bench. A single rough blanket folded at one end held little promise of warmth, but she draped it over herself, trying not to inhale its wet wool aroma. The air was chill and the stone walls slick with damp. A tattered modesty curtain almost managed to hide a convenience in one corner, its odour mingling with the general nauseous taint of the cells.

Heavy feet trudged slowly along the corridor and stopped outside. Frances looked up and saw Inspector Sharrock leaning against the bars with an expression of deep sadness. 'Oh dear me, Miss Doughty, what have you done now?'

'I'm afraid it's a misunderstanding,' she said.

He grunted. 'I can't free you this time. But I'll do whatever I can.' He sighed and walked away.

After the initial shock of her arrest was over, Frances found herself praying for the soul of the man she had inadvertently killed, hoping he would find peace and a better purpose in the afterlife. Even as she turned over the events in her mind, assuring herself that there was nothing else she could have done, she felt inescapably guilty, horrified that a man had died at her hands.

Frances' next feeling was one of frustration. She had no doubt that she would eventually be cleared of suspicion and released, but it was annoying to be trapped in a cell when she needed to be taking action. Her only means of continuing her work was through her agents and as a spirit of determination set in she decided to do just that. Her enforced incarceration would not mean enforced idleness. She could still think.

❧

Her first visitor was Sarah, who brought the solicitor, Mr Bramley, to her cell, together with a welcome basket of food, a quilt, a pillow and a fresh notebook and pencil. 'Not that you'll be here long,' said Sarah defiantly, with a meaningful look at the solicitor as if to say that she expected prompt and effective action.

'Have they questioned you yet?' asked Bramley, who looked increasingly regretful that he had agreed to act for Frances each time they met.

'No, I expect they are waiting for the light to make a better search.'

'I tried looking around,' said Sarah, 'but the police are not letting anyone else near the front of the house. In any case, if I was to find the hammer they'd only think I put one there to save you. Mrs Embleton is in a state, but she's sure you weren't to blame. The police are going to all the neighbours asking if anyone saw what happened, but I don't think anyone did.'

'In your own words,' said Mr Bramley, 'can you describe the incident?'

Frances did her best and he made careful notes.

'And you are quite certain beyond any shadow of a doubt that he had a weapon in his hand?'

'Yes, I am.'

'A hammer, you say?'

'Yes.'

'Can you describe it?'

'Just a plain hammer, I believe. There was enough light to see the shine of the metal.'

'And once you struck him and he collapsed you didn't see what happened to it?'

'No.'

'Did you hear it strike the ground?'

'No I didn't.'

'Miss Smith? Did you hear it?'

Sarah shook her head. 'I wish I had. Just the bang as the club hit his head.'

'Perhaps,' Frances ventured, 'he didn't drop it on the ground, but it fell against his body, or went into the hedge.'

'Perhaps,' said Bramley, 'but Inspector Payne was on the scene hardly a minute or so later and found nothing.'

'Then it must have flown off into some mud or rubbish,' said Sarah. 'It'll turn up.'

'I sincerely hope so,' said Bramley.

Frances' next visitors were Tom and Ratty. How Tom had persuaded Ratty to voluntarily enter a police station she couldn't be sure, as he only did so under extreme circumstances. Perhaps, she thought miserably, this was an extreme circumstance. They brought a bag of apples, but then proceeded to eat most of them themselves. She had been trying to think how the hammer had gone missing, and asked the boys to make a thorough search of the area outside her house and on either side, once the police had left.

'We got other news for you,' said Tom. 'Found out the man 'oo 'as bin meetin' wiv Mr Green. Saw 'im goin' in and knew 'im at once. Can't mistake them whiskers.'

'Oh?'

'Yes, it were your friend Mr Miggs, what writes poems about flowers and that, creepin' in an' lookin' about 'opin' not ter be seen.'

Ratty chuckled at the thought.

Frances helped herself to the last apple before it disappeared. 'I had imagined that it was Mr Dobree who had initially engaged Mr Green and then, after the murder, some agent of his continued the work on his behalf, but I understand it now. It looks like Mr Dobree didn't after all employ a man to work for him and really did decide to investigate entirely on his own. As for Mr Miggs, he was very annoyed when Mr Salter was freed of suspicion and must have hired Mr Green to find out something to his detriment. In doing so he discovered that Mr Salter had a perfect and genuine alibi for his father-in-law's murder, but assumed that he was visiting a mistress. What a nasty vindictive man.' She bit into the apple hard.

'There's more,' said Tom. 'We follered Mr Miggs when 'e come out, 'an 'e 'ad a very nice meetin' wiv Mrs Cholmondeleyson, the rich lady what doesn't want wimmin ter 'ave the vote.'

'I fink Mrs Chummyson likes 'is poems,' said Ratty. 'I read one once.' He shrugged. 'It was all right.'

'I fink she likes Mr Miggs,' added Tom with a significant wink. 'She brought 'er carriage round to 'is place, and the two of 'em gets in an' off they go very cosy together. They was out fer two 'ours. As far as we c'd find out they were jus' ridin' about, 'n dint stop off anywhere. But 'oo knows what went on?' He wiggled his eyebrows suggestively.

'I dread to think,' said Frances, who, despite her lack of experience in these matters, could well understand the attraction that might arise between a rich elderly lady and a young but poor gentleman. If nothing else, Mrs Cholmondeleyson would enjoy bathing in the glow of her literary connection but more worryingly, she was easily able to provide funds to allow Mr Miggs to pursue his obsessions. 'Well, you must keep watch on them both. Have you had any luck identifying the man who cuts ladies dresses?'

'Not yet, we come on the scene once, soon arterwards, but 'e'd run off. Fast on 'is feet, that one.'

'And have you found Mrs Maxwell's cat?'

Tom hesitated. 'Well, yes and no.'

'Ah.'

'That is, we found most of it.'

'Oh dear.'

'Jus' the fur,' said Ratty. 'It's very nice fur. Does she want it back?'

''Cos we know someone who stuffs animals,' said Tom.

'Or it would make a nice collar,' added Ratty.

'Tell Sarah to speak to her,' said Frances, sadly.

A constable peered into her cell. 'You two can go now,' he said, firmly but not unkindly. Tom and Ratty needed no further bidding, and as soon as the door was opened they jumped up and hurried away. 'And you Miss, I'm to take you to be questioned.'

'By Inspector Sharrock?' she asked hopefully.

'Oh no Miss, you'll be meeting the big man, Superintendent Barnes.'

CHAPTER FORTY-FOUR

Frances, wondering how her situation could possibly be worse, was taken to an interview room. She was somewhat comforted to see Mr Bramley, and thanked him for being there to support her. Sharrock was also present, but it was clear that he was only to observe the proceedings. The officer behind the desk was a tall individual of almost giant-like bulk, with a red face and very white hair. Superintendent Barnes looked like a man who could appear wonderfully jovial when it was called for, but this was not one of those occasions. He had bright blue eyes that he used to his advantage, enabling him to look at a prisoner very searchingly, suggesting he already knew all that there was to know, so there was no point in trying to hide anything.

'Miss Doughty,' said Barnes, examining the papers in a folder, 'you are the daughter of William and Rosetta Doughty, born in September 1860?'

'Yes.'

'And until the death of your father you assisted him in the chemists shop on Westbourne Grove?'

'I did.'

'After his death you moved to lodgings in Westbourne Park Road, together with your maid, Miss Smith, and commenced to offer your services as a detective?'

'Miss Smith was once my maid; she is now my assistant.'

'But you have undertaken work as a detective for two years now?'

'I have, yes.'

Barnes turned through the papers in the file. 'With some success, it appears.'

'I like to think so.'

'A few months ago, however, you decided to give up that occupation. Why was that?'

'I thought it was too dangerous. I was shaken by a number of tragic events. But I do carry out enquiries where no crime is involved. Missing pets, for example.'

'And missing men?' he said pointedly.

'I had thought when I was approached by Mr Fiske that Mr Dobree's disappearance had an innocent explanation.'

'Following the discovery of Mr Dobree's body, and the finding that he had been murdered, that should have meant an end to your enquiries, but it seems it did not.' He fixed her with an icy stare. 'Why was that?'

'When Mr Salter was exonerated of suspicion regarding the murder of his father-in-law the family feared that his reputation had been tainted and I was asked to make enquiries to assist in clearing his name.'

'Did that include making a search of the house where the body was found?'

'I wanted to search but I was not permitted to do so.'

'Instead you asked your agents to search for you with the excuse that they were looking for a missing cat.'

'My client Mrs Maxwell will confirm that she engaged me to find her cat.'

'Was there any reason to suppose that the cat was in 2 Linfield Gardens?'

'It could have been anywhere. I should mention that my agents were under strict instructions to harm no property in their searches and to take nothing, instructions with which they complied. As it so happened their actions uncovered valuable evidence the Kensington police had missed. If Mr Dobree's murderer is found they might be entitled to a reward.'

Sharrock made considerable efforts to keep a straight face and almost succeeded.

'You were present when Inspector Payne examined the items found, which included an emerald ring, and this you somehow traced to the Portobello Hotel.'

'Yes.'

'Where you spoke to Mr Harry Abbott. How well did you know Mr Abbott?'

'That was my first meeting with him. We spoke for only a minute. I wanted to know about a guest of the hotel. He refused to help me.'

'Did that make you angry with him?'

'No, I rather expected that response.'

'But you must have been annoyed that he wouldn't help you?'

'I understand what you are implying, but that is quite a common occurrence in my line of work. As it must be in yours.'

'When did you next encounter Mr Abbott?'

'When he followed me to my door and attacked me.'

'Were you expecting to see him?'

'No. It was a shock. I had heard he was missing. I thought he needed help, he was bruised and agitated, but then he attacked me with a hammer. He intended to kill me.'

'A hammer.'

'Yes. Have you found it?'

'No, Miss Doughty, we have not. The whole street has been searched, the drains, the bushes, every nook and cranny where this – hammer – might have ended up. But there is no sign of it. None at all.'

'He had one. He raised it to strike me.'

'Are you sure of that? It was dark.'

'I saw it in the light of the gas lamp.'

'Did you?'

'Yes. I am certain of it.'

Barnes looked wary and closed the file, pushing it away.

'The thing is, Miss Doughty, you have taken a very close interest in the Dobree case right from the start. Inspector Payne has established that despite your insistence that you never met Mr Dobree or, before recent events, any member of his family, you are aware that Mr Vernon Salter is maintaining your mother in an apartment in Brighton. We have further established that the separation agreement between Mr William Doughty and his wife named Mr Vernon Salter as the other man in the case.'

Frances could say nothing and she dared not glance at Inspector Sharrock, however it dawned upon her that if the police knew about the terms of the Doughty separation there was only one source for that information, Mr Rawsthorne, her former solicitor.

He probably suspected that she had been instrumental in his downfall and would not be thinking of her kindly.

'Moreover,' the Superintendent continued, 'it included some information that William Doughty only confided to his family and most trusted friends, his suspicion that Mr Vernon Salter is your natural father.'

Frances heard Sharrock gasp.

'So Mr Salter is far more than a client to you, and you have strong reasons to protect both him and your mother from scandal. It all comes down to the emerald ring. I suspect that Mr Abbott was blackmailing the family who do not want it revealed that Mr Dobree was in the habit of consorting with an actress at a disreputable hotel.'

'I can see that you might suspect that Mr Dobree was the man who purchased the ring, as did I at first, but I have established that it was quite another man.'

'Indeed? And his name?'

'He did not give me his name. But I was introduced to him by Miss Lorna Lee.'

'Ah. So you accepted the word of an actress – a woman of no character. Others may not. And would this man be willing to come forward and repeat his story to a court?'

Frances sighed. 'I doubt it.'

Superintendent Barnes leaned back in his chair and cleared his throat. 'Miss Frances Doughty, I am formally charging you with the murder of Mr Harry Abbott. You are warned that you must say nothing that might criminate you. I will now proceed to take a written statement, after which you will be returned to your cell to await transfer to the cells at Marylebone Police Court, where proceedings will be taken to commit you to take your trial at the Central Criminal Court.'

For a moment the words seemed to pass her by, as if they were just sounds with no meaning. She was brought back to reality by Mr Bramley's hand on her arm. 'I think my client would like a moment to rest, and perhaps if a glass of water could be provided?'

'Of course,' said Barnes. He gathered his papers and rose to his feet. 'Inspector Sharrock, I will leave the rest of the arrangements to you.'

CHAPTER FORTY-FIVE

When Barnes had left the room, Frances sat quite still for a while, until she was shocked back to reality by Inspector Sharrock bringing her a glass of water. The glass rattled against her teeth as she drank. He sat beside her sympathetically for a moment.

She blotted her lips with a handkerchief. 'What will happen now?'

'Constable Stuckey will write down your statement and when you've signed it we'll get you back to your cell. Take as long as you like over it, you can have rests from time to time if you want them.'

'I need to send a message to Sarah.'

'I can arrange for that,' said Bramley.

'When will I be taken to Marylebone?'

'Tomorrow morning.'

Frances had no idea what the prisoner accommodation was like at Marylebone Police Court, or how many visitors she would be permitted there. At Paddington, she knew she would be allowed the maximum privileges in Sharrock's power, and probably more. She had to clear her head and think fast.

'There was a hammer,' she insisted. 'I didn't imagine it. Ask the constables to look again. Either that or —' she wondered suddenly if Inspector Payne, who seemed to have focussed his entire distrust of the female sex onto her, had deliberately removed it. Was he capable of such a dreadful act? 'Would you be so good as to speak to Inspector Payne? He was the first to find the body. There must be some little thing he can recall. Is it possible he picked up the hammer and – in the heat of the moment – has forgotten about it?'

Sharrock grunted. 'I think I know what you're implying. I'll have a word. But I think you're wrong. He's a miserable character, but not wicked.'

By the time Frances had completed her statement, Sarah had returned, together with Cedric Garton, who Frances knew from experience could change from languid aesthete to man of action in an instant if required.

'The police have been all over the street, or at least everywhere a hammer could have been dropped or thrown,' said Sarah. 'Nothing's come up.'

'I've been talking to the neighbours,' added Cedric, 'and there is no one who saw the attack on you. Not surprising if it was just in front of the door and behind a hedge. The people on either side couldn't have seen it. I have spoken to the people opposite who looked out of their bedroom windows when they heard police whistles, but all they saw was Payne standing over the body and the constables running up.'

'It seems to me,' said Frances, 'from the way that I have been questioned, that Superintendent Barnes has made up his mind that there never was a hammer at all.'

'We'll carry on the work,' Sarah reassured her. 'It must be somewhere.'

'If it isn't still in the street then it was taken away,' said Frances. 'Inspector Payne took it, or one of his men. Or someone found it next morning.'

Sarah nodded. 'And if someone just picked it up they might not have known it was important. It might have been someone passing by and not a neighbour. We could put a notice in the papers, ask them to hand it in, no questions asked.'

'Don't you worry,' said Cedric. 'If it's in London, we will find it!'

Leaving some comforting little gifts behind, they had scarcely departed when Vernon Salter arrived. Sharrock, without commenting, showed him to Frances' cell, but she could see him glancing back and forth, comparing the appearance of the two.

Salter perched beside Frances on the bench. He was heavy eyed and spoke with an effort. 'You look well.'

'Thank you, I am. There is a solution to this, I am sure of it.'

'Is there anything I can do to help you, anything at all?'

'I don't think so. Only – please make sure mother doesn't hear of this.'

'I shall protect her, of course. I assume this is all a terrible mistake? Miss Smith told me you had actually been charged with murder. I can't believe you would kill someone!'

'I am responsible for a man's death,' said Frances, the words sounding strange as she spoke them, 'and of course I regret it very much, but he was trying to kill me. If I had not struck him I would have died.'

'The police must be made to understand that!'

'That will be hard unless they find the weapon he used to attack me. At least this will take their attention away from you for a while. But I have learned something of interest very recently. Your father-in-law was seen standing outside the back door of the Lodge room before the last meeting of Mulberry Lodge he attended – I assume he must have climbed up the back stairs – and he was looking out of the little window there. It gives a view of the alleyway and also the yard of the lodging house. There was some kind of criminal activity going on in that house. A convenient place to hide and distribute stolen goods – perhaps the proceeds of the recent burglaries in the area. But did you ever notice any sign that your father-in-law suspected you of involvement in those activities? Have you ever climbed the back stairs of the tavern and looked out of the window?'

Vernon looked mystified. 'I suppose I knew those stairs existed, but I have never had any occasion to go up them. I always used the main stairs to go to the Lodge room, as we all did. The only time I ever went along the corridor leading to the stairs was to visit the gentleman's convenience.' He paused as an idea occurred to him. 'I do recall something. There was one time – it couldn't have been long before Lancelot died – I was at the tavern for a meeting of the Mulberry Lodge, probably the same one you are referring to, and perhaps spent a little longer than was usual in that room.' He rubbed his stomach reflectively. 'When I returned to the lounge bar Lancelot had just arrived and he looked at me very strangely, but said nothing.'

'Did you not travel to the tavern together?'

'We did, but he took a walk around outside first. He wanted to look at some properties. I would have gone with him but for a touch of inner discomfort.'

'Might he have suspected that you had gone to look out of the window – perhaps used it to signal to an accomplice outside?'

'It was not a pleasant look he gave me, that much I can say. I put it down to dyspepsia at the time. I offered him a lozenge but he wouldn't take it.'

'If he was outside the tavern he might have seen someone at the back window, and suspected it was you. Which leads to the question – if it wasn't you, then who was it? The stairs were not restricted to employees. Anyone who used the corridor could have known about them.'

Frances recalled her conversation with the charlady and the subsequent one with Mr Neilson. Events had driven those thoughts from her mind, but they had just resurfaced. 'There is something you could do for me. The Director of Ceremonies for Mulberry Lodge —'

'Mr Pollard, yes.'

'When you arrived for the last meeting was he already there? Had he already checked the Lodge room?'

'I don't think so. We arrived early because Lancelot wanted to look over some properties first. Then he had some business to discuss with Mr Neilson.'

'Ask Mr Pollard if he remembers that meeting. When he went to get the key to the Lodge room from the office, was Mr Dobree there?'

'Very well, I will ask him. Is the subject of their conversation important?'

'No. But I had assumed that your father-in-law didn't know where the key to the Lodge was concealed. He knew it was kept in the office, but he didn't know its new hiding place, and he didn't want to attract suspicion by asking directly, but he did know that Mr Pollard would come and get it to check that all was in order before the meeting. All he had to do was engage Mr Neilson in conversation and wait for Mr Pollard to arrive. Then he would see where it was kept.'

'How astute! I will go and ask Pollard about it at once!' Salter, looking more energised now that he could make himself useful, rose to his feet. He paused, facing her and she could see that his lips were trembling with emotion. 'I promise I will do everything in my power to help you.'

It was in that moment that Frances at last recognised something of him in her own character; a natural sympathy, an earnest desire to do good. There was an awkward pause, then he asked permission to take her hand and she agreed. He begged to be allowed to embrace her as a father, and she agreed to that, too. She rose, and for a few seconds he held her in his arms in a way that William Doughty never had, very gently, very lightly, then he drew back a little, and pressed his fingertips to her cheek. She could see that he was afraid for her, afraid that this was not only the first time but also the last that he might be able to do so.

Frances was left to herself. Sharrock arrived for a brief visit and told her that she would be taken to Marylebone at ten the next morning for the preliminary hearing. Mr Bramley was going to try and obtain an adjournment on the grounds that there was additional evidence to be gathered. It was a depressing prospect but there was nothing Frances could do. A plate of bread and dripping and some hot tea were brought, and this was very comforting. She wrapped herself in the blanket and the quilt that Sarah had provided, and was able to imagine that she was quite warm. Lying on the hard bench she dared not even try to sleep, she needed every moment of time to try to piece together the train of events.

Lancelot Dobree had been led to believe by the vengeful Marsden that his son-in-law was involved in the local robberies. Not wanting to alert the police or reveal his concerns to anyone else without proof, Dobree had decided to look into it himself. While looking around the exterior of the lodging house he had seen something that struck him as suspicious. Someone had stood at the tavern window, acting as lookout or signalling to an associate. Vernon Salter's sojourn in the gentleman's convenience had led Dobree to the conclusion that it was his son-in-law at the window. He had confirmed the view himself by ascending the back stairs and looking out. His conversation with the charlady had revealed that secret gatherings were taking place in the yard of the empty house at the same time as Lodge meetings.

But why, Frances wondered, was this activity taking place only during the Lodge meetings? What was special about those times? What was preventing the criminals from simply meeting in the house after dark? That was an important question that would need further thought. But it did mean that if Dobree wanted to find out about what was happening in the lodging house he would have to keep watch at the time when the Lodges met.

Regarding his own Lodge, the Mulberry, Dobree could hardly risk being seen about the tavern and then fail to go to the meeting. That didn't apply to the Literati; however, it so happened that the next meeting of the Literati was one to which he was invited as a guest. Then he realised his chance, because the ceremony to which he had been invited was a raising. At a raising he could, at a time when anyone would have thought he was secure in the Lodge room, slip out unnoticed under cover of darkness to look out of the window, but it must be done without noise. Few keys are noiseless, but he could overcome that difficulty by making sure that the door was unlocked before the meeting began.

To do so he needed the key to the back door of the Lodge room. The keys had once hung on a board on the office wall, but no longer. Not wanting to ask, he had taken steps to find out where the key was kept. When Pollard came to get the key to the front door of the Lodge room Dobree would have seen him take it from the box.

On the day of the Literati meeting, Dobree must have waited until Mr Chappell had checked that the Lodge room was secure. He then took the back door key, slipped upstairs, unlocked the back door and returned to the lounge bar. His absence must have been assumed to be occasioned by a visit to the gentleman's convenience. Only Dobree would have known the back door was unlocked. Then, in the dark, he would have been able to slip out without making a sound.

But, thought Frances, there was no reason for him to relock the door behind him after making his exit. Far from it, as to do so would have risked making a noise, and he was probably intending to return as soon as he had looked out of the window. From his point of view the best time to relock the door and put the key back was just after the meeting, but by then he had already vanished. When and by whom the door had been relocked and the key returned to its proper place was another puzzle.

What had Dobree seen when he looked out of the window? Transactions in stolen goods? A meeting of a criminal gang?

Whatever it was, he might well have decided to go downstairs and investigate, and this had led to his death. Had the door to the alley been open or shut? And if open, who had opened it?

Frances wondered if the mysterious Cullum had been present, but doubted it. Cullum, she had been told, was a man who paid others to do his nefarious work for him. Dobree, interrupting the thieves, had met his death probably in the alley and his body carried quickly into the yard. But why had this been done? Why had he not simply been left in the alley to be found, appearing to have been killed by a street robber?

Frances had some of the answers but was missing something vital that would tie all the facts together.

CHAPTER FORTY-SIX

She slept little that night. Her mind would not allow her to rest, going over all she knew repeatedly and without respite. A glimmer of inspiration did appear, and then, finally, she sank into an exhausted sleep. She awoke with Sarah shaking her by the shoulder.

'What time is it?'

'Seven.'

'They're taking me to Marylebone at ten.'

'I hope not.'

'Did you find the hammer?'

'No, but we found a witness. Mr Garton's brought her in, she's with Sharrock now.'

'She saw what happened?'

'No, but she did see something. She's a maidservant from up the road. About half an hour before you came home she saw two men in the street arguing. One of them had bruises on his face.'

Frances sat up, as wide awake as it was possible for her to be. 'Abbott!'

'We think so.'

'Who was the other one?'

'She doesn't know. Only saw his back and can't even say if he was young or old. Can't remember how he was dressed.'

'What were they arguing about?'

'It sounded like Abbott was being ordered to do something he didn't want to do. But he was told that he had to, "after your part in that business at the Duke's". She remembered that very clearly, seeing as how it involved a Duke.'

Frances rubbed the stiffness from her shoulders. 'Not a Duke, of course, the Duke of Sussex. The tavern. So Harry Abbott was there that night.' This was the first indication that there was a direct link between the Portobello Hotel and the tavern, and it meant that Harry Abbott had been involved in the death of Lancelot Dobree. Either he had killed him or had helped to conceal the body. It was clear now that Abbott was one small part of a gang operating in West London which stole goods that were taken to a central place, the abandoned lodging house. Abbott's role was to hand over the pickings from the hotel, which explained how the ring had got there, and being a small item, it could have been overlooked in its hiding place. He had, however, unwisely done his own deals in stolen goods, such as the watch. He had been cheating a brutal and unforgiving man, and was badly beaten when found out, then ordered to dispose of Frances as a penance and proof of his loyalty. 'It's a pity she didn't see the other man. He could have been anyone familiar with the tavern, either customer or staff.'

At that moment Vernon Salter hurried in to see Frances and was admitted by the constable. 'I asked Pollard. He says yes, he went in to get the key and Lancelot Dobree was in the office talking to Neilson.'

'So that was how he knew where it was hidden,' said Frances. 'I thought as much.'

'Do you think he unlocked the back door then locked it when he went out and put the key back?'

'He had no reason to lock it. He meant to return after a few minutes. He would have kept the key so he could lock the door later.'

'Then it would have been found on his body or amongst his things. If the killer found the key on the body he would just have thrown it away. How would he have known what it was for?'

'You're right,' said Frances. 'How would he have known?' There was a long silence. 'Only someone who went to that box for the keys and was familiar with them and how they were labelled would have known it was a tavern key. In fact, now I think about it, how did your father-in-law guess which was the right one? Someone must have taken it from his body, recognised it, and come in and locked the door and put the key back, so it looked as if it had never been missing. As if the murdered man had never gone out through that door and looked out of the window and seen what was happening in the yard. It means that someone connected with the tavern is involved with the criminals and wanted to keep that fact well hidden.'

At least one of the gang, Frances reasoned, had to be a member of the tavern staff, and not only that but someone who lived on the premises. That was the reason the gang meetings took place at the time of the Lodge meetings. If anyone had crept about during the night the guard dog, Wellington, would have raised the alarm. At other times of the day, the criminal could never be sure that the eagle eye of Mr Neilson would not discover him. There was only one time when it was absolutely certain that Mr Neilson would not move from his post, and that was when he acted as Tyler for the Mulberry and Literati Lodges. And now Frances thought about it, there was one person she had spoken to who had referred to the Duke of Sussex Tavern as 'the Duke's'.

That person had taken the key from the body and returned indoors and as it chanced, this was during the time when Mr Fiske had been declaiming his address and ringing the bell. The opportunity was seized; the key was quickly turned in the lock and then replaced in its box. It thus appeared that the door had been locked all along.

The other items that linked the body with the tavern were the identifying possessions from the body, the regalia and gentleman's ring, which were so distinctive that the killer dared not try and dispose of them, also Dobree's pocketbook, cards and other items. These were removed from the body, which was then concealed. His house keys, with the identifying fob stamped 'Mulberry House' were later used in an attempt to burgle his home. If the lodging house had remained empty as seemed likely in view of its poor showing on the property market, then the rats would have disposed of both flesh and clothing within days. The killer must have hoped that the body would be quickly reduced to a skeleton impossible to identify. Many a tramp had crawled into an outhouse on a wintry night and not lived to see the morning. The murderer, however, could not have known that Dobree's club foot would give away his identity.

Neither, Frances reasoned, would the murderer have known that Dobree was interested in buying the lodging house, a piece of information that would have prompted an early search. The actual killer, she felt sure, was a very small fish, no more than the paid acolyte of another, a man who controlled and gave orders and made sure to know all there was to know; Mr Cullum. Did Cullum know about Dobree's interest in the property? Was there a professional connection or had he simply been lunching in the tavern and overheard Munro discussing it with his friend Mr Weber? Once he had found out about the murder he would have given orders for the body to be quickly spirited away. It was only Frances' early intervention that had prevented it.

The murder of Munro, which had followed soon after, was no chance. Cullum must have been rattled by the unplanned murder of Dobree. The fact that one of his agents had twice been sent to enquire about the lodging house to make sure it was still unsold was now looking extremely suspicious, especially as it was clear that Munro could identify him. The young property agent, with information that could lead to the controlling man, was a danger to be eliminated.

But who was Cullum? She felt his presence, his influence in everything. She knew his age, but men could look younger or older than the calendar said, and there were many men who fitted that picture. He had been a skilled silversmith, but no one she knew of that age practised that trade. Cullum himself had wanted to give up the toil of silversmithing and make an easier fortune by dealing in stolen goods. He was left handed, but so were many men. He had been wounded in a shooting, but for all she knew he had made a complete recovery with only a scar not readily visible. That incident, an altercation between thieves and killers, would have been kept secret from the law. The only man who might know something was Mr Capper, Cullum's brother-in-law, and he was too afraid to speak out.

There was one undeniable connection between Cullum and the tavern, the estranged son, who had not seen his father since he was a small child, or so he claimed. Had John Capper been sought out by his father and drawn into his schemes, and if so had Cullum revealed his true identity?

Frances realised she had been deep in thought for several minutes, Sarah and Salter standing silently by afraid to interrupt. 'I need my breakfast,' she said, 'and I need to speak to Inspector Sharrock as soon as he is finished talking to the maid. And I must see Mr Bramley, although I expect he will be here this morning in any case.'

Half an hour later Frances was able to see Sharrock, and he listened quietly as she explained her theories. 'During the Lodge meeting when Mr Dobree went missing most of the staff were on view in the bar, there are many witnesses to that, although I believe the manager Mr MacNulty divided his attention between the two bars and was not under continuous observation. Then there are Mr Capper and Mr Spevin. I suggest that all three are brought here for questioning as soon as possible. And could you bring the box of keys from the tavern's office?'

Sharrock glanced at his watch. 'No time to waste.'

'I really ought to be present when they are questioned.'

'That's a hard request. You're due at Marylebone this morning. There's a van waiting.'

'There has to be some way of delaying my being taken away.'

He considered the problem. 'I'll have a word with Mr Bramley and we'll see what can be done.'

Mr Bramley arrived at about the same time as the three staff from the tavern. MacNulty looked deeply insulted, Capper frightened and Spevin sullen. Bramley and Sharrock were in conference for several minutes, and then Bramley went to see Frances.

'Am I to go now?' she asked.

'Not in your state of health,' he said. 'I will go to Marylebone and inform the magistrates of your sudden collapse. You will need rest before you can appear in court.'

'Thank you,' she said, with some relief.

Soon afterwards Frances was brought to the interview room, where Sharrock and a constable were about to speak to MacNulty. The key box was on the table. Sharrock opened the box, took out the key labelled 'I.L.B.' and put it on the desk. 'Now then, Mr MacNulty, can you tell us what door is opened by that key?' Frances glanced into the box and saw that the key to the front of the Lodge room was on the far right of the row of keys, and the hook where the back door key had been was beside it. Once Mr Pollard had taken the key to open the front door of the Lodge room it would have been simple for Dobree to guess which was the one he sought.

MacNulty glanced at the wooden label. 'It's the back door of the Lodge room,' he said.

'And supposing a stranger was to find that key – would he know that?'

'Of course not!'

'So who else other than yourself would know?'

'Mr Neilson, of course. And Mr Chappell and Mr Pollard who look over the Lodge room before the meetings and check it is all secure.'

'No one else?'

'No one else has occasion to know.'

'Who else of the tavern staff other than yourself might go to the box to get a key – any key?'

MacNulty gave this some thought. 'Mr Tetlow might fetch the key to the dining room for me.'

'Does he lodge at the tavern?'

'No.'

'But you do, as do Mr Spevin and Mr Capper. Do they go to the box for keys?'

'Not to my knowledge. I wouldn't ask them to.'

'Might I ask Mr MacNulty a question?' Frances interposed.

Sharrock nodded.

'Mr Neilson told me you supplied the key box. Did you make it yourself?'

'No, I'm not that handy with woodworking and the like. Spevin made it. He does all the carpentry for the tavern.'

'What's she doing here!' demanded Spevin when he was brought in.

'Now then, a bit more politeness would be in order,' advised Sharrock.

'All right, but I haven't done anything!' Spevin was pushed into a chair by the constable, where he sat trying to look unconcerned.

'Let's begin at the beginning, Mr Spevin. How long have you worked at the Duke of Sussex Tavern?'

'I've been at the Duke's for six months. No complaints.'

Frances and Sharrock exchanged glances.

'How long have you known Harry Abbott?'

'Not sure I do know him.'

'Really? Because we have a witness who saw you talking to Mr Abbott on Westbourne Grove Gardens not long before he was killed. You were urging him to do something. Were you telling him to kill Miss Doughty?'

'Don't know what you mean.'

There was a knock at the door and a constable entered with a note for Sharrock. The Inspector studied it carefully and nodded to the constable, who left. 'I think you did know Mr Abbott, and you spoke to him last night. I think he did, at your urging, try to kill Miss Doughty with the hammer you gave him. Quite a distinctive hammer, it's got the name of your father's business on it, so of course you didn't want to leave it lying around to be found, and after Mr Abbott was killed you ran up and took it away. My constable has just found it in your room at the tavern.'

Spevin looked a little less comfortable, but remained obstinate. 'It's just a hammer. I use it for my work.'

'We'll be having a close look at it. Who knows but there might be some dried blood on it. What have you been up to, Mr Spevin?'

'Nothing. And if there is blood on the hammer it's mine. Or I might have killed a rat with it.'

'You'll have to do better than that. Why did you tell Harry Abbott to kill Miss Doughty? Come on, I want the truth!'

'I didn't. I don't believe you've even got a witness,' he added defiantly.

'Let's go back a bit and talk about the night Mr Dobree was killed. What can you tell me about that?'

'Nothing. I was working in the cellars. I've been asked about it before. I don't know anything; I didn't see anything.'

'What about your friend Mr Capper? Where was he?'

'In the store room. I told you.'

'Who killed Mr Dobree?'

'I don't know.'

'Do you know anyone called Cullum?'

'No.'

'Listen Mr Spevin, I think you know a lot more than you're saying, so I'm going to send you back to the cells and let you think about it for a bit. And I'm going to talk to Mr Capper and see what he has to say.'

Spevin shrugged, and was removed.

'I think he was the man talking to Harry Abbott, and I think he took the hammer away, but whatever he's done he'll never admit it,' said Frances. 'The man behind all this is Mr Cullum, the missing partner of Vernon Salter's father. He disappeared in 1857 but I think he is here under another name. He's a vengeful, cold-hearted man and will kill anyone who crosses him. I think he ordered the beating of Harry Abbott and also told Abbott to kill me.'

'But who is Mr Cullum?'

'I wish I knew.'

The constable knocked on the door again. 'Visitor for you, sir, a Mr Wheelock.'

'What can he want?' said Sharrock irritably. 'I don't like that man!'

'Says it's about Mr Capper. He's here on behalf of Mr Marsden the solicitor to look into the situation.'

Wheelock arrived with his inky grin. 'Good morning, Inspector! And to you, Miss Doughty! News is all over Bayswater that you're being had up for murder. I'd have thought they'd have hanged you by now.'

'Not yet,' said Frances coldly.

'I'm here on behalf of Mr John Capper. If you're going to question him I will be here to represent him, but I will have to warn him to say nothing at all until he comes to court. *If* he comes to court, that is, because I don't think you have a case against him.'

'We'll see about that,' said Sharrock. 'Is his friend Mr Spevin a client of yours as well?'

'Spevin? No.'

'I didn't know Mr Capper had appointed a solicitor,' said Frances.

'Well, there's a lot you don't know,' sneered Wheelock.

'Who asked you to come here?' Sharrock demanded.

'My employer, Mr Marsden. That's all I can say.'

'And who asked Mr Marsden?'

'I'm not sure we can give away clients' secrets.'

Frances addressed Sharrock. 'Inspector, when Mr Capper was brought here, did he send a message to anyone?'

'No.'

'Who saw him being removed?'

'We did it as quietly as possible. The tavern wasn't yet open, which was a good thing. The landlord knew about it of course, and there were some people in the street who saw it.' Sharrock turned to his visitor. 'So, Mr Wheelock, it seems that Mr Capper hasn't appointed you to look after his interests and may not even want you to advise him. I think we need to ask him about it.'

Frances had a moment of inspiration. 'Mr Wheelock, am I correct in guessing that Mr Capper has a benefactor – possibly one he knows nothing about? A family member, perhaps, who has become estranged from him and therefore wants his interest kept secret?'

Wheelock's eyes narrowed and Frances knew she had hit the mark. 'I am not at liberty to say.'

'Do you think,' Sharrock asked Frances, 'that the identity of this person is of importance in this case?'

'I think it is the essential piece of information that would solve it.'

'Really?' Sharrock turned to the visitor with a broad smile. 'Well, Mr Wheelock, I think before we go any further we need to know who is assisting Mr Capper.'

There was a hesitation and a sucking of stained teeth.

'Unless you would like me to arrest you for obstructing a police enquiry.'

Wheelock scowled, which was never an attractive sight. 'All I can say is that a man visited Mr Marsden. I have known him visit before. His name is Kennard. He's a clerk of some sort.'

Sharrock turned to Frances. 'Does that name mean anything to you?'

'Yes. He is Mr Johnstone's assistant. He takes notes because Mr Johnstone can't write. Unless —,' another thought struck her. 'Mr Wheelock, does Mr Johnstone not write because he never learned to write, or because he is physically unable to?'

'Oh he's clever enough, educated and all that; but there's something the matter with his hand.'

CHAPTER FORTY-SEVEN

Once Mr Johnstone was safely in custody it was surprising how many people who had been unwilling to speak before suddenly found their tongues loosened. Vernon Salter and John Capper's uncle both identified Johnstone as the missing Cullum. Johnstone's left wrist bore the mark of a bullet wound that had been so destructive that his hand had contracted into a useless claw, afflicted with pain that rendered him unable even to grasp a pen.

John Capper, stung with grief, refused to remain silent under questioning, and admitted that he had been asked by Spevin to carry out some dealings in small packages, which had initially been hidden in the tavern's storeroom. He was aware that Spevin got his instructions from another man, but didn't know who that man was. Capper had not been comfortable about what he was being asked to do, as he was sure it was illegal, but the payment he received was generous, and very welcome in view of his wedding plans.

Mr Neilson's vigilance meant that it was too risky to have the little parcels handed over inside the tavern, and Spevin had been ordered to obtain a copy of the back door key leading into the alley so deliveries could be made unobserved. They knew they would never get Mr Neilson's key, which was as good as chained to him, but Mr MacNulty for all that he prided himself, was less careful. The conspirators had to wait for an occasion when MacNulty was about to supervise a delivery, and succeeded on the second attempt. Spevin had created a distraction by dropping some glassware in the storeroom. The noise and mess had sent MacNulty to investigate and Capper had offered to open the door for him. The key was in his hands for less than a minute, but it was enough time to take an impression using material provided by Spevin. A few days later the duplicate key arrived.

Storing the packages was another difficulty. Once or twice the sharp eye of Mr Neilson had almost caught them out, but then they were informed that since the lodging house next door was empty and likely to remain so, it would become their new centre of operations. Spevin had told Capper that his master planned to buy the house when he could get it for a good price and then it would be a regular thieves palace, masquerading as a lodging house, and they would all be safe and happy. Until then they would make use of the yard.

Spevin had been told that there was a key to the gate of 2 Linfield Gardens hanging on a hook inside the yard, and he and Capper were to scale the wall and take it. He didn't tell Capper how he had found out, but Frances thought that Johnstone must have spotted it on his visit and had ordered his henchmen to take it. This done, they had easy access to the yard, where some loose bricks in the side wall had, after a little further excavation, provided a hiding place adequate for the kind of small items they dealt with. They had easy passage in and out of the tavern at any hour, but timed their activities with the Lodge meetings when they knew Mr Neilson would be at his post. Neither Capper nor Spevin had known that Lancelot Dobree was interested in buying the property. That nugget of information must have come from Kennard, lurking unnoticed in the lounge bar and listening out for anything that his employer would be interested in.

On the night of Dobree's death, Spevin and Capper were taking their usual delivery of stolen goods, assisted by Harry Abbott, when they were interrupted by Dobree standing at the open back door demanding to know what was going on and threatening to tell Neilson. It was Spevin, said Capper, who had struck Dobree from behind with the hammer, and he had tumbled out into the alley. All the conspirators had been alarmed when it was found that Dobree was dead, but Spevin, the coolest-headed of the three, had devised a plan to avoid any suggestion of a connection with the tavern. The body had been taken into the yard, stripped of anything that might identify it, and left in the fuel store, where there was a rats' nest. They had then hidden the property taken from the body, and locked and bolted the gate before retreating over the wall, confident that the house would remain empty for long enough to render the remains unidentifiable. Later, Spevin told Capper that there had been a change of plan and they had to move the body as soon as possible, but before they could, they learned it had been found.

Neither Capper nor Spevin knew who had made enquiries at Munro's to check if the property was still unsold. It could have been Harry Abbott or another of Johnstone's men. Either way, he had been rattled when Munro had recognised him after the murder, and identifying him could have led to his employer. Munro had to be got out of the way before he could talk to the police. His killer was never found but in view of Abbott's timorousness Frances did not think it was he. She suspected that Abbott and Spevin had acted together, Abbott distracting Munro while Spevin attacked him from behind.

Faced with so many fingers pointing in his direction, Spevin grew close as an oyster. All he would admit to after being confronted with the witness was being nearby while Abbott went to try and kill Frances, and retrieving the hammer because he thought he would be blamed for it.

At a conference presided over by Superintendent Barnes, the charges against Frances were formally dropped and she was a free woman. The spider was caught in his own web, and now the captive flies were turning on him. The lodging house proved to be only one meeting place of several in West London, and large quantities of stolen goods were recovered. A new witness came forward to say that he had seen Cullum paying a man to murder David Dunne and had been threatened with death if he spoke out. Johnstone was questioned, but said nothing apart from demands to see his children. They refused to have anything to do with him.

On the day after his arrest Johnstone was found dead in his cell. It was thought that he had had some poison concealed about him for just such an eventuality.

It was some small comfort to Frances to learn at the conclusion of the inquest into the death of Harry Abbott that she was not solely to blame. The savage beating he had suffered at the hands of Cullum's men had resulted in a fracture of the skull without which the blow she inflicted with the club would probably only have stunned him. The verdict was that he had died from a combination of factors, of which Frances' action was only one, and she, in defending her life, was blameless.

Despite the successful conclusion of the enquiry, Frances was not in the mood for celebration. She preferred to sit quietly by her own fireside, in good company; Sarah and Professor Pounder, Tom and Ratty, and Cedric. There were little treats to be eaten, and even some nice sherry to wash them down. It was not all she desired, but it was the best that was possible.

On the day after her release, Mr Fiske came to see her in great good humour. 'I am so happy that we can finally put this terrible tragedy behind us. Of course it is an awful thing, but it is some relief to know that those responsible were such villains and nothing to do with either Lodge. A hammer – how very dreadful! I am pleased that the weapon turned out to be an operative tool and not a piece of Lodge furniture – I dread to think what Mr Miggs would have made of that. So is it determined who wielded it?'

'Not precisely. Mr Spevin is blaming everything on Harry Abbott and John Capper, and Mr Capper insists that it was Spevin who killed Mr Dobree. I am inclined to believe Mr Capper and I think we may yet see a trial of Spevin with Capper turning Queen's Evidence.'

'Did we ever discover where Dobree was going that night?'

'No, but I have my suspicions. If he thought that Mr Salter was involved in the robberies he was probably going to the cottage to see if there were any stolen goods hidden there.'

'But he didn't advise the housekeeper that he was going.'

'No, that was probably deliberate. He wanted no advance warning of his visit.'

'The only concern I have now is Mr Miggs,' sighed Fiske. 'I have heard a rumour that he is writing a new novel called *The Working Tools of Treason*, set in a Masonic Lodge in which the brethren are all the most reprehensible villains. What am I to do? Who would publish such dreadful material?'

'I am afraid he has a wealthy patroness nowadays,' said Frances.

'Oh dear, that makes it so much worse. Who is she?'

'Mrs Cholmondeleyson, founder of the Ladies League Against Female Suffrage. She seems to have taken a liking to his poetry, and, I am afraid, to him.'

Mr Fiske was clearly astounded by this information. 'Mrs Cholmondeleyson? Surely not! She must have taken leave of her senses!'

'Elderly ladies can sometimes do so when a young man charms them.'

'But that is extraordinary! Did you know that Mrs Cholmondeleyson is the former Mrs Josiah Finchbourne?'

'No, I did not. That name sounds familiar. Where have I heard it mentioned? Oh yes, it is a name attached to a charity.'

'Precisely. Finchbourne was a self-made man from humble beginnings, and when he became wealthy he determined to use that wealth to help others less fortunate. He founded the Josiah Finchbourne Home for Destitute and Distressed Children. The home provides education and training in useful trades. It still does, as Mrs Cholmondeleyson provides generous financial support, and it is one of the charities to which the Literati contributes.'

A thought occurred to Frances. 'Was Mr Finchbourne a Freemason?'

'Indeed he was, a very senior Mason.'

Frances reasoned that there was no way Mrs Cholmondeleyson could be aware that the anonymous outspoken opponent of freemasonry was the very poet she admired. It was unlikely that the private conversations of the two had covered any subjects beyond literature and the unsuitability of women to have the vote. Freemasonry, since it was a male preserve, would almost certainly not have been discussed. To expose Mr Miggs' activities to Mrs Cholmondeleyson would have been an act of cruelty, and in any case the only result desired was to have him desist from his annoying activities.

'I suppose Mrs Cholmondeleyson was very fond of her former husband?'

'She was indeed, and most proud of his good works.'

'Is there in her home a portrait of him in regalia?'

'There is.'

'Then perhaps you might suggest to her that she hosts a fashionable soirée and invites poets to read from their work, with the object of collecting funds for the children's home.'

'But then she would be bound to invite – oh, I see. I see. Yes, that is an excellent suggestion. I will mention it at the very first opportunity.'

Mr Miggs's proposed book never appeared, and there were no more pamphlets or letters to the newspapers. A month later came the announcement that he and Mrs Cholmondeleyson were betrothed, the wedding to take place in the spring. In view of the advanced age of the bride-to-be, no chaperone was deemed to be necessary by society and the loving couple were often to be seen in public as he squired her to balls and benefits. Mr Miggs was a happy man. Surely he was, as the fixed smile on his face testified. He was anxious to perform every small service for his lady love, be it supplying her with glasses of wine, or sweetmeats, or carrying anything she felt she did not wish to carry for herself. Love, it certainly was, as his every utterance to her was an endearment, and the lady was showered with terms such as 'my dear little flower', 'my sweetest rose', and 'my dearest daisy', all with the same horrible fixed smile. She, on the other hand, referred to him as 'Miggs!' and she had only to bark that syllable before he rushed obediently to her side.

Sarah's agreement to chaperone a meeting between the nervous lover and his adored lady in Hyde Park ended rather better than anticipated. The gentleman had been very shy, hardly daring to speak, and the object of his affections, while liking his looks, found him hard to appreciate. The assignation had been interrupted by a scream some distance away, a respectable woman having been assaulted by a man who cut off a piece of her gown. The bashful lover suddenly underwent a heroic transformation, sprinting after the criminal, catching him, and placing him in the custody of the park police, so earning the warm approbation of the maiden he admired. He was rewarded with an invitation to pay a visit to her family.

CHAPTER FORTY-EIGHT

Mrs Sharrock poured the tea, and pushed a plate of cakes in Ratty's direction. He was not a lad who despised cake, but he looked at these distrustfully. He glanced at Frances, who picked up her teacup and helped herself to a cake.

'Delicious, thank you,' said Frances, which indeed it was.

Hesitantly, Ratty took a cake, put it on his plate, and stared at it. After a while he poked it cautiously with his finger.

'Now then, young master Ratty,' said Inspector Sharrock, 'I've invited you here to tell you a story – it's a story about a policeman.'

Ratty frowned.

'His name was Walter Atkinson, and he was a constable at Paddington Green station. Active, clever, brave, diligent. Knew his duty and did it. A fine man in every way.'

Ratty said nothing but he didn't look convinced. He picked up his cake and sniffed it.

'One night, Constable Atkinson surprised a burglar and gave chase. He managed to apprehend the man despite being struck on the head with an iron bar. He was back on duty again the very next day. But from that time on he wasn't quite the same man. He was usually a placid type, but he began to have outbursts of bad temper, and complained of headaches. One night his head was so bad he was sent home to rest up.'

Ratty looked suddenly alarmed. He swallowed his cake in a gulp, almost choked, and washed it down with a copious draught of tea.

'Constable Atkinson was happily married with a son, Walter junior, and another child on the way. We don't know exactly what happened that night, but it seems he had a brainstorm. Neighbours heard screaming and crying. Next thing, poor Mrs Atkinson was lying dead, her husband had collapsed in a fit and the little boy – Watty, they used to call him – was missing. He was only about four or five at the time. Police searched high and low, but he was never found. Some people thought he had wandered off and hidden out of fright and starved to death, others thought his father had killed him, too, and hidden the body. Me? I think he was looked after by some street urchins and grew up with them. But it wouldn't surprise me at all if from then on he had a terror of any man in a police uniform.'

Tears started from Ratty's eyes and began to trickle down his face. 'What 'appened to the farver?'

'He was questioned, but he didn't seem to be aware of what he had done. He was unfit to plead, and ended up in an asylum. He died about a year later.' Sharrock took a photograph out of his pocket. It showed a line-up of policemen pictured outside Paddington Green station. 'See that fellow?' He pointed to one of the men. 'That's Constable Atkinson. A good man. He didn't deserve what happened to him and neither did his family.'

Ratty sniffled and used his sleeve to wipe long wet smears from his face.

'Watty's mother has a sister. Married, with three children. She used to look after little Watty sometimes, and thinks she could identify him, even if he's older. I know it's a lot to take in all at once, but if you'd like to meet her, that could be arranged.'

At the trial of Matthew Spevin for the murder of Lancelot Dobree, a competent but not eminent defence counsel made the best case he could. His unfortunate client, he said, was standing trial only because the real culprits, the truly guilty men, were beyond the reach of the law. His client was just twenty-three years of age. When he was fifteen, his father, a hardworking and respectable carpenter, died after a fall from a ladder. The boy, without that firm masculine guidance known to be so essential at an impressionable age, had been led astray by a criminal of experience. Realising too late that he was deeply in the villain's toils, he wanted to put it all behind him but could not. His life had been threatened and he lived in fear, not only for himself but his poor sick mother who relied on his income. Yes, Spevin had assisted the late Mr Cullum in his movement of stolen goods, but that was not the charge here. During one such transaction, at which John Capper and Harry Abbott had been present, the unfortunate Lancelot Dobree had stumbled across their activities. There was no doubt that Dobree had been killed, struck over the back of the head with a hammer, and the prosecution would try to prove that an exhibit brought to court marked with the name of Mr Spevin's father was the murder weapon, but he believed that there was no sound evidence that this was the case. Mr Spevin was not a killer. He was an unfortunate victim. He was not even in the vicinity when Dobree was killed. The defence would maintain that the murderer of Lancelot Dobree was the late Harry Abbott.

John Capper, turning Queen's Evidence in consideration of avoiding a murder charge, said that he was in the alley when Dobree appeared at the back door. It was Spevin, who had been in the habit of carrying the hammer in his pocket when they crept about on their unsavoury activities, who had struck the old man from behind.

Spevin was found guilty of murder and recommended to mercy by the jury. He was sentenced to death but it was confidently expected that this would be commuted to life in prison. John Capper stood trial for receiving stolen goods and on being found guilty was handed a sentence of nine months, which the judge suspended.

'It was the best outcome,' said Sharrock to Frances afterwards. 'Did you know that Cullum left a will with his entire fortune divided between his son and daughter? I've heard that John Capper refused to take a penny of it, but his lady love talked him round. Oh, and speaking of lady loves, I'm sorry to say you missed your chance with Inspector Payne.'

Frances was startled. 'Chance? Whatever do you mean?'

Sharrock grinned. 'I think he rather admired you in his own way.'

'He accused me of being an immoral woman and arrested me for murder!'

'No accounting for tastes. But it seems that his former sweetheart who ran off with a criminal found the new fellow a bit too heavy-handed for her liking and went and turned him in to the police. So the wedding's back on again.'

Rosetta Doughty's health gradually but surely improved, and Frances was able to spend a wonderful week in Brighton with her father and mother. On the balmier days all three, with Rosetta very carefully wrapped against chills, enjoyed carriage rides along the promenade, and they attended some marvellous concerts at the Dome. The best times, however, were when she and her mother engaged in lively conversation, and she found a witty, perceptive and erudite mind that was a brilliant match for her own. On those occasions, Vernon could only sit by and admire them both. Frances also met her brother Cornelius for the first time, a shy, studious youth so much like her in appearance that it was remarked upon that if she had put on his clothes they would have looked almost identical.

'Alicia and I have come to an agreement,' said Vernon Salter as they gathered for a family tea. 'We will separate informally, by a private arrangement. We will no longer live together, and Alicia will have full control of the children until they reach their majority, after which I am sure they will make their own decisions. I will be permitted to see them from time to time, but not in the company of Rosetta.'

'What of the terms of your father-in-law's will?' asked Frances.

'As already provided that will mostly be divided between charities, Alicia and the children. But she has generously agreed that none of the legacies relating to me will be challenged. My annuity will continue, and I will also have the cottage, which will be rented. And I have just had a letter from an old friend, James Felter. His business in Switzerland has been prospering, so much so that he wishes to appoint an agent in England to work on commission. I have agreed to accept the position. We will not be rich but we will be comfortable.'

'Where will you live?'

'Here, in Brighton. There has been too much publicity to continue the fiction that I am Rosetta's brother, so I must take a separate establishment. However, we remain hopeful that one day, when time has passed and the children are grown, Alicia will agree to a quiet divorce, and Rosetta and I can marry.'

On her return to Bayswater Frances received a letter from Mr Fiske, and as a result attended a gathering at the Duke of Sussex Tavern. She had assumed that the invitation was to a social occasion to thank her for her work, however the gentleman of the Literati Lodge looked unexpectedly serious. 'Miss Doughty,' said Mr Brassington, 'we are eternally grateful to you for all you have done. You have preserved the good names of the Lodge in particular and freemasonry in general, and most especially those of Lancelot Dobree and Vernon Salter, who are now both cleared of any suspicion of wrongdoing. We appreciate that as a part of your investigations it was necessary for you to observe some of our ceremonies, and we were of course on that unusual occasion most careful not to reveal to you any secrets of our Craft, which would not have been appropriate, however …' he paused. His fellow Freemasons looked more solemn still. 'I did advise one of our senior brethren of what had taken place and he was deeply concerned that we might have been unwise, and that in some way we had inadvertently either revealed a secret or by our words and actions enabled you to guess a secret which is not to be divulged to any except fellow Masons.'

Frances understood his anxiety. 'I can assure you that I will not reveal anything that took place to another person.'

Mr Brassington did not look as relieved as Frances anticipated. 'I accept that assurance of course, however, I have been told that even your most solemn promise will not be sufficient to ensure your secrecy to our satisfaction.'

'I don't understand,' said Frances.

Mr Brassington paused again, and looked at his brethren. They all nodded. 'We are advised that there is only one way in which we can feel quite certain that you do not divulge any of the secrets of our Craft.'

And that was how, soon afterwards, Frances unexpectedly found herself standing outside the door of the Literati Lodge room, having removed her left shoe, and unfastened the top buttons of her gown. Mr Neilson placed the hood over her head and the noose around her neck, then, sword in hand, he stood beside her. It was time. He knocked on the door to alert the Inner Guard, and the door swung open. Frances stepped off on the left foot, and was guided into the room for her initiation.

Once the ceremony, in which she swore never to reveal the secrets of the First Degree, was completed, she was invited to dine with the gentlemen who were now her fellow brethren, and Mr Brassington, in great good humour, rose to drink a toast to the Literati Lodge's newest member, 'Miss Frances Doughty, a true and faithful brother.'

AUTHOR'S NOTES

In the UK, the 'first floor' of a building is the one immediately above the ground floor, which is at street level.

The Literati and Mulberry Lodges are fictional. Masonic ritual has undergone many changes over the years, and varies from Lodge to Lodge. The details included in this book are a suggestion of what the ritual might have been in 1882. The event described in the final paragraph of the book does have historical precedent.

The Duke of Sussex Tavern and its location, Linfield Gardens, are fictional. The Duke, Prince Augustus Frederick, sixth son of King George III, was the first Grand Master of the United Grand Lodge of England.

The guard dog, Wellington, is named after soldier and statesman the Duke of Wellington, who was a Freemason.

'Quis custodiet ipsos custodes?', a quote from the *Satires* of Juvenal, is translated as 'Who will guard the guards themselves?'

The Ladies League Against Female Suffrage is fictional, however, a Women's National Anti-Suffrage League was formed in 1908 and was disbanded in 1918.

The business of Finewax & Sons on the Portobello Road, the Portobello London Hotel and the Portobello Theatre of Varieties are fictional and not based on any actual businesses past or present.

In 1881, fifty-five-year-old solicitor Edward Bramley lived at 63 Richmond Road (since renamed Chepstow Road), Bayswater.

Thomas Bramah Diplock MD (1830–1892) was coroner for West London and Middlesex from 1868.

In 1811 seven people died in two separate attacks on families in the East End of London near Wapping. A sailor, John Williams, was arrested and hanged himself in his cell.

Charles Jamrach (1815–1891) was the proprietor of a store on the Ratcliffe Highway that dealt in exotic animals. In 1857 he rescued a child who had been carried away by an escaped tiger.

ABOUT THE AUTHOR

LINDA STRATMANN is a former chemist's dispenser and civil servant who now writes full time. As well as the Frances Doughty mystery series, she is also the author of the Mina Scarletti mysteries, set in Brighton. She lives in London.

ALSO BY THE AUTHOR

IN THE
FRANCES DOUGHTY
MYSTERY SERIES

IN THE
MINA SCARLETTI
MYSTERY SERIES

Praise for the Frances Doughty Mystery Series

'If Jane Austen had lived a few decades longer, and spent her twilight years writing detective stories, they might have read something like this one.'

Sharon Bolton, bestselling author of the Lacey Flint series

'I feel that I am walking down the street in Frances' company and seeing the people and houses around me with clarity.'

Jennifer S. Palmer, Mystery Women

'Every novelist needs her USP: Stratmann's is her intimate knowledge of both pharmacy and true-life Victorian crime.'

Shots Magazine

'The atmosphere and picture of Victorian London is vivid and beautifully portrayed.'

www.crimesquad.com

'Vivid details and convincing period dialogue bring to life Victorian England during the early days of the women's suffrage movement, which increasingly appeals to Frances even as she strives for acceptance from the male-dominated society of the time. Historical mystery fans will be hooked.'

Publishers Weekly

'[Frances'] adventures as a detective, and the slowly unravelling evidence of multiple crimes in a murky Victorian setting, make for a gripping read.'

Historical Novel Review

'The historical background is impeccable.'

Mystery People